Winter Witness

A Batavia-on-Hudson Mystery

WINTER WITNESS

A Batavia-on-Hudson Mystery

by Tina deBellegarde

LEVEL
BEST BOOKS

CREDITS:

MAP ARTIST: Sachi Mulkey

PHOTO CREDIT: Patrizia Tersigni

First edition

ISBN: 978-1-947915-76-3

Cover art by Sachi Mulkey

This book was professionally typeset on Reedsy.
Find out more at reedsy.com

For
Denis and Alessandro
With my love

Praise for WINTER WITNESS

"In *Winter Witness*, Tina deBellegarde gives us an evocative debut mystery so lush you'll believe you're strolling the streets of Batavia-on-Hudson, battling the brutal winter's chill, even inhaling the aroma of the town bakery's wares. Through Bianca St. Denis's eyes, we gain an outsider's perspective on the quirks and secrets of a village rife with history and deception, as well as a glimpse into her own loss and heartbreak."—Annette Dashofy, *USA Today* Bestselling Author of the Agatha-nominated Zoe Chambers Mysteries

"Richly atmospheric, *Winter Witness* reminds us of the high cost of family secrets - and the even higher cost of those secrets being revealed."—Liz Milliron, author of *The Laurel Highlands Mysteries* and *The Home Front Mysteries*

"Beautifully written and evocative, *Winter Witness* explores the comforts and quirky charms of small-town life that have drawn so many urban dwellers to the slower rhythms of the Hudson Valley. But *Winter Witness* is far more than a simple cozy mystery; it is also a sensitive and nuanced examination of the nature of compassion, loss, and community... Bianca and Mike make a believable and engaging investigative team, with a balance of complementary strengths and vulnerabilities that never descend into cliché. I'm looking forward to spending more time with them, along with the other citizens of Batavia-on-Hudson, in the future."—Erica Obey, author of *The Curse of the Braddock Brides* and *The Horseman's Word*

"*Winter Witness* is a sly and subtle mystery, full of nuanced observations of life in a small town. Tina deBellegarde's debut novel reveals a masterful understanding of grief, of feeling stuck and lost in life, and the price of keeping secrets. Her Bianca St. Denis is the compassionate outsider who has a journalist's eye for detail and a writer's understanding of human weakness. Watch the mystery be solved and the clues fall into place, the way the lid of a box clicks closed. You'll want the next installment."—Gabriel Valjan, Agatha- and Anthony-nominated author of The *Naming Game*.

"Tina deBellegarde's *Winter Witness* is an accomplished debut, offering well-crafted characters and a setting that pulls the reader in. The story grabbed me right at the beginning and kept me turning the pages all the way through to a satisfying conclusion. I'm looking forward to the next installment in this series."—Carol Pouliot, Author of The Blackwell and Watson Time-Travel Mysteries.

Chapter One

Thursday, December 15

She could have been sleeping, were it not for the gaping gash in the back of her head and the bloody stone next to her limp body.

Sheriff Mike Riley stood alone on the shore of the near-frozen lake. At his feet, Sister Elaine Fisher lay face down, ice crystals forming around her body where it met the shoreline. The murmuring water of the nearby stream imparted a peacefulness at odds with the scene. In the waning winter light, he paused ankle deep in the snow illuminated by the beat of red strobe lights.

Murder seemed so extreme. The villagers would be baffled. Murder didn't happen in sleepy Batavia-on-Hudson. An occasional stolen bicycle, some were paid off the books, but that was hardly worth mentioning. Lately, there had been a handful of amateur burglaries. Murder was another story altogether.

But there was no denying it. Elaine's body was there before him, lifeless on a cushion of snow at the edge of the lake.

Sheriff Riley ran his chapped hands through his salt and pepper hair. A knowing person might have noticed that he used this motion to disguise a quick brush at his cheek, to eliminate the one tear that slipped through.

He feared this day, the day his lazy job would bring him face to face once again with the ugly underbelly he knew existed even in a quiet place like Batavia-on-Hudson. Mike Riley wasn't afraid of death. He was afraid of the

1

transformation a village like this was bound to go through after an act of murder.

He cried for Elaine; though he barely knew her. But also, he cried for the village that died with her that morning. A place where children still wandered freely. A village that didn't lock doors, and trusted everyone, even the ones they gossiped about. Now, inevitably, the villagers would be guarded around each other, never quite sure anymore if someone could be trusted.

He thought he could already hear the locks snapping shut in cars and homes as word of the murder got out. Mothers yanking children indoors, hand-in-hand lovers escaping the once-romantic shadows of the wooded pathways, and old ladies turning into shut-ins instead of walking their dogs across the windy bluff.

Sheriff Riley steeled himself not just to confront the damaged body of the first murder victim of Batavia in over seventy years, but to confront the worried faces of mothers, the defeated faces of fathers and the vulnerable faces of the elderly.

He squatted in the slush, wincing as his bad knee rebelled, and laid his hands on Elaine's rough canvas jacket, two-sizes too big—one of her thrift shop purchases, no doubt. As reverently as was possible in the muddy snow, Mike Riley turned over her body to examine the face of a changing village.

Sister Elaine had no one left, she had no known siblings and of course, no spouse or children. Only Agatha Miller, her childhood companion, could have been considered next of kin. How Elaine had tolerated her grumpy old friend was a mystery to everyone.

The sheriff knew that Elaine's death would rock the community. Even a relative outsider like Mike understood that Elaine had been an anchor in Batavia. Her kindness had given the village heart, and her compassion had given it soul. No one would be prepared for this.

Mike knew from experience that preparation for death eases the grief. You start getting ready emotionally and psychologically. You make arrangements. You imagine your life without someone. But Mike also knew that when the time comes it still slaps you in the face, cold and bracing. And you realize you were only fooling yourself. Then somehow, in short order, work becomes demanding, bills need to be paid and something on the radio steals a chuckle right out of your throat. For a brief second you realize that there are moments of respite from your grief and perhaps someday those moments will expand and you may be able to experience joy once again.

But for now, Elaine's death will be a shock. No one had prepared for her death, let alone her murder.

***

Agatha Miller raised herself on one elbow and looked out the window. More snow. More cold.

"This weather will kill me."

She let her body drop to the pillows. Agatha had made her peace with terminal cancer but it was the ice that had taken her down.

Agatha stretched for the cup of water on her bedside. Her fingers inched toward it, but it remained out of reach. She rearranged herself on the bed and reached her arm out again. Just as her fingers touched the plastic cup, her nurse walked in.

"Time for your pills."

Agatha clutched at the cup, and watched it go over the far side of the table, water splashing to the carpet.

"Stop turning this place into a hospital room. If I wanted plastic cups I'd stay in the hospital," Agatha snapped. "Bring me a glass and my blue crystal pitcher from the breakfront."

The nurse dried the carpet and returned with a half-full glass and the pitcher.

"Agatha, I don't think this is a good idea. You won't be able to lift those. I'll leave the plastic on the side over here."

"Just get the plastic out of here and turn down the heat. It's an oven in here. It's bad enough no one will let me go outside. Now you're incubating everyone's germs for me too. Want to make sure if one thing doesn't kill me, something else will?" Agatha sputtered more to herself than to the nurse.

3

Agatha took a deep drink, enjoying the heft of the glass and the coolness of the water. The nurse returned with a tray: light tea, dry whole-wheat toast, a banana and two pills.

"It's almost five and someone should be here soon," the nurse said over her shoulder on her way out the door.

Agatha took a bite of the cold toast, regretting her outburst.

"Why do I do that? I have become a grumpy old lady just like everyone says," she whispered to the empty room. She took another bite and pushed the plate aside. She hated toast and tea. She ate the banana but her mind wandered to black coffee and a cheese danish. For some reason she couldn't get her nurses to understand that all she wanted was black coffee and a danish. "Stupid, stupid girl," Agatha muttered, surprised to find herself on the verge of tears.

"Why does coffee make me cry but not a hip fracture or cancer? What is wrong with me?"

She finished the banana and reached for the pitcher to refill the water glass. It was too heavy from her awkward angle in bed. She rearranged her grasp and tried again but with no luck. Out of breath, she gave up and receded into the pillows.

Agatha studied the water stain on the ceiling. Bert should have fixed that leak by now. Her stomach lurched in hunger. Maybe she could call Bianca and ask her to pick up some real food at Stella's on her way. How she missed the aroma of the diner. Agatha picked up the phone and started to dial the number from the list at the side of the bed: one for every villager on rotation to care for her. Her eyes caught sight of the calendar on the nightstand. She slipped her glasses on for a closer look. Bianca wasn't scheduled until tomorrow. Claire Koop was due at five, but Agatha had no intention of asking any favors of that busy-body. She placed the phone back in the cradle before it started to ring. She didn't like to ask favors, they needed to be reciprocated. Besides, she had other plans for Bianca.

Agatha was finally ready to tell someone her story and Bianca St. Denis seemed like the perfect confidante. Agatha needed to have one person witness her story, acknowledge her life, someone who might understand

4

but not judge. She was tired of being overlooked. And labeled. Grumpy Agatha, woman of few words.

She wanted to share her thoughts but couldn't decide how far to trust this newcomer.

Not being able to tell her story had made her question her own existence. She needed to share her story, but most of all she needed someone to hear her. This was a need she had just started to face. Once she is gone her story will go with her. What will remain of her? Her son was no longer in her life. Her daughter was distant. Allison was upstanding and solid, but not warm. Agatha took the blame. She had tried to make Allison strong, to prepare her for life's difficulties, to make it on her own and not rely on a man. And she had succeeded.

Sister Elaine had always been there and had never asked Agatha to explain herself. Elaine had taken her in—no questions asked. That was exactly what Agatha had needed at the time but, all these years later, Agatha felt inconsequential, impermanent. She needed to concretize her life now and she could only do that with a willing witness.

Bianca seemed intelligent and caring. And best of all she was another historian. Agatha never lent her books out to anyone but she surprised herself by how readily she shared her books with Bianca.

If she could trust Bianca with her books, why not more? Bianca was a clean slate, had no history in Batavia, no grudge, no agenda. The perfect witness.

***

Bianca St. Denis wended her way through the narrow aisles dropping groceries into her basket as she went: one can of tuna, a small head of lettuce, two oranges, a quart of milk, and two freshly baked rolls. Rudy's Market was lively with the before dinner rush. She treated herself to some roasted artichokes at the deli counter, then moved on to the meat counter. She waited at the end of the very informal line. It was barely a line but everyone was good about waiting their turn. Bianca was grateful she didn't need to keep her defenses up. No one would steal her spot.

Still, she was a little tense since Rudy always seemed a little put off when she requested only one pork chop or a quarter of a chicken. Today all she wanted was two of his homemade bratwursts to sauté with her artichokes.

Bianca enjoyed the homey atmosphere of the market. Rudy's carried all the necessities. Not much variety, but it saved the villagers the long trip into the next big town. She didn't mind waiting on line since Rudy Bauer's wife, Trudy, offered her homemade German baked goods, along with fresh-ground coffee. Today she was serving buttery linzer tarts. At forty-two, Bianca wasn't vain but struggled to keep her sweet tooth in check. Trudy's masterpieces were particularly troublesome.

Bianca sipped and nibbled and waited. Her eyes fell on the hand crank coffee grinder behind the bakery counter. The heady aroma permeated the entire market. She really had died and gone to coffee heaven when she had moved to Batavia; it seemed all the local merchants were trying to outdo each other. No wonder the market was always crowded and the lines moved so slowly. Three years ago this place would have made her blood pressure rise. Today it relaxed her.

Above the grinder was a sign she had noticed the last few times she had come into the store. *"Ask Dad...he knows."* Bianca always found the sign vaguely familiar but she could never place it.

The sign was not the only mystery of the morning. Bianca started to notice that the market was busier and noisier than usual. The half-whispered murmurings were tense and furtive. Through the chatter she noticed a common thread. She heard Elaine Fisher's name over and over. Finally, when Trudy came by to refill the tray of cookies she asked. "Excuse me, Mrs. Bauer, but has something happened to Sister Elaine?"

"Ya, ya!" Trudy nodded vigorously. "She vas murtert. The mahn from za hills vound her by za zee!"

Bianca deciphered what she'd heard to: "She was murdered. The man from the hills found her by the sea."

But it couldn't be. There was no sea in Batavia; there was a river, a stream, a lake and even a creek, but no sea. Bianca assumed she'd misunderstood.

Why had she chosen Trudy of all people to ask? A murder in Batavia? It wasn't possible. Elaine couldn't have been murdered.

"I'm sorry Trudy, did you say murdered?"

"Ya, ya murtert by za zee!"

Then Bianca's college German kicked in and she remembered that *zee* meant lake. Could Elaine have been murdered by Groenmeer Lake?

Now the muttering all around her started to make sense.

"He found her by the lake with a bloody gash."

"She was face down in the icy water."

"Ishikawa found her. He was walking his dog."

"Odd one that one. Never comes out of the woods except to walk his dog around the lake and then he finds a murdered body. Sounds fishy to me."

"I'm locking my doors tonight."

"My wife can't stop crying. Sister Elaine had been her teacher years ago before the Catholic school closed."

"No weapon. Just a bloody rock, Doctor Spenser said."

"You can't kill someone with a rock. What does a young kid like him know anyway?"

"Elaine was so tiny, probably easier than you think."

The line had stopped moving. Everyone hovered in twos and threes. No one even pretended to make purchases and Rudy had made his way around to the front of the meat counter. Bianca wandered the aisles listening attentively. Through the spaetzle and rice she could hear them speculating.

"Who would kill Sister Elaine, of all people?"

"Bert Henderson says her family ring was gone."

"Bert was the one who took her to Albany to get it appraised. He said it was worth a small fortune."

"I'm not surprised. It was a family heirloom, sapphire and diamond, it's been in her family for three generations."

"Let's not forget, there have been a couple of burglaries the last couple of months."

"Those damn kids on their ATVs...I wonder..."

"Those kids are disturbing everything. The deer, the bears and now this."

"Did the sheriff ever arrest anyone for the burglaries?"

"If you ask me, Trevor Streat always seems to be at the wrong place at the wrong time. I never trusted that boy."

Walter Patten walked into the market. Before he could greet anyone, the state senator was surrounded by neighbors shooting questions at him.

Trudy used her considerable heft to make her way to the front of the room and cornered him. She was not just wider, she was taller than Walt.

"Valter, vat are you doing about zis? Zis is a small town. Vee shouldn't vorry about burglary, cazinos and now murter!" Trudy's round face was splotched with red.

Walt, looking to run for governor next fall, took control.

"Everybody calm down. Sheriff Riley is working diligently to track down the killer. I will personally make sure that whoever did this will be behind bars for a very long time. This has nothing to do with casinos. However, we have reason to believe there is a connection between the burglaries and the murder and we will keep the community informed. And next year, if you elect me, I will see to it that mandatory sentencing terms are increased for your peace of mind. If anyone knows anything at all about these events, please see Sheriff Riley immediately."

Walt got applause for his extemporaneous campaigning and then went around shaking hands and inquiring after ailing parents and children away at college. When he made his way to Bianca, he asked how she was making out on the Van Rouse farm all alone.

"It's taking some getting used to but I'm making do, thank you, Walt. Why do you think the murder and the burglaries are connected?"

"The missing ring. Elaine never took that ring off, and it's very valuable, I hear. The sheriff believes that she may have been targeted as an easy victim. She walks the convent's cocker spaniel every dawn and dusk by the lake, rain or shine. Not too difficult to plan. Probably a mugging gone awry."

"I never thought I would move from the city into a hot bed of crime. It's very…disturbing." Bianca shifted from foot to foot, her nerves starting to fray.

Walt pulled out his wallet and handed Bianca a card. "This has never happened around here, and if I have anything to say about it, it will never happen again." Walt waved to the customers as they trickled out of the market, still chatting and gesticulating. No one else stopped to talk to him. Was it because she was there, Bianca wondered? She turned to Walt again to give him her full attention. "Don't worry," he continued, "I am looking out for this village. If you hear of anything or you need me for any reason just call that number, it's my home number."

"I can't call you at ho—"

"That's why I made those cards. This is an intimate community, and we have needs at all hours. Call me, anytime, really."

"Thank you, Walt, I do believe that you will get to the bottom of this."

Bianca stepped out of the market and crossed the street. As she turned the corner, she passed the police station where Mr. Ishikawa, a man who looked to be in his early seventies, sat answering questions from Sheriff Riley. His dog sat at attention by his side, a cinnamon shiba inu, ears perked and watching Mike Riley's every movement.

Bianca changed her mind; no longer interested in walking down a lonely path with a murderer on the loose, she turned and made her way across the street to Stella's Diner.

***

Bianca crossed the street to the diner, the blue lights of the sign a beacon. As anxious as she was to arrive, Bianca didn't walk in immediately. She stopped before the door. Stella's. The town hub. Where warmth, friends and food joined forces.

She remembered how she had discovered the village of Batavia-on-Hudson by chance. Traveling from the city for a teacher's seminar in Albany, she had pulled off the exit for a coffee.

That day she had absolutely needed a coffee...needed...more like a habit she had come to internalize as a need...mile after mile of driving with no rest stop. "Love is the sea with no horizon in sight." Where had she read that? Wasn't it on a chocolate wrapper? Got to stop that chocolate addiction.

Something's got to go: coffee or chocolate, and it definitely wasn't coffee. "Love is the sea with no horizon in sight." Lovely sentiment but all she could think was "Driving was the sea with no coffee in sight." Why were there no rest stops? And so many miles between exits? Bianca didn't want to lose any time getting off an exit but she was desperate for fuel of both kinds. She turned off the next exit labeled *Food Phone Gas Lodging*. At the end of the exit ramp two signs gave her the choice to go right three miles for gas or go left eight miles for food and gas. That left turn and those winding eight miles led to the door of Stella's Diner, voted "The Best Coffee in New York State" according to the sign in the window. How could she pass that up?

Bianca parked her car and dodged enormous raindrops to reach the diner door. Drenched and impatient she waited next on line, but a line that never moved as the tall black man behind the counter chatted up a big bearded guy in an orange hunting jacket. An interminable wait in her wet wool suit.

She turned to the man next to her to commiserate but she found him smiling, really smiling, in a way that warmed his surroundings. She could do nothing else but smile back. His warmth had reached deep inside her and yanked a smile out of her. Deeply buried. A genuine smile. A child's smile.

In that instant her senses clicked on; she smelled the aroma of roasted coffee and the sugar icing on doughnuts. The locals' laughter echoed from the corner competing with the mellow tenor sax of Booker Ervin. The music penetrated her defenses and the fluid notes lodged somewhere between her shoulders.

Her smile invited the stranger to introduce himself. Ernest McCrae, but everyone called him Ernie. Not exactly handsome, but pleasant to look at. He removed his cap to speak to her, his dark hair lightly specked with grey. He wore a jacket with *Ernie's Lawn Service* embroidered over his heart. Not what she would expect in a savior, but there you have it.

They chatted about coffee and doughnuts and rain. Bianca had never been able to recall most of the details of the conversation; her memory had recorded the impressions, the sights, sounds and smells of that day. But she remembered the most important thing he said.

"The day I was lucky enough to return from Vietnam, I decided I would never have another bad day. I would make every day a good one. I chose to be happy."

Bianca recalled how his deep brown eyes had danced. She was warmed by the smile lines that creased his face. Normally Bianca would have called these worry lines but she knew she would be wrong. Ernie's lines were smile lines.

For days afterward, Bianca found her mind wandering to Stella's. She was distracted in her classrooom thinking about the sunflower field she passed on her way back to the thruway from Batavia. She dusted off her jazz collection and found her Booker Ervin album and played "You Don't Know What Love Is" over and over again, trying to conjure up the vaguely nostalgic feelings she had tapped into at Stella's. The opposite of free-floating anxiety, Bianca had experienced free-floating tranquility.

That Sunday morning, Bianca told Richard about Batavia and Stella's. She worked it into their morning coffee and newspaper conversation. "Why not get out of the city...take a drive in the country...fresh air...autumn foliage...it would be good for us."

And they had. She directed him to Stella's after a couple of wrong turns and he had been charmed. It was unpretentious and homey, like his childhood memories of Québec.

Funny how the world shifts, Bianca thought now, standing once again before the diner door. We witness it and yet we still remain oblivious to the seismic shifts. Like the underground rumblings of nascent earthquakes, no one notices until one day everything changes.

Standing there, Bianca realized why her first instinct had been to run to Stella's. Even as a newcomer, she knew it was the heart of the village and that she would find comfort behind those doors this evening.

Chapter Two

Friday, December 16

Sheriff Mike Riley stepped away from the mangled deer on the icy pavement. Red snow melted at his feet. Sweat rolled down his back despite the frigid morning temperature.

Mike stared at the steam rising from the broken body, mesmerized, remembering his partner's body all those years ago. He took another step back, his breathing accelerated under the strain of the graphic memory. *A fresh death.* Waves rushed in his ears, the metallic smell of warm blood turned his stomach.

A clap to his back jolted him. His vision cleared. He looked up to see the flickering lights on his deputy's car, the red pulse reflecting on the snow.

"She looks pretty bad. She must've been hit by a truck. Probably speeding too," his deputy said.

Tall, blond and athletic, Vera Weber was a perfect partner, even if she wasn't Sal.

Mike nodded his head to clear the cobwebs. He shivered, his senses finally acknowledging the cold.

"You'd think they could've at least moved the body." Vera walked around the deer. "I never get used to these hit and runs. Even hunting isn't this brutal. Everyone's such a good shot around here."

Vera knelt and grabbed the hind legs, waiting for Mike to mirror her motions at the front.

"Mike, come on. Let's move her over and get out of the cold already."

Mike blinked and nodded. He squatted and reached out his hands. They still trembled. He quickly clamped his hands around the front legs before Vera could see.

One hundred and fifty pounds of dead broken weight, but they managed to hoist her onto the embankment.

His breathing steadied somewhat. The episodes hadn't stopped but were briefer and less frequent now. Once he regained his composure, Mike switched to all business.

"Vera, I'll meet you at the station later. Could you call the DEC to retrieve the carcass while I run down to Stella's? I promised Bert Henderson I would meet him there. One of his tires has a slow leak. I was on my way to bring him my jack when I came across the doe. Then I'm heading out to the convent, I need to ask the nuns a few questions about Elaine."

"You don't really think—"

Mike didn't stick around to hear the rest. He jumped into his truck and jammed it into gear. He slapped his wipers on but his vision remained blurry. He shouldn't be driving. Pulling around the bend, he stopped on the shoulder where he was out of sight. He rested his forehead on the wheel seeking the relief of a cold surface.

He did the breathing exercises they had taught him: breathe in for seven seconds, hold for seven, out for seven. After three sets, he lost patience. How could he still be having anxiety attacks six years after Sal's death? How could he ever be a decent sheriff if he couldn't handle the sight of some blood? He had been fine last night when he was dealing with Elaine's bloody head injury.

But Mike knew it wasn't the blood. It was the contorted limbs that had gotten the better of him. Just like Sal's arms and legs, skewed to unnatural angles after the fall.

Breathe in for seven seconds, hold for seven, out for seven.

He picked up his head and peered over his steering wheel.

From his vantage point at the top of the hill he could see the whole village. Batavia-on-Hudson lay peacefully before him. The steeple of St. James the

Elder was the most prominent landmark at the end of the two short blocks of Main Street. This tiny village, quietly tucked into the Catskill Mountains, was now home. It was a miracle, really, that he felt most settled in a place he and his wife had escaped to only six years earlier. He may have been a transplant from New York City but he felt a part of this cozy village. The old brick facades gave him a sense of security and permanence.

But what a difference a day makes. He had always loved that song but today he understood it better than ever. The tranquility laid out before him was in danger, and on his watch. He stared a little longer, willing the view to work its charm.

The blue sign at Stella's Diner flipped on. Eugene would be putting on the first pot of coffee. A couple of pickups splashed in the slush of the near empty streets. Smoke swirled out of chimneys; many of the locals still heated with wood. The red school house now turned market, the two-room Carnegie Library and the old movie marquee proclaimed the history of the town. In the village square, where Main Street met Van Patten Street, the thirty-foot Christmas tree swayed under the weight of snow on its needles. Beyond the square, the Batavia Creek meandered and led Mike's gaze to the bluff at Miller's Point. The locals loved the view from the bluff, but he still believed the top of Main Street offered the best vista of the Hudson River.

His musings had calmed him. His breathing was quieted now and mirrored the tranquil view. He eased the truck back into gear and cruised down Main Street, still asleep under a blanket of fresh snow.

***

In the early morning light, Bianca St. Denis guided her small foot on the narrow farmhouse stairs, stairs her husband could never use without first turning his body sideways so his entire foot could fit on the treads. She smiled as her head easily cleared the beam. Richard had always tilted his head slightly. These images slipped into her thoughts as they had every morning for the last year. Not so painfully now, but with a soft familiarity she hoped would never fade.

Bianca turned into her kitchen and her smile broadened at the sight of her yellow cabinets glowing in the morning light. Richard had surprised her one spring day. He had painted the worn cabinets a bright yellow to match her daffodils.

Her eyes avoided the papers stacked by the phone in the front hallway. No need to think about that now. Time for coffee.

She filled the kettle with bottled water, and made another mental note to get the well water tested. She turned the knob until she heard the click-click-poof of the gas igniting and placed the kettle on the burner.

Bianca turned toward the front window, her favorite view. They had managed to preserve the original glass. She loved how the wavy panes made the snow undulate. In spring, the window transformed her garden into a Monet painting.

She picked up Richard's plaid scarf from the peg by the front door and wrapped it loosely around her neck. Outside, she was greeted by the morning sun's reflection off the snow. With cold air whipping her face, she stacked firewood in her arms.

Bianca stomped the snow from her feet and fed some cedar kindling into last night's embers. She reached for yesterday's newspaper to fuel the fire, but her eye caught an image of Sheriff Mike Riley. Two articles on the front page were dedicated to him. He had delivered a baby Monday after managing to get his truck through the snow up Route 17. Responding without knowing what awaited him, he had delivered Batavia's newest citizen, Stephan Michael Jacobs. That same night he had been the guest of honor at the Eagle Scout ceremony. The photo was charming. With his shy smile captured surreptitiously for the camera, he towered over the two young men in their crisp uniforms. She finished the article about how Mike had been the youngest Eagle Scout his Brooklyn troop had ever produced. She took one more look at his crooked smile, then crumpled the paper and tucked it under the kindling. It ignited immediately.

The fire sputtered, smoked, and cracked, then engulfed the wood.

Bianca knew she had just enough time to fill the birdfeeders before the rumbling kettle whistled. She dragged a large seed bag out the back door, tripping over the cat on her way out. Shelby didn't seem to mind, nor did he budge. The door clacked shut behind her. A doe in the far corner of the yard jerked her head up but didn't move. They stared at each other for a moment then the deer put her head down and continued rooting through the snow under the apple tree.

Inside, Bianca balanced the filter on the rim of her mug and dribbled hot water over the coffee grounds. She lingered over the smoky aroma and planned her day. First, she needed to pick up her eggs from Dekker's farm. Bianca had volunteered to bake her Java Cakes for the upcoming Winter Solstice Festival. They were her personal favorites. Pineapple, coconut, banana and orange zest. Rich and moist, topped with orange cream cheese icing.

After picking up her eggs, she'd have breakfast at Stella's before a visit with old Agatha Miller. Her writing would have to wait until the afternoon again. Since her visits with Agatha these last few weeks, her writing schedule had suffered. Was she avoiding the writing, she wondered?

Revisions were hard, she told herself, she was just hitting a snag.

Bianca turned to the picture of Richard on the windowsill above the sink. She had his picture in every room so she could talk to him wherever she happened to be. His dark eyes paid close attention to her every word.

"Good morning, love. It's really cold today, but you were right about the ash logs burning long and hot. I need to ask Bert to cut more for next season."

Bianca gently watered Richard's succulents.

"So I'm volunteering now...what do you think? I know it must make you happy. Better than sulking in the house. I'm still helping out with Agatha. I never thought I'd last this long, given her disposition. But in an intimate village of this size you have to take the good with the bad. Now that I'm putting myself out there, I see how it's more like a family. Nobody's going anywhere, so we all have to get along." Bianca carefully tipped enough water into the base of each plant on the windowsill. "But today's visit with Agatha is going to be more difficult than usual. Her dear friend, Sister Elaine, died yesterday." Bianca hesitated to say the "m" word. Murder.

"I also got lassoed into the ACE Club and I'm baking for the Winter Solstice. Yes, you heard me, the village celebrates the Winter Solstice. Who would have thought this old village could be so New Age?"

Bianca kept talking as she snipped the dead leaves off the gardenia.

"Eugene at the diner tells me that the celebration was started to create a community event everyone could attend regardless of denomination. The whole village turns out. To think we've been missing it these last few years."

She moved on to the African violet. It seemed to have more dead blooms than usual. Her gaze dropped to her manuscript sitting on the desk below the windowsill. She picked up a letter abandoned there two days ago, her most recent rejection from an agent. Kindly worded but still a rejection. She heard herself sigh as she dropped the letter.

She wanted to count her blessings; at least she had the time and a place to write. It had been Richard's gift to her, a peaceful place to finally write her first novel. It was the deciding factor for their move to Batavia three years ago.

A delicate film of dust lifted as she rifled the pages of her manuscript. Why hadn't she been writing as much lately? She shook her head. But she knew why, she had found herself thinking more and more about starting a new project. She felt guilty about abandoning her book. It had been on the back burner for many years, and now that she had the chance to write, it had stalled. Had she outgrown it?

Maybe this afternoon she would spend just a few minutes on an article she had promised the *Gazette* about the history of her German Colonial home, a rare style in this Dutch area. She loved the old stone Palatine farmhouse despite the fact that it hadn't been preserved properly. When they purchased it the beams had been hidden by a drop ceiling, the floors had been covered with linoleum and an addition had jutted out one side, ruining the original symmetry. She and Richard had done their best on their budget to bring it back to life.

Yes, she would work on the *Gazette* article this afternoon. It was probably good to clear her head and finish this overdue project for the newspaper so she could get back to her novel.

Her gaze skittered back to the other pile of papers, the ones stacked near the phone. She looked at Richard again. "Maybe I should be looking for a job, a real job, right now. What do you think?"

"Do what you love," she imagined him answering. "Give the book another month and see how you feel then. Those bills aren't going anywhere."

The clock chimed. Bianca roused herself from her musings. She took a moment to feed Shelby. She ran her hands through his thick orange coat while he ate. He loved the attention, even while eating. When he finished, he licked his lips then looked up at her and blinked. She was sure he was telling her he loved her. She blinked back. She really did love this creature. He was a constant connection to Richard who had named him after Carroll Shelby and his famous sportscar, the Shelby Cobra, his dream car.

After feeding Shelby, she ran upstairs to dress. Habit brought her hand up to caress the hand-hewn beam in the spot where Richard had occasionally hit his head. The low ceilings of the ancient farmhouse had never been a problem for her, and they kept the house cozy and warm. Richard had had to be vigilant but hadn't always succeeded in navigating the small house.

She chose a comfortable outfit of jeans and a soft brown turtleneck. As she left the bedroom, Bianca caught a glimpse of herself in the mirror. She had skipped her makeup as usual, just a little mascara to accentuate her amber eyes. They were her best feature and she preferred to keep them the center of attention. She tucked her short brown hair behind her ears. Her hair refused to be predictable so she wore it in a carefree pixie. Not bad for forty-two, she thought. Her gaze moved down over her sweater and jeans and she decided that tomorrow was a good day to start a diet. Only five foot two, Bianca didn't have a frame that could carry any extra weight with elegance. Her enjoyment of good food was an obstacle. She had neither the power nor the inclination to overcome it. So today she would have her favorite breakfast: croissant and coffee at Stella's.

Downstairs, she bundled up, rushed passed her cluttered desk, and slammed the door behind her.

A notice of foreclosure flew off the stack and fluttered to the floor.

Chapter Three

Eugene Wilkins flipped the switch; the neon blue flickered for a while then settled into a steady glow. The ice blue snow on the front walk turned a darker hue. He paid little attention to his own reflection in the front window. The only black man in the village, Eugene was so tall that he cast a shadow over the patrons who sat at his counter.

He watched the sign come to life as he did each morning. It reminded him why he got up each day and assured him his place in the universe. Stella had loved that sign; she had always wanted to see her name in lights, she used to say.

Stella. The grief he felt was an old friend. He'd watched his wife diminish before his eyes until she simply disappeared.

Someday, his friends tell him, someday the wound would heal. He hoped they were wrong. The day he woke up with no pain for Stella, he would have lost her for good. It was all that remained, like the ghost pain of an amputated limb.

Eugene started each day with good intentions. Some days he even fooled himself. Some days he had a spring in his step that felt almost genuine.

He hobbled around the diner, his bad hip clicking on occasion. As he walked, he worked out the kinks and put the first pot of coffee on for the early crowd. They wandered into Stella's from seven o'clock on, more like roommates than patrons. They shared their first cup of coffee together, old men all of them, and all widowers except one, who'd never married. "Still looking," he told everyone.

Eugene warmed up the espresso machine, took some croissants out of the freezer, and turned on the oven. Cappuccino and croissants. Years ago he and Stella had never served such fancy fare. Now the weekenders and the youngsters were keeping his business alive, so on the menu, next to grits and homemade buttermilk pancakes, were warm croissants and cappuccino. He hated to admit it, but he enjoyed them too. He snuck an espresso every morning before the regulars showed up.

**

At the end of her long driveway, Bianca waved to her neighbor across the way. Claire Koop was a tall slender woman, a little older than Bianca she suspected, and a tad matronly in her dress and demeanor. She wore corduroy pantsuits year-round. It seemed that she had one in every color. Bianca had admired Claire's suit one day in the aisle at Rudy's Market.

"Thank you. I made it myself." Claire had beamed.

"I never learned to sew. It must be hard to work with corduroy." Bianca admired anyone who could create something out of nothing.

"Oh, I couldn't get along without my trusty Singer. I make all my own suits. And I love corduroys. They are so soft and comfortable. And I can dress them up when I need to. Although there's not much that is too formal for corduroys around here." Claire had seemed charmed by the attention.

Bianca noticed that the navy blue cords Claire wore now for Christmas decorating suited her: practical, warm and soft around the edges.

"Good morning, Claire," Bianca said as she approached her neighbor's driveway.

"Good morning." Claire passed Bianca a string of Christmas lights as she unwound the tangled one in her hands. "I don't like to gossip but, I heard that Mike Riley brought Mr. Ishikawa in for questioning about Elaine's death." Claire started up the step stool. "I never trusted that man, always keeps to himself. Never talks to anyone."

"I'm sure it's just routine procedure. He *is* the one who found her. It seems natural the sheriff would need to ask him a few questions."

Claire took the string of lights back from Bianca. "Poor Agatha, she was

20

absolutely crestfallen when I told her."

"I didn't know you were the one who had to break the news," Bianca said.

"Well, someone needed to tell her. We couldn't keep her in the dark. I rushed right over there as soon as I heard about Elaine."

"I would have thought her daughter or the sheriff might have done it."

"I did run into Allison on my way out. She wasn't grateful at all that I had come to break the news. She said she had come into town to tell her mother, acted as if I had done something wrong. With that tone in her voice. How was I supposed to know she was on her way? I figured the sooner the better."

"It looks like snow again, what do you think?" Bianca changed the subject, and weather was always a favorite distraction in Batavia.

Claire ignored Bianca's question. "And did you hear that Sheriff Riley picked up Trevor Streat again?"

"No, I hadn't, but I'm not as…tuned in as you are." Bianca chose the most delicate phrase she could think of to describe Claire's talent for knowing more than just about anyone in a village where everyone knew everything already.

Claire scooted closer to Bianca, as if the chipmunks might overhear. "I have it on good authority that this time he was cuffed and brought in to the station. I would just die if he were my son."

"Poor Rebecca." Bianca could think of nothing else to say. She found it natural to empathize with the boy's mother. "So, Claire, are you baking? I certainly hope so."

Bianca changed the subject once again. She didn't want to encourage Claire and her stories. She wanted to arrive at her own opinions about her new neighbors. Once Claire got hold of a snippet of what might be gossip, she could embellish a fish story like no one else. Claire fished too, like most of the locals, though she rarely needed to exaggerate. She had won the village fishing tournament eight out of the last ten years. Everyone wanted to know her secret. But on this she was silent.

Bianca had learned to keep on Claire's good side while not divulging too much. Unless of course she was hoping to spread some news to the village, then she would confide in Claire and swear her to secrecy.

***

Bianca turned up the street toward the village. Her morning walk was the highlight of her day. She rarely missed it. Today she enjoyed the long winter shadows, gold light rising late over the crest of the hill. Rays broken by the eerie denuded trees, like sentries on the lookout for the enemy. She indulged all her senses. In the country air everything was brighter, greener and richer in texture. The dark greens of the pines were darker still where the trees met: rich, almost black.

She walked on the frosty shoulder to avoid Bert Henderson careening down the road in his red pickup. Her path offered a delicious crunch and she could indulge her new hobby of identifying animal tracks. Deer, rabbit, and raccoon all revealed their peregrinations on the forest floor. She walked slowly, lingering over the sweet musky scent of the pine stand and of the damp crystallized smell of snow on its way. Richard had taught her how to predict snow. He had helped her recognize the nuances of the winter air until she could identify the correct level of dampness and cold to anticipate a snowfall. He used to brag to his relatives back home how her nose made her an honorary Québécoise. She could smell snow.

A rustle behind the next pine startled her. Bianca's stomach fluttered. Bert had sighted a bear on this road just yesterday, he had said. A chipmunk poked his head out from behind the tree. His tail standing straight up in alarm, he ran for his life across the street. Bianca relaxed and smiled at her own foolishness. She had come to learn that sound traveled unencumbered in the countryside. She could hear her neighbors as they chatted on their porches. The wind passing through bare branches was remarkably loud without the competing noise of the city. A buck snorting in the woods sounded as if he were breathing down her neck. She was surprised each day by the myriad sounds of nature.

At the bend in the road, Bianca was almost clipped by Bert Henderson's truck. He waved and pulled over to chat. Bert's skin was weathered from working outdoors and Bianca remained stumped over his age. His close-cropped hair offered her no clues either. He could have been anywhere from forty to sixty.

She liked Bert but they came from different worlds. "I guess if someone doesn't work enough they gotta go looking for exercise," he'd said to Bianca more than a few times. The puzzled look on his face told her that he couldn't understand her fascination with walking. She supposed his work was so physical he couldn't imagine someone looking to tire themselves out this way.

"I stopped by a couple of times yesterday and I missed you. I've been making my rounds to see what everyone needs. I'll be cording up wood for Claire this afternoon." Bert turned his head and nodded down the path toward her neighbor as he lit a cigarette. "And Mike called me to plow out the sheriff's station, but I have some time tomorrow if you want me to come by and split more kindling."

Bert never used the phone. Bianca found that most of the locals didn't. They preferred to drop in and hope for the best. It was like a step back in time, a step Bianca didn't mind taking.

"You've split enough kindling to last through the end of the season, I'm sure. But when you have the time could you stack the rest of the firewood near the back door? And then we can talk about harvesting some wood to season for next year. But no rush on that, Bert."

Bianca's property was larger than the average lot. She kept Bert on to mow, plow, and cut firewood, but mostly because she didn't have the heart to let him go. She didn't mind doing the yard herself, it would be hard work but she could use the time to think. Although she wasn't sure if she was up to the challenge of intimate time with her thoughts. Still, she couldn't ignore that money was tight. She would really need to consider letting him go soon.

Once again, she pushed the thought away.

"Okay, if you say so. I'll make a point of coming by at the beginning of the week." Bert stretched his neck a little farther out the window. "A real shame what happened to Sister Elaine."

"It seems like more than a shame. I mean, it was murder."

"Do you really think it was murder and not just an accident from a mugging? That ring was valuable. I should know, I was with her when she had it appraised for the insurance company. Seems clear to me that someone had their eyes on that ring and in the scuffle it would be easy for a frail little lady like Elaine…" Bert didn't seem able to continue.

"Whatever happened, Elaine died an unnecessary death."

"Ain't that the truth." Bert took another puff of his cigarette. "Well, Bianca, I gotta go. I'm on my way to meet Mike. He's helping me with my bad tire then I'm off to the Blanchard estate. They're having a big shindig next Wednesday and they asked me to cord up some wood and spruce things up a bit."

"Isn't that during the Winter Solstice? I thought everyone in the village was going to the festival," Bianca said.

"I sure wouldn't miss it, but you know how the Blanchards are. They're city folks and not what you would call comfortable with the most of us. And, besides, they're not locals…I don't think they really fit in. Don't think they'll be missed either," Bert answered.

Bert took a last drag on his cigarette and threw the butt out the window. Then he grabbed the pack off the windshield and counted his cigarettes before deciding to light up another.

"I'm stopping for a coffee at Stella's before I head out. I don't suppose you want a lift?"

"No thanks, Bert, I'll walk as usual." Bianca preferred walking but she also hesitated to accept a ride from Bert with Claire in view. The entire village knew Claire was sweet on Bert, even though he noticed nothing.

"Suit yourself. I'll see you down there." Bert's tires spun then finally grabbed the pavement as he pulled off the shoulder.

***

Bianca turned away from Bert's receding truck and made her way up the hill to the Dekker farm. She walked past the faded sign of a red hen holding

24

a basket of eggs. The cross outs showed the economic realities of raising chickens. The prices inched up a quarter at a time with this season's price of a dollar twenty-five marked prominently. Bianca figured it was a bargain.

Her eyes scanned the Dutch colonial and rested on the lace curtains in the dormer windows jutting out of the gambrel roof. Bianca assumed the curtains were handmade since Frederika Dekker was a talented seamstress. The house was much too large for the two of them but it had passed through Kurt's family and her husband would never think of leaving, Freddie had confided to her last week at the library. They had bumped into each other in the stacks. Freddie had been perusing the baking books as usual and Bianca had been skimming a book about the architecture of the village. Freddie had proudly shown her the chapter on their home. The Dekkers were true natives to the area, they had lived in Batavia for generations.

Bianca lifted the knocker and let it strike twice. Kurt was expecting her and was quick to open the front door. He wore a long grey beard that belied his age. Although only in his mid-fifties, Kurt looked as old as the surrounding hills and most villagers referred to him as Old Farmer Dekker. Each year he was cast as Rip Van Winkle in the Founder's Day skit. It seemed to Bianca that he remained in character year-round. Bianca thought he looked rather silly and she took pains not to giggle each time they met.

"Good Morning, Kurt. Am I too early?"

"Morning, Bianca. Nope, three dozen, got 'em right here. Took 'em off the nests myself this morning."

"Perfect! Look at those! They're beautiful!"

Kurt looked pleased. "You won't find eggs this beautiful anywhere else in the winter. Look at those brown eggs! Rhode Island Reds lay them. We spoil our girls. We keep it nice and warm in there for them, and we leave a light on, like Motel 6." Kurt chuckled at his own cleverness. "Are you baking for the village meeting or for the festival next week?"

"It's for next week. I'm baking and freezing in advance. I'm not sure I'll be at the village meeting."

Kurt had been bagging the egg crates but stopped in mid-motion.

"Everyone needs to go to the meeting. Casinos are a no-brainer around here. Any kind of development needs to be encouraged. The resorts are almost all gone, the family businesses are closing left and right as youngsters leave town, and the ones who stay have no work."

Bianca decided not to contribute anything, and Kurt hadn't paused long enough to allow her to voice her opinion anyway.

Kurt paced and his arms slashed the air as he continued. "My son hasn't worked in years." He paused at this. "Look, no one knows better than I do how lazy Stewart is, but there is nothing for him around here either. Casinos will bring us jobs and tourists. I don't like outsiders here anymore than anyone else but...um...well, I'm sorry...I didn't mean you...I mean...you know what I mean...but we need tourism."

Through his beard Bianca could see pink splotches dancing on Kurt's cheeks.

"I bet you're like my wife and her friends who worry about what kind of bad elements the casinos might bring. Am I right?"

Bianca hesitated a little too long. She had purposely not shared her opinions on politics with the locals. In fact, she'd planned on missing the village meeting. She wanted to stay out of it and not show her cards. Now she was on the spot.

"Well, I haven't made up my mind yet," she answered with little conviction in her voice.

"What's the matter with you, woman? We need jobs here—plain and simple."

"Oh Kurt, please stop harassing Bianca." A soft voice saved her just in time. "Pretty soon she won't want to come up here if you badger her with politics every time she shows up." A childlike sense of comfort welled up in Bianca at the sight of Kurt's wife in a starched white apron.

"Please excuse the mess, I'm just finishing up a batch of marmalade," Freddie said as she wiped her sticky hands on a crisp white dishtowel. Her eyes were red and swollen, Bianca noticed. No doubt she'd been crying for Elaine but Bianca hesitated to bring it up and start her weeping again.

Intent on getting to Stella's for her cappuccino, Bianca turned down the offer of coffee. She slipped on her backpack, now satisfyingly heavy with the warm eggs, and headed out again.

Chapter Four

After Kurt's tirade, Bianca realized if she took the snowmobile path through the woods she could shave a few minutes off her walk to Stella's. It was rough terrain and she had sprained her ankle last winter when the snow had disguised a rut, but it had its advantages; it was beautiful, it was quiet, and she was safe from drivers like Bert.

She entered the woods but a loud crack quickly stopped her in her tracks. She almost turned and ran when she realized that a deer had beaten her to it.

Bianca felt silly but her fear was close to the surface, suddenly realizing that if in fact Elaine had been murdered, then she shouldn't be walking alone on a deserted pathway.

The frightened doe bounded away from her with its white tail upright and fanned out in alarm. Bianca felt guilty. She had recently read how deer should not be spooked in winter because they needed to conserve their energy. Bianca would make it up to her later by putting out some feed.

She picked up her pace and before long Bianca was on Main Street. She turned left to walk the last half block to the diner. At the corner, entangled in a circle of smoke, Bert was getting out of his truck. She waved before bringing her hand down to shield her eyes from the bounce of sun off the snow.

She stepped off the curb and sniffed. The cold humidity foretold of snow later.

A truck careened into the empty parking space by the curb in front of her and blocked the blinding sun. It skidded to a stop on the ice. Like hidden wires in a circus act, instinct yanked Bianca back up to the curb.

She caught her breath then opened her mouth to scold the driver but was silenced by the sheriff's emblem emblazoned on the truck door.

Mike Riley slammed his door. "Are you trying to get yourself killed?"

Bianca stammered a few sounds, not sure what she had done wrong.

Mike continued red-faced, "Don't you look before stepping into the street? Didn't you see me?" He persisted without pausing for a breath, "You aren't in the city anymore. Around here we look before crossing the street. I don't want to be scraping you off the pavement!"

He stopped his rant when he arrived at the curb. Towering over her she could see how easily he could use his height to assert his authority.

Her embarrassment fluctuated with anger and she couldn't formulate a proper defense. Finally, she tilted her head to look up at him, her eyes liquid with the threat of tears.

He flinched briefly and broke eye contact. He took a deeper breath then turned back to meet her eyes. She found his gaze uncomfortable. It lingered just a little too long. Bianca concentrated on keeping her eyes open, afraid a blink might initiate a tear.

"I mean…you really need to be…more careful," he said more quietly, still staring and then dropped his eyes.

"I'm sorry, Sheriff. I—"

"Forget it. Just be more careful." Mike quickly sidestepped Bianca to greet Bert.

Her cheeks burned. She tucked her face into her scarf. And then, as she turned to walk away, Bianca finally allowed herself to blink.

***

Mike stared at the front of Bert's truck. It was hard to tell, it was a well-worn Dodge, but Mike thought he saw some fresh damage.

"Mike, you okay today? You nearly took Bianca right off the curb. That's more like my kind of driving. Have you been drinking this morning?" Bert showed him a big grin, obviously enjoying turning the tables on his friend.

29

"I'm not in the mood this morning, Bert. That woman is exasperating. Walking off the curb like that, with her head in the clouds." Mike pulled the car jack out of the back of his truck.

"Well, you gotta cut her some slack, she's a city girl, what do you expect? But she's a good lady, so was her husband. They always treated me right, they did." Bert flicked his cigarette into the snow and squatted by the bad tire. "Thanks for stopping by. Nadine took my car jack, along with everything else, when she left. I've been meaning to replace it, but you know how that goes."

"Hey, no problem. I'm just fired up this morning, what with Elaine and all. Don't mind me. I probably shouldn't be around people today." Mike handed him the jack.

Bert assembled it, shoved it under the truck, and started pumping. "So, it was murder then, huh?"

"That's what we're trying to figure out." Mike offered nothing extra.

"Mike, you can tell me. I won't blab."

Mike was in no position to talk about the investigation yet, and he needed to ask Bert some questions later about it anyway. Mike knew only one other person who would blab more than Bert and that was Claire. Two peas in a pod. Mike wondered when Bert would open his eyes and see what everyone else saw so clearly.

He decided to change the subject. "Bert, what do you know about a deer hit on Route 17 last night?"

Bert put his hands up in mock surrender. "Don't look at me, I was in bed early last night."

Mike liked Bert, he was the real deal, but Mike didn't believe him. His friend needed to clean up his drinking if he wanted to move on with his life. He took another turn around the vehicle while Bert was occupied.

"Are you checking out my grill? I told you I didn't hit that doe. Probably one of those guys from the city. They drive around here like they own these roads. They poach, then clear out, leaving a trail of damage."

"Look, hitting a deer is no crime, it's bound to happen around here, we just need to be careful, especially at night…and if we've been drinking. Next time it won't be a deer, you know what I'm saying, Bert?"

"You're talking to me like I did it." There was an edge to Bert's voice.

Mike ignored the remark. "And dead deer need to be moved out of the road, they can cause another accident, even if you just call the station or the DEC." He was determined to get his message across.

"Nobody around here is going to call a conservation officer, Mike, you know that. Everybody's got a secret and they don't want the authorities around."

Mike's brows shot up.

"You're different, and I don't mean we have any crazy secrets either. This is a small town, what kind of secrets could we have? But you know, someone shoots a deer out of season, or takes one without a license. The usual."

"Then call the station and we'll move it. A deer in the road is dangerous, especially at night and in bad weather."

"Hand me the lug wrench already, would you? Are you here to change a tire or are you here to interrogate me?"

Mike handed him the tire iron and watched him remove the lugs, then Mike swapped out the spare for the damaged tire.

In no time they were finished. Nice and easy. The day was getting better, it seemed to Mike. He might even step into Stella's for a coffee. Or maybe not. Bianca St. Denis was in there and he had had enough aggravation for one morning. He would need to say something to her. He was out of line before, but he wasn't ready to admit it. What would he say, anyway? *Sorry, I was just getting over an anxiety attack and you were at the wrong place at the wrong time.* Doesn't inspire much confidence in your sheriff. Probably better to get his coffee at Rudy's Market today.

He hoisted the tire in the back of Bert's pickup then he made another turn around the truck. He stopped and yanked a tuft of coarse fur out of the grill. Damn booze. "Bert, we need to talk, seriously."

Ignoring Mike, Bert walked away to shake hands with Big Ben Sawyer. His truck had just pulled up with a carcass strapped to the back.

"Wow, Ben, what a beauty. What's that, an eight pointer? I haven't gotten me a buck in two years." Bert circled the truck as he admired the deer.

Mike noticed that Bert's frame was dwarfed by Ben's bear-like physique. Mike had always been relieved that Big Ben was one of the good guys. Mike was a little over six feet but Ben was twice his girth.

"Well, you better get hunting then, Bert, we're running out of time," Ben said, reaching over to shake Mike's hand.

Mike decided one dead deer was enough for the day and made his escape. Bert's lecture would have to wait for another time. But it would have to be soon. Bert was slipping again.

Chapter Five

Bianca's heart still pounded from her close call with Mike Riley. She shook the sheriff's image out of her head and stepped into Stella's, setting off a jingle from the bell tied with fishing line above the door. The ring alerted the locals. Some acknowledged her with a nod or a smile then went back to their food and conversation.

The aroma of coffee and sizzling bacon welcomed her to claim her usual seat, the one in the corner of the counter across from the grill. She may not have been sitting at a table with the locals but her seat had advantages: quick coffee refills and a chance to chat with Eugene when things slowed down. She sat in this same seat every day and hoped that by dint of patience and persistence her presence would wear away the invisible line between the counter and the tables.

City living had taught Bianca patience. Traffic moving so slowly she lost her sense of time as she watched the lights, red, green, yellow and red once again. Long lines for everything from dry cleaning to take out food. Waiting rooms where doctors fined her for being ten minutes late but sat her down in their waiting room for two hours with an outdated copy of *Architectural Digest* and the invasive voice of local news anchors warning of further traffic delays.

So without fail, Bianca dug deep each morning, deep into her winter storage of patience, and made her daily pilgrimage to Stella's. She followed the neon star in hopes that it would lead her to acceptance and to a seat in the heart of Batavia. Stella's, where her status would change like the flick of a switch from passing through to staying put, from outsider to neighbor, from one of them to one of us.

Eugene was grumpy and too busy to talk, so she grabbed yesterday's well-worn paper by the register and waited for her coffee.

Bianca had recently relinquished her *New York Times* for the *Batavia Gazette* although she refused to give up her subscription to the *Book Review*. The *Gazette* was down to earth and pertinent to her new life in a way that the *Times* could never be. It was published every afternoon Monday through Friday. Not quite the *New York Times*, but she reveled in its quirky stories, and made a point of reading it each day to stay on top of the mild disturbances and frequent celebrations of the village.

Today one of the eastbound lanes of the Vanderkill Bridge was closed for repairs. A village meeting was scheduled for Saturday night to discuss the pros and cons of casinos and condo development. Water damage from the last hurricane had delayed completion of the Community Center. The long awaited ribbon-cutting ceremony would be Sunday at noon. The Village Board was pleased to announce that the upcoming Winter Solstice events would be held at the Community Center in Fisher's Park followed by fireworks launched from Miller's Point. There was a short article about two black bears wandering around the outskirts of town; Sheriff Mike Riley speculated that their winter denning had been disturbed by snowmobile and ATV use in the vicinity. The police blotter had only two entries: Police responded to a false alarm at the bowling alley last night which they believed was caused by an electrical surge, and Trevor Streat, 18, of Batavia-on-Hudson was ticketed last night for exceeding the speed limit eastbound on Route 17.

No news regarding Elaine. Bianca supposed a small town paper didn't have the resources to make last minute changes to their copy. Not that the whole town wasn't buzzing with the news already.

The rumble of a pickup outside the diner interrupted Bianca's reading. As the muddy truck pulled up to the curb, the rack of a deer inched into view. The glassy eyes and protruding tongue of the carcass made Bianca shiver. As much as she embraced country living, her city sensibilities got the better of her during hunting season.

The bell above the diner door chimed as Big Ben Sawyer's massive orange body blocked the doorway and a chorus of welcomes greeted him; excitement over the eight-point buck sending an envious ripple through the room. Bianca couldn't understand how one could gain pleasure out of killing. And Ben of all people. He was the village president, and a successful business owner. His antique co-op attracted buyers from all over. He didn't fit her vision of a hunter, or an antique dealer either. But here he was slapping more orange backs and exchanging hunting stories.

Bianca returned to her paper. She settled in to read "The Last Page," a weekly column by her new friend Olivia Last. Bianca had been drawn to the strong single woman who managed to make a living as a writer. Recently they had developed a weekly coffee meeting where they shared and critiqued each other's writing. Olivia was working on a novel too, it had been in the works for four years. It relieved Bianca to know that she wasn't alone in agonizing over her first novel. So far Bianca had only shared short stories with Olivia. Maybe next week she would offer her the first few chapters of her book. Bianca looked forward to a reader who wasn't an agent. Olivia was kind, looking to find something nice to say, while still offering sage advice.

Olivia's column today was entitled "Winter Witness." Bianca had found this winter to be the hardest so far. It had arrived early and hit hard. Everyone was complaining. The topic was worn out and it was only mid-December. But Bianca read on, giving Olivia the benefit of the doubt.

The unending snow and cold: it seems to be all the village talks about. We worry about our pipes. We warn each other to keep the walkways salted and the parking lots sanded.

We start out the season welcoming the flurries of pure whiteness and the snap in the air. We jump on our skis and snowmobiles in excitement.

But within weeks the cold and snow wear us out. Like the ice on Groenmeer Lake, we start to crack. Our joints ache, our gutters dam up, and our cars won't start.

I walked past the frozen expanse of Groenmeer Lake last week. I missed the swans rippling on the water, the herons gliding, the turtles and frogs plopping. I tucked my head deeper into my hood and prayed for an early spring.

Since we hold the power to see the beauty or the curse of winter, why don't we choose to reclaim the joy of winter?

Yesterday I walked past the lake again to see the clamor of fisherman and children breaking through the ice to witness the teeming life below.

Let's not allow ourselves to be deceived by winter as merely a season of death or dormancy. It is uniquely in winter that Nature sheds her modesty and permits us to peer through her lace curtains on illuminated windows.

With proper intention we can enjoy the life only the winter months can offer us and the white forest floor is the perfect backdrop to witness the inner workings of that world. Deer walk, run and root through the snow. If we are patient, we can catch them crouching down to settle in for a sleep. Squirrels and chipmunks scurry about. Bright cardinals and blue jays pop against the white snow.

Be in the moment; stop yearning for spring and the thaw. Experience life as it can only be experienced in winter. I challenge you to truly bear witness with intent: to be a winter witness.

Bianca picked her head up from the paper and focused on her reflection in the mirror behind the coffee machine. Olivia always seemed to see the joy in her surroundings. Even as Bianca attempted to follow her newfound interest in meditation and mindfulness, she encountered difficulties seeing the good in some situations. After reading Olivia's column she always felt enriched, a better version of herself.

Bianca slipped her hand into her backpack and retrieved her notebook. She took a moment to compose her thoughts then jotted them down on the last page. She would need to get herself a new book tomorrow. She had shelves of notebooks filled with musings, story plots, characters and snippets of eavesdropped conversations. As a teenager, when she had finally admitted to herself that she was a writer above all else, she had purchased a dozen notebooks small enough to fit in pockets, purses and backpacks. Never knowing when a thought would strike her, she had worried that she would lose the kernel of a good story if she didn't memorialize it immediately. Richard had found it endearing and had bought her new notebooks every Christmas, but he had reminded her that if she didn't write it down it wasn't lost. Richard had believed that worthy thoughts were never lost. If she had created them and they were good, they would always come back to her. Mostly, she found this to be true, but she had never been willing to risk it.

Today she wrote about her winter revelations. Olivia's analogy of bare tree branches against the snowy forest floor as lace curtains on illuminated windows sparked an idea for a scene. Above that were noted a few colloquialisms she had overheard from the local ice fishermen yesterday morning. She had sat next to them at the counter sipping her coffee and had heard every word they had said but had understood nothing. Eugene had needed to translate for her that waxies, mousies and spikes were bait.

Reading "The Last Page" reminded her that it was time to consider Olivia's suggestion of becoming a reporter at large for the *Gazette*. When she had given up teaching in the city for writing in the country she had also given up financial security. Writing for the *Gazette* would give her flexibility and some added income. It would also take time away from her book, but at least she would be writing.

The fragrance of coffee distracted Bianca once again. She realized no one had served her. She continued to wait patiently, or she tried at least. "Patience is a virtue, and virtue is its own reward..." or so she'd been told, but she had yet to witness this phenomenon for herself. Eugene caught her eye and quickly splashed some coffee in her cup as he rushed past to flip some eggs.

Bianca debated whether to drink the coffee or ask for her cappuccino and croissant. She cleared her throat and paused. Today was as good a day as any to start a diet, she decided, and took a few sips from her cup. Besides, Eugene was distracted today. Elaine's death, no doubt. He was a natural mourner, obviously still not over his wife's death. Eugene seemed to feel things more acutely than others. She empathized now that she was experiencing her own grief.

A man dressed in an orange hunting jacket broke away from Ben's group and sidled up to the counter, placing his cup down. Bianca turned with a smile but his eyes were focused on Eugene.

"Fill 'er up."

Eugene brought over the pot along with some cream and sugar.

"Listen, Gene, I need to replace my Weatherby hammer. Any suggestions who could help me out? Since Raymond's closed up shop I'm at a loss."

Bianca took another long sip of her coffee and cleared her throat. "Actually, my husband was a tool hound and I'm sure I have a hammer you could have. I couldn't use all his tools if I tried. I don't know what most of them do, really." Bianca smiled, pleased with herself.

"No—" Both Eugene and his buddy cut her off at the same time.

"Really, I don't mind, it would make me feel better if his tools were put to good use," Bianca insisted.

The hunter turned to Eugene, shrugged and then turned back to her.

"Ma'am, you don't understand, I need a new hammer for my old shotgun. It's part of the action…uh…the triggering mechanism, I need to replace the hammer." He attempted to demonstrate what he meant with his hands.

"Oh. Oh, I see." Bianca could feel the warmth creeping up her neck. "Of course, how stupid of me." She looked down at her coffee cup only to find one last cold drop at the bottom of the cup.

Bianca buried her face in the newspaper and flipped through the pages absently, but at a mere twelve pages she found the *Gazette* inadaquate cover for her discomfort. Frustrated, she stopped at the crossword puzzle and stared at the print until Eugene and his friend wandered away. She felt her face cool down and decided to keep her mouth shut next time.

When she finally ventured a glance over the paper, she found steam swirling above her refilled cup.

Chapter Six

Agatha's house was only a few doors down from Stella's. Bianca wound her way up the path and passed the faded nativity set. The porch railing gave slightly under her weight as she used it to steady herself on the ice. She knocked. No answer. She knocked again and let herself in. The air was warm and stale with the smell of mothballs and cooking. How long had the windows and doors remained shut, Bianca wondered?

She stepped into the front hallway and walked past the phone nook under the staircase. At the end of the hall, she entered the den, now converted into a sick room. The knot in her stomach reminded her that Elaine was considered Agatha's only real friend. She tried on her cheeriest voice.

"Good Morning, Agatha."

Agatha didn't answer right away but handed her a chipped jelly glass. "Good, I'm glad you're finally here. I need some more water to take my pills. Nurse Ratched left them for me."

Bianca hesitated. "Agatha, I'd like to express my deepest condolences."

Agatha stared at her but said nothing, her expression blank.

"I know you and Elaine were close."

"I said I need some water to take these pills."

"*Chop wood, carry water.*" Bianca remembered her Zen mindfulness exercises. She went into the bathroom and filled the glass with water from the tap. As Bianca offered her the glass, Agatha looked first at the glass and then at the bathroom door. She opened her mouth; her bright brown eyes staring Bianca down and then hesitated and said, "Thank you."

Agatha gulped her pills down with an enthusiasm at odds with her reputation as a reluctant patient.

Bianca scanned the room, looking for an opening in the silence. Agatha was far from frail looking. She sat ramrod straight and even in bed it was obvious that Agatha was a tall woman. Next to her bed Bianca noticed her uneaten breakfast.

"You didn't eat your breakfast. No appetite?"

"Nothing coffee and a danish couldn't fix."

"I know what you mean. I didn't get what I wanted this morning either. Should I make you something else? Eggs maybe? I just picked up fresh ones from the Dekkers."

"Forget it, I'm over it."

"Alright then, what would you like to do today, Agatha? Should I read you something?" Bianca called from the kitchen where she was tucking her eggs into the refrigerator.

"It's okay with me if you feel like reading—there are some books in the next room," Agatha answered.

Bianca peeked around the corner to a makeshift library. Upon closer inspection she realized that this had been a dining room at one time. There was a breakfront in one corner, a serving table in the other and Agatha's worktable was a burled wood and black lacquer dining room set. The bookshelves were crammed with books every which way with more piles precariously perched on the floor. *"This is a person I can get along with,"* Bianca thought as she scanned the shelves. Agatha had an impressive library of local history books, documents and maps. She owned books and loose articles by Alf Evers, the local historian of the Catskills. Her inventory included several books on the Roosevelts, the Progressive Era and the Gilded Age.

Bianca called to Agatha, "Some of these same books are on my shelves, or rather in storage. I have been meaning to read Evers' book on the Catskill Mountains but never got around to picking it up."

"Borrow it if you want. Dry as a bone, I think. Just make sure you return it. There's nothing I dislike more than someone who doesn't return a book."

"Thank you, I will borrow it then!" Bianca called out from the other room.

She peeked her head around the corner and spoke directly to Agatha. "You have been so generous lending me your books. I will treat them as my own and I promise to return them all. The local history is really why I love living in the Hudson Valley. There's a story at every turn. Our own churchyard has Revolutionary War soldiers buried there. And the Crossroads Inn actually served as a makeshift headquarters for Washington for two weeks. How can you not love this place? But here I am telling the village historian about local history. I've been known to talk too much."

Bianca returned to the bedroom with the book on the Catskills and a John Cheever book. She put the Alf Evers book in her backpack and sat down to read.

"How about Cheever? I love him and I haven't read *Bullet Park* in ages. I'm not sure if I remember it."

"Things are not what they appear," Agatha mumbled.

"How's that?"

"That's the point of the book," Agatha said, her exasperation barely concealed. "Things are not what they appear."

"Oh, well maybe you want me to find something you haven't read?"

"You won't find anything in this house I haven't read at least twice. That's why I own them. Worth reading. Not like what they publish nowadays. Go ahead. I can hear it again. Don't mind being reminded that I'm not the only one suffering. Misery likes company as they say. Which reminds me, before you sit down, open that window and let me breathe some fresh air. I don't know what everyone is afraid of. I broke my hip, what that has to do with the window I can't begin to understand. Between Nurse Ratched and Allison the Hun I can't get any fresh air anymore."

Bianca chose not to remind Agatha that she had already been sitting when she asked her to open the window. But since Agatha was willing to talk to her in complete sentences Bianca figured she was making progress. She got up again and reached over the bed to open the window. It stuck at first but then she gave it a good pull and it opened wide. She sat down and turned to the first page of the book. "Well, alright then, let's see."

Bianca started reading and found herself immersed, forgetting Agatha completely. After a few minutes she became aware of the rumble of Agatha's irregular breathing. At that moment Bianca realized how much of living was done in complete privacy, with no witnesses. Now this reading, that she intended for someone else, had become personal and private as she read on alone. The book was speaking to her now. Its opening pages tapped into her deep-rooted issues about her first marriage. She wrestled with bitter feelings she hadn't experienced for years.

Bianca closed the book and gently placed it on the nightstand.

Agatha's eyes fluttered as she came through the twilight between sleep and wakefulness. Bianca could see her trying to focus and gather her thoughts; trying to figure out whether it was morning or evening. Agatha rubbed her eyes, her hands ribbed with blue veins, the skin so thin and crepe-like Bianca almost expected to hear it crinkle.

"What's going on? Still reading?" Agatha wanted to know.

"Oh, no. This book has got me thinking."

Agatha nodded but didn't say anything.

Finally, Bianca couldn't stand the silence so she filled it in.

"I forgot how sad this book is. Cheever exposes the failure of the American dream."

"Keep talking. You don't sound like you're finished to me."

"Oh, well, I'm just thinking back, I don't want to bore you."

"You're the only one who has said anything to me of any interest. Everyone thinks that because my body is frail, my mind must be too. They all speak a little too loud and seem afraid to venture past the weather and my bathroom habits. Go on, go on..."

Bianca knew Agatha was a woman of few words and did not want to be too chatty, but she plunged ahead.

"Before I met Richard I had been divorced. My ex-husband enjoyed living in suburbia but I didn't fit in with him and his friends. Of course we had bigger problems but it caused real distance for us, or at least for me. I felt everyone was busy buying things as a way to show how happy they were, but then it wasn't enough so they bought more things. I wanted to keep my car for years and drive it to the ground. I was comfortable with that choice and yet sometimes, when I would arrive someplace, I'd notice that my car was the oldest in the lot. I found I was second-guessing myself. I didn't like that feeling. When Richard and I got together we decided on a different environment. We moved back to the city where we both originated. We loved it there but eventually we tired of the pace and decided this quiet village was more what we needed. Especially for me and my writing."

"Remember what I said. Things are not what they seem. Don't let the countryside blind you with its pretty landscapes. We have plenty of sadness, deception and materialism going on here too. Drinking, gambling, it's a disease. And now they keep talking about casinos. Be careful what you wish for. Well, I'll tell you what they're wishing for. Disappointment, empty bank accounts, drinking, abuse and sadness if you ask me. Ah!" Agatha waved a hand in front of her face as if shooing a fly. "You didn't ask me."

Bianca had no idea Agatha had so much to say and was afraid of breaking the spell so it was her turn to remain silent in the hopes of not sending Agatha back into her shell.

Instead of talking, Agatha shooed away another fly.

"Go on, Agatha. I would like to hear what you have to say. I admit that I haven't had too many real conversations either since Richard died. A lot of polite chats but not much more."

Bianca paused at the thought of how her life had changed in such a short time. When Richard was alive everything had been different. They had rarely needed anyone else. They had talked and read and tried new things together. They had created a world so intimate, so their own, that there hadn't been enough space for others.

"But Richard's gone now," Bianca finally said.

Agatha hesitated before speaking up. Her face screwed up as if in pain.

"Ah...but I'll just sound like a grumpy old lady. That's what I am, right? That's what everyone says, don't they? Well, then I am. And I have a right to be. No one knows what burdens we each carry. I carry mine and I'm sure you carry yours. No need to waste your time. Too late to do anything about it anyway."

Bianca decided to try a new tactic. "Well, I thought we were having a conversation. You just want to take the easy way out. But I guess when you're sick you have the right to be grumpy."

Agatha's eyes widened, surprise registering on her face and Bianca thought maybe some respect too.

"Keep reading and I'll talk when I'm ready," Agatha conceded.

Bianca reluctantly opened the book and started to read.

Chapter Seven

"I was a misfit," Agatha interrupted Bianca's reading. "I never fit in, I was always on the outside. Still am. So I know what you mean. I understand all too well what you went through then and what you're going through now."

Bianca placed the book on her knee inserting her thumb to save her place.

"First," Agatha continued, "I was unlucky as a young child to have too much, and I didn't fit in with the others. When we arrived from the city I snubbed the other children who had much less. So I had no playmates, lots of toys and no playmates. Later, after we lost everything, I was too ashamed to approach them and they no longer wanted me."

"I had no idea that you came from out of the area. I thought your family was an institution around here. Didn't all the land in Miller's Point belong to your family at one time?" Bianca asked.

"It still does, mostly." Agatha straightened herself in the bed. "My family came up from the city shortly after the turn of the century. I was just a child. My father was trying his hand at the leather tanning business. He saw how lucrative the tanneries had been and picked up a closed tannery on the Hudson for a song."

"But I thought the tanneries went bust once the hemlocks had been overharvested. Wasn't the bark necessary for tanning the hides?" Bianca asked.

"You know your history, young lady. But my father took up with a partner, Harold Fisher, who had developed a new tanning chemical that didn't need hemlock bark. They were convinced that their new system would revive the depressed tanning industry. They were all set to make a fortune."

"Harold Fisher? Any relation to Sister Elaine?" Bianca immediately wished she hadn't asked. Agatha had brushed away Bianca's condolences earlier. But to her surprise, Agatha answered.

"He was Elaine's father. The two of us girls came to this town together. We were complete strangers here. She was older than I was so we were never playmates, but she was the kindest person you'd ever want to meet." Agatha's eyes misted slightly. "She was there at every turn, whenever I needed her. Over the years she had her share of troubles, but she never lost her faith. Never saw the bad side of anyone." Agatha turned her face away from Bianca and looked out the window. "Maybe my mistake was having no faith."

Bianca sat quietly until Agatha turned back around, took a sip of water, and to Bianca's relief, picked up her story.

"But early on we had it good. I'll never forget those first few days. It was autumn. We came up north on the Ulster and Delaware Railroad. The car was new and had a heady wood smell. I loved everything about that trip: the sounds of the train and the scenery of the passing Hudson River. I remember being so excited that our home would be overlooking the river.

"When we arrived at the Ashokan Station we took a horse-drawn coach ride up to the Catskill Mountain House to stay the last week while they were putting the final touches on our house. The Mountain House was everything you could imagine. Have you ever seen the pictures?"

Agatha pointed to a print on the opposite wall and continued her story as Bianca walked over to take a closer look at the pen and ink drawing.

"It was elegant and majestic. Full of the rich and powerful. And the hubris of the time. You could smell it. In the French perfumes, soft leather, rich woods and imported foods."

Agatha sat there quietly for a moment, lost in thought. When she started her voice was little more than a whisper, tentative. Bianca tucked in closer.

"Everyone in my father's circle thought it would last forever. No one knew then how the world would change. Some of those same people we shared dinners with later resorted to a bullet in the head when they lost their fortunes. My father didn't even have the courage to do that. One day he just walked away and no one ever heard from him again."

Agatha paused, eyes glazed. She extended her glass and Bianca refilled it. Agatha sipped and cleared her throat.

"But at that time we were all ensconced in luxury. My father moved in elite circles. That week alone I met the painter Winslow Homer and Theodore Roosevelt. Can you imagine how I felt, such a young girl, being introduced to the vice-president of the United States?"

Agatha didn't wait for an answer. She was in her own world now.

"That first night at the Catskill Mountain House my father was entertaining a group of guests with his stories of Africa. He was in his best form, keeping everyone's interest with his stories. Charming everyone with his infectious laugh. No one could resist George Miller, with his dark wavy hair and a dimple on each cheek when he smiled. And he always smiled. He was disarmingly boyish-looking. He had a way of making you want to believe everything he said. When he told a story, you were there. During his safari stories you could almost feel the sand scratch your throat and the cool relief when the rains finally arrived. As he spoke, you would feel the adrenalin rush of spotting an oncoming lion before he raised his rifle for the fatal shot.

"Everyone else receded into the shadows when my father was present. I was so proud of him, and those nights were some of my fondest memories before everything went wrong. Staring up at him I could picture myself falling in love with a man just like him. Big and strong, yet kind and funny."

Agatha's storytelling acquired a gentle rhythm, like a lullaby. A tiny smile curved at the corners of her mouth.

Bianca slipped her hand inside her sweater pocket. Her fingers played with the cover of her notebook. She was itching to take notes.

"He was weaving a tale about a big game shoot and along came Mr. Roosevelt, asking questions. My father never blinked and never even hinted that he was the least bit surprised that the vice president had just joined his fans. Before the night was out he and Teddy Roosevelt were having cognac and cigars. On my way up to bed my father pulled me over and introduced me. I was struck dumb for a moment but I remembered how proud I was that he was my father, that everyone at the Mountain House thought George Miller was the most interesting man in the room, even with Roosevelt present. To this day I believe that some of Roosevelt's safari stories were borrowed from my father. I suppose all safari stories sound alike but still, that's what I believe."

Agatha paused, thinking.

"In fact, I have Roosevelt's book on my shelf inside. He tells a story about how he and another hunter were charged by a rhino. They landed three shots between them that didn't seem to penetrate. They were sure they were done for but stood their ground with no other option but to shoot, knowing that running was futile. The rhino kept charging and finally dropped just thirteen paces before reaching them. That's my father's story word for word. I know because it was one of my favorites as a child and I remember him sharing it that night. I guess that's the benefit of success, Roosevelt made history and my father just disappeared."

Agatha twisted the sheet in her hand into a ragged knot.

"The vice president was leaving the next morning for Vermont, so they shared breakfast and discussed politics before he left. When my mother and I arrived at the table my father asked me if I had anything I wanted to ask Mr. Roosevelt to address when he returned to Washington. I'm sure he was merely entertaining the vice president but I took him seriously. I remembered something my parents had debated a few weeks back and I asked him if he could do something to help the labor unions.

"Roosevelt sat back in his chair. I could feel the redness creeping into my face; sure I had humiliated myself. He looked at my parents and then broke out with a jolly laugh.

"'Well imagine that! A real Progressive right here in the belly of the business elite! I must say you surprise me with that one!' he finally said to my relief.

"He went on to Vermont and a few days later President McKinley was shot. My love of history and politics was cemented the moment my new friend was sworn in as President of the United States. To this day I like to think that I had something to do with his lean to the left. It's our little secret—"

Agatha was interrupted by the sound of the back door opening.

"Mom?"

Allison Miller walked in through the mudroom with the mail.

"So I suppose we will keep reading tomorrow, Bianca." Agatha's voice had turned curt.

Allison put the mail on the nightstand and poured herself a cup of water. She offered no kiss and no hug. She wasn't a pretty woman, Bianca noticed. Her harsh angles could only be described as handsome. But she was perfectly turned out. Her hair recently colored a soft shade of auburn and cut into fashionable layers and she wore a suit expertly tailored to flatter her large but attractive frame. Allison's expensive grooming gave her a cool, classic agelessness that did not betray what Bianca suspected was a woman in her sixties.

Bianca tugged at her comfortable outfit and fidgeted with her worn scarf. She quickly inserted herself into her oversized parka, her eyes zeroing in on the quickest exit out the mudroom door.

"You must be the newcomer. I'm Allison Miller, Agatha's daughter." Allison held out a manicured hand for Bianca to shake.

"Yes, I'm Bianca St. Denis and I suppose I am the newcomer until someone new comes along and takes my title. Agatha, I should be going now but I'll be back tonight."

Bianca shook hands then made her way to the kitchen to retrieve her eggs from the refrigerator. Without putting them in her backpack she returned to Agatha, said her goodbyes, and walked out.

***

Bianca was beginning to understand how Agatha had come to occupy the position of Village Historian. She was disappointed Agatha's story had been interrupted but she was anxious to go home and check her mailbox. Before heading home she stopped at the bench in front of the post office, cleared the snow with her mitten and took a seat. Her notebook was out in a flash and in her tiniest print she jotted down whatever she could remember of Agatha's story. Roosevelt, the Mountain House, the timbre of Agatha's voice, and the light in her eyes. When Bianca's memory was exhausted, she pocketed the book and stood up. She inhaled deeply, glad to be out of the stifling atmosphere that had fallen over Agatha's room when Allison had arrived. She turned to the right and headed home, contemplating her unlikely new friendship.

Bianca rounded the last curve toward her house and stopped at the mailbox. Nothing yet. She turned down the bend in her driveway and as she neared the house she saw the white tail of a deer as it leapt back into the woods. She remembered her earlier promise and went to the shed to find the leftover deer feed from last winter. She walked over years of hobbies searching for the bag: a hot air balloon basket, honey bee frames, skis, a torn sail, three hiking poles, two recurve bows, and a leather quiver with some arrows. But no deer feed. She was sure that Richard had stored it in the shed at the end of last winter.

She decided to put Richard's bow aside to see if someone could use it, maybe Bert. It was a waste sitting idle in the shed. She kept looking among the gardening tools until finally she found a pail hidden in the far corner. When she opened it she discovered the corn. Not as much as she had thought but enough for a couple of days. She found a wooden box on the shelf and filled it with the feed. As the grains dropped into the box it reminded her of the sound trapped in a rain stick. She remembered getting one for her son when he was just a child at The Museum of Natural History. He loved to turn it over and over to hear the sound it made. To Bianca it seemed that he kept turning it to reassure himself the sound was still locked inside and that he could summon it at will. He carried it everywhere for weeks. She realized how much she missed him. She was looking forward to their weekly phone call. Bianca would make sure to tell him Agatha's story about Roosevelt.

Bianca envied Agatha. She had been an eyewitness to an era long gone, with a personal library full of her notes and journals of the times. Then

Bianca stopped in her tracks. An idea was forming. The hair on her arms stood on end. She recognized that sensation. It was a good sign. It meant she was on to something. She felt better already.

She took the box of feed and dragged it out to the middle of the field all the while calling out to the deer she knew were watching her from just inside the tree line, "Now Dasher! Now Dancer! Now Prancer and Vixen! On, Comet! On, Cupid! On, Donner and Blitzen! Come and get it, dinner's on!"

Chapter Eight

E ugene left his buddies and walked over to Bianca's seat by the counter. He poured her a fresh cup of coffee. Bianca could always rely on Eugene to have fresh coffee even late in the afternoon. No stale or burnt brews here.

"How's Agatha? I heard you've been visiting with her. That's very nice of you." He popped a croissant into the small toaster oven by the coffee machine.

"You mean it's nice of me because I'm not a native?" Bianca asked, a bit more curtly than she intended. Allison had gotten to her.

Eugene didn't seem bothered by the remark. "It takes a special kind of person to deal with her is all that I meant. She isn't the easiest person to spend time with, but we love her."

Bianca's demeanor softened. "I'm sorry for being short with you. I met Allison Miller earlier today and she treated me like a complete stranger to the village. It's been three years, when will people stop treating me like I just moved in?"

"In her defense, you've only just started peeking your head out of your farmhouse these last few months."

"You're right, of course. Some nerve you have frustrating my right to be indignant."

Eugene just smiled and handed her the warmed up croissant. "On the house, neighbor."

"Thanks, Eugene." Bianca split open the flaky crust and watched the steam rise from the center.

"Agatha is tough as nails but we've had nice visits. She seems to be recuperating well. I read to her, she sleeps, we talk."

"You talk? Together? You mean you both talk? Well, you are special then! What do you talk about? I suppose she complains about the state of the village and the world?"

"Oh, this and that, nothing in particular." Bianca fiddled with the corner of her croissant before dunking it in her coffee. For some reason she felt that she had said too much already. She didn't want to breach Agatha's trust even to such a kind man as Eugene.

"Eugene, can you give me an apple danish and a cup of coffee to go?"

"You've got quite an appetite, young lady."

"Oh, it's not for me. I thought I'd bring it to Agatha."

Eugene squinted as he took a closer look at Bianca. "I have a newfound respect for you, Bianca."

"Gee, thanks Gene. You mean I've had it all wrong when I thought you already liked me?"

"I always liked you but now you intrigue me. Here's a cheese danish—that's what she likes." Eugene wrapped up the food and walked her to the door.

Bianca had planned a walk on the Miller's Point bluff, but she had decided that a quick stop at Agatha's wouldn't detain her too much. As she passed the VFW hall she nearly bumped into Ernie McCrae's golden retriever. Bianca was afraid of big dogs but Tillie was different; she was like an oversized bunny, soft and playful. And now that Bianca thought of it, Tillie bounced a lot too. The retriever sniffed around Ernie's landscaping truck and then around the bushes searching for something to chase. Bianca walked by and patted her on the head. Ernie waved, managing to look attractive even bundled up in his workclothes. He was at the top of the cleared walk, leaning on a snow shovel talking to Sheriff Riley. Mike was frowning, Ernie was smiling and nodding. That was Ernie, always smiling, just like the first time she met him years ago when she discovered Batavia. Bianca waved back but put her head down and scurried along when Mike Riley turned to follow Ernie's gaze.

In front of Agatha's house Bert was shoveling, a cigarette dangling from his lips. Bianca greeted him but scooted quickly past him to avoid a long conversation. Bert was fond of taking long breaks from his work to discuss anything from bear sightings to back pain remedies.

She walked up Agatha's front steps, knocked and let herself in. As her eyes adjusted to the dark entryway she discovered Rebecca Streat in the front hall in a fuchsia coat and hat, her pink suede gloves in hand. Rebecca was seated at the secretary in the phone nook under the stairway jotting some notes in her planner. She closed it. The Streat Realty crest was engraved in gold on the cover. Bianca could hear Agatha in the other room wrapping up a phone call.

"Bianca, what a nice surprise!" Rebecca came out from the shadows of the nook and seemed genuinely pleased to see her. Under her coat she wore a tight denim mini-skirt with a pair of high boots that Bianca suspected would not be very useful in the snow. Bianca enjoyed Rebecca's optimism and refused to judge her taste in clothes. Bianca had read somewhere that good moods were contagious, even to oneself. That if you smiled and laughed enough, even if you had to force it, it was easier to feel good; the leap from bad mood to good was narrowed. So Bianca decided that Rebecca's positive demeanor was better than negativity, even if perhaps not entirely sincere.

"Are you here to relieve me so soon?" Rebecca asked.

"No, I was just dropping in to see Agatha for a moment. I'm not due back for another hour."

Bianca walked into Agatha's room as she hung up the phone and put down her pen and pad.

"You're early, is Rebecca Streetwalker still here?"

"Yes, Rebecca is here. She's at the desk. I just stopped in with a quick delivery." Bianca laughed to herself at another one of Agatha's sardonic nicknames. She extended her arm like a schoolboy presenting an apple to his teacher. Agatha took the blue starred bag from Stella's and opened it. She peeked at her coffee and danish and then put the bag on the side table.

"You shouldn't have bothered."

"Oh, it wasn't a bother—"

"The coffee is probably cold and the danish will be stuck to the wrapper,"

Agatha interrupted.

Bianca stopped short. How had this happened? How had she overstepped her boundaries so quickly? She couldn't believe her ears. Foolish of her to think that someone could change overnight, and arrogant to believe that she was the one who could bring about the change.

Rebecca walked in with Agatha's unopened mail from the phone nook.

"Would you like me to sort and read your mail for you?" Rebecca asked.

"No, I can read my own mail, thank you very much. The T.V. remote is all I need."

Bianca stuttered her excuses and left. The foolish feeling of insinuating herself where she didn't belong stayed with her until she reached the bluff.

Slowly, the quiet flow of the Hudson River straining under sheets of ice worked its magic. She reminded herself that this was why she had moved here. She turned and walked into the snapping wind.

***

Bianca wasn't looking forward to returning to Agatha's after her last encounter but her walk had put her in a good frame of mind so she let herself in at five o'clock as scheduled.

Agatha slept peacefully. Almost too peacefully.

The television hummed quietly in the corner with a talk show. Bianca found the remote and turned it off. She sat down and picked up the Cheever book on the side table. Next to the book was this afternoon's danish wrapper. All that remained were a few crumbs and the empty coffee cup. She smiled to herself. People don't change, it's true. Agatha still loved her coffee and cheese danish, and Agatha still had an acerbic tongue. *Plus ça change...*as they say.

She reached over the bed to crack the window the way Agatha liked it then she carefully pulled the blanket up to Agatha's chin before she sat back down.

The curtains bellowed over the bed.

The lighting was weak. Bianca reached over to the sconce above her head and turned it on; one bulb worked, the other didn't, but it was enough to read by.

The filigree sconce was more ornate than the rest of Agatha's décor. Actually, Bianca noticed, Agatha's home didn't have a décor. The house was a mishmash of clashing styles ranging from patio plastic to fine antiques.

Bianca sat on a simple wooden folding chair but the side table was made of delicate inlaid wood. Agatha's mattress rested on a bare metal frame but it was prepared with fine white linen sheets and the two pillowcases were intricately hand-embroidered with pansies. They reminded her of the needlework she had agonized over as a child to please her grandmother. Agatha's desk chair was Chippendale and the Japanese dining room set in what was now the library was surrounded by peeling white laminate bookshelves. Persian rugs barely concealed the green shag carpet underneath while gray file cabinets were tucked into any available space.

The schizophrenia of the décor was enough to give Bianca a headache so she went back to her book. After a few minutes the complete silence in the room disturbed her. She finally stood up and leaned over Agatha to listen for her breathing. Agatha awoke with a gasp and startled Bianca in turn. The two of them jumped.

"What are you doing? Trying to suffocate me? Don't get any ideas!"

"Oh! I was…just opening the window."

"Oh, it's you. When did you get here?"

Bianca sat back down. Feeling like a fool was starting to become a regular situation lately. "About a half hour ago. I've been reading."

"Not depressed enough I suppose, so you keep reading Cheever?"

They were both quiet for a moment, then Agatha broke the silence. "By the way…the danish didn't stick to the wrapper and…the coffee wasn't terribly cold. The blanket is useful too."

"You're welcome," Bianca said, suppressing a smile.

Chapter Nine

Bianca sat quietly reading a local history book published by the Batavia-on-Hudson Historical Society in 1898. Meanwhile, Agatha watched television. Bianca reread the same passage three times. Agatha flipped channels, resting a few moments on a program and then moving on. She too seemed restless and distracted. It reminded Bianca of a young couple on their first date, awkwardly deciding when to hold hands for the first time. Bianca didn't know how to pick up where they left off yesterday before Allison arrived. She was still not sure whether Agatha would show her fangs, and she was in no rush to be barked at. Since Richard died, her emotions were too close to the surface. She did not want to find herself in tears with this woman.

They continued this silent tug of war for twenty minutes.

Finally, Agatha mumbled, "So do you want to hear the rest of the story or am I just boring you?"

Bianca closed the book without replacing the bookmark and sat up straight like a schoolgirl at story time. "I thought you'd never ask."

"Okay, prop the pillows behind me so I can sit up and tell the story properly."

After Bianca fluffed up the pillows, Agatha continued her story.

"My father had been prosperous enough, and lucky enough in the past to believe he could revive a dying industry. Any previous failures were forgotten. Of course, this also meant that he hadn't learned from his mistakes. This could be a useful trait for an entrepreneur, someone who needs to have a vision unsullied by pessimism. My father and his associates succeeded spectacularly and they failed in spectacular fashion as well. But the success was all they cared about and all the rest of us cared about too, I suppose.

"It all started so well. After those glorious days at the Mountain House, Father brought us to our home. It was a beautiful Greek revival overlooking the river. The only other Greek revival building in the area was the Village Hall. He wanted to be associated with its authority and prestige, he said. He wanted the villagers to recognize him as a "founder." He named his stretch of land Miller's Point and added our home and the company housing to the tannery buildings, and created a little hamlet within the village. The house overlooked the entire area, like a plantation. Our house was perched with a sweeping view leading to the bluff above the river.

"He and Fisher had recruited immigrants out of New York City to work the tannery. They lived in the company housing at the foot of the hill. In fact, many of the families are still in the area: the Koops, the Talentis, the Hendersons.

"At first it was a booming little area, and the village benefitted and boomed along with us. The trains brought workers and materials. Eventually the laborers brought their families to Miller's Point. Their children attended the local schoolhouse and their wives shopped in the village. But mostly the workers kept to themselves. The Italians with the Italians, the Germans with the Germans and the Irish with the Irish; the village was glad they had a little money to spend but immigrants were no more welcome then than they are now.

"The activity of a reopened tannery was good for the village and initially we were welcomed. My father even took it upon himself to promote the village of Batavia. He arranged for Fisher to run the tannery and my father daydreamed and worked tirelessly on developing the town. He hired a developer to put his dreams into reality. It was my father who got this town a theater, a bandstand in Fisher Park and a rail stop. His company housing was modest but designed like a garden city and he had plans to add more. He had visions of making a metropolis of the area and he intended on being the father of the new and improved Batavia. He even found us sister cities in an effort to make Batavia more international and sophisticated."

Bianca noticed that Agatha had inherited some of George Miller's storytelling skill. Her eyes sparkled and much of the fragility in her voice had disappeared.

"The first two weeks I spent hours reading in the library and in the formal gardens. Then my parents put me in school. Originally they had hired a personal tutor to come live with us but he never arrived. He had taken another position overseas. While my parents searched for a suitable candidate my father convinced my mother that it was a good idea to send me to the local school as an ambassador for the family.

"I remember my first day at the school. It looked exactly the way you've seen old schoolhouses on television; it was the little red brick building that is Rudy's market now. I thought it was quaint until I walked inside and saw my classmates. They were the dirty little children of my father's workers, and they were farmers' children and worse. I was dressed in an imported dress and shoes, and I didn't want to sit next to any of them. I had been taught to be a lady but my classmates were children."

The wind kicked up outside and introduced a chill into the room. Agatha rearranged herself on the bed, took another sip of water and tugged the blanket closer to her chin. Agatha's hands were stronger than Bianca expected. She kept a tight grip on the edge of the blanket as she talked.

"My first day the teacher placed me in the front of the room and introduced me. I was on full display and I enjoyed being that special person I had been groomed to be. The girls stared at my dress and when I took my seat a couple of them grabbed at my dress to feel the fabric. I enjoyed being singled out. If I had only known that I would have been far better off with a plain dress and no attention. It wasn't until later that I understood that all I wanted was to be a part of the class, but by then it was too late.

"For that first year I rebuffed anyone's attempts at befriending me. I sat in the back outraged that I had to be there at all. The boys with their dirty hands and frogs, the girls with their common clothes and speech. I went home and cried every day but my mother could find no one to tutor me this far from the city and each day my father insisted on sending me back.

59

"So every day I was sent right back to the schoolhouse to pout in the back of the room. The teacher did her best to make me feel comfortable but she had so much to handle. Students with real problems needed her more than I did."

The tempo of Agatha's voice had slowed and she did not seem to notice Bianca. Agatha was far away.

"There was another loner in the back of the room, Thomas Brennan. He was in turn ignored or harassed. At least my classmates wanted me; it was I who rebuffed them. But poor Thomas was rejected completely. His father drank and beat his mother. This by itself was not that uncommon, but—"

The phone rang. Agatha didn't make a move to answer it. After a few rings Bianca picked it up and passed it to Agatha. She waved her hand in front of her face motioning that she didn't want it. Bianca answered instead.

"Miller residence. Hello Claire...yes, it's Bianca...of course I'll tell her...we will figure something out...don't worry." Bianca hung up the phone.

"Claire Koop is stuck in Albany at a doctor appointment and won't be able to relieve me until at least eight o'clock."

"You mean Koop the Snoop is going to stand me up again? Last week it was the dentist that made her late, or so she said."

"I could stay until Claire gets here if you'd like, I don't mind." Bianca hoped that Agatha accepted. It was nearing six o'clock and she hated to leave Agatha's story up in the air again.

Agatha thought about it a moment.

"Honestly, Agatha, I don't mind," Bianca prompted.

"It's up to you, Bianca, I'm just rambling now. I'm sure you don't want to hear anymore."

"On the contrary, Agatha, I am interested. I had no idea about your history."

"Nobody does, and I liked it that way. But you're...different than the others."

"Well, thank you," Bianca said, pleased that she had been able to crack the person nobody could get along with. "Please keep going. You were saying something about Thomas and his parents. Please."

Agatha's face went blank and for a moment Bianca thought she would end the story there.

"Thomas was wounded and never recuperated, I think. But I didn't learn his entire story until much later. I heard what the children said but I didn't care, I was so absorbed in my own misery."

Agatha blinked once, then twice before continuing.

"Thomas's father was unusually cruel, and one day his wife took a knife to him. She didn't harm him very much but she got her message across. Eventually she left town with another man, leaving the five children behind with the father. Thomas was the youngest. For all the father's cruelty, it was the mother's infidelity that the town found an outrage. Children heard the things their parents gossiped about and our classmates would never let him forget what his mother had done."

Bianca noticed a flush creep up Agatha's pale neck and face. She offered her the water glass but Agatha ignored her and continued.

"Things were bad but I never saw the signs that things would soon be getting worse. What no one knew was that along with success came recklessness and my father was slowly gambling away money that should have been reinvested in the business.

"Elaine's father, the managing partner, couldn't keep them out of debt. He didn't have enough funds to pay their creditors. One month he would pay the workers and one month he would pay the creditors. Eventually the balancing act all came crashing down."

Agatha's words were clipped now. Her voice cracked and she took a drink of water.

Now Agatha seemed to become aware of her audience and her voice had returned to a near whisper. And then she stopped. Silence draped over them but it was an appropriate silence, not awkward. They both sat there a few minutes enveloped by their thoughts, and it was okay.

Finally, Agatha spoke up, "Bianca, I know you go to Stella's pretty regularly. Could you deliver this envelope to Old Man Quirke?"

"Of course. And I can find him at Stella's?"

"He's one of Eugene's regulars, Lester Quirke, you can't miss him. He's the one with the pet skunk and the bowtie."

"He has a pet skunk with a bowtie?"

"No, Lester wears the bowtie. The skunk is just an ordinary skunk."

Bianca refrained from commenting that she didn't think any pet skunk was ordinary.

"I'll take care of it tomorrow." Bianca took the envelope and sat back down to silence again. She tried to muster up the nerve to ask Agatha what she had waited all day to ask. She fidgeted, thought of a few openings but couldn't settle on one she thought Agatha wouldn't shoot down out of hand.

"Out with it. What's on your mind?"

Bianca admired Agatha's frankness. There was a lot she could learn from this woman.

"Agatha, I know we don't know each other very well but I stayed up all night thinking about this." Bianca fidgeted with the envelope in her hand. "I don't quite know how to say this but what would you think about letting me write your story? A book based on your story?" Now that she had started, she dove all the way in, the words rushed out in her enthusiasm. "I am a writer...well, I've never had a book published but that's a formality...a matter of time I have to believe—"

Agatha's mouth dropped, her eyes welled up.

"I'm sorry, I should never have presumed. It's just that you have such a rich story."

Now Bianca couldn't stop. Her nervous habit of talking too much when uncomfortable took over. She was on autopilot and she had no idea how to stop her mouth.

Bianca continued, tripping over her words. "I would love to memorialize it. I have been searching for the right historical subject and of course, I would fictionalize it and change the names. Just use it as inspiration...silly idea, I know...your life is private. I don't know what I was thinking."

Now that the words were out it dawned on Bianca just how preposterous it was to make this particular request of this particular person. Agatha was the last woman on earth who would allow her private matters out in the open. Why had this seemed like such a good idea last night?

In the end, Bianca's nervous habit was no match for Agatha's silence. So she stopped talking and in the deep quiet that echoed after her cascade of words she started to think of ways to extricate herself. She could kick herself for opening her mouth and now she had just agreed to stay late. How was she going to sit here all that time?

"Okay."

"Did you say okay?"

"Okay."

So there it was, she had done it. She had gotten Agatha to agree. Bianca sat back, satisfied. And to Bianca's surprise, Agatha seemed relieved.

Chapter Ten

Saturday, December 17

Buffeted by the wind, Bianca walked down her driveway with her head down. She had wrapped herself up tight but the wind insinuated itself into every possible stitch just the same. Luckily, her walkway had mysteriously been shoveled again. Though neither had ever admitted it, she suspected either Bert or Ernie.

Bianca's driveway was a long one, and it was a true gift to awaken after a stormy night to a cleared path.

Today Bianca walked alone. The villagers did not consider this walking weather; the cold and the snow were bearable as long as the day was blessed with sun, but today the sun was absent.

Despite the cold, Bianca looked forward to her new routine of delivering a danish and coffee to Agatha. When she approached the house she could see that the snow-shoveling elves had hit Agatha's path too. Was no one safe from these do-gooders?

She turned up the walk, smiling. Bianca was savoring this moment; she was about to embark on her new project, one she was sure a publisher would love. Best of all, one she knew she would love.

This morning Bianca hadn't had enough time to read further into the journals Agatha had given her. Knowing she had another audience with Agatha had made it easier to tear herself away. Last night she had stumbled home from Agatha's house with her arms full of journals and other materials, just the tip of the iceberg. Today she would bring home another batch of journals. She couldn't wait to get her hands on all of it. She would have months of reading ahead of her.

Today she planned to take notes if Agatha would allow it. She was almost giddy as she approached the steps.

But something was amiss. Her smile disappeared.

She stopped short at the sight of two cars in Agatha's driveway. One car she didn't recognize but the other belonged to Sheriff Riley. She blushed, remembering their last encounter.

Suddenly nauseous, she climbed the stoop. The door opened under the weight of her knock. She made her way to the back bedroom to find young Dr. Spenser and Mike Riley hunched over Agatha.

Agatha's labored breathing caused Bianca to release her own breath, not realizing she had held it since she had arrived. Relieved now that the doctor was here, she had originally jumped to the worst conclusion.

She was trembling slightly. Was it her rattled nerves or was the room cold?

She tried to ignore how much this scene reminded her of the other scene from last year. Bert hunched on the ground, Bianca wondering whether he had discovered another rabbit warren or snake den while mowing. But when Bert had heard her steps on the gravel he had stood up and turned. It was only then that Bianca had seen Richard. What she remembered most of that day wasn't the sight of Richard on the ground, it was the expression on Bert's face.

The floor creaked as she stepped through the door. Sheriff Riley and Doctor Spenser turned around and the scene suddenly changed. Bianca had once again fooled herself into seeing what she wanted to see. There had been no rabbit warren or snake den. Richard was dead. Agatha too was dead. That much was now obvious.

The window beside Agatha's bed was wide open. Small hills of snow had accumulated on the window frame. Her pretty embroidered pillow was soaked and her nightgown was wet through. The drenched sheer curtains clung together in spots and Agatha's gray hair was plastered to her face.

As Bianca stepped further into the room she could see Agatha's nurse crying in the corner. It had been the nurse's sobs she had heard. How her senses had deceived her.

Bianca searched Mike's face, as she had Bert's face all those months ago, looking for the relief she craved. Instead she found the truth.

She turned and left the room. She walked out of the house and down the street. She walked out of the village and out of the sight of another loss.

She kept walking. Not sure if she was going home or just going away, but she was going. She was going as far as possible from the reality of Agatha's death, each step bringing her closer to the reality of Richard's.

***

Mike stood alone in the street, his hand shielding his eyes from the morning light bouncing off the ice. He watched Bianca's back recede. Now that he found himself outside, he was no longer sure of his intentions.

When Bianca had looked at him in there, it had been a mere instant, but he was sure her eyes had pleaded with him to do something.

Those eyes. The second time in two days that he had put pain there. Her amber eyes filled to the brim.

Then she had turned and left so quickly. He had acted on impulse, but a delayed impulse. He stood in Agatha's wet, cold bedroom and argued with himself to follow Bianca or to let her go and finally his instincts won.

Once outside he hesitated again. Bianca's already small back got smaller. He watched her race down the street, tripping over a distracted Tillie who was crouched behind a bush preparing to pounce on a cardinal in Ernie's front yard. Mike lurched forward in a futile gesture to rescue her and watched as Ernie's hand shot out and caught her just in time.

Ernie. Always at the right place at the right time to lend a helping hand. It was as if he had a sixth sense for the needs of others. That quality could certainly come in handy for a sheriff. But Mike had to work hard at it. Ernie was a natural. No wonder everyone loved Ernie. Always there, always smiling. And so comfortable with women. He had what the ladies called a sensitive side. Mike found it irritating that he missed cues Ernie picked up so easily.

"Ah, hell," Mike said to himself, "what do you have against Ernie? He's never done anything but help you and welcome you to this town. Take a lesson from him and remember to smile more. You can't blame someone for being more likeable than you, if you don't even try."

Bianca's parka was just a small dark stain on the distant snow now that Mike had hesitated so long. He could never catch up. Not without looking ridiculous and not without falling on the ice.

What did he want to say to her anyway? That he was sorry? How pathetic. Sorry that Agatha died? That's ridiculous. Everyone knew she was dying. Or did he really want to apologize for acting like such a jerk to her at Stella's?

"God, Mike, you nearly brought the poor girl to tears," Mike whispered to no one.

Watching her eyes fill up had made him ache in a way he hadn't in a long time. The way he used to feel when his wife needed him. Like the time when she broke her leg water skiing on their honeymoon. Or how eight years ago she had cried on his chest until his shirt was soaked through after the doctor had told her she'd never have children. Sad as those days were, he missed them. The days when Maggie had been vulnerable and needed him. When Mike was the only one who could allay her fears. When she turned to him and confided her weakest moments. When Maggie was his first and last thought each day.

Now she rarely confided in him. She was too busy with her new agency to keep him up to date. He rarely saw her now that she kept a small efficiency apartment in the city.

He had thought that starting over in Batavia would have given them a second chance. A chance to put their childlessness behind them. They had both needed a fresh start. He had needed to move past his old precinct and the trauma of his partner's death. And Mike had been naïve enough to think that Maggie needed to move past her business partner. He was supposed to run the city office so Maggie could have more flexibility to work from home. But it seemed they liked working together more than she liked being home. She claimed a fledgling business needed to be nurtured like a child.

So there it was, Maggie threw all her maternal instincts into her business. At first he thought it was good for her, to help keep her mind off things but eventually it became her life. Over the years Mike had heard his buddies complain how their wives ignored them for the children. Maggie would have been one of those for sure, so now she poured her heart into her business instead. She made good money, great money even, much more than he did. But at what cost? He feared she didn't need him anymore, not to support her, and not for a shoulder to cry on.

So, Mike wondered, had it been Bianca's vulnerability that struck a chord with him? Who was this woman who was hurt so deeply by a stranger's passing, and whose eyes were so quick to tear up?

Sure, he knew that Richard and Bianca St. Denis had purchased the Van Rouse Farm; not much went unnoticed in a village of this size. And he had seen them on Main Street on rare occasions. He had even been formally introduced to them at a village meeting once. But like the other villagers, Mike knew almost nothing about those two.

He watched as Bianca finally disappeared into the wooded path at the end of the street.

A crackle roused him. His dispatcher's voice came over the radio on Mike's hip. He turned back toward the house and yanked the radio off its holster, grateful that his musings were cut short by reality. Mike always opted for reality when he had the opportunity. He preferred not to have his thoughts meander. There was no telling where they would lead.

Chapter Eleven

The Batavia-on-Hudson Alliance for Community Engagement, or ACE as everyone preferred to call it, had met the third Saturday of every month for the past twenty-seven years without fail. As the founder and longstanding president, Agatha attended every meeting until her recent operation.

Bianca looked around the table. The local realtor, Rebecca Streat, in her tight red sweater, was the consummate networker and made a point of being visible in as many community organizations as possible.

There were others. Her neighbor, Claire Koop, volunteered for most events. Of course she would, Bianca realized, there was gossip in abundance at these meetings. Her friend, Olivia Last, the *Gazette* reporter, had to be there. Ernie McCrae, everyone's landscaper and the neighborhood good Samaritan, was always generous with his time.

Frederika Dekker was also at the table. Freddie offered a friendly face and a quiet voice. She rarely spoke up or contributed ideas but she was a great worker bee.

Agatha's absence reverberated in the room. Today Rebecca Streat stepped up to lead the group under the circumstances.

Today's meeting was held on the second floor of the Bench and Mug Bakery & Café. Sitting at the window, Bianca was distracted. From her vantage point she could see all of Main Street and straight up Van Patten Street until it turned by Ben's Antique Cooperative. Rudy's Market across Main Street was active as usual. She could see high school students emerging from the library to grab snacks at Rudy's Market. The flower shop was busier than usual. Eugene was out in front of Stella's throwing more salt on the front walk, his limp a little more visible today. Directly across from Stella's, on the corner of Main and Van Patten, the pharmacy's green and white striped awning flapped in the wind. Ernie and his retriever Tillie were passing just as the awning was ripped from the old man's grasp for the third time. Bianca watched as Ernie gave the pharmacist a helping hand.

The movie theater was run down; the paint was peeling, and the marquee lacked certain letters so you had to fill in the blanks for yourself like a television game show. The sight of the lovely old building in disrepair tugged at Bianca's emotions. She was saddened by its neglected beauty of bygone days and the stories it could tell, ignored by the villagers as they walked passed every day, forgetting its history and elegance. It seemed to Bianca that they were so used to its worn presence, that it conjured up no sadness or outrage for them. They went on about their business, never giving the old theater a second look.

Bianca was always shocked at how the world around her persisted in its daily routines when she had been so completely disrupted by death. Her walk earlier had led her into the depths of the wooded path and she had lost track of time. Eventually she had emerged at the edge of town tired, cold, and hungry for lunch. When she had checked her watch she had realized she was late for the ACE meeting. Bianca had decided it would be a good distraction. Besides, she could almost hear Agatha bellowing that the ACE members had never missed a meeting since its inception, they sure as hell shouldn't miss one now just because someone was dead.

The group allowed themselves a few moments at the start of the meeting to express the appropriate sorrow for an old woman's death. They all had been briefly disturbed by the announcement of Agatha's passing, but it had been expected for so long. Some seemed relieved, a couple even confessed to a little niggle of guilt from their relief.

Why Agatha always insisted on opening the windows, especially during last night's storm was a mystery to everyone who battened down the hatches in this weather. The deputy said the window wasn't just cracked but wide open. Is it any surprise that she had succumbed to the cold and snow?

Rumor had it there was snow all over her bedroom. She was so fragile, how could she expect to withstand the elements? They speculated that she must have fallen asleep before the weather turned so bad, the cold finishing her off in her weakened state.

Then, out of nowhere, the conversation took a different turn.

"Not surprising that the cold got to her so quickly since she was halfway there already," Olivia started.

"Yea, she was pretty cold to begin with," Freddie added.

"They won't need to keep *her* body on ice at Dawson's Funeral Home," Claire finished. All three broke out laughing. Bianca could see the effort they were making to tame their hearty laughs but they were unsuccessful. Even kind Ernie couldn't suppress a quiet snort. Only Bianca and Rebecca remained stoic, trying to figure out what to do next.

Finally, Rebecca brought them back to respectability.

"Ladies, you know it's not nice to speak ill of the dead."

"You're right of course, Rebecca." Claire fidgeted uncomfortably in her seat after having been caught acting unladylike.

"I don't know what came over me," confessed Freddie, whom Bianca never expected to behave this way.

Little giggles erupted here and there as they tried to recover their poise and focus on their paperwork. Rebecca glowered at them while they hid behind their agendas. Bianca was relieved to find herself smirking. It was a good sign.

"I've found that a little black humor always seems to take the edge off dealing with death." Bianca looked around for agreement.

"True. Funny how we avoided the subject of Elaine's death entirely. See, I did it there again. I said death and not murder. Nobody wants to think about murder. So we distract ourselves," Ernie said.

"Isn't it true? We just want things to go back to normal and laughing is as close as we can get right now," Olivia added.

"How can things go back to normal with an unsolved murder?" Freddie asked, fear creeping onto her face.

"Olivia, you spoke to the sheriff's office for the *Gazette*. What do they have to say? Any leads?" Ernie asked.

"They are investigating it as a theft is all he told me. Her ring was valuable, it was an antique and the stone alone was worth quite a lot."

"Well, we all know there are some sticky fingers in this town." Claire seemed a little too pleased to point this out.

"But that still doesn't explain the murder. Why would anyone kill her?" Freddie persisted.

"Maybe she had her own secrets," Claire offered.

"Now we are just gossiping. I think the sheriff will do a fine job investigating. I for one prefer to think that it was a horrible mistake and no one was meant to get hurt," Freddie said.

"I think it's time for more coffee." Ernie scooted out of his seat and took the empty carafe downstairs to the bake shop.

"We should get back to the business at hand." Rebecca handed out a sheet to everyone as she spoke. "Here are the most recent expenditures on the festival. We are running a little over budget, as you can see, but nothing to be concerned about."

They moved on to committee business, wrapping up last minute details of the Winter Solstice festivities. They started by arranging for additional chair rentals; last year they had been short. They worked on finalizing the evening agenda. This year a rare lunar eclipse would occur during the festivities and a viewing would need to be added to the schedule. They did one more pass at the menu for the evening, and arranged to borrow cooking utensils for the Community Center kitchen since there hadn't been time or money to stock the kitchen before the event.

The meeting wore on with these details as Bianca nodded, lost in her own thoughts, staring out the window, watching the villagers go about their daily routines.

***

Allison worked her thumb into the soft brown leather cover of her agenda book. The stillness of the funeral home unnerved her. She looked around the director's office, her gaze tripping over the drab curtains and a nondescript landscape on the far wall. A grandfather clock towered over the room. Tissues in pretty boxes were tucked everywhere. She certainly wouldn't be needing those. Allison considered crying in public the worst of weaknesses. But she helped herself to a cup of water. It bubbled out of the cooler and immediately chilled the paper cup in her hand. She brought her cool hand to her forehead.

She sat down again in the overstuffed chair. Her eyes rested on the dated wallpaper for a moment. She found the repetition of the flocked floral pattern oddly soothing. Allison suspected they hadn't updated it for that reason.

She opened the planner in her hands and reviewed her schedule. She had a full day as usual. After finalizing the funeral arrangements, she needed to speak to Bert about the house. He was supposed to have worked on the leaky roof last week. He had never been organized but he had gotten worse since his wife had left. Allison had no patience for inefficiency. She ran the largest hotel in Albany, how hard could it be to sort out a few handyman jobs on a calendar? It just wasn't that much to ask.

Next, she had an appointment at the realtor's office. Rebecca Streat had arranged for her to meet with the developers before their presentation at the village meeting. Allison considered Rebecca frivolous and unprofessional, but she had to admit Rebecca was a great saleswoman. The Janus Group had approached Allison two and half years ago with tentative plans for a riverfront condo complex. She and Rebecca had been in negotiations with them ever since. It bewildered Allison that her mother had refused to sell the valuable land on Miller's Point. She had been forbidden to even broach the subject.

Her mother admonished her just the other day, "I hate to disappoint you, but I'm not dead yet." Just like her mother to be so blunt.

The nosey villagers would surely judge her for attending the village meeting tonight. But her mother was dead. Nothing Allison could do sitting at home could change that, and she didn't care what the villagers thought anyway. She had waited years for this and she'd be damned if she was going to blow it now.

Allison had no intention of being tied down to Batavia with a rundown riverfront property facing the railroad tracks and a handful of old buildings. She had never been interested in living in the village. It was beautiful in many ways. It was her home and she loved it, but she also felt trapped by it. The intimacy of the neighbors, the inability to outpace the past. It was stifling. She had always longed for the liberating anonymity of the city and she had taken her first opportunity to move out. When she had landed a trainee position at the Tavers Hotel in Albany, it was her ticket out of Batavia. The Tavers was the finest hotel in the state capital. Local politicos and businessmen worked deals at the bar and married off their daughters in the Banquet Hall.

Her stomach startled her with a loud growl, she looked out of the office door to see if anyone had heard it. She had skipped breakfast and now it appeared she would be skipping lunch. She was nauseated by the sweet floral scent that hung in the air. There were no flowers anywhere in the office; perhaps the fragrance was permanent, she thought.

She closed her agenda. Again her fingers sought out the supple Italian leather. The smoothness distracted her as she remembered splurging on the agenda and the matching briefcase her first week at the hotel. Then, after surviving her probationary three months, she went into debt for a new wardrobe. Her smile quickly retreated as she thought about the twenty years of long hours she had given to Tavers. She had never had time for dating, and love had almost passed her by. She did fall in love once and came close to marrying, but he was her underling and their relationship had not survived the uncomfortable power dynamic. There had never been anyone else worth mentioning.

The clock chimed twice. Her appointment had been at one thirty. Where was this man? How long must she be kept waiting? Small town businesses, they think everybody has all day to chat over tea and crumpets. It's a miracle anything ever got done in Batavia. This would never happen if she ran the place. Not that she'd work in this profession. The hotel business had been sacrifice enough.

A Porsche key fob peeked out of the leather bag on the floor and reminded her that her sacrifices had paid off in some ways. She was in the enviable position of being extended more credit than the average person, although she had grown weary of her servitude to the debt as well as to the social obligations. It was an expensive and exhausting lifestyle. Plus the hotel had overlooked her repeatedly for promotions, and given them to men brought in from other hotel chains—less capable and less experienced men. She had waited long enough.

Allison snapped the agenda shut. Her patience exhausted, she shot out of the chair and stomped through the office door. She was having this meeting, and she was having it now, or she would move her mother's body elsewhere.

Chapter Twelve

Bianca entered the oasis from the biting cold. A faint rhythm of ocean waves was lapping against a shore. Occasionally a harp strummed or a bell chimed. The stage had been set for a perfect meditative moment. Colorful shawls draped the lamps and lent a soft glow to the room.

Upon arrival, each woman took a yoga mat from the corner and stretched. Bianca squatted and rolled onto her back, not exactly graceful but already more agile this week than two weeks ago when she started.

Some of the women closed their eyes but Bianca continued to observe through the mirror. Olivia walked through the door and they exchanged smiles. She squatted easily and started to stretch. Bianca could think of no better way to describe Olivia than to call her down-to-earth. Her hair was starting to show some gray but it was a shimmering gray. Bianca admired her for that. On Olivia it somehow looked youthful. She wore no makeup as usual, but her bright smile and gentle gray eyes were adornment enough. The dress code at the *Gazette* seemed pretty casual and it suited Olivia who usually wore jeans and sneakers, probably purchased in the junior petites department, Bianca suspected.

Vera Weber arrived next, looking athletic and attractive without her deputy uniform. Vera was a well-loved local that many felt could handle the sheriff's job as capably as Mike Riley. When the position opened, Deputy Weber filled in as Acting Sheriff seamlessly, but when the time came to fill the position permanently, the village recruited Mike for the job.

Now that the village was facing murder, many were relieved they had a seasoned city detective sitting in the sheriff's office. Vera was good at resolving community disputes. Fence encroachments, poaching, disorderly conduct were the disturbances that she handled with panache. She knew everyone, had grown up in the village, and was famous for her diplomacy and sensitivity. She knew everyone's past and everyone's baggage. She knew when to push and when to pull back. But Vera had never been tested under these new circumstances. Mike on the other hand had no finesse for the nuances of village life, but as a team they had all the bases covered.

Rebecca and Freddie walked in the door. Bianca looked around. Everyone was comfortably dressed in sweats except Rebecca who wore a revealing leotard. A few more women Bianca recognized from around town settled in. Then Ernie McCrae showed up. He put his hands together and gave the group a shallow bow then he took off his sneakers and made himself comfortable on a mat.

The instructor entered the room. She reached up and tied her long curls into a ponytail, then she joined them on a mat.

Her fluid voice never rose above a whisper as she talked them through each motion and breath. The sound of the music washed over them.

Slowly, slowly she awakened their bodies with her whispers.

Come into the moment.

As they stretched she continued.

Be mindful.

The tightness of their bodies gave way slowly.

Lift your hearts.

They stretched beyond the tips of their fingers and toes.

Extend your breath.

They lifted their bodies off the mat with ease.

Seek balance between softness and strength.

Their movements became more confident and deliberate.

Find a place where strength and calm can dance together.

Bodies still relaxed but exhilarated.

And back to center.

They paused.

Journey a little deeper.

They pushed themselves a little more.

Maintain elegance and ease.

They pulled back.

Release your stress. A long extended exhalation.

They stretched to the sky, then doubled over and touched the mat with their fingertips.

Bianca found herself immersed. She followed the movements, losing all track of time.

And back to center.

Cross-legged on the floor they shut their eyes and stayed quiet for two long minutes.

Turn your body awareness to the neighbor on your right.

They formed a circle facing each other's backs. They started gentle massages on neck and shoulders as the music slowly disappeared and only the faint splash of water from the fountain in the corner remained.

They opened their eyes.

Bianca discovered she had shed her insecurities and was refreshed. She was glad she hadn't skipped this yoga session, as she had been tempted to do. She had left the ACE meeting tired and had almost headed home, discouraged. Yoga turned out to have been just what she needed to put things in perspective.

The group passed Japanese teacups hand to hand around the circle until everyone had one. They all took one sip. This was their sharing circle where they counted their blessings, literally.

The young instructor started the blessings. "I am blessed with my new electric teapot so I can indulge in a quiet tea meditation with you." Then she took a sip.

Freddie's usual joyful face still glowed but with peaceful resignation rather than her usual exhilaration. "I am sad today."

Everyone nodded sheepishly in support.

Freddie continued, "It is easy to lose sight of my blessings today. The passing of two of our town elders back to back has taken its toll. But I can say I feel blessed to have known them as long as I have." She stopped talking as her eyes started to well up.

Another sip.

Olivia was blessed with a new assistant to ease her workload at the *Gazette* and Claire was blessed with a new Christmas tree Bert had set up in her living room this morning.

"I was blessed with a new litter of puppies last night," Vera shared.

It was Bianca's turn. "I was blessed with a visit from three deer in my yard this morning."

Next came Rebecca. "I am blessed…with…I am blessed with." Her inability to answer saddened Bianca, and she could see a wave of empathy make its way around the room on everyone's face. Finally, Rebecca pushed forward. "I was blessed with a new listing yesterday."

Ernie quickly picked up after her. "I am blessed to be here."

Once they were done sharing they sat around and chatted while they finished their tea.

"What this tea needs is a cookie," Olivia said as she drained her cup.

"You only want a cookie? You have real restraint. I want a piece of cheesecake," Freddie declared.

"Oh no, I keep thinking about the apple pies I'm baking for tonight," Claire offered as she stretched to keep her mind off dessert.

"What about Freddie's lemon cake? Absolutely delicious! One of my favorites and Tillie's too!" Ernie said. Freddie blushed at the compliment.

"Well, I had a croissant at Stella's this morning and I'm still picking crumbs out of my hair but I wouldn't mind another," said Bianca as she ran her hand through her hair.

Olivia joined in, "I love the croissants at Stella's!"

"Here we are at yoga and all we can talk about is cakes and cookies. I think we have a dessert problem," said Rebecca.

"You can say that again," Freddie said.

"We have a dessert problem!" They all chanted at once.

"We certainly do, we don't have any," Olivia responded.

Everyone laughed and got up to gather their street clothes. Bianca found a spot on the bench next to Olivia. "That was a much needed session. I'm glad I came."

"Why would you miss it? Yoga keeps my head on straight. It's more about my frame of mind, not just the physical." Olivia tied her laces as she spoke.

"It certainly cleared my head today. These two deaths are shaking me up. Do you have some time later? I want to run something by you."

"I have to get some work done at the *Gazette* when we're done here, but if you give me a head start I can meet you there in about an hour."

"That sounds perfect. See you then." Bianca stood up and wound her scarf around her neck.

While everyone finished dressing, they decided that for next class they would start a dessert rotation. Freddie's lemon poppy seed cake was unanimously volunteered.

As Bianca stepped out the door she could hear Olivia shouting behind her, "I've got dibs on lemon cake as my blessing for next week!"

***

Rebecca hurriedly grabbed her things and tried to catch up with Bianca but couldn't manage it in her heels. She had hesitated too long waiting for an invitation from one of the cliques that had developed in the yoga group, but none came. As each of the ladies left she waved and said goodbye but no one asked her to linger and chat, or to grab a coffee.

A brilliant sunray peeked through the barely separated curtains to illuminate Ernie and the yoga instructor. They were in the corner with their heads together discussing various meditation techniques. Rebecca remained shadowed in the other corner trying to look busy and indifferent.

Rebecca had been hoping to make a friend of Bianca, she was also hoping to make her a client, but why not both? She would have liked to gossip over a cup of coffee with her as if they were old friends. She liked Bianca's casual demeanor, so different from her own, she found her refreshing and easy. Rebecca felt her own approach to life was too high maintenance. The smiles and constant flirting, the high profile clothes, the ongoing dieting.

Sometimes she wished she could go back to the fork in the road, wherever it had been, when she had made her choices. She wished she could retrace her steps and choose a more comfortable, easygoing path. All had been choices she had made freely and yet somehow she felt trapped by a game of her own making. Bianca seemed to glide through life, able to navigate without contrivance. She wondered how liberating it must be to let your hair down and go through life being your true self.

Rebecca also felt a connection to Bianca as a non-native to Batavia. No matter how much Rebecca had volunteered and networked, she had accumulated acquaintances but not one friend. Perhaps this common background was enough to start a friendship with Bianca.

As she made her way down the V.F.W. steps she decided to stop at the bakery and pick up something special for her meeting with Allison Miller and the Janus Development Group. Maybe some fruit tarts or pastries. Of course Rebecca couldn't eat any of it, all that butter didn't fit in to her diet, but she would take one and break it up and pick at it as she usually did with all foods not allowed on her diet. The trick was not to make anyone uncomfortable.

She walked over the bridge keeping her head down. The Bench and Mug Café was on the second floor of the bakery. She didn't want to look up and risk being seen by Freddie and Claire sitting in the window, chatting over coffee as they did after every yoga class. Everyone's favorite spot in the café were two facing loveseats in the front window where you could watch village life and the snow falling. Rebecca loved that seat herself, she had sat there many times doing work, sipping a fresh brewed cup of Guatemalan coffee, no cream, no sugar, but alone. Always alone.

She stepped into the bakery. Soft jazz played in the background. The scent of warm butter, cinnamon and coffee welcomed her. It was the kind of place you entered with anticipation and were reluctant to leave. Some customers nursed one cup of coffee while reading for hours, never rushed. Individually brewed coffees coupled with daily baked specials had made the café a sensation. The Bench and Mug had only been in business for eight months but everyone seemed to think it would remain a permanent fixture on Main Street.

Rebecca admired the flakey pastries and placed her order. With her warm package in hand she walked the rest of the block to her office to do a little cold calling before her meeting with Janus. Cold calling. What an expression. It was a cold, lonely endeavor. Reaching out to people who didn't want to talk to her, pretending she was their friend. Making a nuisance of herself, trying to create trust where once there was nothing. What kind of a life was it to rely on complete strangers, to be forever pandering to make ends meet? Groveling and wooing at the same time. With women she needed to be disarming. With men she needed to be flirtatious; making unspoken promises they both knew she could never fulfill. Riding a fine line so as not to upset Owen and his ferocious temper.

She was exhausted. All the work for an occasional sale and then nothing for months. Rebecca was not obsequious by nature and every day it took a piece of her soul to pander to others in a town that rarely noticed her.

She picked up the phone and started her daily ritual, the bag of warm pastries sitting beside the phone.

Eventually the fragrance wore her down and she ate one.

Alone.

***

The gold lettering on the *Gazette*'s window was faded. Not a surprise considering that the historic marker next to the building stated that it was the first newspaper in Onanda County, founded in 1826. Bianca walked in to find the temperature wasn't much warmer than outside. Olivia and two others were wearing gloves as they worked at their desks. Olivia looked up, and with her ready smile motioned Bianca to come and sit near her desk. Her smile may have been warm and inviting but it held back just a little.

"So, Bianca, what's on your mind? No more news in town, I hope? Agatha and Sister Elaine are enough, thank you very much."

"Nothing, unless you see news in Walt Patten taking advantage of the town panic to do some early campaigning."

"No, that's pretty standard for Walt. So handsome with those green eyes, but always campaigning." Olivia tapped out a few words then turned and gave Bianca her full attention. "You know, Bianca, for years I wished I had more exciting things to write for the *Gazette*. Now I'm writing about the deaths of two friends, and one was a murder. I realize now I'd rather be writing garden club news. I just don't think I can find anything positive in this day."

"Olivia, some things cannot be smiled through, I guess. We just have to live through them and wait. And hopefully the pain will pass."

"I guess you're right." Olivia fidgeted with the paperclips on her desk.

Bianca looked around the office. "It looks like you have a full staff today. Do you usually work on weekends?"

"We work when there is news and this weekend unfortunately there's plenty. If I weren't so upset, I would consider this fun."

"Olivia, listen, can we talk privately? I wanted to talk to you but I don't want to interrupt your work."

"Great excuse for a break, let's walk over to Stella's and warm up."

Olivia called over her shoulder as she pulled on her parka, "Bianca has a breaking story; we are heading out for coffee to discuss."

"Hey! Hey, wait a minute!" the others objected.

"Condition of anonymity and all that…See you later!" She turned to Bianca with a mischievous smile. "Quick, let's get out of here."

Their boots crunching the pavement, Olivia shoved her hands deep in her pockets and turned to Bianca. "So, what's the secret?"

"I don't know. I just have a strange feeling about all this."

"I'd be surprised if you didn't. Murder is pretty unsettling business."

In a few steps, they had crossed the street and arrived at Stella's. The bell jingled as they entered. Bianca lowered her voice as they took counter seats in the corner. Eugene poured them two cups of coffee. They never looked up so he moved along.

"No, it's more than that. I'm uncomfortable with how the neighbors are talking about Trevor and the man who found Elaine. You know the sheriff is questioning that man again right now in the police station."

"Who, Ishikawa?"

"Yes. Next they will call in Trevor and then me." Bianca took a deep gulp of coffee, skipping her usual cream and sugar.

"Why you?" Olivia stirred in a half-teaspoon of sugar and a few drops of cream.

"Because I'm another outsider and because I was with Agatha Friday night."

"But Agatha wasn't murdered," Olivia said matter-of-factly.

Bianca moved a little closer to Olivia. "I can't help feeling that it's more than a coincidence that Agatha and Elaine died only two days apart."

"Bianca, do you know what you're saying? You think there is a geriatric serial killer out there?"

"Very funny. I think Elaine and Agatha were too connected for them to die so close together just out of coincidence. And one of them was clearly murdered. What if both of them were murdered? What if this wasn't just a mugging gone wrong? What if someone wanted them both dead?" Bianca took another sip of coffee and was suddenly startled by its strength. She reached for the cream and sugar. "When Agatha died I was taken aback but I didn't think there was anything fishy about it at first. After all, we all know how sick she has been. But the more I think about it, I just don't know."

Quiet for a bit, they sat watching their neighbors speculating about Elaine's murder. Then there was a hush as Ishikawa stepped out of the station with his dog. All eyes were on him as he made his way down Main Street and turned in front of Stella's window on his way up Van Patten Street.

"See what I mean? This is when being an outsider is uncomfortable. Do you know anything about him?"

Olivia lifted her eyebrows at Bianca.

"Right. Now I'm doing it." Bianca shook her head and took another sip.

They sat in silence for a moment.

"So, do you want to know or not?" Olivia looked conspiratorially at Bianca.

"Yes, I do." Bianca didn't hesitate.

"Well, I don't know much, just the basics. He seems harmless enough but he has never made an effort to belong. He has lived in the cabin in the hills for as long as I can remember. He walks his dog every day, twice a day, past my house and around Groenmeer Lake. He comes down into town for supplies occasionally. He doesn't linger, just gets what he needs and goes back. All I know is that his name is Kenzo Ishikawa and he was an internment camp detainee during World War II." Olivia sat back from the counter. "I have to admit that not knowing much about him before never bothered me, I figured he just wanted to be left alone, but under these circumstances, I wish I knew more."

"At Rudy's Market I heard some people talking about him and Trevor. I just feel uncomfortable. I feel that everybody sees me that way, a suspicious outsider. You don't really think it was someone local, do you?"

"Stop being so paranoid, everyone in town likes you and even if some people are a little too clear about who is a long-time local and who is new to town, they don't have any gripe with you. They just need time, but they will get there. Until then, I guess we have to be realistic about how people will react when their peace is threatened. All of the sudden a sleepy town finds itself in a murder investigation, the locals will look askance at people they don't know very well. I'm sure they can only assume the murderer is a stranger, how could they come to terms with a childhood friend doing this? It somehow seems less scary if the threat is from the outside. But don't worry. What could they do, try to drive out all newcomers? You, Doctor Spenser, the Blanchards, Emily and her mom, Rebecca? For that matter the real old-timers around here consider Rudy and Trudy from the market newcomers and they arrived thirty years ago."

"I know you're right, Olivia. But the whole situation has just unsettled me. It's a matter of timing, I guess. I wonder if I made a mistake. Maybe I should consider moving back to the city."

They finished their coffees and left their money on the counter. They waved to Eugene and pushed through the door into the bracing cold.

Olivia's voice was swallowed by the wind. She turned her head to speak to Bianca. "I'm not ready to lose my new writing partner. You're not going anywhere, young lady. I think you should try to relax. I'm not dismissing your concerns; we are all on edge because of this, and we need to get a handle on ourselves before we start pointing fingers. Besides, Mike told me he would be questioning many of us for any kind of insight we might have. So don't be surprised if he questions you, it's not personal…then again, maybe it is." Olivia gave her a knowing look.

They stopped in front of the *Gazette* window.

"Don't start with that again. But maybe you're right, I'm probably overanxious and making something out of nothing." Bianca's heartbeat quickened. The thought of being questioned made her uneasy. Or was it the thought of having another awkward encounter with the sheriff that was bothering her?

A tapping sound on the newspaper window caught their attention. The editor was motioning for Olivia to come in.

"Oh no, what now?" Olivia groaned. She turned to Bianca. "I'm going to cover the ribbon cutting. Will you be there?"

Bianca had forgotten all about the Community Center ceremony. "Of course, I'll see you then. Thanks for listening."

Olivia smiled one of her winning smiles and turned into her office. As she entered she was hit by a bombardment of crumpled paper balls. Dozens. They must have been preparing them for her the entire time she was gone. Bianca watched through the window as Olivia giggled all the way to her desk, flailing like a kid caught in a snowball ambush.

Chapter Thirteen

Bianca collected her mail at the mailbox at the head of her driveway. As she walked down the long drive she flipped through the envelopes. The monthly newsletter from her old school district would be nice to review. A few pieces of junk mail; apparently she had won a million dollars. And, of course, a couple of bills. She found one from ABC Storage and when she opened it she found the quarterly bill with a carried over balance from last quarter.

Once she arrived in the house and took off all her layers she took a closer look. The total bill was more than she had expected. How had the last bill fallen through the cracks? Her car insurance had also gone unpaid but luckily she had picked it up fast enough to avoid a lapse of insurance. Not that she needed to drive the car very much around the village. She hoped she would never be forced to part with Richard's old convertible.

She needed to take a long hard look at all her expenses. Did she really need to keep this storage unit? All that remained in there were the books. Boxes and boxes of books. Their old place had been lined with bookshelves but Richard had only just started building shelves in their new home. With no place to put them after their move they reluctantly hid them away in storage. Now she needed to make a decision.

She glanced at Richard's image on the desk. "You're right, I'm calling Bert."

She got on the phone and made arrangements for Bert to pick up the storage key and get the books with his pickup. She told him she would leave the house unlocked. He was to let himself in and drop off the boxes tomorrow morning while she was working on ACE errands. They negotiated a reasonable price for this, one of many odd jobs Bert had been doing for her since Richard passed. Then she called ABC Storage to cancel the contract as of the end of the month and she wrote out a check for the remaining balance. She licked the envelope as she walked back up her driveway. She raised the red flag on the side of her mailbox to signal the mailman to pick it up tomorrow.

Back at the house she took off her boots and warmed up before the fire.

"That's more like it, don't you think, Richard? I just have to take the bull by the horns and stop over-thinking things. You were always so good at that. I can't keep ignoring my problems and think they will just go away."

She put on a pot of tea water and returned to the rest of the mail. She sorted through the junk, put aside the sales circular for the market, and found a flier with the words *CasiNo!* written inside a large red circle with a line through it. As she picked up the junk mail to throw it away a letter fell to the table.

It was from the bank. Her stomach made a tiny flip. Her eyes darted up to search for Richard's photo on the window sill.

"I thought my financial troubles were over for today," she whispered to him.

She dropped the letter on the table. After refreshing the cat's water, she rearranged the already orderly spice rack. She looked up at him again. His eyes met hers.

With renewed courage she picked up the letter again.

Maybe they had finally approved her request for a loan modification. For two months she had waited for an answer. Bianca couldn't wait much longer, she needed to lower the mortgage payments and get back on track. She wasn't able to make any progress on the phone. They kept telling her she needed to wait, an official answer would arrive in the mail. Now she hoped it was resolved.

She opened the letter.

We regret to inform you...

Never a good start to any letter. Bianca took a deep breath and kept reading.

We regret to inform you that our underwriters were unable to approve your recent request for a loan modification. An agreement can only be entered into by the mortgagor, Mr. Richard St. Denis. Since your name is not on the mortgage we cannot negotiate a modification of the terms of the loan.

We have returned your most recent payment. Since the mortgage payments are overdue only a full payment of arrears will be accepted. No partial payments will be accepted.

We apologize for any inconvenience.

There was a knock at the door. Bianca looked up from her letter, unsure that she wanted to deal with anyone at the moment. But courtesy won out. Through the window she saw Sheriff Riley.

She tucked her hair behind her ears, tugged on her sweater then opened the door.

***

Mike stood on the stoop, waiting for Bianca to answer.

He assumed she was home. The light was on, and he could smell the logs in the fire.

The smoke mingled with the snowy crispness and transported him to his childhood days at his grandparent's farm in Illinois. As a boy he looked forward to the snow covering their vast fields, the smell of the fire, and the lights on the enormous trees he and his grandfather would cut down every year at Christmas.

He had a wood-burning stove now, a new model he had taken great pains to pick out. It was the centerpiece of his living room, but Maggie made such a fuss about the mess that he rarely used it.

When the door opened, the warmth engulfed him. Not just the heat from the fire, but the coziness of the room. The house was reminiscent of an earlier age, comfortably worn and faded, but inviting. Snapshots of quiet evenings in the Illinois farmhouse slipped through his memory. Reading in front of the fire, or playing silent games of chess with his grandfather while his grandmother's gentle clanging in the kitchen foretold of pot roast and dumplings or meatloaf and mashed potatoes. Mike still had his grandfather's worn copy of Moby Dick on his night table.

Bianca's front door opened directly into the kitchen. A golden glow from the sun setting on the yellow cabinets illuminated it. The fire danced, and steam rose from a mug perched on the edge of the old stove.

He suddenly had an overwhelming desire to settle into the rocking chair by the stove and sip tea late into the evening with this woman.

But she remained standing and didn't offer him a seat.

"Good afternoon, Sheriff. What can I do for you?"

She sounded so formal. Mike began to regret stopping by.

She didn't offer a seat but she did step aside to let Mike enter a little further into the room. He stomped his feet on the rug to ensure he left most of the snow behind. Then he stepped gingerly into the amber room. The frigid air still enveloped him as he walked in, and once it had made its way into the house, the cold asserted its own presence.

"Sorry to bother you, Mrs. St. Denis." Now *he* sounded formal.

"Is anything wrong?" she asked.

"Not at all, why do you ask?"

"Well," she shrugged, and made a motion with her hand toward him, "I don't usually have the sheriff show up at my door. So I thought maybe...something else had happened."

Mike could kick himself. Why was he so bad at this? "I see. No. Well."

Bianca was staring at him with a perplexed look on her face. "I don't mean to be rude but is this important? You've caught me at a bad time."

"Oh, I see. No, it's not important. I mean, it is. I just wanted to check on you. You were pretty upset this morning and this was the first chance I had to stop by."

Mike watched her slowly close and then open her eyes. Her small hand tentatively reached for the tip of her short hair and then quickly tucked the lock behind her ear as if suddenly shy. "That was very nice of you. Thank you." She took a deep breath. "I was upset, naturally. I was caught off guard by Agatha's death. But I'm fine now. Thank you for stopping by." Bianca's hand groped for the door knob.

Mike turned and instinctively reached for the knob. At his touch, Bianca quickly pulled her hand away, leaving Mike to open the door and step out into the cold once again.

Chapter Fourteen

C laire formed the meatloaf with confidence. Her secret ingredient was nutmeg.

The surest way she knew to show Bertie how much she cared was to cook for him. Twice a week she prepared one of her carefully orchestrated meals which looked and tasted simple and pure. Perhaps too much so, thought Claire. Maybe he didn't realize how much work she was putting into these meals. They weren't simple at all, and he certainly seemed unaware of just how impure her objective was.

Before starting on each dish she would contemplate a subtle flavor enhancer. Today her string bean casserole was topped with home-fried shallots and her chicken was rubbed in a blend of hand-ground white pepper and coriander seeds then stuffed with garlic scapes she had frozen from her garden this summer. She decided Bertie would appreciate roasted potatoes that were perfectly simple but seasoned with her own dried tarragon, his favorite herb. Finally, her apple pie was sprinkled with pats of home-churned butter, a healthy squeeze of Meyer lemon juice and a pinch of coarse salt before it was topped and baked.

She slid the meatloaf in the oven and took out three apple pies: one for Bertie and two for tonight's meeting.

Claire was starting to perspire, she hoped she had allowed herself enough time to freshen up and change into fresh corduroys before Bertie arrived. She quickly topped the string bean casserole with the fried shallots and placed it next to the browning potatoes.

She cast a look around to make sure the kitchen and dining room were tidy, then she scooted up the stairs to change. No sooner had she touched a hint of pink to her lips when she heard Bertie's truck pull up. She parted the lace curtains to peek on the driveway. Bertie remained in his truck, his head resting on the back of his seat, smoking a cigarette. He looked deep in thought and Claire wondered what was on his mind. It seemed that he never got a break. She worried about him. Then he bent down over the glove compartment out of view. Suddenly, he came back up and took the last tug on his cigarette and in one motion threw the cigarette out the window and opened the door to let himself out. Claire dropped the curtain. Her heart pounded: had she been caught peeping? She put her palm to her face to cool the flush as it rose to her cheeks.

The doorbell rang and Claire hesitated to answer. What if he had seen her? Like a high school girl…when was she going to grow up? How could he possibly find her attractive when she was so insecure?

"Claire? You in here?" Bert let himself in.

Claire couldn't hide anymore. She took a deep breath and went down the stairs.

"Bertie? Are you here already?" She hoped her voice sounded casual.

"Am I early? Sorry about that. What time is it?"

"Never mind, just come on in and have a soda." She never served him alcohol. Claire believed he could quit. It was a matter of discipline. She could help him with that. She could help him in so many ways. She was good for him. If only she could make him see that.

"Claire, do I smell meatloaf? Umm, have I worked up an appetite today. The Blanchards really had me working. I was setting up their Christmas lights for their big party next week. I put up a fifteen-foot tree in their living room. You've never seen such a thing. All the way up to the cathedral ceiling!"

"How exciting, I bet their parties are elegant affairs." Claire started settling into their evening together.

"Well, I think they're too big. Mrs. Blanchard said something about eighty people coming to this shindig. It's a fundraiser for some big politician they're supporting. Her last fundraiser brought in thousands of dollars she said. Could you imagine?"

"Well, who are they raising funds for? The governor? Or maybe Walt? He wants to run for governor. Don't keep me in suspense, Bertie."

"Beats me, I don't know these guys. One is the same as the next for me."

Claire was disappointed with only half a story but kept a cheery disposition.

"Well, that sounds like a nice day. Decorating for the holidays. Not too strenuous."

"Let me tell you that was only the beginning. I spent the rest of the day fixing the pool house. Did it need work! I don't think they have ever used it since they bought the place." Bertie sipped at his soda and took his usual seat in the armchair by the fire. "A bit silly if you ask me. Their son failed himself out of college and so you know how they teach him a lesson? They have me fix up their pool house for him to live in. That'll teach him, don't you think? I sure never had any help with anything my whole life. Least of all from my parents. But the Blanchards pay me well and it's none of my business."

"Bertie, I don't like to gossip but doesn't the Blanchard boy hang out with Trevor Streat? He's up to no good, that one. Maybe he should find some work and forget about school. School's not for everyone. I think I heard he likes to fix motorcycles, isn't that right?"

"Now that you mention it, he was working on an old Italian bike in the garage when I arrived. I think he said it was a Ducati."

"What's wrong with a Ford?"

"Claire, Ford doesn't make motorcycles."

"Well, they should." Claire finished the last of her soda, the ice clanking back into the bottom of the glass as she placed it on the table.

They continued their chat as Claire put out the food and Bertie set the table. This was her favorite time. They had established a routine of setting the dinner table and doing the dishes together. As she handed him the cutlery her hand brushed against his. She pulled it away quickly hoping that he hadn't thought it was intentional. What was wrong with her, she was so awkward tonight.

"So sad about Agatha, isn't it?" Claire muttered the first thing that came to her mind.

"I guess you can call it sad when a grumpy old lady with cancer dies four years after the doctors said she would pass. I just call it expected."

"Bertie, really! We mustn't speak ill of the dead," Claire said with a smirk. Trying to avoid a repeat of her behavior earlier in the day.

"Says who anyway? I'm not saying anything that's not true. She was old, she was nasty, she had cancer, and she was supposed to die years ago."

"Well, she *was* difficult," Claire conceded.

"Difficult doesn't even begin to cover it. Remember when she had that fight with Sister Elaine? I mean really, who could fight with Elaine, God rest her soul?"

"That's true, but I never really understood what that was about. I know they have some history. I heard it had something to do with Agatha's son."

"You mean her daughter?"

"No, I mean her son. I don't like to gossip, but awhile back I heard that Agatha had a son that she gave up for adoption years ago. Rumor has it a local family adopted him."

"Who is it? Does he know she is his mother? All that property on Miller's Point, I bet he would like to know. Especially now."

"There are quite a few possibilities, actually. The resort owners at Groenmeer Lake have a son about that age, Edward and Elizabeth Streat do too. Hmm, let me see, Stewart Dekker is too young but—"

"I don't want to talk about Stew Dekker," Bertie snapped.

"Of course, of course, I'm sorry, Bertie." Claire was dizzy with her missteps. Stewart Dekker had stolen Bertie's wife and good riddance if you asked Claire but she had to consider Bert's pride. She changed approach.

"Then again, even you and Ben Sawyer are about the right age."

"What are you talking about? I know who my parents are. And Ben is the spitting image of his father. Now you're just talking nonsense. If one of us was a Miller, we'd know about it, we would." Bert paused. "But, I have to admit, it does make you think."

When the food was all set out, the aroma of garlic, tarragon and shallots was so seductive Claire was sure that at least subconsciously Bertie was aware of her intentions.

He served himself heaping amounts of food and Claire beamed as he took seconds and then thirds. Claire watched Bert eat with gusto. Unable to talk with his mouth full, they ate in silence for most of the meal. The silence was fine with Claire, she could almost believe they were an old married couple.

"Oh yeah, Claire, I brought you something. I almost forgot."

Claire's appetite vanished. In all the years they had known each other he had never brought her a gift. Could he have realized that her birthday had passed unnoticed a couple of weeks ago? As he fished in his pocket she tried to imagine what he could possibly have gotten for her that would fit in there. She dared not believe it could be a piece of jewelry, but allowed herself the indulgence of thinking that it might be some other type of trinket.

He eventually pulled out a crumpled piece of paper and pushed it to her side of the table.

"The Blanchards' maid gave me some lunch today and she made the best cranberry muffin thing I ever had and I told her so and she offered me the recipe, which I thought was pretty funny. Don't know what she thought I would do with it, but she speaks with an accent so maybe we weren't communicating too well. I figure you like cooking, so I brought it to you."

Claire opened the paper to find a recipe for scones written in a neat script. She mustered up a smile and said thank you.

She got up from the table and went into the other room with the excuse of getting the pie. Once in the kitchen she leaned against the counter to catch her breath. She busied herself removing the pie and warm plates from the oven, taking comfort in the clang of dishes and the scent of warm apples.

She brought him his slice and focused on the French vanilla ice cream melting as she walked to the dining room. Claire ate her small slice silently, afraid her voice would betray her disappointment. How had she allowed the thought of a gift to enter her mind? She was embarrassed by her childishness.

How could the whole village see inside her heart except Bertie, snickering like they did in seventh grade when Bertie said he wanted to sit with her at lunch. She had boasted to her friends that she had a lunch date with Bertie.

Then he had shown up with his math homework unfinished and looking for help. Her classmates had teased her for weeks. Those girls had gone from best friends to mere classmates that day.

Bertie was done with dessert and stood up to start cleaning.

"Claire, you're not going to waste this pie, I hope?"

"I'm not hungry anymore, I ate too much meatloaf."

"You don't mind if I finish it, do you?" he said as he grabbed his fork and finished it in two bites.

They quickly cleaned up. It was almost time to get to the meeting. Claire was relieved that this one night at least he didn't go straight to McLoughlin's for a few beers. She pulled on her coat and grabbed her car keys off the hook at the door. She took one pie and Bertie took the other. As they approached her car they both realized that Bertie had blocked her in the driveway.

"It doesn't make sense to take two cars down the road, jump in mine since I'm blocking your car." Bert waved her over.

"Okay," she said, trying to sound casual. She climbed into his truck and balanced the pies on her knees for the three-minute ride. She sat up straighter as they pulled passed the Village Hall with all her neighbors congregating outside. She almost felt like she was on a date when the door on her side stuck and Bertie had to come around to give the door a tug and let her out.

"Thank you, Bertie."

"Sorry about the door, Claire. You go on in, I'm going to have a smoke and say hello to Big Ben before the meeting starts."

Claire walked in alone with the two pies stacked one on top of the other.

Chapter Fifteen

Bianca wiped crumbs from her fingers and looked for a seat at the back of the Village Hall. It had been a difficult choice at the bake sale table. Bianca had settled on Eugene's simple coffee cake piled two inches high with crumbs.

She was pleased with her choice but now her battle to tame the crumbs began. Despite all her good intentions she was forever losing her food battles in public: gooey cheeses, crumbling crackers, and greasy finger foods. She avoided the lemon poppy cake since she made it a rule to never eat anything with poppy seeds in public. The pecan pie would have required finger licking, another no-no. She enjoyed the crumb cake as long as she pretended not to notice the Hansel and Gretel trail left behind in her wake.

Bianca took a seat in the back of the room, a perfect position to observe. She balanced her notebook on her knee. She ate a large crumb off the top of the cake and took a look around.

Not large, the Village Hall was a Greek revival from the early nineteenth century. It had never been out of use, and it certainly showed its age. The village managed to have the maple floors and the wainscoting waxed regularly, and tonight they gleamed.

Framed pictures of the U.S presidents lined the walls, along with village evacuation routes in the case of flooding. The dropped ceiling was the only architectural anachronism Bianca noticed.

She tightened her sweater. The potbelly stove in the middle of the room radiated some heat but the building remained drafty. She sipped her coffee and warmed her hands on the cup.

Bianca sat people-watching, one of her favorite pastimes. Rebecca Streat took charge of the bake table; her perpetual smile greeted everyone who walked in the door, and she sold at least one dessert to everyone.

Rebecca's maroon hair was in a tight bun, and along with her tortoise shell glasses, she looked more like a reserved librarian than a realtor tonight. She spiced it up with a neckline just a tad lower than professional, and a suit that fit just a tiny bit too snugly on her lovely figure.

Agatha's daughter was alone in the opposite corner eating a sliver of pecan pie with no apparent mess. She had a presence in the room without actually mingling or making eye contact. Bianca found that even at a distance Allison made her uncomfortable. She tried to ignore the feelings bubbling to the surface as she absentmindedly brushed the last of the crumbs from her pants.

Eugene Wilkins was offering Trudy Bauer his seat. Always the gentleman and despite his bad hip, he wouldn't sit if a woman needed a chair. If you weren't paying attention you might believe that Eugene was without a care but as a mourner herself, Bianca recognized the telltale signs: the lapses in conversation, the daydreaming, the occasional catch in his voice.

Ernie McCrae arrived still wearing his snowplowing clothes. He quietly took his lemon cake, and with his golden retriever sat in the back just a few chairs over from Bianca. Tillie stared up at him, her tail wagging furiously as her eyes darted between Ernie's face and the cake in his hand. Ernie hiccupped a tiny laugh, shared his cake with her and then smoothed the top of her head. When he looked up he caught Bianca watching him. He smiled and raised his coffee cup.

Big Ben Sawyer was working the room as usual with his hearty handshakes and deep belly laughs. When he approached Allison Miller his voice no longer carried across the room. He must have been offering her his condolences. Was it Bianca's imagination or did Allison's cool demeanor seem to warm slightly?

Claire Koop and Freddie Dekker were chatting. It sounded as if they were exchanging recipes. She was talking to Freddie, but Claire's eyes were busy searching and finally rested when they found Bert making his way into the room.

Rebecca stopped Bert at the door. She used all her charm and sold him a slice of lemon cake and a bag of truffles, and then pulled him back by the arm before he left the table and gave him the last piece of her pecan pie, waving away his attempt to pay for it. He walked away a bit dazed, wending his way around the room until he found one of the few empty seats. He tipped his cap to Bianca, sat down next to her and absentmindedly handed her his bag of truffles.Taken by surprise, Bianca started to thank him but Bert had already turned to his right to chat with Ernie.

Out of the corner of her eye Bianca noticed Rebecca abandon the bake table. She moved to the coffee station where she fiddled with the coffee urn, the sugar and the cream. When she was done tidying up, Rebecca stood there sipping her coffee while reading the meeting agenda. Bianca could see that Rebecca's eyes were not skimming the paper at all. She was concentrating, almost squinting. Bianca followed Rebecca's gaze and noticed Allison Miller, Senator Walt Patten, and the developer having a quiet conversation at the far end of the table. Finally, Walter's assistant came over pointing to her watch and Walter walked up to the podium.

Owen Streat, Rebecca's husband, walked in. Tall, with striking blue eyes, most of the ladies noticed him when he arrived. He looked around with obvious frustration until he found Rebecca. When he reached the coffee station he bent to kiss her, she gave him her cheek and they stood quietly for a moment as Big Ben leapt to the podium to start the meeting. Rebecca looked around and placed herself in the only remaining seat in the room next to Father McCardle, leaving Owen alone by the coffee.

***

Ben Sawyer turned on the mic. The meeting was about to start and as usual there was standing room only. Batavian residents were nothing if not diligent in their civic responsibilities.

"Welcome, neighbors! Before we get started we would like to thank everyone who donated baked goods for our sale. The proceeds will be going toward the village weather station. We remain a little short of our goal and with tonight's proceeds I believe we will finally make it a reality." The crowd applauded.

Bianca turned to Bert. "Did he say a weather station?"

"Yep, he did indeed. The high school science club plans to man a weather station at Miller's Point. It started out as a science lesson but the idea just took off, it did."

"But what about national weather services? Is a weather station really necessary?"

"Oh, it's necessary. The last couple of hurricanes caused serious damage. The river and the creek flooded so quickly that by the time the national warnings made it to us, it was too late. That was before your time. We're overdue, we are. I'm hoping the weather station will be up in time for the next big storm." Bert took a swig of coffee, something akin to a deep beer chug. With his coffee in his hand he motioned to Bianca's knee. "What're you writing in there? I seen you scribbling away. Anything interesting?"

Bianca closed her notebook, she didn't want to reveal that she was taking notes on her observations of her neighbors. "Oh, it's nothing, just taking some notes for an article I'm thinking about writing for the *Gazette*."

"Oh yeah? I didn't know you wrote for the *Gazette*. What side of this fight are you on anyway?"

Bianca hesitated a moment to compose a diplomatic answer when Ben tapped the mic to gain the wandering attention of the audience.

"I'm going to call this meeting to order and Sister Concetta will lead us in a moment of silence and the pledge. Thank you, Sister." There was more applause as everyone watched Eugene help the nun up from her chair and to the front of the room.

The applause was polite but guarded. Sister Elaine usually led the prayer before the meetings. Bianca remembered last month when Ben had called her up to the podium as usual. The two of them had been a sight. Quite a bit over six feet, two hundred and fifty pounds with a beard that could have used a trimming, Ben had dominated the front of the room in red and black plaid. Sister Elaine couldn't have weighed more than ninety-five pounds in her gray pantsuit. She had no adornment but the family ring she had always worn on her left hand. Where Ben was like a beacon in the room, Sister Elaine had faded away, almost ethereal.

Sister Elaine had looked up at him. "My, how big you've grown since eighth grade, Ben." Everyone had chuckled remembering Ben's reputation as a troublemaker in school. Stories of how tiny Sister Elaine had managed to keep him in check were always batted around at gatherings. Despite his exploits, he had been every teacher's pet. He was called The Mayor even back then; now he was the Village President. In Batavia it seemed that the more things changed, the more they stayed the same.

A brief squeal of the mic caught Bianca's attention.

"A moment of silence as we each pray for our dear departed Elaine Fisher and Agatha Miller." Sister Concetta bowed her head and everyone followed suit.

After a few moments Sister Concetta lifted her head, turned to face the flag, and started the pledge. Everyone picked up with her, some slower than others, some racing ahead.

"Thank you, Sister. Tonight we have two brief presentations in a series. State Senator Walt Patten is here to speak to us about the advantages of adding class III casino gaming to our area. Then the Janus Development Corporation will discuss a proposed timeshare development right here in our village. Both projects promise to bring much-needed job opportunities and tourism."

Walt Patten spoke first. Elegant and certainly on the right side of handsome, it was obvious to Bianca how Walter was able to make it in politics. His amiable disposition and his soft hazel eyes made him easy to listen to even when you didn't agree with him. He discussed the jobs that would be created in the region and he reminded the crowd that a casino would provide much-needed tax relief. This information sent up a positive murmur and heads nodded all around.

Walter wrapped up. "I want to end with a pledge to work with you drafting a convincing letter to the governor to help him see that casino gaming is the way for us to reclaim the title of Hospitality Capital of the Northeast and to urge him to put it to a referendum vote."

A young man stepped up to the podium as Walt took his seat. He sported an expensive haircut and a more expensive suit.

Bert leaned over to Bianca again. "I wonder if he knows that we don't take too kindly to outsiders. We certainly don't trust young slick ones."

The presentation was brief but packed a punch when he unveiled a beautifully designed mock-up of a five-story condo to mixed sounds of approval.

Ben returned to the podium. "Okay, ladies and gents, the floor is open. Let's hear what you have to say!"

The first person to pop out of his chair was Old Farmer Dekker. Everyone laughed, clapped and then playfully booed him off the floor before he could finish his first sentence. Kurt's friends were more than a little familiar with his rants in favor of the casino.

"We know what you think, Kurt!"

"*And* he's off!"

"Not again!"

Father McCardle stood up and raised both his hands as if giving a blessing. As the room quieted down, a sigh or two escaped from the ladies in the corner. It was no secret that Father McCardle's looks had helped rebuild attendance at St. James the Elder. His sandy hair slipped over his left eye. It was said that he was sinfully handsome for a priest, the fresh blush on his cheeks proof that Liam McCardle was uncomfortably aware of his status.

"Thank you, Kurt. I'll take over from here." Everyone laughed. Kurt sat down clumsily but didn't seem too hurt by the not-so-gentle ribbing his friends had just given him.

With a smile, Father McCardle began. "I am not against gambling per se but..." He was interrupted by laughter and snickering as everyone considered the small and not-so-small sums many of them had lost to his exceptional poker skills over the last few years. "But we cannot forget that we are a community and it is morally wrong to benefit from the weaknesses of our neighbors. Casinos prey on weakness. Gambling will change the character of our village. Is the economic benefit worth it?"

Sister Concetta chimed in, "I agree with Father McCardle. But I want to add that we must protect our children. They are the weakest of our community and they are our primary responsibility."

Allison Miller shot out of her chair.

"Sister, let's remember that children are raised by their parents. It is their responsibility, not mine, to protect them."

Freddie Dekker stood up and offered her thoughts. "Allison, let's face it, you haven't really lived here full time in years and those of us who do need to consider the bad elements that would creep into Batavia."

"What bad element are you worried about? Gambling is already going on, what do you think happens in the back room at McLoughlin's Pub?" Here Allison settled a blatant look on Father McCardle. As she turned to nod in Bert's direction she said, "Drinking? That happens in the front room at McLoughlin's. We aren't even ashamed enough to hide that. Staying out all night and cheating on spouses? We all know that happens too." Allison was discreet enough to avoid looking at Stewart Dekker or Bert's ex-wife, Nadine.

"Freddie's no match for Allison, she should quit while she's ahead."

As if she heard Bert's whisper, Freddie took her seat.

Claire Koop spoke up next. "The only consideration we should have right now is jobs. Many of us lucky enough to work have to hold down more than one job to make ends meet. We need jobs. Here. Now. Everything else is irrelevant."

Emily White stood up. She looked about seventeen years old but was poised and confident beyond her years.

"Ms. Koop, I don't think we can focus only on jobs. Studies show that there is an increase in addictive behavior when access is increased. Local casinos would be too much temptation for those with gambling and drinking problems already."

Ryan McLoughlin, the pub owner, jumped up at her remarks. "Young lady, we need jobs, and we need patrons! Period!" Ryan's unruly red hair shook as he spoke.

This got the group riled up and everyone broke out talking at once. Many got out of their chairs.

Ben tapped the mic a few times to no effect. Finally, he stuck two fingers in his mouth and blew.

"Whoa! Ben! For Christ's sake!" said Bert. He turned to Father McCardle. "Sorry about that." And then he nodded to the nuns and sat down.

"Okay, everyone, we need to be able to discuss this calmly. Remember, we are all friends here no matter what happens. Now, if we are ready, who would like the floor?"

Margaret Blanchard raised her hand but didn't wait to be called on. She stood up.

"We are so lucky to be living in such a lovely place as Batavia. Do we really want to see these kinds of changes? Shouldn't we be looking to add something cultural to this area? More concerts and exhibits would bring in tourism as well, don't you think?"

"Batavia may be lovely for you, Mrs. Blanchard, but not everyone lives in a mansion on the hill. Some of us live down by the tracks. The view isn't quite so nice while we sit around waiting for a job," Stew Dekker called out, slumped in his chair, arms crossed over his chest.

"Well, you gotta get out and find a job, they don't come looking for you, they don't!" Bert called in response.

Stew shot out of his chair, looking for Bert.

Ben took two swift strides over to Stewart and put his hand on his shoulder. He took Ben's warning and sat back down. Nobody argued with Big Ben, certainly not someone of Stew's small stature.

Eugene Wilkins slowly stood up. "All I know is that I want to preserve my peace. I don't live in a fancy house but I live here for a reason. I don't want this place to change."

Things quieted down for a few moments. Some mumblings here and there. Ben took the floor. "Well, we have heard quite a bit about the casinos. Do we have any questions or comments for Janus regarding the condo proposal?"

Eugene stood up again. "I have a question. Five stories seems high around here. Where could that be built and not be in the way? You said something about the riverfront but I don't like the idea of blocking everyone's view of the river."

Ernie McCrae spoke up. "I agree with Eugene. Five-stories just won't fit in around here. I walk with Tillie on the bluff every day. Lots of us depend on the river as a place to sit and think and regenerate. I don't consider the riverside a luxury, it has become a necessity for me now."

The young man from Janus took the mic. "If we want to attract a certain type of buyer we need to offer them something more than housing. Batavia offers a view and hopefully soon a casino will be built in the area. It's your most valuable asset. There are other towns that would like to see a project like this but they have nothing to offer."

As things quieted down Ben called the meeting to an end. "If we have no more to say, I suggest we all go home and think about these proposals and reconvene next month to pick up the discussions. Thank you, and good night. And let's make sure all the desserts are spoken for before we leave. I'm counting on you!"

Chapter Sixteen

Bianca brushed the last of the crumbs from her lap and stood up. For the first time that evening she noticed Mr. Ishikawa in the corner of the room alone. He was heading toward the door. She excused her way through the crowded room until she reached him.

"Mr. Ishikawa, hello, I am Bianca St. Denis. I don't think we've met."

"Hello, yes, nice to meet you. You live on the old Van Rouse Farm."

"Yes, I do."

"Very lovely there. I'm glad it is being cared for again."

"We, I mean, I try."

"Oh yes, my condolences."

"Thank you. You have had a difficult time these last couple of days too, I hear. I think it's been hard for you after finding Sister Elaine's body."

"It's never easy to encounter death first hand."

"I mean the villagers are not always so easy to get along with."

"They just have strong opinions about who is considered a true Batavian. I've had some hardships over the years, my wife passing, some financial burdens, like everyone else. The town though has always been respectful of my privacy."

Bianca suspected that was a nice way to say that the village didn't make his problems their own.

"Did you know Sister Elaine well?"

"No, but we would run into each other almost every day when we walked our dogs. She always had a kind word."

Bianca was curious about this elusive man but she could think of nothing more to ask him.

"Goodnight, it was nice to meet you." With a nod he left.

Bianca shoved her notebook into her coat pocket and made her way to Ben. She quickly jumped into her question before he had a chance to corner her about her opinion on the casino.

"Ben, I ran out of deer feed. Any suggestions where I could get more?"

"Sure, I've got just the place. Go down Route 17, east out of town about four miles just before the bridge. You tell them I sent you, they will take good care of you."

Emily poked her head into their conversation. She had long, chestnut colored hair that almost reached her waist. It was so abundant that only ingrained etiquette prevented Bianca from touching it.

"Sorry to eavesdrop, but I have read that feeding deer in winter is not a good idea."

Ben's considerable brows shot up.

Emily continued in her reasoned manner. "Apparently it interferes with their natural ability to digest. They gorge themselves to make reserves before the winter sets in and then throughout the season their bodies are able to digest tough twigs and brush. But when we provide feed that they wouldn't normally get in nature, their bodies can't digest it and they actually starve with a full belly."

Bianca was horrified and looked at Ben, pleading for him to disprove Emily's theory.

"Emily, I think you've been reading too many books. We have been feeding deer around here every winter since forever. Can't have deer starving before the hunt, now can we?"

Now both of them looked at Ben, appalled.

"Hey ladies, now you know I'm just kidding...just a little hunting season humor. Please forgive me." Walter Patten walked over, smiled at the ladies and interrupted Ben with a question in his ear.

"Excuse me, ladies," Ben said, relief registering on his face as he walked away.

Olivia filled the void left by Ben.

"So, will I see any of you at the lake bright and early tomorrow morning?"

Bianca nodded, she was looking forward to hiking and clearing her head in the morning air.

"I can't be there. Mike asked me to work that shift at the station, he has to attend a political breakfast with his wife," Deputy Weber said, her eyes scanning the room. Vera was always alert, always on the job. Bianca felt guilty just being in the deputy's presence, as if she might be caught doing something wrong.

Rebecca overheard and joined their little group. "I wouldn't miss it. I've never been more fit since I started hiking." Rebecca walked around the group and tilted her head to Bianca.

"Bianca, do you have a minute?" They moved to the side and left the other ladies chatting.

Just as they put their heads together, Owen appeared.

"Rebecca, I need to talk to you." He was brusque with his wife and ignored Bianca. With a steady smile, Rebecca allowed him to turn her away by the arm. In an attempt to give the couple some privacy, Bianca swung around to head back to the other ladies and walked directly into Mike Riley, splashing some of his coffee onto his blue chambray shirt.

At first Bianca didn't notice the coffee but she did notice that he was out of uniform. His faded shirt set off the grey in his eyes in a way that the dull brown uniform could never do.

He looked down at his shirt.

"Sheriff, I'm so sorry. I wasn't paying attention," Bianca sputtered, handing him her crumpled napkin.

"It was my fault. I shouldn't have been standing in the middle of the walkway." He blotted his shirt absentmindedly.

They both apologized and danced from side to side trying to walk around each other.

Finally, they gave up.

"Listen," Bianca started, "I am very sorry about how rude I was when you stopped by the house. It was so nice of you, really. Thank you."

"I understand. I shouldn't have dropped by unannounced." Mike took a sip of whatever was left in his coffee cup.

"No, it's not that, I had just gotten some bad news in the mail and I hadn't any time to digest it before you arrived."

"I'm sorry to hear that. If I can help in any way—" Mike offered but Bianca quickly interjected.

"It's not the kind of thing the sheriff's office can help me with but thanks. I'll be fine. It's just been a tough day. I was starting to find a friend in Agatha, a friend and..."

"And?" Mike's warm interest helped her open up.

"This is going to sound selfish, but Agatha and I were going to start working on a book and I am sad that I won't be able to collaborate with her." She hadn't realized until she said it that she was doubly saddened by Agatha's death. To add to her confusion, she found herself confiding to the person she knew the least in Batavia.

Compared to the rest of the villagers, Mike Riley was an enigma to Bianca. He kept to himself more than the others. He wasn't part of the old crowd. Mike was different. He was accepted but still stood apart. Bianca suspected that it was partly his own choice. It must be hard policing your friends.

They chatted comfortably. The awkward exchanges they had shared recently faded away for the moment. Mike focused all his attention on Bianca, it reminded her of how Richard had listened with all his being when she spoke.

"Sounds like it would have been an interesting project, yet Agatha was...uh..." Mike searched for the right word.

Bianca let him off the hook. "Yeah, I know, she was something special, and I suspect it would have been challenging to work with her, but you had to see how animated she was about all of this."

Despite her comfort Bianca slowly discovered that she had trouble meeting Mike's eyes. They were impossible not to notice tonight. The more she thought about it the more self-conscious she became. Then, over Mike's left shoulder, she noticed Claire trying to eavesdrop. And behind Claire there was Olivia smiling broadly at her. Vera Weber caught her eyes next, then averted them almost immediately and made her way to the dessert table.

"Sheriff, would you excuse me, I need to take care of something." Bianca suddenly needed to escape the conversation.

She sidled up to Olivia.

"What are you smiling at?" Bianca asked. Her tone of voice implied that Olivia better have a good answer.

"He is handsome, isn't he? In a straightforward kind of way. Not like Owen Streat or even Father McCardle for that matter but...just the same," Olivia said. Claire nodded in agreement.

Bianca pulled Olivia away from the others.

"Olivia, come and grab a coffee with me, would you? I wanted to talk to you about that column I'd like to write for the *Gazette*."

"Sounds wonderful! We are always looking for contributors," Olivia said as Bianca led her by the arm toward the table by the door. As they arrived at the desserts, Vera left with the last bag of truffles.

"What are you doing? Don't say those things in front of Claire. You know how she gossips," Bianca whispered urgently.

"But it's all true. We would love to have you write for the *Gazette*," Olivia said with a smirk.

"That's not what I mean and you know it."

"I didn't say anything except that the sheriff looks good out of uniform. Just an innocent observation...that I believe you share."

"Olivia! He's married and so am I," Bianca scolded.

"You're not married," Olivia said, then immediately scrunched up her face in apology.

Bianca was startled by the remark and it showed.

"I'm sorry, I didn't mean it that way. I mean that it's not preposterous for you to find a man interesting. And you shouldn't feel guilty."

"I don't feel guilty because I'm not interested in anyone." Then for good measure Bianca added, "And he's married."

"Yeah, well, that's up for debate."

Bianca gave her another look. "Wow, the gossip around here...I wonder what everyone says about me."

"I'll tell you what they say. Apparently the sheriff's truck was spotted in your driveway today. It has led to some speculation," Olivia said with a smile.

"Let me guess…"

"Yep, you guessed it, Claire. You know how it is…she doesn't like to gossip but…if you ask me you're going to have to be more discreet if—"

"Olivia, this conversation is over."

Olivia apparently didn't think the conversation was over. "Don't look now but it looks like you have competition."

Bianca turned around just in time to notice Deputy Weber sharing her truffles with the sheriff.

"He's what, forty-five? She can't be more than thirty-five. What do you think, is she too young for him?"

Rebecca arrived at the dessert table. Bianca took the opportunity to change the subject.

"Rebecca, you wanted to talk to me?" Bianca offered.

"If you have a minute, let's sit where it's a little quieter. Olivia you don't mind, do you?"

"No, not at all. I think this conversation was over anyway." Olivia smiled kindly at Bianca and left.

"Bert tells me that Richard was interested in selling part of your parcel last year. I'd like to make some proposals on how to get this land to make money for you. Who couldn't use extra income, especially us women? We need to make ourselves self-sufficient. Don't you agree?"

Bianca couldn't argue with that logic considering her financial concerns of late.

"Well, your timing is superb. Now is a good time to discuss it. When did you have in mind?"

"How about tomorrow morning? After the hike, I have some papers to prepare and then I'm free. What do you think? At my office or your house?"

"Let's meet at my house, we'll have tea."

As they made their final plans they stepped out the door to the snow falling once again. The last hour and a half the snow had accumulated quickly and

Bianca could see everyone slipping and sliding their way home. She and Rebecca were among the last to leave. Rebecca fussed with her fur-lined hood and tiptoed her way to her car in her heels. Bianca tracked through the snow in her sturdy Timberlands, smiled up at the dark sky, and turned toward home.

***

Bianca enjoyed the first few minutes of her walk but began to have some misgivings after losing her footing a couple of times. The dark was punctuated with patches of moonlight as the clouds swept across the moon. Ernie had offered her a ride home; now she wished she had taken him up on it.

A howl pierced the woods. The clouds moved in once again and she found herself in complete darkness. She pulled her coat tighter and picked up her pace. She needed a distraction. She considered each of her neighbors. Who would want to see Sister Elaine dead? And what about Agatha? How could these deaths have happened so close together without being connected? But try as she might, she couldn't see the connection. If Trevor and his friends had something to do with Elaine's death then what about Agatha? Now that Bianca knew that Agatha was the Miller heiress, she thought inheritance could be a motive, and that could only lead to Allison. Was Allison capable of killing her mother? And what would Elaine have to do with it? Many of the villagers suspected Kenzo Ishikawa, but again, why? What reason could he possibly have? Bianca could think of nothing. She was sure the villagers were just more suspicious of an outsider. Unless Sister Elaine had her own secrets, as Claire had said earlier.

She heard crunching tires in the street and a beam of headlights slowly approached.

"Jump in!" Mike Riley said as he leaned over from the driver's side to call out the passenger window. Face to face with the sheriff, she felt silly contemplating these outlandish suspicions.

Bianca waved him off. "I'm fine."

"No you're not."

He reached a little further and opened the door of the truck. "Hop in, I mean it. You wouldn't want to cross an officer of the law, would you?"

Bianca climbed in, happy to give in this time.

"Thanks."

"Not a problem. You owe me one, that's all."

They rode in silence for a moment. He adjusted the heat until she stopped shivering.

"So, you're a writer?"

"Well, not yet, I haven't had a book published yet."

"You're young yet. Give it time."

"Not so young anymore, I'm afraid."

"Oh come on, you're younger than I am."

"That may be so, but the cemetery at St. James apparently thinks I'm old enough to start considering my final resting place before it's too late. I just got their flier in the mail the other day. What do you say to that?"

"Well, who am I to argue with the Church?" They both laughed a comfortable laugh.

"Just the same, getting published isn't everything," Mike said.

"Easy for you to say." The truck had warmed up enough so that Bianca could make out the scents which permeated the cab: his pine tree air-freshener, which didn't seem necessary since the cab was neat and clean; a hint of clean cologne, something lemony and woodsy with maybe a hint of lavender; and his doggie bag of pecan pie and lemon poppy cake.

"Look, really, you write, don't you?" Mike persisted.

"Yes, I write." Bianca didn't talk to many people about her writing, she tended to keep it to herself but she was interested in what Mike had to say.

Mike turned his truck down her long driveway, the snow heavy on the pines lining each side, creating a canopy of green and white.

"Well, from what I'm told, if you write then you're a writer. Publishing is beside the point, just icing on the cake. You write for yourself."

He slowed to a stop.

Bianca smiled to herself at Mike's encouragement. Richard had been her champion but without his supportive words she sometimes forgot why she wrote.

"Thank you for that. It's something I need to keep reminding myself. It seems that as a writer it's hard to be taken seriously, or even to take yourself seriously, if you don't get recognition or earn a living doing it."

"Well, keep at it and I'm sure you will someday. Don't lose faith. Oh, and something else." Mike reached over her lap and opened the glove compartment. "I didn't have the chance earlier but I wanted to give you my card. I know you're fairly new around here and…I know you are alone now so…I want you to feel comfortable calling if you need anything."

"Thank you." Bianca took the card and slipped it in her pocket.

"Both numbers are on there, the sheriff's office and my personal number. Use them if you need them."

"Thank you again." Bianca hesitated with her hand on the door.

"Mike, do you really think that Trevor could be responsible for Sister Elaine's death?"

"I can't say what anyone is capable of doing. I have seen things in my years with the NYPD that I wouldn't have believed if I hadn't witnessed them first hand."

"Don't you think it's odd that Elaine and Agatha died at almost the same time?"

"I know this has been hard for you, but Agatha was sick, plain and simple. And as far as Sister Elaine is concerned, I really believe it was about the theft of a valuable ring. She must have put up a fight and it ended badly. Vera and I have been working on this. We have a couple of angles we are developing. Stop worrying. We will get to the bottom of this." He picked up the slice of pecan pie in one hand and the lemon poppy cake in the other. "Which one do you want?"

"I can't take your dessert."

"I'm giving it to you. In my experience, a good piece of pastry can soothe most things."

"Thank you, then." Bianca took the lemon poppy and stepped out of the truck. She waved to him. But he didn't budge.

"I'll leave once you've gotten safely in the house."

Bianca walked the last few steps to the door, inserted the key and opened the door. Then turned and waved again. He waved back and started down the long drive. Bianca watched the red lights disappear through the canopy of trees.

Chapter Seventeen

Sunday, December 18

The L.O.C.A.L. hikers made their way around the shore of Groenmeer Lake every Thursday and Sunday, rain, shine or snow. It was a four-mile hike from Miller's Point, across the bluff, through the woods and around the lake's shore. Rebecca's stylishly fitted ski jacket stood out in fuchsia with a white fur-lined hood but otherwise they all looked like fat, lumbering bears in their oversized parkas. Everyone carried a walking stick as a way to gauge the snow and to steady themselves.

They walked in twos: Bianca and Olivia, Claire with Freddie, Margaret chatted away with Rebecca, and Emily walked beside her mother, Monica.

"So who are the L.O.C.A.L.s exactly?" Bianca asked.

"L.O.C.A.L.s are the Ladies of a Certain Age League members. I founded the club when I turned forty. That year my doctor determined I was cancer-free after my chemo and radiation. When I was sick I had a lot of time to think," Olivia said.

"Like a mid-life crisis?" Bianca suggested.

"More like a mid-life epiphany," Olivia clarified. "I had been bitter about not finding my soul mate and it occurred to me that I had put my life on hold while I waited for the right man and that was a waste." Olivia paused as she navigated an icy patch. "Our mission statement says that L.O.C.A.L.s are ladies who refuse to be kept down because they are women or because they are no longer young. Nothing radical, but a sort of quaint, safe feminism for a small village."

"My kind of feminism. What else do the L.O.C.A.L.s do?"

"Besides things like hiking and biking, we travel, and challenge ourselves. We went scuba diving last year in Mexico on a cultural trip to see the ruins. Freddie was the star of that show. We tried some rock climbing two years ago, Rebecca was most adept at that and still goes with Trevor on occasion. Believe it or not, Claire wants us to try flying lessons next summer and we all agreed to put some money aside for that. But I'm still trying to convince them to go skydiving. We are also taking steps away from dependence on men. Last year we took classes in car mechanics and sweating pipes. Next we are going to learn to lay tile."

"Calling yourselves ladies rather than women is to embrace your femininity, I assume?"

"You're giving us too much credit. We call ourselves ladies because otherwise we would be the W.O.C.A.L.s. Doesn't roll off the tongue exactly."

"Definitely doesn't have a good ring to it, you made a wise decision."

"Thanks, I have to agree."

"I've enjoyed the hikes so far. Are you accepting new members?" Bianca asked.

"Are you over the age of forty and willing to try new things?"

"Should I be raising my right hand and swearing to tell the truth, the whole truth and nothing but the truth?"

"Good, you're in then!" Olivia turned and pretended to knight her with her walking stick. "See Rebecca to pay your dues."

"Thank you, milady." Bianca made a clumsy attempt at a curtsy in her snow-pants.

They continued walking, quietly enjoying their muffled footsteps on the snow and the intimate giggles coming from Emily and her mom.

"Olivia, the reality is I too am looking at things a little differently since Richard died. I hadn't realized how much I had insulated myself. We always tried new things, but always together. Some new challenges would be good for me. But I have to admit that skydiving might be more than I'm ready for," Bianca confessed.

"You don't have to start with skydiving, don't worry. But it's time to start planning our next trip, so think about that. We would like to plan something special for next year, it will be the club's five year anniversary."

Up ahead Emily had thrown herself into the snow and was flapping wildly in a messy attempt at a snow angel.

"So how exactly does Emily qualify as a Lady of a Certain Age?" Bianca asked.

"We all started out at about the age of forty but Emily is such an old soul it only seemed right to let her in. Besides, she and Monica are inseparable," Olivia said smiling at the ladies up ahead.

As they made their way around the bend and came out of the woods they noticed the road leading to the bridge over the Groenmeer Stream was closed off. There were flashing lights in the distance.

"I wonder what's going on down there?" Freddie said.

"I know the sheriff's been patrolling the area lately to stop the kids with their ATVs and snowmobiles running through the paths. They are trespassing and there have been a lot of complaints lately. I don't like to gossip but some people think that those kids are responsible for the two burglaries last month. Maybe they are staking out the houses from the woods and then breaking in when no one is home," Claire said.

"They are doing no such thing! Claire, really, the things you say sometimes! They are just kids having fun. As L.O.C.A.L.s I thought the idea was not to get stuck in our old ways of thinking. Aren't we supposed to be rejuvenating ourselves? Don't you remember doing fun and naughty things when you were young?" Rebecca snapped.

Bianca felt for her, it musn't be easy to have your son the target of constant gossip. She wanted to go to Rebecca's defense but had no idea how to help.

"Actually, no. I have always followed the rules. That's what they're for. I never got in trouble a day in my life," Claire said proudly.

"Probably never had any fun either," Rebecca mumbled, obviously still a little unnerved.

Bianca whispered to Olivia, "Getting a little heated there."

"It's understandable. Rebecca's son, Trevor, is known as the leader of the

ATV gang and she always needs to defend him. No fun being a mom of a teenage boy, I suspect. And with Owen always at the farm in the good weather, and it's no secret he drinks away most of the winter, she's on her own most of the time."

"Isn't that where Mike found Elaine?" Freddie was pointing to the commotion by the lake.

"It was right near there, behind the trees. Isn't that what I read in the *Gazette*?" Claire turned to Olivia.

"I hope they've found some evidence to put this all to rest." Margaret shivered as she spoke.

"They interrogated the nuns at Saint James yesterday. Can you even imagine?" Claire warmed up to the subject.

"Well, you never know," Rebecca said.

"I still put my money on Ishikawa. He seems suspicious and they held him for over an hour. I wonder why Mike let him go?" Claire continued.

Olivia stopped walking and turned to Claire. "Maybe because he's innocent, Claire. Mr. Ishikawa found Elaine, so naturally Mike needed to ask him some questions. It doesn't mean he did anything wrong. And what about motive? What motive could he have to kill a nun?"

"Same as anyone, that ring," Claire said with a confident nod.

Chapter Eighteen

Bianca put down her pen. She had managed to scratch out an outline for her *Gazette* article. She was relieved to have managed that much despite her wandering mind. She neatened up her desk. That was all the writing she would be doing for now. Rebecca would be arriving soon.

She stoked the fire then turned to the shelves in the kitchen and chose a vintage vase from her collection of McCoy pottery. The yellow lilies she had just picked up from the florist would show beautifully in the tall, green vase. And if she turned it just right no one would see the hairline crack. She found her emergency tin of Royal Dansk Butter cookies and warmed up some water for tea.

Bianca looked over at Richard's photo above the kitchen sink.

"I could see myself becoming friends with Rebecca. What do you think? I know she doesn't seem like my kind of person on the surface but I'm drawn to her positive nature. And she seems fragile to me. Like she might need a friend."

Bianca pulled the tea mugs from the cabinet and then placed the creamer and sugarbowl on the table. "And for someone so comfortable with her sex appeal, occasionally Rebecca seems uncomfortable in her own skin. We are all so complicated, don't you think? There is so much more to each of us than meets the eye."

Bianca considered her own insecurities. Feeling like an outsider and being without Richard had tapped into an extreme loneliness that she was reluctant to face. Volunteering and trying to wedge herself into the community had been Bianca's armor. Agatha, on the other hand, had spent a lifetime keeping the villagers at a distance, carrying her animosity and shame all alone. It seemed no one had known her story or her pain. Her privacy had been her armor.

What was Rebecca's story, Bianca wondered? What armor had she chosen?

The doorbell rang and Bianca let in a bundled Rebecca, the fur on her hood standing up frozen. Bianca offered her a pair of the knitted slippers she kept by the door, Quebec-style.

"These booties are adorable! It's so nice to be able to take my heels off. And it's good to have some girl time once in a while and let our hair down, don't you think?" Rebecca precariously balanced on one high-heel boot as she took off the other.

Rebecca seemed to relax immediately as she took off her boots. Perhaps Bianca had gotten a glimpse of Rebecca's armor after all.

Rebecca handed her a brown parcel.

"A treat, how nice. The package is still warm. What's in it?" Bianca untied the string. "Croissants, my favorite! How thoughtful, Rebecca."

Bianca offered Rebecca a seat near the woodstove as she poured the Earl Grey.

Rebecca tiptoed around the curled up cat and settled into a rocking chair.

The quiet was soothing and familiar, they both seemed to forget this was a business call.

"Wow, look at this recurve! Is this yours?" Rebecca admired the bow leaning in the corner.

"Oh no, that's Richard's. I couldn't handle that one; it's got a fifty-pound draw. Do you use a bow?"

"I do target practice with my son. I keep trying to bond with him. I'm not always successful, but at least it helps me stay in shape."

With gusto Bianca took a bite out of a croissant. Rebecca broke hers into little pieces.

Bianca found herself admiring Rebecca in a new light. She may have been a bit self-absorbed about her appearance but she was also active and healthy, a trait Bianca admired. Rebecca was feminine but she was strong and independent, and was trying to be a good mother to a difficult child.

Bianca felt the warmth of new affection brewing.

"Rumor has it we have another major storm heading our way tonight," Bianca said.

"I am so tired of this weather. It is really hurting my business. No one thinks about buying or selling real estate in a storm."

"I know what you mean. My finances aren't in great shape right now either."

"It's so hard being a woman, isn't it?" Rebecca mused, almost to herself.

"Yes, isn't it?"

"It must be even harder for you since Richard passed."

"It has been. I have prepared for so long. Because of our age difference it was only reasonable to assume I would be alone. But this happened much sooner than I had ever expected. All my preparation wasn't enough. I still wake up and reach over to find his side empty. Sometimes I catch myself setting the dinner table for two." Bianca stared down at her cup and absently stirred her tea. "And of course, finances are tough. Together it seemed like we could always manage. Alone it seems insurmountable. These years were supposed to be for my writing but now it seems my funds will be short. In fact..." Bianca started to confide then thought better of it.

"I know, Owen and I fight over finances all the time. He is very old-fashioned and he doesn't think women should work at all. And he only gives me a small allowance and nothing at all to Trevor. My job makes all the financial difference for me. But even with my income, a couple of times a year I get in such a jam I have to pawn a piece of jewelry. It's so embarrassing. So I found a tiny shop all the way in Albany where no one knows me. He's fair; he deals in antique jewelry and other things, but it pains me to part with my grandmother's pieces."

"I know what you mean. My grandmother always warned me to have a backup plan. This time, though, I miscalculated." Bianca poked at the fire and considered sharing more but was too embarrassed.

"I have a secret little nest egg in a bank in Albany." Rebecca showed no reservations about confiding in Bianca. "I've been stashing money there for years to send Trevor to college. He isn't a good student so his father doesn't see any point in paying for school. But he's a good mechanic, so Owen's bright idea is to keep him on the farm. For Owen it's a win-win. Trevor sees it as an easy way out of school. But I see it as a waste of my son's life. He will never be able to meet his potential while he's under his father's thumb. He'll be graduating high school soon, at least I hope so, I never know with his grades and his attendance. But I've only got enough saved up for the first year of college."

Rebecca's confession laid the foundation for Bianca to commiserate.

"I have an issue too. It looks like my house is going to end up in foreclosure if I'm not careful. The bank won't negotiate with me since my name isn't on the mortgage. They won't even take my money unless it is the full arrears and I'm in no position to do that."

They fiddled with their mugs and croissants, both lost in thought. The hiss of the fire and Shelby's quiet purr the only sounds.

"Luckily my name is on the deed. I'm beginning to think I might need to sell the house and move back down to an apartment in the city."

"Don't be hasty." Rebecca kicked into business mode. "First of all, selling the house isn't the end of the world. I know you don't want to hear it but it's more than you can handle anyway. It's not the kind of house meant for a woman alone. And second, you're better off renting an apartment here in the village. Much more affordable than the city. I can find you a lovely place in one of the nineteenth century buildings right on Main Street. It might need a little sprucing up but the period details in these buildings are incomparable." Rebecca was in her element. She was making a deal. "Let me see what I can do. I have a couple of buyers who are looking to relocate onto hobby farms. They would love it. I could get you almost double what you two paid now that you and Richard have done so much work here. This town is just the kind of hideaway city folks are looking for lately. A beautiful village on the Hudson. Virtually undiscovered. Affordable. We are going to make it on the map in the near future. You mark my words." Rebecca was beaming. Finally, she took a breather.

"Well, now who's being hasty? I'm not ready to list my home yet. This was my dream with Richard and I'm not ready to give it up. I'm going to

124

start looking for a job first."

"Well then you better hope the casino bill gets passed because no job around here will pay you enough to cover your back mortgage payments. Listen to me. I know. Finances are a problem for a lot of people out here. We haven't yet recovered from the economic slow-down this region took after the resorts died. That's why we need the casino and the condos. Tourism is the only sure bet to stimulate the economy. I haven't caught my pedals for years. If I don't make a sale soon my grandmother's art deco broach will need to go into hock like her bracelet did last Christmas."

"No, don't do that! That would be such a shame. These things should stay in the family. I have admired that broach since the first time I met you. It reminds me of a pendant my grandmother had. We'll find another way. I may not be ready to commit on listing my house but I am ready to sell some of my land. I have another thirty acres just west of the path. That's the parcel I'm thinking of selling."

"Don't wait too long to think about selling your house. Once in foreclosure the banks won't get you what I can get you." Rebecca let that sink in for a moment. "But I won't push you, obviously you're not ready. Selling a house is an emotional decision more than a financial one so…"

Bianca did her best to hide it but she knew the emotion was starting to show on her face.

Rebecca changed the subject just in time. "I don't know about you, but I'm still shocked by Elaine's death."

Although not thrilled with Rebecca's choice, Bianca was relieved to have the subject changed.

"That's no ordinary death. Elaine was murdered."

"What did the sheriff tell you?" Rebecca asked.

"I haven't spoken to the sheriff."

"I thought you two were friendly. You were in a tête-à-tête last night."

"It wasn't a tête-à-tête. We were just chatting about…about the meeting. But Walt Patten told me that Sheriff Riley is interrogating the entire village for clues to what happened."

As they spoke, Bianca stoked the fire again. She lifted an oak log with the poker to replace it on the irons. Then it rolled off the iron, still blazing, and landed on the floor tiles in front of her. Bianca jumped up but the poker was still in the stove and she dislodged another log with it. She froze in place but Rebecca quickly donned the welding gloves by the woodpile. She lifted both logs and placed them back safely in the stove.

"Rebecca, you were wonderful! Thank you! I don't know what went wrong with me. I was so clumsy and then I froze up. I don't know what I would have done if you weren't here."

"It's nothing. You would have come to your senses and did what I did. I just got there first. Everything is fine now, stop worrying."

"Oh, but I do worry. Bert told me a story last winter of the farm house on the other side of the lake that burned down as a result of just this kind of accident."

"I remember that, it was awful. They were sleeping and didn't close the stove properly and the log rolled out and before they knew it, the place went up. Luckily, no one was hurt."

Bianca sat back down and took a long swig of her tea and finished her croissant for good measure.

Rebecca brought them back to the matter at hand. "We were talking about your excess acreage. I can get you some cash for that and the bonus is you will stop paying taxes on it."

They talked at length about Bianca's options and decided on a course of action, a price and a commission. Bianca's land abutted the old Miller Point property. Rebecca informed her that its location made it valuable to anyone interested in the larger plot.

"Just between us, the Janus Development Group is looking at Miller's Point seriously for the condo development. Allison is hot to sell. And it's almost a done deal. If we play our cards right, we might be able to interest them. Most realtors will say the trick to real estate is location, location, location. But you have to pair that with timing, timing, timing. And you have both."

"Do you think it could be that easy?"

"Leave it to me. I'll draw up the listing papers for you to sign and bring them by in a couple of days. In the meantime, I will feel things out and see if we can't get Janus interested." Rebecca stood up to leave. Bianca felt better already. Rebecca had managed to quell some of her worries.

Bianca brought out Rebecca's coat, scarf and gloves. Juggling all the pieces, she dropped a glove. They both bent down to retrieve it at the same time, bumping heads as a result. They giggled like two middle schoolers. Bianca relished the sensual feel of the supple pink suede as she passed the glove to her new friend.

"Rebecca, thank you. You have really put my mind at ease. You're a lifesaver, in more ways than one apparently!"

Rebecca trudged carefully up the snowy path and into her Jeep. As Bianca watched her leave, she considered this puzzling village. For a community so social and connected it seemed that there remained a great many secrets. Her conversations with Agatha, and now Rebecca, had given her a hint of just how much remained hidden from the public eye. As Agatha had said, we never really know what burdens each of us carries, what battles we are fighting. Things are not always what they appear.

Chapter Nineteen

Bianca stomped her boots and clapped the sides of her parka to remove the excess snow before stepping into Stella's. She headed toward her usual seat but Monica White, Eugene's new waitress, had beaten her to it and was already cleaning the corner of the counter.

Monica worked quickly. She appeared to be delicate but she had to be pretty sturdy, Bianca thought, to carry those food trays laden with lumberjack breakfasts. She buzzed around the diner so efficiently, it seemed as if she had always worked there.

Before Bianca realized it, Monica grabbed the pot from behind the counter and poured Bianca a cup and then removed the pencil from her bun, ready to take her order. Bianca had hardly settled in but she was determined to get her order straight this time.

"Thanks for pouring so quickly but I was hoping to get a cappuccino."

"Sure! I guess I got a little carried away. The morning rush is pretty hectic here for such a small town," she apologized with a broad smile. "You're the first person who didn't want a full octane splash. I stopped asking. It was slowing me down."

"I'm sure you don't have to run around so much. The locals are used to Eugene meandering over to help them. You are more efficient than anything they're used to." They both looked over at Eugene who was seated with his early morning breakfast buddies. His arms were draped over the seat back, his long legs stretched out in front of him creating an obstacle course for the waitress.

"Thanks, I try. I became a city girl these last few years. I haven't adjusted to small town living, I guess." Their eyes met in understanding. Two city girls. There was an unspoken bond among this type of expat Bianca realized. It was like two sports cars acknowledging each other on a country road. They knew they shared something special even if they were very different; the drivers smiling fleetingly at each other as they lifted their hands slightly from the steering wheel or flashed their lights briefly as they passed.

In no time Bianca had a rich cappuccino with a cloud of foam on top. As she sipped, the local gossip floated around her. She flipped open her notebook, her pen at the ready in case she overheard something worth commemorating. She found that a snippet of conversation could start her writing at any time. An interesting turn of phrase, a funny exchange, a foreign accent or a country drawl.

Eugene's buddies were lamenting the local doctor's absence. He had gone down south to care for his ailing sister.

"There's no telling how long he'll be gone," Eugene said.

Some of the others chimed in. "Why doesn't he just bring her up here to his place. Makes more sense if you ask me."

"No one asked you," they ribbed.

"I've been going to the same doctor for decades, I have no mind to change doctors now."

"And I'm certainly not going to that boy they brought up here. He's younger than my grandson."

"Yeah, old age has a way of making you uncomfortable when your doctor's not around. Young people think old people don't travel because we're boring. We don't travel because we want to stay near our doctors," Eugene said.

"Speak for yourself! I'm not old! Of course, I don't travel anymore either," said one of Eugene's buddies. He wore a three-piece suit, a loop of watch chain dangled from the vest pocket. He had removed his hat and coat but a hand-knitted scarf remained wound around his neck. He was animated when he spoke and occasionally he secured the ends of the scarf as they loosened.

"You're right, Lester, you're not old. You're ancient! Who are you fooling?"

The old man hacked a hearty laugh that showed his badly fitting dentures.

Bianca caught a snippet of a German accent. Trudy Bauer was sharing some gossip with Bianca's neighbor Claire in the corner by the window.

"I don't like to gossip," Claire confided in hushed tones, "but I hear Trevor Streat is in trouble again. Apparently the sheriff figured out that he was the leader of the kids who have been tearing up the woods by the lake and the quarry with their snowmobiles and three-wheelers. He was detained for trespassing and for property damage."

With some difficulty understanding Trudy's English, Bianca realized that they were speculating about Trevor's future. They both doubted he would amount to much. Trudy suspected he had something to do with the spate of local burglaries over the last few months.

"What with Elaine's murder unsolved it makes you wonder," Claire said. Then the conversation turned to his mother, Rebecca.

"She's a good real estate agent, I hear, but obviously working mothers don't make the best parents. And the way she dresses—no wonder she makes good sales," Claire continued.

Bianca rolled her eyes and Monica shrugged back.

Reaching over to refill the sugar bowl she whispered, "I've always been a single working mom and I think I did a good job. Emily's a pretty good kid, I think."

"Emily is delightful. She's smart and so helpful. You did a fine job indeed. I was a single mom for a while too and Ian turned out just fine. I guess people believe what they want to believe."

"People also see what they want to see. Emily says that Trevor's not as bad as the adults make him out to be." She bought herself some time to talk by refilling the salt shaker. "He just likes a little attention."

Bianca unscrewed the pepper shaker and handed it over. "Small town gossip, I'm not used to it. I guess I shouldn't let it bother me so much."

The bell above the door announced another customer. Bianca watched Doctor Spenser settle into a seat. Eugene's buddies blustered around for a change of topic.

"Back to work." Monica turned and cleared off a spot on the far end of the counter.

***

Bianca pushed her coffee aside and dug into her tote bag for the stack of journals Agatha had given her. Some were dog-eared, some crisp and new. She flipped through them, reading snippets until she could find some order. On the surface they appeared to be journals, daily entries with notes as to weather, gardening tips, medical notes, reminders for errands and household repairs, responses to her voracious reading, heart-felt musings, and of most interest to Bianca, ramblings related to her past. It seemed to Bianca that Agatha hadn't started out with the intention of writing about her past. Rather, something in her daily entries would spark a memory and she would jot it down. Agatha had written almost every day and seemed to have a conversation with her journal, or perhaps with herself, Bianca imagined.

After her initial perusal of the diaries Bianca stacked them in chronological order and decided to dig into the worn ones first. These were probably the most important ones if Agatha had reread them enough to wear them out.

The journals started in nineteen seventy-seven. Just four years ago. That would have been about the time of her cancer diagnosis. Had it taken her that long before she was willing to tackle her past? Had her illness prompted her to face her mortality? Coaxed her into reaching back and organizing her feelings?

Bianca opened the first journal, a black and white marbled composition book like the ones she had used in grammar school. Agatha's script was tight and precise yet still pretty, a bit fanciful even. That surprised Bianca; she was expecting to find something more spartan and practical.

March 21, 1977

Today I read some passages from The History of the Decline and Fall of the Roman Empire. *How sobering to be reminded of our impermanence, whether we be individuals or the most powerful empire in the world. The fall of the Millers started so quietly, never signaling the turmoil to follow.*

One morning my mother didn't send me to school. I was so relieved. I spent the day reading in the library. Such an innocuous beginning.

That afternoon I heard Mr. Fisher and my mother in a heated discussion but I couldn't make out what was being said. I remember thinking how odd it was that he was talking to my mother and not my father. But the thought was fleeting.

That night my father was absent from dinner. He often had business or social responsibilities that took him away from home so I thought nothing of it. But still, it was always a disappointment for me when my father missed dinner. I was Daddy's little girl. Mother barely looked at me that evening, she had no appetite, and was short-tempered.

The next morning, she kept me home again. This time I was uneasy. I knew my mother never wanted me to attend the local school but she would not defy my father even if he were out of town. I enjoyed another free day reading until that evening. Mr. Fisher came over again and this time the noise came from outside the house. My mother was crying and Mr. Fisher was outside trying to calm the workers. My mother locked herself in her room and wouldn't tell me anything. The crowd didn't leave for hours.

I stayed home the rest of that week and Mrs. Fisher and her daughter Elaine took care of me; fed me, made sure I bathed and tried to help me sleep through my nightmares. Elaine was a young novitiate with the Sisters of Saint James the Elder at the time. They tried to get my mother to eat a bit and sent for the doctor who gave her sedatives. I had to learn what happened from them. My father had disappeared, he had taken with him whatever money he hadn't gambled, and the business had had to close its doors. The workers hadn't been paid in three months and the shopkeepers wouldn't extend them any more credit. The entire community was up in arms.

Eventually, Elaine took me back to school and managed to get my mother to come out of her room a few hours every day. Life slowly developed a routine, sickly as it was.

But life without Father was colorless.

It was the beginning of the end for us.

Bianca sat back and returned to her coffee. She understood now why Agatha was against the casino. Her entire family had been ruined by gambling and she had lost her beloved father as well. She jotted some thoughts in her notebook, added sugar to her coffee, and resumed her reading.

March 24, 1977

Today, jammed in the back of the secretary drawer, I found Mrs. Condon's obituary. According to the clipping, her legacy was being the first schoolteacher in the Batavia-on-Hudson little red schoolhouse. She did not have much of an education herself but certainly enough to teach the children of this remote village of immigrants. But she brought more to the school than education. She brought kindness and compassion. Mrs. Condon made my school experience bearable. She protected me the best way she knew how from the other children.

I remember returning to school after my father left. It was humiliating. I was a pariah. The tables had turned on me overnight. The girls huddled in corners whispering about me. The boys laughed out loud and pointed. No one would sit near me. One girl ran out of the school crying because she said my father had ruined their lives. Years later I learned that she had been right; her father had been forced to leave town to work up north logging. The family had had to fend for themselves; they had no income except what the mother brought in from selling eggs. The father never returned.

Another boy threatened to come to my house with his uncle to kill my father. His uncle didn't believe that my father had disappeared. They thought we had been hiding him.

My classmates no longer found me an enigma to admire from afar. They pushed me into the mud and ruined all my dresses. They pulled the hair ribbons out of my hair. They stole my school supplies and in their place they deposited their hate. Every day I would find something in my desk: a spider, a dead bird, cow dung, even a snake. It got to the point that I shook with tears every time the teacher asked us to take something out of our desks. Even when nothing was there, I cried out of relief. Mrs. Condon scolded the children and checked my desk every day but the children managed to sneak things into my desk despite her vigilance.

When I tried to defend myself they spit horrible insults at me. Their anger, pain and fear were wrapped up in those insults. Later, when my life more resembled theirs, I began to understand the enormity of what my father had done, of how the

133

actions of one man could impact the lives of so many. Just as he had been hailed a savior at first, he had become responsible for devastating the economy of the entire village.

His hubris had led to this. His arrogance had allowed him to believe that he was special and untouchable. I had seen him bounce back from failure before but I had been too young and too isolated to see how his failures impacted others.

Bianca found it hard to imagine Rudy's as the little red school house from Agatha's childhood. Now the market aisles were jammed with gossiping neighbors and the shelves overflowed with delicacies. She pictured Agatha's teacher trying to manage an unruly class of diverse backgrounds and ages. She must have been a saint. Bianca remembered how challenging her teaching experience had been under the best of circumstances and counted her blessings. She turned the page, anxious for more.

March 31, 1977

Today is Mother's birthday.

I walked to the cemetery and brought her a small bouquet of daisies as usual. For all her pretentions she loved the simple daisy. Probably an echo of her more modest days before she met my father. The empty space next to her, set aside for my father, was hard to ignore and more painful than I'd like to admit after all these years.

My mother never recuperated from the shame of my father's actions or his abandonment of us. She lost her mind, I'm sure. She would wander out of her room on occasion calling out for him casually as if he were in the other room. Then, when there was no answer, she would turn around and lock herself in again.

At a young age I learned the difficult lesson that we are not alone in this world even if we want to be or pretend to be. The dynamics of our existence preclude the possibility of any real isolation. When friends and relatives advise us against certain actions it is not merely to save us from a mistake, it is to immunize themselves from the inevitable impact of that mistake on their lives. We cannot pretend to operate in a vacuum. We exist in community and we must act with everyone else in mind. Others are not only our witnesses but also co-actors in our story. My father wanted to be the leading man, and then he walked off the stage.

The clang of dishes disturbed Bianca's concentration. Eugene may have been jovial, but he wasn't always graceful. She sipped her coffee, now cold, and considered the last journal entry. Agatha was reporting not only her experiences, but also her lessons. She certainly had a keen understanding of living in a small community. Bianca felt she too was beginning to unravel the lessons of small town life, both the blessings and the burdens.

Chapter Twenty

Doctor Robert Spenser sipped his coffee and read the *Gazette* at the counter. This afternoon's headline of course was Sister Elaine's murder. From his corner of Stella's he could hear the agitation in everyone's voices as they speculated about the murder.

Lester Quirke was boasting that Mike Riley had questioned him since he was one of Elaine's dearest friends. Unfortunately, he had nothing of value to offer the sheriff. But Lester did have some gossip to share with the locals. He had it on good authority that the owners of the Groenmeer Inn said they saw Trevor and his gang of friends riding around the lake that night. They had complained to the sheriff many times in the past about the noise and they were convinced that Trevor was up to no good.

Old Man Quirke certainly enjoyed being center stage, Robert noticed. Dressed in his striped suit and bowtie, he looked like a vaudeville performer. He was certainly old enough to be one.

Lester also heard that Ishikawa's dog, Tengo, was the one really responsible for finding Elaine. Angelica, the convent cocker spaniel, was circling Elaine's body whimpering when Tengo had led Ishikawa straight to them.

Robert Spenser sat wondering how he came to find himself in a village of only nine hundred and seventy-two people and his first two jobs were preparing coroner reports: one for a woman who died of hypothermia in her own bed and another for a murdered nun in her nineties. He arrived in Batavia two weeks ago and had yet to see any living patients.

The bell rang as Lester Quirke left the diner. Robert heard a whistle outside just as Monica arrived at the counter again. She poured him another cup of coffee, smiled and moved on. His eyes lingered on her as she walked away and then he went back to his coffee and paper. The Community Center ribbon cutting was today at noon. Maybe he should go to that and see if he could get the locals to warm up to him. Maybe follow that up with the Winter Solstice celebration later in the week. He was hoping that the reason he didn't have any patients had to do with the exceptional health of the Batavians but he suspected it was more complicated than that.

Someone somewhere must have a sore throat or a backache. He hadn't expected it to be an exciting place to work but he had expected to work. Maybe he could run a special of some kind: two physicals for the price of one, or free flu shots with a checkup. Pretty pathetic, but it made him chuckle. Monica walked past with the coffee pot in her hand and raised her eyebrows at the sound of his laugh.

Great, now the locals will think he's nuts too. Sobered by Monica's expression, he wondered that if he was having trouble attracting patients how he would ever be able to attract a date.

Fresh out of his residency three years ago Doctor Spenser had joined a large practice in the city. He had tried but he couldn't enjoy practicing medicine in such an impersonal manner. It wasn't the fast-paced environment that bothered him but the anonymity of the entire experience. One late night reading the paper with his beer, he had come across an ad from the Town of Batavia soliciting resumes from doctors, and on the spur of the moment, he had sent his in. The advertisement had been for a long-term temporary position. This had bothered him at first since it would require another change in the near future but now he thought it was his graceful way out of the situation if it didn't work for him. In theory, Batavia would suit him just fine. He just needed patients.

The bell above the door jingled. When he looked up he spotted Bianca St. Denis on her way out. He liked Bianca. She had introduced herself at the village meeting, one newcomer to another. He appreciated her efforts to make him feel welcome.

He smiled and waved. She hesitated at the door then walked back over to the counter and took a seat next to him.

"Good morning, Doctor Spenser."

"Please, call me Robert."

"Okay, Robert, I will. I'm so glad I ran into you. I was hoping I could see you."

Robert felt a little guilty over his relief at finally having a sick patient to treat.

"Well, I am due to open my office in about fifteen minutes. I'll go over as soon as I am done with breakfast. Or is this urgent?"

"I'm sorry, I'm not sick. I wanted to talk to you."

Robert grinned. She was apologizing for not being sick. "Sure, what's on your mind?"

"Another cup, Bianca?" Monica was poised with the pot over a cup, waiting for Bianca's answer. Bianca hesitated and took a moment to stare at Monica.

"Yes, coffee is fine and maybe a corn muffin. I'm getting hungry. Thanks, Monica."

"Coming right up!" Monica poured and left.

"She's nice, isn't she?"

"Who, Monica, ye…yeah she's very nice." Dr. Spenser blushed, hoping Bianca hadn't noticed. "So what did you want to talk about?"

Bianca leaned in. "I have a couple of questions about the deaths of Agatha and Elaine."

"There isn't much to talk about, but try me. Pretty cut-and-dried, both of them."

"I don't understand how Agatha died."

"I know sometimes it is hard to accept the death of a friend but she was ill and weak. The Doc told me before he left town that her body was wracked with cancer. And that open window was more than her body could sustain. My report concluded that she died of hypothermia. It was all about that window."

"That's just it, the window. It doesn't seem right to me."

"It does seem odd that in her condition she would open the window like that before going to sleep."

"Robert, that's just it, I agree with you. It bothered me all night but as I

138

awoke this morning, in that twilight between wake and sleep, it finally came to me what was strange about the scene."

Robert got a little closer to hear as Bianca's voice dipped.

"She liked the window open but she wasn't able to open it herself and she certainly could never have opened it that wide. Allison would not have done it because she insisted on closing and locking the window whenever she was there. And Agatha complained to me that her nurse set the heat too high and refused to open the window. She used to ask me to open it for her whenever I arrived."

"But the window was wide open. How do you explain it then?"

"Well, I can't explain it except—"

"Except what? Do you think someone did it on purpose?"

"Maybe. I didn't think too much about it at first, but Elaine's..." Bianca hesitated, "murder has got me wondering."

"But what does one have to do with the other?"

Monica dropped off Bianca's corn muffin, cut in half and warmed with butter on the griddle. The crisp, brown edges were almost enough to distract Bianca from her concerns about murder. She broke off a hot piece and popped it in her mouth before she continued.

"Of course, it might be a coincidence, but this is more than two old women dying two days apart. These are two best friends with a complicated history that goes back to their childhood and even to their fathers who were partners in a failed business."

"Is that so?" Robert thought about this and finished his eggs. "I didn't know their history. It does seem like more than a coincidence when you put it that way. But why? Why would anyone murder Agatha Miller? A dying woman? What secret, what power could she have over someone to prompt such an act?"

"I don't know but it seems the community is satisfied with the idea that she was weak and dying and that the cold coming in the window got the best of her. I suppose it could make sense that she gave up and was tired of all her suffering. But I don't see it that way. Maybe as an outsider I saw Agatha in a different light, and maybe she sensed that too. She was confiding her life history to me, as if it were an urgent, pressing thing for her to share. And I just don't feel that she would have been willing to let go before she finished telling her story. It just doesn't make sense to me. If you knew her you would have seen that she was not frail at all."

Bianca took a deep breath then continued.

"I remember when my grandfather was ill and dying. He didn't allow himself to go until his whole family had made it to his bedside. He had wanted to say goodbye to each and every one of us. Once he had done that, he went peacefully." Bianca paused, remembering how she had handled her grief over her grandfather's passing by writing about the very scene she was describing. She had used it to launch a short story about the afterlife. It had been an uplifting story that left her feeling blessed for having had him in her life for so long rather than cheated over his loss. "I believe that we have a great deal of control over our time of death and I believe that Agatha did not let go. That she had enough strength to at least pick up the phone. I don't think she gave up either. I guess what I mean is, I don't think she committed suicide. If I'm right, that leaves only one other option."

Doctor Spenser shook his head and took a deep breath. "I don't know, two murders back to back here in Batavia? Seems far-fetched."

"I agree. It's farfetched but not out of the question, you have to admit. How does a woman die of hypothermia in her own bed? And Elaine's murder, could anything be more senseless? For a ring? No matter how valuable. They could have mugged her and left. She couldn't have put up much of a fight, she is...was...a tiny little thing."

Robert thought about this for a while as he turned his cup around in its saucer.

Bianca sat back and looked around at her neighbors all tensely engaged in conversation except one. An old man walked over to the opposite end of the counter after a brief moment with Eugene. He was stooped but it was obvious that he had been very tall at one time, maybe even as tall as Eugene. His light eyes coupled with his fair skin revealed the remnants of a handsome youth. He sat alone and did not look interested in participating in the town talk. When Eugene walked past her seat, she stopped him. "Eugene, who is that man? He looks so familiar, but I can't put my finger on how I know him."

"He's not much of a talker, that one."

"His face is familiar, maybe someone I knew from the city?"

"I doubt it. He says he was a Batavia local but I don't remember ever seeing him around these parts."

Doctor Spenser shrugged. "Don't look at me, I don't know anyone, and at this rate I never will."

Bianca hated that feeling of knowing something but being unable to retrieve it.

She turned back to Robert. "Where were we?"

"You were suggesting that we have more than one murder on our hands. But what's the connection? I mean specifically? Why kill these two ladies? Can you see any logic behind it?"

Bianca sat back in her chair with a huff. "No, I just don't. I can't come up with a single motive, unless it's sheer hatred of old ladies."

"Agatha's case seems pretty straightforward. She was a typical hypothermia victim: she was old, ill, and frail. She was on multiple types of medications which increased her vulnerability to hypothermia. Thousands of seniors die every year as a result of hypothermia, many in their own homes. To make matters worse she was exposed for up to fifteen hours to the brutal cold and snow, and she was wearing only a nightgown."

"That's another thing that doesn't sit well with me, I don't understand why she didn't have a blanket over her."

"That's easy to explain. As hypothermia sets in we experience a burning sensation. In fact, it's not uncommon to find hypothermia victims with little or no clothes on because they try to strip themselves as a way to combat that feeling of extreme heat."

"And why didn't she call anyone?"

"I don't know, but hypothermia is disorienting. The elderly succumb very quickly and don't even realize it. They get drowsy and confused. She may have picked up the phone but she probably couldn't remember anyone's phone number. So when you put all the pieces together it really does point to hypothermia. But I don't think you're really disputing that, are you? What you're asking is if someone exposed her on purpose?"

"Maybe. I think it's worth considering."

After a few moments of nibbling her muffin crumbs, Bianca started up again. "About Elaine's death, did you see anything odd there, anything that might lead to a different motive than her ring?"

"Not much there either. The sheriff said that the scene offered very few clues because a light snow had fallen that morning obscuring any evidence on the ground. To make matters worse the two dogs trampled the whole area. The time of death was very difficult to establish too."

"I thought that was fairly reliable. At least that's the way it looks on television."

"Well, we don't have very sophisticated forensics capabilities here to start. But based on heat loss, normally a dead body loses heat at about one and a half degrees an hour. But since she was outside in this frigid weather it's harder to determine how much of her heat loss was time, and how much was the cold. Older people lose heat faster, and smaller bodies do too. Elaine's body temperature was about ambient temperature. Once a body reaches ambient temperature a reliable time of death can't be established. She could have been killed Thursday morning around 5:00 or 6:00 a.m., or even as early as 10:00 p.m. Wednesday night. Unfortunately, it just makes Sheriff Riley's job that much harder."

"No one has come forward with anything useful?"

"Nothing, except the guests at the Inn said the boys were making a ruckus in the woods all night."

"Was anything found at the scene? Anything useful to the investigation?"

"Well, some beer cans were found by the dock, not too far from the body, which I assume came from Trevor's group. And a match book from the bowling alley was found behind the trees near her body."

"Trevor used to work at the bowling alley, didn't he?"

"I didn't know that. Well, that doesn't look too good for Trevor, does it?"

"No, it doesn't. I feel so bad for Rebecca. Even if Trevor had nothing to do with this, it's going to be difficult for them."

"Well, Bianca, do I need to warn Deputy Weber about you? Are you trying to take her job?"

Bianca laughed. It felt good. She didn't realize how tense she had become. "I don't mean to put you in a bad position by asking you all these questions."

"Well, I probably shouldn't have said so much to you. It's not like I have much experience in these types of investigations. I really don't know what the protocol is." Robert emptied his cup. "Look, Bianca, if you have concerns you should see Sheriff Riley about them."

"Yes, I suppose I should."

Bianca absently broke off more crumbs from her muffin. She ate the last couple of pieces and took a final sip of her coffee. "I have to run some errands now but will I see you at the ribbon cutting later?"

"Yep, I was just thinking about that before you arrived. I'm going to close the office for a half hour and stop by. It's not like anyone is banging down my door."

They smiled knowingly at each other then they walked out together and went their separate ways with the promise of sharing a hot chocolate at noon.

Chapter Twenty-One

Bianca ran her errands by making her way up one side of Main Street and down the other and ending with a turn up Van Patten Street to the hardware store to buy a washer for her dripping kitchen faucet. Despite the town mourning, it was hard to be too somber with Christmas tunes piped through the streets. Bianca found herself humming a few bars here and there.

On her way back down Van Patten, she stopped at the tree lot between Rudy's Market and the Overland Pharmacy to pick out a Christmas tree from the Boy Scouts. She had finally decided to take Ian's persistent advice to get a tree. It was bound to cheer her up. Christmas lights decorated the outer rim of trees, lit despite the daylight. The boys huddled around a bonfire sipping *heisse schokolade*, German hot chocolate, from Rudy's Market cups. Trudy made it out of semi-sweet chocolate bars melted with milk and topped with her hand-whipped cream. It was a local treat the villagers enjoyed this time of year. She was looking forward to her own cup during the ribbon-cutting ceremony.

She circled the lot and finally decided on a squat balsam with fresh needles. She ran a branch of needles through her gloved hand to release the distinct sweet fragrance. Making her decision did cheer her up and she was glad for it. She paid the boys and arranged for them to keep the tree on the side until she could get Bert to pick it up and deliver it for her.

Finally she stopped at the library. She passed under Andrew Carnegie's portrait in the foyer and warmed her hands over the old circular radiator in front of the main desk. It clanked and hissed in all its ancient splendor.

Emily was shelving books on the far side of the room. Bianca waved and headed for the mystery stacks. She planned on reading some Raymond Chandler. He had been on her reading list for years. She was finally going to treat herself today. She was thrilled to find *The Big Sleep* on the shelf and checked it out with Mrs. Abernathy, the head librarian. Bianca longed to linger. The old library had charm and great reading chairs, but she didn't want to miss the ribbon cutting.

With her errands done it was almost noon and she headed to the end of town for the ceremony. When she arrived at the Community Center she had to walk around Trevor fidgeting with the throttle on his snowmobile. A small bag attached to the back of the seat held his tools. He looked engrossed in his repair.

"Hello, Trevor." With no answer forthcoming, Bianca moved on.

Trudy offered her a cup of hot chocolate with extra cream. She savored it as she waited for the ceremony to begin. Bianca marveled that so many of the villagers had taken a few moments to attend.

Ben and Walt were the usual ceremonial hosts. They worked the crowd, not the least bit bothered by the cold. They were a great political team, Bianca thought. Walt more refined and sophisticated while Ben was everyone's buddy.

Claire hovered around Bert, talking over their hot chocolate cups. He looked dazed and unhappy to be there. She took some pills out of her purse and he knocked them back with a swig of chocolate. Claire hung close to Bert, darting glances around the gathering crowd, not her usual social self.

Rebecca was helping serve hot chocolate with Eugene. She was making him laugh and that was a good thing. Eugene had been close to Elaine and respected Agatha. He wouldn't be doing too well after losing them both. Rudy and Trudy were warming up a fresh batch of chocolate; it was going fast.

Doctor Spenser was handing Monica White a fresh cup of hot chocolate. Monica's cheeks were pink. Was she cold or blushing? Bianca wasn't sure, but she noticed that neither of them walked away. She watched them sipping their chocolate in silence. Bianca was happy to sacrifice her hot chocolate date with Robert Spenser for a higher cause.

The morning crowd from Stella's had migrated over, the postmaster was there, the owners from the Crossroads Inn, the high school principal, and Mr. Overland from the pharmacy. Bianca did notice that no one from the Groenmeer Inn was in attendance, Kurt and Freddie Dekker were missing too, as well as Allison Miller. It was odd for anyone with any standing in town to miss these Chamber of Commerce events.

At noon they all moved to the front of the new brick building, designed to complement the local architecture. Walt and Ben were separated from the crowd by a wide red ribbon. After saying a few words of welcome they thanked Streat Farms for donating the bronze plaque that was to be embedded in the corner of the building dedicating the Community Center to Agatha Miller and Elaine Fisher.

Everyone turned as they applauded. The Streat family had chosen a spot next to one of the bonfires for the benefit of the elderly Streats who were sitting as guests of honor, a blanket draped over their knees. Owen, Rebecca, and Trevor towered over the elderly Elizabeth and Edward Streat. Elizabeth's deep eyes and her lovely smile lit up with the attention. Edward nodded modestly and turned and pecked Elizabeth on the cheek. Everyone applauded with renewed vigor.

Walt handed Mrs. Streat the mic. She blushed and tried to pass it to her husband who waved it away, shaking his head, and before the mic could make its way to Owen he settled his piercing blue eyes on Rebecca who quickly picked it up.

"Streat Farms and the entire Streat family are happy to honor the memory of two very special people. Agatha Miller and Elaine Fisher will be missed. They were active community members and it is only fitting that the new Community Center be dedicated to them and their untiring work for Batavia."

With that Walt and Ben each took hold of one side of the large ceremonial scissors and sliced through the ribbon.

***

146

Sheriff Riley watched the red ribbon hit the snow and thought of Elaine's blood on the snowy bank of the lake. He wasn't at the ribbon cutting as a social event, or even as a political one, he was there to keep an eye on his neighbors. He had the unfortunate job of having to ferret out which one of them was a murderer. He knew there was a chance that it was a random and arbitrary event, maybe a mugging by a stranger that went terribly wrong, someone passing through. But he knew better. It was much more likely that it was someone they all knew and someone who targeted Sister Elaine for a very specific and probably very personal reason.

He couldn't say that he wasn't baffled though; who would kill a little old nun, and one as sweet as Elaine? He didn't know who yet, but he knew someone had wanted her dead. Sheriff Riley knew from experience that things on the surface were deceiving. Elaine appeared to be a sweet innocent person, but then again all the neighbors seemed that way. He knew that in order to get to the truth, he would need to reach below the surface and ignore what he thought he knew about his neighbors. With a murder to solve, all bets were off. At least one Batavian was not who he appeared to be. So the sheriff watched and watched, and prepared to ask more questions.

Kenzo Ishikawa wasn't at the ribbon cutting. Mike didn't think he needed to read anything into that, Ishikawa had never been social in this village. Although, in light of recent events, Mike couldn't honestly say that Ishikawa's solitary life didn't pique his curiosity.

Ishikawa had answered Mike's questions with the fewest words possible. Yes, he saw Elaine many mornings when they walked their dogs. No, he did not know her very well. No, he saw and heard nothing unusual at the lake that morning.

Mike had run out of questions to ask this quiet man with the protective dog by his side. Ishikawa had offered nothing new with his answers. Although no alarms had gone off in his head, Mike hadn't liked the way he remained so guarded; his behavior had made him look suspicious, as if he had consulted a lawyer and was warned not to incriminate himself. It smacked of guilty behavior. His alibi was nonexistent, he was home alone that night and he had walked the dog alone on an empty lakeshore in the morning when he found the body. But he lived a solitary life, could he be faulted for that? And he had no obvious motive, but then again no one had an obvious motive. So far the only motive they could find was a stolen ring. Deputy Weber was looking into the theft and checking out possible fencing locations to see if that led anywhere.

The sisters of St. James weren't present today either, but they were all old or infirm and not expected to come out in this weather. Mike had questioned them too; if anyone was likely to have a gripe with Elaine it would be one of the women she lived with, someone she was close to. The nuns told Mike that Sister Elaine walked Angelica, their cocker spaniel, early every morning and every night before bed.

Although the sisters were the ones most likely to have a motive, their health constraints certainly would rule out opportunity since most used a cane or a wheelchair. Elaine would usually return for morning prayers, they had said. Nobody had given it much thought when she hadn't arrived on time because she had come in late after the high school concert the night before. They assumed she had gotten a late start. Mike had looked around at what amounted to a geriatric ward at the convent and couldn't picture any one of those frail ladies killing Elaine, and again, to what end?

He had also approached Agatha's friend, old man Quirke, since he knew everything about everyone. But this time he knew nothing. And the owners of the Groenmeer Inn were so focused on their anger at Trevor Streat these last few months that Mike couldn't get any other details out of them. All they cared about was Trevor and his friends running through the woods and over the lake, upsetting their guests with the noise and garbage they left behind. The ATVs were disturbing the denning bears too. The bear sightings were making the guests skittish, it was hurting business. The innkeepers were so unnerved by Trevor they suspected that he was responsible for the murder, possibly while attempting to steal her ring. The Talentis were conspicuously absent today. As business owners, it seemed odd to the sheriff that they would skip this community and networking event.

Bianca St. Denis was off to the side by herself, scribbling notes into her ubiquitous notebook. What was she up to, he wondered?

Today he needed to speak to a few more people. He decided to start with the Streats and get it over with. Mike wondered if Trevor could really have done this. Mike's sense, honed over eighteen years with the NYPD told him that Trevor was no murderer. Mike knew tough. Trevor didn't measure up. He seemed more like a kid trying to get his parents to pay attention. But Mike needed to turn over every stone, and Trevor and his friends were on the lake on Wednesday night. And to be honest, young kids who like to get into trouble wouldn't mind getting their hands on a valuable ring to bankroll their bad habits. Trevor's gang had the closest thing to a motive so far. They also had the opportunity and the means; they were certainly capable of overtaking Elaine.

Mike wasn't looking forward to interviewing the Streats. Mike was uneasy around Rebecca. Despite himself, he found his eyes wandering over her body, even in Owen's presence. Not wise, but Rebecca was the type of woman you notice, she made sure of it. It was impossible to not pay attention to her.

As far as Owen was concerned, Mike didn't trust him, never had. His cop gut told him something was off. No surprise that Trevor turned out to be difficult.

He hated to upset the elderly Streats, they were a modest and unassuming couple. Elizabeth's maternal nature was accentuated by Edward's generosity. They reminded Mike of his own grandparents.

The sheriff made his way over to the family and discovered that all of them were visibly uncomfortable in his presence. Owen straightened up to his full height of well over six feet and looked even more ominous than usual in his bulky parka. The elderly Mrs. Streat blushed, her husband grabbed her hand to comfort her. Trevor fidgeted from foot to foot and Rebecca fiddled with the belt of her coat. Mike's radar started to buzz.

"Good afternoon, everyone. As you know my deputy and I are going around asking everybody anything they might know about Sister Elaine's death. I know this has been a difficult time for the village. I was hoping I could ask you a few questions that might help us figure things out."

Everyone nodded but no one said a word.

"Let's start with you, Mrs. Streat." Mike turned to Elizabeth Streat and bowed down a little to bridge the distance from her wheelchair. "As I understand it, you and Elaine were good friends for many years. Do you know anything that could help me out here? Anything at all? Did anything seem wrong lately, did she have any problems you could share with me?"

Elizabeth stammered her way through a few sentences which revealed nothing helpful. "Elaine was her usual cheery self, even more chipper than usual the last day or so." Elizabeth's eyes started to tear up so Mike switched his attention.

"Rebecca, I was hoping you could shed a little light for me. Your office is directly across from the convent. Did you happen to see Elaine Thursday morning? The sisters don't know what time she got in from the high school concert Wednesday night or what time she left Thursday morning. I was hoping you might have seen something."

Rebecca toyed with the tips of her long red hair. "I sometimes see her walking the dog but I don't remember seeing her Wednesday evening or Thursday morning."

"Trevor, can you tell me what you were doing on Wednesday night?"

At that moment Owen put his hand out in front of Trevor to stop him from answering. "Wait just a minute. I hope you don't think you're going to question my son about Elaine's murder. Trevor may get into some scrapes but he is not a murderer."

Mike took a small step back and to the side of the group; taking the least threatening stance he could while still maintaining authority.

"No, Owen, relax. I'm just—"

"Don't you tell me to relax. You come around here questioning my family like we were criminals." Owen took a step closer.

"Owen, the sheriff is just doing his job. He didn't accuse us of anything."

"Rebecca, did I ask you to say anything?"

Elizabeth grabbed her son's hand but Owen pulled it away, unwilling to have his anger tempered.

"Owen, please let the sheriff ask his questions so we can get it over with. We have nothing to hide. I just want all this horror to go away. Trevor, we know you didn't do anything, just answer the sheriff." Elizabeth's voice was strained as she coaxed her grandson to cooperate.

"Grandma, I don't need you or my parents to protect me. Nobody ever seems to care what I do and now everybody is looking out for me? You're just protecting your name and the farm. Well, you have nothing to worry about because I didn't do anything."

Mike's mind was scrambling. He needed to gain back control of this situation.

"Trevor, no one said you did anything. I was hoping you saw something out there that would be helpful, is all."

Trevor paused. Mike waited.

"Look, sure I was riding around the lake on my ATV with my friends. I know you told me not to, but we're not doing anything wrong. That land is just wasted, nobody's using it. What's wrong with just riding around a little bit?"

Mike wanted to set him straight. Trevor was trespassing, he was damaging property, he was in possession of open containers of beer in public, and he was disturbing the peace. For that matter, he was disturbing the bear dens. The sheriff had a litany of complaints against him but it was a matter of picking his battles and today murder was more important than trespassing. So he kept his tongue for now. "Right Trevor, what time did you get out on the lake?"

"Around eleven. We had a pizza at the bowling alley and then we went out to the lake."

"Did you see anything out on the lake while you were there?"

"Yeah we saw snow, trees, the lake."

Mike didn't lose his patience. Didn't even blink. "What did you guys do out there?"

"I told you, we drove around."

"Anything else? Were you drinking or smoking by any chance?"

"I told you, we were driving around. Who's going to sell me alcohol around here? Old man Lutz gives me a dirty look any time I go near his liquor store. And what does that have to do with your investigation anyway? I thought you were looking for a murderer or is that more than you can handle? We all know you can't hack the hard stuff. That's why you came here in the first place isn't it? New York too tough for you?"

Mike ignored the insolence and the embarassed gasp from the elderly Mrs. Streat.

He moved on to his next question. "What time do you think you got off the lake?"

"I don't know. I didn't check my watch."

"Can you guess?"

"No, I can't. I didn't know I would have to answer any questions so I didn't take notes," he spat.

"Sheriff Riley, I can answer that question. I heard Trevor come in around one o'clock," Rebecca said.

"Okay, are you sure about the time?"

Rebecca hesitated. "I couldn't sleep. I was watching some TV when I heard him come into the house and then go into his room," Rebecca said. "I guess I fell asleep. But...but I remember turning to look at the clock when I heard him come in."

Mike wasn't convinced about anything he had heard from the Streats but he knew better than to push it at the moment. He flipped his notebook shut. "Thanks for all your help. Let me know if anything else comes to mind." Mike gave nothing away; as he turned and left them, the Streats seemed more nervous than when he'd arrived.

Chapter Twenty-Two

After the ceremony some locals lingered and chatted around the hot chocolate, some went to Stella's or Rudy's to continue their conversations in the warmth, some returned to work. Mike walked into the Community Center and made his way over to Bert Henderson. As Elaine's chauffeur and the town's all-round handyman, he was next on Mike's list to question.

"Hello, Bert. Claire, could you give us a minute?"

Claire nodded and reluctantly walked away from their circle. But Mike looked over his shoulder and realized that she was barely out of earshot, if at all. He didn't mind so much, it was more important that Bert felt comfortable. He turned back and for the first time noticed that Bert wasn't himself. Usually jovial, with a smile and ruddy cheeks, today Bert looked ragged, pale and fidgety. He fumbled with his cigarettes, pulling one out and then returning it to the pack. He repeated this a few times until Mike finally offered to move outside so he could have a smoke.

"Thanks, yeah, I would like that. Trying to quit. Again. Not succeeding though. Boy, do I regret the day I started these things." Bert quickly moved out the door and lit up. He took a deep draw and then another. As far as Mike could see he never exhaled.

"Bert, I just need to ask you a few questions to help me with the investigation into Elaine's death." Bert looked around, dropped his cigarette, and stomped on it. And before he had completely put it out he lit another.

"Okay, Mike, shoot."

"Well, I know you drove Elaine around. I assume the last time you did was Wednesday night after the Christmas concert, am I correct?"

"Yeah, yeah that's right. Wednesday night after the concert," Bert sputtered.

"And what time would you say you left the auditorium?"

"I don't really know the time we left. Didn't look at my watch, I didn't."

"Can you approximate?" Mike asked.

"Yeah, well we left after a little bit."

"Well, by a little bit do you mean a few minutes after the show ended? A half hour?"

"I'm sorry, Mike." Bert shrugged.

Mike scribbled in his notebook and shook his head. Bert drew another long puff. His hand trembling from the cold.

"Okay, think a minute, do you remember if you stopped to talk to anybody or did she? Did you take Elaine back to the convent alone or did you give anybody else a ride that night?"

"Look, we all left pretty soon after the show. I gave Claire a ride home too, and I had Elaine home by nine. She's an old lady, needed to get to bed."

"And what did you do after you dropped her off?" Mike was beginning to feel that he was making Bert nervous. Maybe it wasn't the cold that was making his hand tremble.

"I stopped by the bowling alley on my way home."

"How long were you at the bowling alley?"

"Well, about...," Bert started.

"It couldn't have been very long because he returned to my house around nine thirty for a nightcap," Claire interjected. She had followed them outside and now had rejoined them.

"Is that the way you remember it, Bert?" Mike asked, doing his best to hold Bert's evasive eyes.

"Yeah, it's just the way Claire said." Bert now was so obviously uncomfortable there was no way for Mike to ignore it.

"And what time did you leave?"

Quickly, Claire pulled in closer to the sheriff and with not much more than a whisper said, "Sheriff, we are a little embarrassed. We don't want the neighbors to talk, this being a small town and all. Bertie didn't leave until late morning and, well, we are just a little shy about sharing that information. If you know what I mean." Claire blushed.

Claire wasn't the only one blushing; Bert's cheeks had regained more than their natural ruddiness. The down side of policing a small town is that when you know everyone's business they also happen to be your friends and neighbors. And Mike was surprised to stumble on this piece of town gossip and wished he didn't know who was sleeping with whom.

"Okay, Bert, thanks for your time but I may have some more questions for you later."

"Sure, sure." Bert made for his truck without saying another word to anyone.

***

"Sheriff Riley, could I talk to you a moment?"

He turned so fast that he almost walked into Bianca as she was rushing to keep up with his long strides.

"Oh, sorry." Bianca blushed. "I guess we're making a habit of bumping into each other."

"My fault entirely. Did you say you wanted to talk to me, Mrs. St. Denis?"

"I prefer Ms., and you should call me Bianca."

"Okay Ms. Bianca, how can I help? Do you have information for me?" Mike asked with a smile.

"Well, Sheriff, I have a couple of things I wanted to run by you."

"I prefer Mr., but you can call me Mike." He surprised himself at how one could find an uplifting moment at the most stressful of times.

Bianca blushed again. "Mike, I want to discuss a few things that have to do with the murder."

"Let's find a more private spot."

He gently took her arm and guided her to the corner where he put his back to the wall in order to keep an eye on everyone mulling around and Bianca could speak more privately.

"I happened to overhear some of your conversation with Bert and Claire. I hope you don't mind?"

"Overhearing is a village pastime I have come to terms with, so please go ahead."

"Well, I know Claire and Bert are really lovely people, they are my friends and all. But if I'm not mistaken she said that Bert was at her house from Wednesday evening until the late morning?"

Mike nodded his agreement.

"But Claire lives directly across from me. I never saw Bert's truck Wednesday night after the concert or the next morning."

"Are you sure his truck wasn't there?'

"Well, it *was* there at dinner time before the show, he has dinner at Claire's every Wednesday and Saturday night, but afterwards he dropped her off and left. I watched the truck drive away."

"She said that he returned later."

"That's just it, he never did as far as I could tell."

"How can you be so sure?"

"I had trouble sleeping and was sitting in the rocker by my bedroom window until after midnight. The moon was so bright, it was like daylight. I could clearly see that there was no truck there. And in the morning I stopped by Claire's house to drop off some mail that was delivered to me by mistake. Claire is very modest and I don't think she would have invited me in if Bert had spent the night. And there was still no truck or tire tracks in the morning snow."

"You noticed that there were no tire tracks?" Mike's voice carried more than a hint of skepticism.

"I'm pretty observant, it's something I take pride in."

"Is that what you're always jotting down in your notebook?"

"Sometimes I jot things like that down, but other times it's more random, just observations that I find interesting. Something I might expand on in my writings." Bianca felt the conversation was losing focus. "Look, I'm not trying to cause trouble but I'm as worried as anyone else about what happened here and I think we need all the facts straight. I can't imagine why they would lie but I'm pretty sure they were not telling the truth. I suppose it's possible that he returned much later after I fell asleep and maybe he left very early in the morning before the snowfall but..." Bianca trailed off. She felt so guilty saying anything at all but she knew something wasn't right. Friends or no friends, there was a murderer on the loose.

"You're right, it could be that he arrived later and left earlier, but it's not what they said." Mike thought about it a few seconds and then turned back to Bianca.

"You said you had something else you needed to talk to me about?"

"Yes, it's about Agatha," Bianca began, but Mike was no longer paying attention. Where he was absorbed and attentive moments ago, his eyes now followed Trevor and his family as they left the grounds. Distracted, he didn't notice that she had paused. When he finally turned his attention back to Bianca, Deputy Weber appeared through the door, calling after him.

Vera waved him over.

"Excuse me one moment, Bianca."

Vera whispered a few words into his ear. Mike nodded as Vera filled him in, then she quickly turned and left.

"I'm sorry, we'll have to finish our conversation later. This can't wait," Mike called out to Bianca as he followed Vera out of the Community Center.

Chapter Twenty-Three

Flashing lights. Again.

Bianca's skin crawled.

Why were they here now? What next? What could possibly have happened, outside her own door this time?

She kept walking in a haze until she reached the truck with the flashing lights parked next to her mailbox. She didn't recognize the vehicle at first. As she got closer she realized it was a DEC truck, not the sheriff, not the dreaded ambulance. She never wanted to see an ambulance come down her driveway again.

Why would the Department of Environmental Conservation be at her house?

When she neared the mailbox she saw a doe, dead on the ground. She must have been hit. Another reason Bianca preferred to walk the country roads. She never knew when a deer would leap out in front of her car, especially at dusk.

One of the two DEC officers walked over to Bianca after finishing a few words on his radio.

"Hello, ma'am, is this your residence?"

"It is. Was that doe hit by a car?"

"We don't think so; no obvious trauma. She is considered a suspicious death. The second one we've found in two days now. We'll have to bring her in for an examination to establish a cause of death." He jotted something in his notebook. "You've been feeding the deer, ma'am, am I right? I see feed in your front yard." He was smiling politely, but his voice was stern.

"Well, yes, I have. I hope she hasn't starved to death. I tried to get more feed but we have had quite a lot going on around here lately and I never got around to it. I try my best to help though."

"Mrs.—"

"Ms. St. Denis," Bianca corrected him.

"Ms. St. Denis, it seems that the problem isn't that you aren't feeding the deer enough, but that you are feeding them at all. The DEC has been trying to educate the public about the damage done by feeding the deer."

"But, I don't understand. Don't we want to help them survive these long winters?"

"Naturally we want to help but we are limited by what we can do. When deer congregate at a feeding location they spread disease, they also overeat the natural environment surrounding the artificial feed, which in turn diminishes the natural feed in future years, and they can starve. They become dependent on the feeding sites people provide. But worst of all, the feed we give them cannot be digested properly and it eventually kills them. I'm sorry, ma'am, but it looks like that's what happened here."

Bianca's eyes welled up with tears and she nodded. "Is there anything I can do?"

"Are you or your husband hunters?"

"No, I never hunt and…my husband stopped hunting years ago."

"I will not fine you this time because it doesn't look like you were luring deer for hunting purposes but please don't continue to feed the deer and please educate anyone who will listen." He reached into his truck and handed her a DEC pamphlet on the dangers of feeding deer.

When they finished talking, the officers heaved the deer on the pickup. Then they climbed into the truck and left Bianca standing there.

She retrieved her mail, avoiding the spot where the deer had lain, and slowly walked down the long driveway, fighting back tears.

Emily had been right. Emily had told her and Ben at the meeting that they shouldn't feed the deer. They had both ignored her. Ben had even ridiculed Emily for reading too many books. She must apologize to Emily when she saw her next. Now two deer had died, maybe more. Bianca had murdered a deer. She couldn't even kill a spider without closing her eyes and saying "I'm sorry" aloud as she squished.

Bianca made fresh boot tracks down her driveway. She remembered when Richard used to walk ahead of her in the snow. His large footprints would create a safe place for her to step. Now she needed to make her own way.

The train sounded in the distance as it passed through the village. The train no longer stopped in Batavia as it did years ago. The station had been decommissioned and was now a mechanic's garage. The village hadn't been able to raise the funds to buy it back and restore it. Maybe someday, she hoped. It was a shame to let a beautiful historic building fade away unnoticed. Another whistle. It was a comforting sound just the same.

She opened her door and took one step inside.

Only one step, because that was all she was able to do. The kitchen and living room were full to the brim with boxes. Boxes and boxes of books wound around the kitchen wall and filled the living room. She could barely tiptoe her way through and when she reached the corner she found the Christmas tree in the stand. Bert had delivered everything at once! He did exactly as she had asked but she couldn't move. She had never calculated how many boxes were in storage or that they might not fit on the main floor of her small house. The tree was the last straw. How could she live like this? She would have to line every room with bookshelves in order to unpack all of these boxes.

Once again her eyes stung, she was finding this winter a trying experience.

The books towered above her head and there on the very top was Shelby settled in as king of the mountain. He looked down at Bianca and then yawned his approval of the situation.

Bianca smiled back and sat down on the nearest box.

***

The phone rang at precisely six o'clock as it did every Sunday evening. Bianca ran to pick it up unable to suppress a smile.

"*Ohaiyo gozaimasu*," she stumbled in Japanese. The fourteen-hour time difference meant that Ian called his mom before he left for classes on Monday mornings. It was a nice routine they had developed since he had arrived in Japan for his studies two years earlier. Something for her to look forward to every week.

"Hey, good morning, Mom." Ian's voice was gravelly with sleep. Bianca could hear the chopping sounds as Ian made himself breakfast. She pictured him with the phone tucked in his shoulder and his curls standing up and unruly until his shower could tame them.

"I really needed this phone call today, Ian," Bianca confided.

"Why, what's up, Mom?"

"Do you remember me mentioning my new friend, Agatha?"

"Sure, I remember Agatha, she's the grump. But now she's your friend?"

"I know, she is, um, was a grump, wasn't she? Well, she died and it really hit me hard."

"I'm sorry to hear that," Ian said, a genuine note of sadness in his voice.

"I don't really understand it because I hardly knew her. But we were developing a bond. She told me a few stories about her childhood, and I don't think she had shared them with anyone else. I was so excited to tell you about them this week. She met Teddy Roosevelt and her family established Miller's Point with the old tannery. She answered so many questions I had about the area. It was like having a private history lesson. So I found myself being the confidante for a grumpy, dying woman, developing an unusually close bond in a matter of a few weeks, and then she just dies."

"I know it must be hard, Mom, but it sounds like it was expected."

"But that's just it. I don't think it was as expected as everyone thinks. I've been sitting with her the last few weeks and she was fine. It just doesn't add up."

"What are you saying? That you think there was something fishy about her death?"

"Well, yes, I guess that *is* what I'm saying."

"I don't know, Mom, that's a pretty big deal. How did she die?"

"Doctor Spenser says it looks like hypothermia."

"Hypothermia? But I thought you said she was bedridden? Didn't she have cancer or something?"

"Yes, she had cancer and was expected to die years ago. She's only been bedridden recently because she was recuperating from a hip fracture. But they found her in bed all wet and frozen from the open window."

"So you think someone opened the window to kill her?" Ian said incredulously. "It seems like an awfully uncertain way to try to kill someone."

"I know, I know, it sounds ridiculous. But the strange thing about it Ian is that someone else died too."

"Another death?" he mumbled through his mouthful of breakfast.

"Not just a death, a murder. Her name is Elaine Fisher, she's an old friend of Agatha's and she was found murdered by the side of the lake a couple of days ago."

Ian swallowed. "Murdered? Are you sure? It seems unlikely that someone is going around killing old ladies in a small village."

"No, this was definitely murder. Someone hit her in the back of the head with a stone. The sheriff found the bloody rock near her body." Bianca's voice caught in her throat, tears started to well up. It was too much to have Richard gone and Ian far away, and now this.

"Mom, are you there?" Ian asked through the silence. "I'm sorry you are dealing with this. Do you need me to come home?" His voice developed a mild panic. "You don't think you're in any danger, do you?"

"Are you suggesting that I'm the next logical target of this geriatric killer?"

"Well, you are getting up there you know," Ian played along. Bianca enjoyed the gentle teasing. It helped her keep things in perspective.

More composed, Bianca answered, "I just don't know what to make of it. And, well, you know, I miss you and Richard."

"Maybe you should be thinking about a trip out here soon."

"Not now, I have to watch my money and get myself a job. Then we can talk about a trip."

"Mom, I don't want to sound insensitive but I think you might be a little fragile these days. And no one can blame you. What does the sheriff say about the murder?"

162

CHAPTER TWENTY-THREE

"The woman's ring was stolen so he believes it was a mugging gone wrong."

"Well, although I'm not happy about it, a mugging sounds a lot less dangerous than two murders. Didn't you say some kids were breaking into houses last month? It's probably more of the same." Bianca heard silverware clanking and water running. He must be washing up after breakfast. Bianca smiled; at least he didn't leave dirty dishes in the sink.

Ian paused then asked, "Mom, have you made any new friends? You know, people your own age you can socialize with? I would feel better if you had a busier social life. And I don't mean volunteering and baking either."

"Well, Olivia Last and I have hit it off real well, and we have been getting together on a regular basis for a glass of wine or coffee. We also critique each other's writing, which has been a real blessing for me. She and I are kindred spirits, I think. And Rebecca Streat was here this morning, we had tea and a chat." Bianca didn't mention that it was really a business meeting but she had enjoyed Rebecca's company. Bianca would like to think that they had a friendship developing.

"I'm glad to hear it, Mom, that's more like it. Get some rest tonight. And like you always say, things will be clearer in the morning. It's hard to face difficulties at night, especially if you're alone."

"You're right. It's probably nothing and I'm blowing things out of proportion. So, enough about me. Tell me what's new with you."

Ian filled Bianca in on his week, his courses, his new apartment. She had been to visit him the year before so she was able to envision it all. She loved to hear about the foods he ate and the places he visited. Last weekend he went up to Nagano to ski with his friends. They were a nice bunch; she knew them all. This week Kyoto had its first snowfall of the season. It was incredibly beautiful he said, tempting her to visit. Maybe next year she could plan to spend Christmas in Kyoto with him. Bianca couldn't help thinking what a blessing it had been when Ian had received the scholarship to attend university in Kyoto. A dream come true for him.

When Ian finished catching her up, he asked about her writing.

"I'm working on a new project now but it's in the infant stages, I'll fill you in as it progresses, or if it progresses at all." Bianca decided to hold back on the details. Agatha's death had changed everything.

She signed off reluctantly with a promise to get some rest and do something nice for herself this week. Ian gave her a final reminder: "Remember what I said last week; get yourself a Christmas tree. You won't regret it."

Bianca looked across the crowded room to the tree crushed in the corner behind the tower of boxes. She decided not to tell him she had already taken his advice, and it hadn't turned out quite as he had planned.

***

After Bianca had moved some boxes into the mudroom and brought a few boxes upstairs she was able to get around the kitchen and warm up dinner.

She no longer cooked every night. She and Richard had made their meals more than for nutrition, they had communed over them. They planned their menus together and prepared their dishes with gusto.

Sometimes they shared the kitchen and cooked together. Sometimes one of them treated the other. Presented it like a gift. And it had been received as a gift. Then they would talk through the meal and long after. She often baked for him and they would have a slice of cake with tea and finish their night reading across the table from each other. Still sharing their space, fully aware of each other, but no longer needing to talk.

These days Bianca cooked a small meal every few nights and then relied on leftovers. The joy of cooking had gone flat for her. Where she used to effervesce over their fresh garden harvest in summer and specialty shops in winter as she planned their meals, now she prepared quick and simple meals for one.

But winter demanded warmer, richer foods. Last week Bianca had tentatively entered into stew and soup territory again and she had to admit she enjoyed it. She ordered two small pieces of lamb from Rudy's Market, and picked up a turnip and two leeks. With these she had made a Scotch Broth from Richard's recipe.

Soul food.

Her first taste was surprising; it was like Proust's madeleine cookie, throwing her back to their intimate moments together. She hadn't realized how much she missed the flavor of his food, not just his company. She had been compounding her grief by denying her senses. At first she felt guilty about enjoying the stew without him, but with each spoonful she realized that the aroma and texture were a way to refresh her memory of Richard.

Tonight she warmed up the remaining leftovers of the hearty soup and dug in with some crusty bread.

"Here's to you," she said. Richard's photo smiled in response.

Always unsure whether she could eat alone in complete silence, she picked up Agatha's journal.

April 12, 1977

Today I found a box of Allison's childhood memorabilia. In there was a picture she colored for me of a rolling green field and an enormous sun. Green and yellow. The picture was special then because it held only those two colors. For me green and yellow have always been reminders that there is someone out there to share our path. It also conjures up nightmares of how that path can diverge into dangerous territory.

Green and yellow always make me think of Thomas.

How he helped me in the early days through my shame.

He was the only reprieve I got from the harassment at school. My scandal had now overshadowed his and I am sure he was relieved to fade away unnoticed. Finally he was invisible and left in peace. He sat in the back of the classroom in silence. He never participated in the spiteful behavior of the other children.

Bianca chilled at the story, remembering the faraway look in Agatha's eyes when she first mentioned Thomas Brennan alone at the back of the classroom. The boy whose mother's life was so awful she took a knife out on her husband.

Bianca slipped the bookmark back in place, wandered over to the fire and stoked the logs, unsure whether she was up to reading more. The flames swirled around the log, mesmerizing her but the tug was too strong. Before long, she sat back down and opened the journal where she had left off.

One day I sat alone unable to do my work because I had no supplies left, my classmates had taken them all. I tried to hold my head up but I couldn't stop the tears. I couldn't listen to the teacher. I was angry that my life had fallen apart and I was angry that I couldn't enjoy my history lesson. My father had stolen that too—my love of learning.

Just as my classmates left the room for recess and I believed I could breathe a moment of respite alone, Thomas walked over to me from his cubby in the back of the room. He never approached anyone. He had something in his hand and I started to sweat, steeling myself for the worst. But when he arrived at my desk he held out his hand and in it was a chewed up pencil and two crayons, a green one and a yellow one.

He kept his hand out. He never spoke.

He waited there until I mustered up the nerve to take them from him. Then he bent down and kissed the top of my head and left. Never saying a word.

I can still smell the grass and the damp spring earth steaming from the hot sun, the scent wafting through the classroom window that day. A green crayon and a yellow crayon. The grass and the sun. He gave me two gifts that day; he gave me tools he could not afford to part with and he gave me hope that I would not have to be completely alone.

Thomas and I were drawn to each other by our status as outsiders and at one point we had become inseparable. Two wounded creatures limping along together. We kept to ourselves. Eventually the rest of the class got bored with us. And we were grateful to be forgotten.

After my father's scandal had died down somewhat, the rest of my school days involved being ignored by everyone and eating a silent lunch with Thomas under the elm tree or in the back of the room on cold days. Mrs. Condon gave up trying to assimilate us into the larger group. I imagine she was relieved we had each other, as pathetic as it was.

I found Thomas' silence peaceful and I too came to speak less and less. Talking was painful; it only led to more sadness. Silence allowed us to push the hurt aside and pretend for brief moments that it didn't exist. And yet it was amazing how much we communicated.

Over the years Thomas and I built on this unlikely friendship. Drawn to each other's grief. Afraid to be alone.

It took time but Thomas did start to talk to me. First monosyllables, then short sentences. Sometimes he expelled whole narrations of sadness in one sitting, like a painful birth.

When we were sixteen we started fumbling around in the fields behind the school. We had no other outlet, no one wanted us. We deceived ourselves into believing that our mutual isolation was attraction.

The story ended abruptly. Bianca turned and found a few blank pages. Then a page with only a doodle of a hillside and a sun.

She flipped some more and found two lines stranded alone on a blank page.

I thought my childhood had been hard and sad. But it was later that the true sadness started.

She turned to the next page and read some more.

At eighteen I was pregnant for the first time. We understood nothing about how to prevent conception. Who would tell us? His Irish Catholic father? My emotionally unstable mother? I had lived such a sheltered life and Thomas had been wounded at such an early age that I realize now how limited he was. Maybe he wasn't even right in the head.

The pregnancy changed him. He went from a vulnerable boy to an angry man. He started drinking. Then he found his voice and he blamed me. It seemed that all his anger from all the years finally bubbled to the surface and escaped; like a runaway train, no brakes to stop the ugliness. Then he forced me to get a back-alley abortion. Somehow I survived it.

We stayed together. We knew nothing else. But now we had become reminders of each other's past and mirrors of each other's despair. All we saw reflected back was our dirty history.

I could not look at him without knowing that he knew my secrets. He threw it back in my face. What my father had done, how I thought I was better than the rest of them, how my mother was a madwoman.

My second pregnancy ended in a miscarriage when Thomas graduated from cruel words to cruel actions. He drank and beat me until I lost the baby. Sometimes when I look back at it I think he was afraid of bringing children into a world that had been so cruel to him as a child.

Bianca stopped when she read this remembering Agatha's gravelly voice and her expression of submission when she had allowed herself to step back in time. Bianca stood up and walked around, the story had made her restless. She needed to do something to clear her head.

She made another cup of tea. She brought it back to her desk and took a sip. It was bitter. She had let it steep too long.

By my third pregnancy I ran away, unable to withstand the drunken fits any longer. I had nothing. No job, no skills and no money. I went to the church that night, hid in a pew and cried myself to sleep. Elaine came to my rescue again, she found me there in the morning. She took me to the convent for a few days and then she arranged for me to work at The New York State School for Girls, a facility for "incorrigible" girls.

By working there, I had a place to live, I was well fed and I was allowed to get care and to give birth in their maternity ward. I was expected to guide the girls and organize their chores. We kept a garden and cooked and ate together. I was no different than the other girls but I was older and I had a reputable upbringing. I was like a big sister.

Thinking back, those days were a fairly peaceful respite. For all the trouble the girls had ahead of them they could not deny their youthful natures. It felt good to witness their optimism and it was good to be needed. I realize now that, though brief, it was a happy time.

Before I gave birth, Elaine found me local adoptive parents through the church of St. James. When I delivered I had twins. The adoptive parents were farmers and couldn't afford to take them both so they took my boy and left me Allison. I had no idea what to do with her so I remained at the school where Allison and I grew up together. I didn't leave the grounds for years. I became a recluse.

It's true what they say, that we become our mothers.

Muffled sounds coming from the floor caught Bianca's attention. The cat wrapped himself around Bianca's ankles. She picked up Shelby and stroked him twice before he decided he had had enough and jumped down. Bianca got up from her desk, the cat trotting behind her. When Bianca looked back at him, he stretched his full length, then plopped to the ground and twisted on his back, inviting her to scratch and play. She indulged him briefly, enjoying the thick golden coat. When she stood up, Shelby slipped ahead of her into the kitchen and led her to his food. She put some treats in his bowl and then added some hot water to her tea.

The more she thought about it, the more Agatha and Elaine seemed connected in ways that made their back-to-back deaths uncomfortable.

Bianca walked into the hallway and found her parka on the peg by the door. Deep in her left pocket she rummaged around until she found what she was looking for. Two cards. One said *Walt Patten, State Senator,* with the seal of New York. The other had a raised sheriff's star emblem and said *Mike Riley, Sheriff, Onanda County.* Both had offered to be available to talk at any time. She looked at her watch. Nine thirty-five. Too late? Bianca convinced herself that it was still an acceptable time to call. She looked at Mike's card, then put it down and dialed Walt.

"Thank you for calling Senator Walt Patten. I am unavailable to take your call at the moment. As your senator please know your concerns are my first priority. Leave a message and I will respond as soon as possible."

After the beep, Bianca hung up.

She picked up Mike's card, put it down. Absently warmed up her tea again. And then picked up Mike's card. She turned it over and she thought she smelled of hint of his cologne. On the back was a handwritten number.

She dialed, she listened for the ring. After five rings she decided to hang up. Relieved. She had tried, right?

"Hello?" a woman's voice answered. "Riley residence, hello?"

Bianca slammed down the receiver.

Chapter Twenty-Four

Bianca's embarrassment chased her out of the kitchen and as far from the phone as she could get. She sat down at her desk. She opened her manuscript, grabbed a pencil and started reading. Only chapter seven. Her edits were going slowly.

At the end of the first paragraph Bianca realized that she had absorbed nothing. She was not in the right frame of mind to edit. She pushed her chair back and walked in a circle around the living room. She saw the *Gazette* on the corner table.

Bianca plopped in her favorite armchair, picked up the newspaper and turned to the crossword puzzle.

She made her way through the first few clues pretty easily. Then she got stuck on 26 down: *without the accent you have a ruckus or brothel in Italy*. This one should have been a gift; she spoke Italian, although she was somewhat rusty. She moved on to 26 across: *these are often used at 26 down*. Stuck again. She moved on to 41 across: *swimming weasel*. Ah! That one she got. Otter. She quickly jotted it down. 38 across: *planet named after sea god*. They all should be so easy! Neptune. Now she could figure out 26 across: *without the accent you have a ruckus or brothel in Italy*. Casino! Now on to 26 across: *these are often used at 26 down*. Chips! Click, click her brain went and she made her way through the rest of the puzzle.

Bianca found puzzles so satisfying; she enjoyed the mechanical way her brain worked on the challenge. And a finished puzzle was clean and neat. Unlike life, it allowed itself to be solved, and wrapped up.

Bianca looked around for the next distraction and picked up her new library book but found herself having to reread the passages. She put the book down; she wanted to give Philip Marlowe the proper attention he deserved.

She picked up the large envelope on the side table. Olivia's notes on a stalled short story Bianca had developed last year. She quickly reviewed the notes in the margins, nodding in agreement as she went along. Olivia had seen how complex the story was and had gingerly suggested that what Bianca really had was two stories.

"Richard, Olivia is right, of course. These are really two stories. You always said less was more. It seems so obvious now that she pointed it out." She smiled at his picture.

She turned her attention to the television. Bianca skipped through the channels, not really seeing nor listening. On automatic. She stopped when the screen held the image of young George Bailey. *It's a Wonderful Life* was her favorite Christmas movie. One she watched every year while decorating the tree with her son. They both knew the story so well they would work their way around the tree finding the perfect location for each of the ornaments while reciting the lines of the movie. It was a tradition, one that was on hold while Ian lived in Japan.

Bianca opened the box of Christmas decorations by her armchair and sifted through the ornaments until she found the string of lights. She untangled them. Then she wound around the tree passing the lights behind the tree and resting them on the branches until she could run around the other side and pick up the trail since Ian wasn't there to receive them.

On the television young Mary reaches over the soda fountain counter and whispers into George Bailey's bad ear.

"*George Bailey, I'll love you till the day I die,*" quoted Bianca happily as she wound and wound until the entire tree was covered with lights. She plugged it in to make sure she had no bald spots. The twinkles brightened up the room despite the clutter. She almost forgot there was another storm brewing outside her window.

Bianca glanced at the screen, the saddest scene in the movie. The pharmacist receives a telegram that his son has died and sends George to deliver capsules inadvertently filled with poison. George doesn't know what to do and he sees a sign on the wall that reminds him what to do: *"Ask Dad...he knows."*

The missing piece of the puzzle from Rudy's Market! The sign on the wall behind the coffee grinder was the same as this one in the movie. Bianca was perplexed that she hadn't recognized the sign. She chalked it up to it being a year since the last time she saw the movie. But deep down she knew she was suppressing her holiday sadness. No longer able to make holiday memories with Richard or Ian.

Bianca carefully unwrapped her vintage collection of ornaments. These she placed on the top half of the tree. The remaining ornaments would be for the bottom half where they were fair game for the cat.

"Oh, this old thing? Why, I only wear it when I don't care how I look," Bianca said as she grabbed the edge of her robe and swished it around like Violet did in her sexy dress in the scene. It wasn't as much fun without Ian and Richard to laugh at her antics.

The sounds from the storm competed with the television. The wind was furious. It shrieked around the house and settled with a howl in the stovepipe. The lightning flashed like old flashbulb cubes, flickering as if someone were playing with the light switch. Then a clap of thunder. Had she really heard thunder? During a snowstorm? She didn't enjoy storms as much now that she had to ride them out alone. Nothing will happen, she would tell herself. Or the house could get struck by lightning and burst into flames.

Bianca continued to recite the lines of the movie but her enthusiasm was waning. It was getting harder and harder to face this lovely holiday ritual without Ian and Richard.

The broadcast was interrupted for a weather update: *lightning and thundersnow with one to two inches of snow accumulating per hour.* Thundersnow? She had never heard of it. Everything about her new home was baffling her lately. Thundersnow sounded like a super hero with very loud powers. Intense snow and sleet were expected around midnight. It was nine o'clock, and as far as she could tell the snow and sleet had been going on for at least an hour. Funny how weather reports were always a little late in Batavia.

When the movie returned, Jimmy Stewart and Donna Reed were dancing the Charleston, the gym floor opening behind them to reveal a pool. They danced closer and closer to the edge. Bianca waited for this scene every year. The lights on the tree flickered twice before the TV screen flashed off, along with all the house lights. She would miss her favorite scene.

She busied herself finding and lighting candles. Once that was complete she had nothing left to do. She knew she couldn't concentrate on her book. She stared at the flicker of the candle flame, trying to be mesmerized by it. It swayed and held her attention for a while but her mind was not quiet.

Alone in the farmhouse with a murderer on the loose, and a thunder snowstorm outside her window. Not the way she liked to spend an evening.

Her house felt empty and ominous. The emptiness was misleading, she knew. It held her fears, and regrets, her guilt and her self-deceptions. The connection to Agatha had been severed by death, possibly a murder. She felt a bit the immigrant, unmoored. Why had she not been there for Agatha? Maybe if she had stayed longer on Friday night, Agatha would still be alive. Why had she not remained home that spring morning? Richard had said he wasn't feeling quite right; she should have realized that he needed her at home. She should have insisted that they go to the hospital.

He had died alone.

Alone.

Because she had to run errands. Errands she couldn't remember and that no longer mattered. She had let him down.

Bianca decided to put an end to this long day.

She checked the woodstove as Richard had always done before bed each night. She bent and blew out two candles and with the third still flickering a path, she started up the first step. Then she turned around and walked back to the kitchen and to the front door.

She paused briefly. Resigned, she turned the deadbolt.

Then she dragged herself up the stairs.

Lying awake, staring at the ceiling, the lightning flashes let in sufficient light to allow her to see the outline of the room. She stared and stared, but sleep would not come. Her mind raced with thoughts of missing rings, snowy bedrooms, and old friends bound by a turbulent past.

The thunder was subsiding but it was replaced by the yapping and howling of coyotes. First two, then three or four. Eventually a pack. The noise was unbearable; they must have cornered a weak deer. Maybe one weakened by bad feed.

It sounded as if they were tearing the deer apart.

Bianca covered her head with the pillow and buried the sounds with her own sobs.

Chapter Twenty-Five

9:42 p.m.

Allison Miller closed the curtains, she wasn't afraid of thunder and lightning but she was no fan.

Once the power went out she realized that she had no idea where to find candles at her mother's house. She no longer knew her way around. But she was considering spending more time in Batavia. Things were different now.

With her mother gone she could finally sign the deal with Janus Corporation. The sale would change everything for her.

No more servitude. No more selling her soul.

If she invested the funds from the sale carefully she could finally start her own business, one that would bring a modest income. Maybe she could slow down enough to live a life that wasn't just about working and not having any time to enjoy her earnings. She was fed up with the whole lot of them. When she had received the phone call telling her that she had been passed over once again for the promotion, she had been enraged. Allison knew then what she had to do. Something she had contemplated for a long time but never had the nerve to do, and she had finally gone and done it.

She was relieved but a bitter taste still remained, it wasn't without some regrets. Now she waited for the phone call that would make it all worthwhile.

***

9:57

Walt Patten put down his scotch; maybe he shouldn't keep drinking if he wanted to finish what he had started. Now that the way was clear, Allison Miller would sign the papers and the deal would be done.

Bringing the condo development would be the first step in establishing the casino. And he needed the casino. He owed people and he had no choice but to come through. His political career depended on it, and his time was running out.

It should be smooth sailing from here.

Walt picked up the papers on the edge of his desk and leaned closer to the candle. He was alone in his office tonight. The storm raging outside. He had lost track of time as he had scrambled to put the papers in order. Now he was stranded at the office. He would be spending the night on the couch, but it was worth it.

Walt picked up his scotch again, took a swig and dialed Allison's number.

***

10:02

Claire Koop removed her corduroy headband. She had worn her hair pulled back all day. Her scalp tingled. A mixture of pleasure and pain.

She poured herself a brandy, the strongest drink she had in the house. She had to reach for it behind her homemade jam jars on the bottom shelf, where she didn't think Bertie would find it.

She sipped and then her sips turned to gulps.

She had lied to the sheriff that morning. She had lied to the sheriff.

But she'd had no choice.

Bertie could not be left alone in this. Now perhaps Bertie would see that Claire could be trusted. He needed her, and now she finally believed that he knew it too. After all, he had followed her lead when they were talking to the sheriff. It had done some damage to her reputation but it had been worth it. What was done couldn't be undone so it was a matter of keeping their heads and moving forward.

She paced the living room floor, jumping every time the thunder clapped.

Finally, she stopped before the phone and dialed Bertie's number.

Once again, it rang and rang.

She decided to call McLoughlin's. She had to make sure he didn't get drunk tonight. Drinking had done enough damage this week.

***

10:14

Bert Henderson dropped his tired bones onto the sofa. He sank deep into the cushion, the old sofa springs giving under his weight. Nadine had taken most things of value from their home and he had furnished his apartment above McLoughlin's Pub with Salvation Army bargains. He pulled the space heater closer to him and cracked open the beer he had carried over from the fridge.

The phone rang again. He ignored it again.

He should take his truck out to the lake and try to remember exactly what had happened. But a serious storm was brewing out there. He couldn't leave. Tomorrow he would need to drive around the lake again and jog his memory.

All he could remember was that Nadine had shown up at his door Wednesday night. He couldn't believe his eyes; he had always known that she would come back eventually.

Then his eyes had focused behind her. In the hallway leaning on the wall was Stewart Dekker. They had come to claim her alimony and the child support. Bert was in arrears, and they needed the money. That's how she had said it, "we need the money." He'd be damned if any of his money would make its way into Stewart's pocket.

He had tried to keep his composure. He had tried, but he hadn't succeeded. He had begged her to leave Stewart. He had apologized for being late with the money.

But she had turned and walked away, threatening to take him to court. To her receding back he had yelled his promise to her that if she returned he would stop drinking and he would find more money.

He remembered that much. Then he had gotten into his truck and opened the first beer of the night. He remembered stopping on the dock at the lake and stowing his bottle of bourbon in his parka pocket and sitting on the bench. He remembered hearing the snowmobiles squealing in the woods, and he remembered a bear. And then he didn't remember anything.

He woke up in his truck, parked near the dock.

Now he opened another beer with trembling hands and sat in the darkness. He preferred sitting in the dingy apartment in the dark. He wanted no reminders that it wasn't the home he had made with his own two hands, the home he had made for Nadine.

The beer was souring his stomach, or his anxiety was. The beer was warmish.

And the heater was cold.

***

10:21

Rebecca Streat dropped her briefcase on the bed. It had been a long day.

First the interrogation at the ribbon cutting and then a disappointing day at the real estate office.

She locked her bedroom door. She and Owen no longer shared a room. Until of course he had some drinks and then he would knock until he woke her and she would let him in. She had learned early on not to resist. It only backfired. She could not afford to have visible bruises in a small town where everyone talked. No one would sell or buy through her if she looked like a pity case.

She was hopeful that tonight he wouldn't come knocking; he had fallen asleep in the armchair as soon as the power went out.

She was relieved, and she was surprised when they hadn't argued over what she had said to the sheriff. She had come home prepared for the abuse, he usually took every opportunity to berate and humiliate her. It rarely took much, most of the time he invented it.

Tonight he had avoided her completely. She hoped he wasn't storing up his anger for one of his yearly blowouts. But, she had done what needed to be done, and with the help of her lawyer she would be free of him soon.

She scrubbed her makeup off and lathered her nighttime moisturizer on her face, making sure to put extra on her neck and cleavage. But she did it by rote, not with her typical attention.

She rubbed the cream absentmindedly and then brushed her teeth with a vengeance. She didn't stop until her gums bled. She had to remain steadfast in her position that Trevor had returned at one a.m. Owen had glared at her, incredulous, when she had said it. But the sheriff hadn't noticed, she was sure. Trevor never returned home before his curfew. She had had to cover for him, what else could she have done? She was his mother. Who rides around a lake in the freezing winter all night?

She knew she was doing the right thing. Her son hadn't killed Elaine. Everyone was always so quick to blame everything on him. They judged him too harshly. They didn't know the vulnerable little boy he had been, and she was sure still was. If he would only confide in her like he used to.

It was almost as if he wished no one loved him at all. But she did love him. She did everything she could for him. She gave him as much money as she could spare. In fact, she gave him more money than she could afford to give him. But kids need money, how could he get on without it? He always seemed to need more and more; she had no idea what he spent it on in this sleepy town. With nothing to do, of course he would lash out once in a while. She remembered how restless she had been in high school.

It was just a phase. He would outgrow it.

✳✳✳

10:47

Trevor Streat refused to answer the phone. His mother had picked up three calls for him already tonight but he didn't want to speak to any of his friends. He knew what they wanted to say and he didn't want to hear it. He would fix everything tomorrow. He just needed some time to sort things out.

Tonight he was more concerned about saving his skin.

Trevor hunkered down in the corner of his room. Even in the darkness he wouldn't take his eyes off the door.

Any minute his dad would be walking in that door, pulling off his belt.

But this time Trevor was ready for him. This time he wouldn't get away with it.

He wasn't afraid of him anymore.

***

11:17

Kenzo Ishikawa struck the match. He lit the tea light in front of his wife's shrine. Then he knelt and touched his forehead to the tatami mat and tried to conjure up her face.

No longer able to see her clearly, he remained there as a form of punishment.

But his attention wandered. Thoughts of the last few days filled his restless mind. The scene in the sheriff's office played over and over in his head. His mind was usually disciplined enough to allow thoughts to float in and eventually float out. He had learned that not resisting was the key. But today the thoughts floated in but wouldn't float out.

Had he handled himself properly? Should he have behaved differently? Had he made the situation worse by being so reticent?

He wondered and worried. Would he need to leave here too?

***

11:58

Bianca stumbled around the casino floor, breathless. The deer ran frantically in circles, trapped. The lights flickered. Music and clanging slot machines accompanied the sound of the doe's stomping and snorting.

Bianca desperately searched for a door to offer the deer an exit. But no matter where she looked, she found no door. The doe was tearing up the room, bucking in fear. Bianca's manuscript pages littered the floor.

181

At a wide carpeted staircase the deer galloped up the steps in an attempt to escape but instead got further entrapped in the bowels of the building. Bianca wanted to run but she was mesmerized and followed the deer up the stairs.

The doe climbed to the top floor. Freddie and Claire crossed Bianca on the stairs, screaming. Bert fled his apartment, leaving the door gaping wide. The deer ran into the apartment and headed for the sliding glass doors and the balcony overlooking the Hudson. Finally spotting freedom, the doe leapt out the door and over the balcony.

Bianca opened her mouth to scream but no sound came out.

The deer was gone.

Bianca ran down the stairs. When she made it to the front of the building she backed away at the sound of howling and the gruesome rending of flesh. A pack of coyotes was tearing the doe apart, limb from limb, teeth grabbing hold and ripping out her guts. Spilling from her ruptured body was undigested corn feed.

Bert was kneeling by the deer's side. He stood up. He looked at Bianca and then looked down. Bianca followed Bert's gaze. On the pavement was Richard.

A loud screech startled Bianca. She whipped her head toward the sound.

The sheriff's truck pulled up to the curb and blocked her view of the body. Bianca, relieved, looked up to thank Mike. But she was stopped by the slam of his truck door. He ran around the truck and started yelling.

Chapter Twenty-Six

Monday, December 19

Mike shot up in bed. It was just a dream. Again. The mangled body on the pavement. Would he ever be able to forget the image of his partner in pieces?

Poor Sal. So much pain, so many bad choices. Would Mike ever stop asking himself if there was more he could have done? Had he missed something? He was afraid he knew the answers to those questions; he just wasn't willing to face them.

He reached over to the other side of the bed. Empty. Cold. Then he remembered, Maggie had taken the late train back down to the city last night. She hadn't even asked him to drive her to the station, she had just called the taxi.

He longed for a warm, crowded bed again.

He rolled over. He wanted to sleep but didn't want to close his eyes. Didn't want to invite the dream again.

He looked at the clock. It was just past midnight.

Today he would need to make some real progress on Elaine's murder. He couldn't let the village down. Batavia wasn't just part of his territory, it was his home. These neighbors were his friends.

He wondered how Bianca was doing at her farmhouse alone, worrying about the murderer Mike hadn't apprehended yet.

Mike found himself thinking about Bianca more and more. He needed to stop that. Maggie would be back home tonight. He needed a clear head. They needed to stay on track; their marriage had enough distractions. Even if Maggie refused to admit it.

***

Eugene listened to Bianca's dream with a knowing look, aware that these dreams would haunt her for years to come as she grieved for Richard. How raw and easily aggravated was the pain of losing your partner.

Eugene sensed that Richard had been Bianca's soul mate; he recognized the signs. When they had first arrived in Batavia they had eaten breakfast at Stella's every Sunday morning. They would sit across from each other and they would acknowledge nothing outside their table, they could have been in any diner in any city.

In Eugene's opinion, Bianca's nightmare was a symptom of her current insecurities. Obviously, she was a woman in transition.

Nonetheless, he had to admit that the dream seemed more bizarre than most.

The bell over the door rang and the tall stranger from yesterday walked into the diner. He tugged off his coat and hat, hung them up by the door and took a seat not too far from them.

"G'mornin', Captain, what can I get you today?" Eugene put two fingers to his forehead in a mock salute.

"Coffee and toast will do it," the stranger grunted.

"Coming right up. Excuse me, Bianca."

Before the man could hide behind his newspaper, Bianca closed her notebook and extended her hand.

"Hi, I'm Bianca St. Denis, and you are?"

The man hesitated, but he offered his hand and shook.

"Thomas Brennan." Then he immediately tucked into his newspaper and ignored her.

Bianca frowned to herself. What was it about this man that rang a bell? Then it hit her.

This was Thomas Brennan. Agatha's Thomas. The boy in the back of the classroom. The man who beat her, the man she ran away from.

Bianca's pulse quickened.

Why now? Why would this man appear in town this week? What was he doing here? Did he know Agatha had died? Or worse, did he have something to do with it? Bianca knew she should stop feeding her suspicions about Agatha's death, but she also knew something was amiss. She just knew it.

***

Mike leaned over his desk toward Bert who was huddled in the wooden chair on the other side.

"Why did you lie to me, Bert?"

"Mike, Mike I don't know. I just don't remember anything."

"What happened? Tell me from the beginning. Tell me the truth this time."

"Look, Mike, after I dropped off Elaine and Claire, I went home. A few minutes after I got home there was a knock on my door. I opened it and found Nadine. Couldn't believe my eyes." Bert choked up and had to pause.

"Then I see that Stew was there behind her, waiting for her, protecting her. Protecting her from me. Can you believe it? Protecting my wife from me. When she first arrived I thought she had come back to me, Mike, I really did. Every night I think it will be the night she'll come back to me." Bert was visibly crying now. Trying to hide it, but not succeeding.

"Then what happened?" Mike was firm. He wanted to believe Bert, it was hard watching his friend fall apart, but he needed to get to the truth.

"When I opened the door and I saw her there it was like a dream come true, it was. But you know what she wanted, Mike? Do you know what she wanted? She wanted more money. She said I was behind on my child support. She was there to collect more money and Stew was there to back her up. Instead of getting a job, he was in my hallway shaking me down for money. Before I knew it I was begging her to stay. I was cussing at Stew. And then they left. Just like that. They came in, turned my life upside down and then they walked out." Bert dropped his head to his hands, as if it were too heavy for his neck. Shaking, sobbing.

"What happened next, Bert? I know this is tough for you, do your best."

"Well, I just left the apartment. I got in my pickup and went for a drive. I didn't know what to do. I stopped by the lake, had some beers on the dock and then a few nips. I got a little scared when I realized I'd dozed off a couple of times. I probably would've frozen to death out there, I would've. So I got myself to my truck, drove to the other side of the dock behind the trees to sleep it off. I didn't want anyone to see me like that. I didn't want Nadine to find out I was drinking again. I'll never get her back if I don't stop the drinking. I know it, but I just can't seem to do anything about it."

Mike flipped through his notebook, jotted some notes. He definitely needed another cup of coffee.

After a minute Bert continued with no prodding.

"It was hard enough to quit before, and I was making some progress. But now that she's gone, all I want to do is drink."

Mike just sat there without a word; he wasn't letting him off the hook this time. Bert had lied to him once, this time he wasn't going to make it easy for him. He could wait as long as it took for Bert to finish.

"I woke up before dawn still drunk, but I went home and went right to sleep. I swear, Mike, that's the truth. I swear this time it's the truth."

"Why didn't you just tell me this? Why the story about going to Claire's?"

"Mike, the murder happened on the lake, I spent the night and the morning on the lake drunk. I don't remember a thing. Claire made that up, she was covering for me, I guess. She's a good friend but I suppose that means she thought I did it. Maybe I did, maybe I didn't. I don't know, Mike."

"What did you see on the lake? Tell me something, anything to help me turn my attention to something else, to someone else. Give me something I can work with."

"I didn't see anything." Bert's voice cracked, his eyes wide. Mike saw fear in those eyes. "But, I heard something."

"What did you hear?"

"I heard some ATVs and snowmobiles. And I remember now that I saw a bear. I definitely saw a bear. Could the bear have done it, Mike? You know their dens have been disturbed this winter."

"Bert, no, I don't think the bear did it."

"But, Mike, listen, Mike. Maybe it was the bear. You know how the conservation department keeps warning us not to disturb them, not to antagonize them. It makes sense!"

"Bert, calm down. You're grasping at straws. A bear did not do this."

Mike massaged his temples. This wasn't getting any easier.

"Look, Bert. We didn't see any bear tracks out there but then again the snow made it hard to tell."

"See what I mean? Anything is possible. You have to admit. Huh, Mike?"

Mike wanted to change the subject; Bert was hardly making sense. "What time did you hear the ATVs, Bert?"

"The whole time, it was driving me crazy, all night, all night, even when I was sleeping. I was drunk but I heard those noises all night long."

"Bert we found bowling alley matches, some beer cans and some cigarette butts at the scene. It just doesn't look good for you, Bert. They're your hand-rolled cigarettes. And the beer cans, they're Old Milwaukee. Everyone knows you're an Old Milwaukee man, Bert."

"I didn't kill Elaine. I couldn't hurt her."

"Bert, you don't remember, how can you be so sure?"

"I know I didn't do it. Check my truck. Check my house. I wouldn't lie to you."

"But you already did, Bert. You already did."

Chapter Twenty-Seven

Eugene served Thomas Brennan and then resumed his conversation with Bianca.

"I'd say that Freud would have a field day with your dream, Bianca. You've covered everything in there from the village controversies to your distress over your dead deer to your fear of coyotes. And, of course your grief over Richard. Did I miss anything?"

"No, that about wraps it up. Don't you think that was enough for one night?" The sarcasm in her own voice did not fool her. Apparently, it wasn't enough for one night. She had neglected to mention Mike showing up in her dream.

"No, No." Eugene held his hands up in mock surrender. "You had a hell of a night. Did you get any sleep at all?"

Bianca pushed her cup out in front of him and Eugene refilled it for the third time.

"I guess that answers my question."

"It was a difficult night before I even tried to sleep. I was kidding myself that I could decorate my tree without any backlash. Ian and I always trimmed the tree together and I thought I was used to Ian being away, but that was when Richard was around. Now they are both gone and it's harder."

"Sure it is." Eugene scraped the burnt crumbs off his charred toast with a butter knife. The ash fluttered to his dish like black snow. "You'd think I could get decent toast in this place. I've got to speak to the cook."

Bianca smiled. Eugene was known for great breakfasts but everyone knew he had a tendency to burn the toast.

"Listen Bianca, I wouldn't read too much into your dream except that you're still shocked by Agatha and Elaine's deaths…and, if you don't think I'm too forward for saying it, also Richard's death. I don't think you can rule out how that kind of grief becomes a part of your everyday life, how it colors everything you do, how you have to fend it off constantly. These recent deaths no doubt have brought your pain over Richard closer to the surface. I know it has for me, and I lost Stella eight years ago. Your pain is fresh. And you have to allow for that." Eugene poured more coffee for both of them.

"All I ever want to do is talk about Richard, but most people here barely knew him. It's so sad to feel he is being forgotten." Bianca added cream and sugar in her coffee and looked up at Eugene. "I envy you in a way. Everyone here knew Stella and remembers her. You at least have the option of talking about her."

"You would think so, but most people never bring her name up to me. It's like they're afraid I might break down. But I can handle it. I miss her and talking about her would make her feel close. I'm sure they have good intentions, but I'm hungry to talk about her."

"I agree. The last thing I want is to forget."

"I think no one wants to cause me pain. But I would welcome stories or just an easy conversation about her. It would keep her spirit alive." Eugene restlessly flipped through the paper and stopped at an ad that looked like the flier Bianca received in her mailbox. *CasiNo!* in bold letters took over an entire page. "Bianca, are you a local?"

"What kind of a question is that? I try to think of myself as a local, but according to many villagers, I'm not. I thought I could count on you at least."

"Of course you can. I mean, are you a member of the Ladies of a Certain Age League, a L.O.C.A.L.?" Eugene grinned and pushed the paper over to her side of the counter.

"Oh, I guess I'm a little sensitive when it comes to this subject. I was officially made a member on Sunday, why?" Eugene pointed to the small print at the bottom of the ad. *Paid for by the Ladies of a Certain Age League.*

"Well, I didn't contribute to that ad. I didn't even know they were doing it. I think Olivia got a little carried away. From what I can tell, the ladies of the League are not of one mind politically. It seems that Olivia, Monica and certainly Emily aren't in favor of the casino but Claire and Rebecca certainly seem to be. I wonder how they feel about this ad. And I really don't want everyone to know my politics."

"Get used to it, Bianca. There is no way to live in a small village like Batavia and keep your views hidden. It's not possible. Just be ready for a heated debate with Kurt Dekker whenever he's around. But he won't hold it against you, don't worry." Eugene took the paper back. "If you're against the casino and condo so much that would explain how they made their way into your dream. I know some people are worried to death about them coming to Batavia and ruining our peace."

"I am not in favor of either one but they shouldn't haunt my dreams. I'm no Kurt; I have no passion about this one way or the other. In fact, you're the only one I've told that I would vote against these projects. Let's face it, I didn't move to the country to be surrounded by those things, but I also understand how the locals need jobs and tourism." Bianca paused before adding, "I think they entered my dream for another reason."

"And what would that be?"

"Timing."

Eugene shrugged.

Bianca took a big gulp of her coffee, settling in to explain her theory. "It seems that we can't escape discussion about the casino and condominium lately. The word *casino* was even a crucial piece of my crossword puzzle last night, go figure. I wonder if it was all just front and center in my mind when I went to sleep. And of course when I awoke from that crazy dream they were still on my mind. I've been thinking that maybe my subconscious is at work here. Don't laugh, but I think my dream has something to do with these deaths. I think my dream was a message."

Eugene's eyebrows shot up, a smirk started to wiggle along the outside of his mouth.

"I told you not to laugh!"

"I didn't, I didn't...well, almost. I'm sorry, Bianca, go on."

190

"My grandmother, my mother, my sister and I, we all have had premonitions and dreams that have proven true over and over again. It's a standing joke in my family that the women are witches. This time I think my dream is telling me something."

"Look, I won't dismiss that. My grandmother was kind of..." Eugene hesitated. "She was kind of special that way too. I could tell you some stories. But where do you think there is a link? Elaine didn't have anything to do with either project. Agatha maybe. She was sitting on some land that could have been developed, but we all know she was very much against both projects. There was no chance she would sell to Janus." Eugene kept talking while he wiped down the counter then refilled Bianca's cup. "I don't see how her opinions about these developments could explain her death though. The doctor said she died of hypothermia. Elaine was murdered but has nothing to do with the projects. Agatha had some possible connection to the projects but wasn't murdered."

"Well, it could provide a motive," Bianca blurted.

"I don't understand. How could the developments be a motive for Elaine's murder?"

"I'm not talking about Elaine." Here goes. Bianca was now telling the third person in town about her suspicions. Hopefully none of them was the killer.

She looked up at Eugene. *Really Bianca, Eugene is no killer.* "I'm not convinced that Agatha wasn't murdered. We know that Allison supports both projects. And now that Agatha is gone Allison would inherit and she could sell. From what Rebecca tells me the tannery and the estate sit on acres and acres of prime Hudson River property. It has to be very valuable."

"But that's always been the case. Assuming what you say is true, what could have changed to prompt Allison to act now?"

"Maybe Allison was tired of waiting?"

"I don't know, Bianca. It sounds more like the plot of a movie than something that might happen in Batavia. Allison isn't known as warm and fuzzy that's true, but murdering her own mother?"

Outside the front window something caught Eugene's eye. Bianca followed his gaze and saw an old man. Not more than five and a half feet tall, he was leaning over and talking. Was he talking to a child, or a dog, Bianca wondered? The bell above the diner door signaled his arrival and he walked in to warm welcomes.

Eugene smiled. "Well, here comes Lester finally. He never showed up for his dinner last night. We served short ribs, his favorite. I wonder what kept him away."

Eugene raised his voice in welcome. "It's the Quirke himself. Where have you been? The place hasn't been the same without you." Eugene brought a cup and the coffee pot to the table where his buddies sat by the window.

Lester took off his parka to reveal a brown three-piece suit and yellow bowtie. "I've been busy, I may be old but I have things to do, places to go, people to see." Lester took a swig of his black coffee. "Tell you the truth, Dolly's been under the weather. But she's on the mend now."

"So, that's Lester Quirke?" Bianca asked when Eugene returned.

"The one and only."

Bianca reached behind her counter stool and felt inside her backpack. Sure enough, she found a large envelope stuck inside her book.

"I had completely forgotten that Agatha had given me this envelope for him the other day. I feel terrible. What with all the commotion lately I never remembered."

"No one can fault you for that. But you might as well give it to him now. You never know what it could be. They were old friends, literally. She was probably returning some documents from her Historical Society research."

"I'll wait until he's had his breakfast. I don't want to interrupt him and his friends. His wife's been sick. Let him relax and enjoy himself."

Eugene snorted a laugh which evolved into a guffaw. "Dolly's not Lester's wife, she's a skunk!"

Chapter Twenty-Eight

Sheriff Mike Riley and Deputy Vera Weber walked up the steps to the Streat home. Although it now showed its age and was in need of a coat of paint, the stately farmhouse remained one of the finest homes in the area. Mike dreaded upsetting the elderly Streats but his dispatcher had called in a domestic dispute. Out here, surrounded only by fields, the call could only have come from another family member. Mike figured Edward and Elizabeth were probably pretty upset already.

No one answered Mike's repeated ringing so he showed himself in. He found a living room in disarray; lamps knocked over, the mirror above the fireplace shattered; shards strewn everywhere.

He did a quick once over. No blood.

Mike and Vera kept their hands on their weapons and made their way deeper into the cavernous house.

Mike's skin tingled from the dissonance of the chaos around him coupled with silence. A shadow of a movement caught their attention. Mike signaled Vera to wait.

Muffled sounds grew louder as Mike approached the kitchen. At the table he found Edward comforting Elizabeth; both hunched over with age and sadness. They appeared unharmed. Still no Trevor, Rebecca or Owen. He waved Vera into the kitchen.

"In the bedrooms," Edward whispered and pointed to the back of the house.

Mike passed through the study. He stopped short and pulled his pistol from the holster. The gun cabinet door dangled from the hinge, the empty slot in the row of rifles an ominous warning.

He motioned Vera to hold back again and then he pushed open the bedroom door and extended his pistol.

Droplets of blood on the beige carpet had already started to dry. Mike's temple throbbed.

He followed the trail to the bathroom door. Blood smeared the handle. He pressed his ear to the door. Whimpers. He turned the doorknob, sticky with blood.

Inside, Rebecca was crouched on the floor, crying silently, holding bloody tissues to her nose. She had a bruise developing under one eye. Runs crept down both stocking legs and her blouse was torn at her shoulder.

She cringed when the door opened but didn't look up.

"Rebecca," Mike said gently.

This time she looked up and when her eyes met Mike's, she broke down.

"Oh, God. I thought you were Owen," Rebecca sputtered through her sobs.

***

Deputy Weber searched the cabinets looking for tea bags. She rummaged through decades of clutter until she finally found them in a faded tin in the uppermost cabinet. Rebecca, in a fresh change of clothes, accepted a cup but put it down without taking a sip.

Vera had called Doctor Spenser when Mike left to track down Owen, Trevor, and the missing rifle. The doctor was upstairs administering a sedative to Elizabeth. Edward refused to leave her side. It angered Vera to see what Owen and Trevor had put this elderly couple through.

Vera took a seat across from Rebecca and waited.

After a quiet moment Rebecca opened up. "He just let loose. He went from room to room tearing things up. He's never been this bad before."

Obviously, this was not new behavior for Owen. How Rebecca had kept things secret in such a small town was surprising to Vera. She hoped against hope that Batavia was not about to witness more violence. And Mike was right in the thick of it. She gently tried to pry more out of Rebecca.

"Rebecca, do you know what triggered Owen's outburst?" Vera asked. She sat tucked in close and tried to make this interrogation as intimate and unthreatening as possible.

Rebecca shrugged, but did not elaborate.

Vera gave her time to respond, looking around the room for a distraction. Faded wallpaper curled in the corner, the linoleum had a worn spot in front of the kitchen sink. It had been years since she had been here. The beautiful farmhouse used to be perfect, never a thing out of place. She remembered how the Streats used to host enormous lawn parties. Every harvest they would have apple bobbing, scarecrow contests, pumpkin picking. Owen used to drive the hayrides. She felt a flush rise to her cheeks as she remembered the crush she had on him as a young girl. She would fight to sit as close to him as possible. He was too old for her, of course, but she couldn't resist his blue eyes and the lock of hair that fell in his face when he leaned over. But that was a long time ago. Whatever happened to the idyllic life on Streat Farm? Maybe it had never been as wonderful as it had appeared back then.

Vera shook herself out of her reverie and tried again with Rebecca. "Did Owen take the rifle with him?"

Rebecca swallowed hard and nodded without looking up.

"Do you know where he is?"

Rebecca shook her head violently.

"Rebecca, please think. Did he say anything that would suggest what angered him or where he would go?"

At first Rebecca said nothing. Vera waited patiently until Rebecca broke her silence.

"He was yelling. He wouldn't stop saying horrible things."

"I know this is hard, but what did he say?"

"Terrible things, but that's not unusual. He called me a slut. It usually doesn't take much to set him off, but he rarely goes this far. This time he had it out for Trevor. He called him a filthy kid. He kept repeating 'Not my kid. My son wouldn't act this way.'" Rebecca hiccupped as she tried to suppress her cries. "Then he said that Trevor would ruin us all, and he would make sure this never happened again."

She broke off and slouched over the table. "Trevor, my Trevor. What is he going to do?"

They both jumped at the crackle of Vera's radio.

It was Mike's tired voice. "Vera, we've found Trevor."

Chapter Twenty-Nine

Bianca stared across the counter at Eugene.

"A skunk? Agatha did say something about a skunk, didn't she?" Bianca remembered. "A skunk is no ordinary pet."

"Lester is no ordinary guy."

"Honestly, I never thought of a skunk as a pet." Bianca shook her head, smiling.

"Well, I don't think Lester did either until he found her a couple of years ago, hurt on the side of the road. She was a baby and he nursed her back to health. Now she won't leave his side. I think secretly Lester enjoys adding some panache to his image."

"If she doesn't leave his side then where is she now?"

"He won't let her go into the shops so she wanders around until he whistles for her and they walk home together."

"That must be quite a sight."

"I'm surprised you've never seen them." Eugene scraped down the grill now that the morning rush had subsided.

"I haven't exactly been a regular around town until recently."

Bianca looked across the room. Lester was taking a break from entertaining his friends and was eating his eggs and pancakes with gusto. He had a slight build and didn't seem able to handle the Lumberjack Special but nonetheless he was doing a good job.

It was late morning and Lester's friends had left one by one. He sopped up the last of the maple syrup and blueberries off his plate as Bianca approached.

"Good morning, Mr. Quirke. You don't know me but—"

"Aren't you a sight for sore eyes? I certainly don't know you, young lady. But any friend of Eugene's is a friend of mine." He motioned her to take an empty seat. "My name is Lester. Nobody calls me mister. Some people call me Quirky, some people call me Lester, and some people just call me crazy. But nobody calls me mister. And what is your name?"

Bianca wasn't comfortable calling her elders by their first names but she certainly wasn't going to call him quirky or crazy. She settled on Lester.

"Hello, Lester, my name is Bianca St. Denis."

"Ah, now I remember, I heard through the grapevine that you bought the Van Rouse house."

"That's right. My husband and I moved in three years ago."

"A penny for your thoughts, young lady." She wasn't sure, but Bianca thought he had just winked at her. She enjoyed being called young lady for a change, especially from this eccentric cliché-wielding old gentleman.

"Well, I was sort of a friend of Agatha's."

"Is that so? Well, blow me down! Agatha made friends in her old age? I guess she felt drastic times called for drastic measures. I wouldn't believe it if I hadn't heard it straight from the horse's mouth."

"Before Agatha died…" Bianca hesitated.

"Ah yes, dear girl. What a shame to lose someone so young and gutsy. You could only take Agatha in small doses, but she was the real deal that one." He shook his head sadly, "Dying so young like that."

Bianca's reaction must have prompted him to continue.

"You know, I'll be a hundred years old next spring. Makes everyone else seem rather young and spry. Even Agatha. We went way back, the two of us. Batavia won't be the same without her. She had moxie, that one!"

Moxie. Bianca hadn't heard that word since she was a little girl. Her favorite uncle used to tell her she had moxie. She made a mental note to jot the expression into her notebook.

It suddenly hit Bianca that she was talking to a very old man. From afar he seemed lithe and fit, but upon closer inspection she could see just how deeply his wrinkles had settled in, they had obviously been there a long time.

"Let me extend my condolences Mr...Lester."

"Thank you, dear. That's very kind of you." Lester raised his cup at Eugene. "But no use crying over spilt milk. Besides, it might be a blessing in disguise." Despite what he said, Lester's rheumy eyes got rheumier.

"I also have an envelope for you. Agatha asked me to give it to you." Bianca pushed the envelope, now dog-eared and ragged from her backpack, across the table to him. "I'm sorry it took me so long. I have to confess that I forgot about it, what with—"

"Of course, say no more." Lester's dentures clacked between his words. He carefully unsealed the envelope and peeked at the contents.

"Well, well, I see. Timely as usual, that Agatha." Lester looked up at Bianca. "It's a new will."

***

Mike made it to Lois Lanes within minutes and had been trying to bribe Trevor with fries and a soda since he arrived. Mike knew Vera would have been a better choice to get information out of Trevor but she had her hands full with Rebecca. He gave Trevor some space and some time to eat before he started. He had to ride the delicate line between urgency and success. He needed to know where Owen had gone with his rifle, and he needed to know if there was any connection to Elaine's murder. He also knew Trevor might just shut him out completely if he took the wrong approach.

After a few minutes he asked, "Trevor, you seem okay. Are you?"

"Yeah, yeah. I'm alright." The fries crowded his mouth but he answered anyway.

"Can you tell me where your father is?"

"I don't know."

"Trevor, is that true?"

"I know you don't believe anything I say, but it's true."

"Trevor, you haven't always told me the truth, now have you? But I need the truth now." Mike's voice rose just enough to signal he was serious but not threatening.

"I'm telling you the truth. The last I saw him was at home."

"Then tell me what you know."

Trevor looked up at Mike but didn't say a word.

Mike felt like Trevor was ready to break. He knew that he should try to help him save face, it was hard for a teenager to back down from a tough stance. At this point their bad relationship had settled into something of a habit. It wouldn't be easy changing that attitude even under these circumstances. But Mike was in a rush. The clock had run out for codling and cajoling.

"Trevor." Impatience was seeping through Mike's voice. There was an angry man with a rifle out there; Mike was afraid he was running out of time.

"Dad was yelling as usual but..." Trevor started to take a sip of his drink.

Mike grabbed the soda out of his hand. "Keep talking."

"He was yelling at Mom but this time he was yelling about me. About how I had disappointed them again, and how he was going to stop me before I completely ruined the family. Then he smashed the gun case open and took out his rifle. I climbed out my window and came here to hide out."

"You ran all the way out here? That's four, maybe five miles." Mike wasn't buying it.

"Not if you take the woods. And not if there's a rifle behind you."

"And how did you get in here?"

Trevor shrugged.

"Now is not the time to keep secrets, Trevor. Your father is in a rage with a rifle and we have an unsolved murder with you at the scene. And now I'm starting to understand Jackson's confused complaints about break-ins here at the bowling alley with no actual evidence of a break-in. You have a lot of explaining to do. My patience is wearing thin. So start talking before I bring you in."

Chapter Thirty

J ackson Parker stood behind his bowling alley bar vigorously polishing glasses. He was fuming but he gave the sheriff some space to talk to Trevor. No one wanted to get to the bottom of all of this more than Jackson. He was tired of Trevor and his antics. Worst thing he ever did was hire that kid. First he missed shifts, then he gave away soda and beer to his friends. But once the register started coming up short, Jackson had had enough. Granted, there was no proof but it could only have been Trevor. He was happy to be rid of him.

But Trevor was like a bad cold. Jackson couldn't seem to shake him. When he opened up today he found Trevor hiding behind the pinsetter. Jackson had been oiling the lanes. He turned off the machine when he heard a noise behind the lanes. He went to investigate with a wrench in his hand, the closest thing he had to a weapon, and there he found Trevor.

Jackson had taken his time bringing down the wrench.

Trevor had begged him not to tell the sheriff and Jackson had seriously considered cutting the kid a break. He wasn't sure the sheriff was what the boy needed, maybe better parents, maybe a good beating, but not the sheriff. But with a murderer on the loose, Jackson wasn't sure he had that much compassion in him. When the sheriff's dispatcher called to say they were on the lookout for Owen and Trevor, Jackson didn't hesitate to reveal Trevor's whereabouts. Jackson wouldn't hide a possible murder suspect. Then he called his wife, Lois, and told her to take the day off.

***

Vera poured Rebecca another strong cup of tea. She felt less pressure now that Trevor was found. But she couldn't get complacent. Mike said they still didn't know where Owen was, or where his rifle was for that matter. This wasn't over yet.

Vera sat back down at the pine table. Rebecca's body had transformed once she had heard that Trevor was safe. Exhaustion replaced her adrenaline rush and she could hardly hold her head up.

Vera hated to persist, Rebecca had been through so much already, but she had no choice. "What started this?"

"Yesterday the sheriff questioned us about Elaine's murder," Rebecca whispered.

"Go on. The sheriff's office has been talking to the entire village. How did that trigger this episode?"

"Owen's been upset about what I said to the sheriff, or what I didn't say."

"Rebecca, I need you to explain yourself." Vera grabbed Rebecca's arm, gently but firmly.

Rebecca shook her hand away but with little enthusiasm.

Vera waited.

"I told the sheriff that Trevor came home the night Elaine was killed, but I lied."

Vera's ears pricked but all she said was, "I see." Vera's mind was racing, trying to figure out how to pass this information to Mike without alerting Rebecca.

"That doesn't really explain why Owen's so upset, I don't think he would be so violent because you protected your son. Is there more to this?" She stalled.

Rebecca nodded weakly. "Owen believes that Trevor is ruining this family. Owen refuses to take any responsibility for how the farm has declined since he took over and he's always looking for a scapegoat. Trevor is his latest target. Of course Trevor does get into trouble, at school and with the sheriff, I know what people say. But Owen has started denying that Trevor is his son. He thinks I sleep around. It's not true, Vera." This time Rebecca looked up.

Vera nodded to encourage her to continue and pushed the teapot across the table to her as if they were sharing a pitcher at a bar.

"He thinks Trevor did this to Elaine and he doesn't want suspicion to fall on the family. He thinks that because I covered for him, blame will make its way back to us. He wants Trevor to turn himself in and take his consequences!"

Vera's mind was scrambling now. She needed to get on the radio with Mike right away.

"Look, Rebecca, I know how hard this must be for you as his mother but—"

"You have no idea! Is your son being accused of murder? Don't say you know because you can't possibly know! He could not have done this!"

Chapter Thirty-One

"**A** will?" Bianca had no idea that she had been carrying Agatha's will in her backpack since Friday. Lester compounded her dismay by revealing he was Agatha's lawyer. Lester's gnarled hands and sunbaked skin looked like they belonged to a farmer.

"Agatha warned me to expect a revised will. Honestly, I forgot about it too. Let's take a look, shall we?"

"Well, I don't think I should be…"

"Nonsense, if she didn't trust you she certainly wouldn't have given you the envelope in the first place." He opened the flap and showed Bianca. "Look, she didn't even seal it."

Lester's wild eyebrows shot up at her. "How do I know you haven't looked at it already?"

Red crept into Bianca's face. "No, I didn't…," she stuttered.

"Relax, I'm just pulling your leg." Lester removed the document from the envelope, the papers vibrating slightly from the mild tremor of his hands.

Agatha's writing, so weak and yet so defiant, filled three pages. The dark blue scribblings looked decorative from afar.

Lester took his reading glasses from his vest pocket and perched them on his nose. A faint scent of mothballs wafted from the envelope. He slid over in his seat a few inches to take advantage of a shaft of morning light. He flipped through the document and stopped at the third page.

"Looks like she mentions you here."

Surprise registered on Bianca's face.

"Don't count your chickens." Lester's dentures slipped a little on the word

204

chickens. "Just a few old books, it seems."

"I wasn't…" Bianca didn't know where to look.

"I'm sorry again. My sense of humor is as delicate as a bull in a china shop," Lester said grinning, his brows peaked like an owl's.

Bianca sat back in her chair and started to relax. She found Lester funny now that she was getting the hang of his humor and his exhaustive use of clichés. She supposed when you're a few months away from being a centenarian you're entitled to a few quirks, and Lester certainly lived up to his name.

He pulled up his glasses to read more closely. "She really likes to stir the pot, that one. She's packed a few surprises in here. Allison isn't going to be too happy, I can tell you that."

The morning rush was over and Eugene came over. He straddled a chair as he sat down to listen, his head and arms resting on the chair back. Bianca realized that she was the only one in the room experiencing any discomfort over sharing Agatha's secrets.

"Looks like she's leaving the bulk of her estate to the Sisters of Saint James."

Eugene whistled. "Wow, no one expected that, I bet."

"Least of all Allison, I'm sure. Says here Allison is to get the old Miller house but all the rest—the old tannery, the company housing and most of the acreage—is to go to the nuns."

"While she was being so generous, did she leave me anything? I need to replace my furnace, it's been clanking for weeks, going to go any minute," Eugene inquired with a smirk.

"You're barking up the wrong tree there, Eugene, but she did leave something to Bianca. And it seems she has all her ducks in a row, too. It's all signed and witnessed properly. Looks like her nurse, Marla, and her husband took care of that."

Wes Montgomery's smooth jazz guitar strummed out of the turntable behind the register. Eugene's musical choices usually had to compete with town gossip, but in the near-empty room Bianca's thoughts meandered with the music. The idea of Agatha's books both thrilled and exhausted her.

"Penny for your thoughts?" Lester asked in his pithy way.

"Lester, did you say you knew that she had revised her will?"

"Yes, she called me on Friday, said she was having it delivered."

"That's the day before she died. Do you mind me asking who else knew about it?"

"Your guess is as good as mine. But my experience is that Agatha always played things close to the vest. I don't think she would have advertised this."

"Do you think she told her daughter?" Bianca asked.

"No way to tell. Agatha and Allison weren't particularly close, so my first reaction would be no. On the other hand, Agatha never beat around the bush, she would have wanted all her cards on the table. Allison is a bit of a bully but no one scared Agatha."

"Would she have told Sister Elaine?" Bianca leaned in a little closer. Waiting to hear if what she started to suspect could possibly be true.

"Elaine was her best friend and I wouldn't be surprised if she told her. After all, this would have been a very big deal for Elaine. Actually, it makes sense, Agatha owed a lot to the sisters and especially Sister Elaine."

Lester stood up and was wrapping himself in his parka and scarf. He perched his knit hat on top of his head so it came to a peak. "I don't mean to leave you in the lurch, young lady. I need to get to the post office so I will leave you to your own devices. It was a pleasure to make your acquaintance. Let's chat again soon."

He waved to Eugene, grabbed the envelope and walked out. Once outside he put two fingers in his mouth, screeched a whistle and then slipped his gloves on. As he walked across the street Bianca saw the skunk waiting for him on the other side. Dolly wore a badly knitted red sweater. Tufts of black and white fur spiked out of the dropped stitches. When Lester made it across the street, Dolly waddled into lockstep beside him until he reached the post office.

Bianca and Eugene watched in silence until the odd pair were out of view.

"What are you thinking, Bianca? I see the wheels turning in your head."

"Well, if Agatha changed her will just before she died, maybe someone did know about the new will."

"Certainly doesn't look good for Allison."

CHAPTER THIRTY-ONE

"That could explain what changed," Bianca mumbled.

"I'm not following."

"Remember earlier you said Allison was in line to inherit all along, so what had changed? Well, this did." Bianca's voice rose in excitement. She was speaking faster, and her leg was jiggling. "Eugene, I've got to take care of something right away. Please put my breakfast on a tab until tomorrow."

She jumped into her parka and was half way out the door as Eugene called after her.

"Go ahead, but you better have something good to tell me tomorrow…I'll be waiting."

Chapter Thirty-Two

Trevor decided to go for it. He told them the truth.

"I have a key to the back door," Trevor said. Better off admitting to breaking in. Maybe the sheriff would back off.

In two quick strides Jackson made his way to the other side of the counter. "What do you mean, you have a key? You turned your key in when I fired you." Jackson inserted himself between the sheriff and Trevor then brought his flushed face down in line with Trevor's. His hands, knotted into fists were down by his side, knuckles white. Trevor looked to the sheriff but got no clear message that he would prevent Jackson from swinging.

The moment stretched out until finally Sheriff Riley gently corralled Jackson and got him far enough away so that the counter was a barrier between them.

"Trevor, Jackson's right, we need to know how you got hold of a key."

Trevor reluctantly mumbled something. What the hell—they'll find out anyway, he figured.

Now Jackson was yelling, his temper on full display.

"Did I hear you say Olsen's Hardware? Fred Olsen would never make you a copy of my key!"

"He didn't, he thought I was making a copy of my house key. I told him my dad sent me because I lost mine and couldn't get home to do my homework after school without one. He's pretty gullible, that one."

"You watch your mouth, Trevor Streat," Sheriff Riley lashed out. "You're in enough trouble as it is. Folks around here are trusting. But you know that, don't you? That's how you figured out you could con Olsen. You're a

Streat after all, one of the finest families in this town. No one would suspect a Streat of being underhanded."

Trevor smirked and a grunt escaped him. Disgusted with his own family, he couldn't understand how the Batavians thought so highly of them.

"So this isn't the first time you've been here after hours. You're the one drinking my beer and leaving crumbs." Jackson paced the floor behind the counter. "I knew something was wrong. No jimmied locks, nothing really disturbed but I knew something wasn't right. Here I was yelling at the janitor for doing a lousy job, I'm thinking he's pilfering a beer here and there but this is too much! Boy, do I owe him an apology." Jackson stopped in his tracks; he looked up suddenly, his eyes screwed up in anger. "Mike, you better get this kid out of my sight."

***

Mike took Trevor by the shoulder and escorted him to the back of the bowling alley and sat him down on one of the aisle bumpers. Mike remained standing in order to maintain the upper hand. He knew Trevor talked the big talk but he was starting to display some weakness, his voice had cracked a couple of times, his right hand was furiously ripping at the cuticles on his left hand. Mike knew it was a matter of time and Trevor would break down crying. The young ones all cried in the end.

Mike's radio sputtered. "Mike, I need you to call me on a private line right away. I'll be waiting at the Streat's for your call." Vera's voice had an urgency that Mike didn't like.

"Trevor, I'm going to give you a minute to compose your thoughts. Then we are going to start from the beginning and you are going to give me the truth this time or you're spending the night in jail for obstruction and you'll stay there until I figure all this out without your help."

Mike walked up to the phone on the wall near Jackson and gave him a hard look and a nod in Trevor's direction and then dialed the number in his notebook. Jackson nodded back. The phone rang once and Vera picked up right away.

"Vera, what have you got?"

"Mike, Rebecca told me she lied to you," Vera whispered. "Trevor never came home the night of Elaine's murder. Owen went ballistic today because he wants Trevor to turn himself in and take his consequences. Rebecca was covering for him. And Mike...Rebecca thinks her handgun is missing."

"Mike, are you there?"

Mike turned, his heart thumped. An ugly taste rose in his mouth. Had he really underestimated this kid? Was he stupid enough to turn his back? Had he fooled himself into believing that in a small town like Batavia kids are kids and don't do cruel, awful things?

But he had turned his back and now Trevor was gone. And Rebecca's gun was missing.

Chapter Thirty-Three

Dr. Spenser typed the final entries into the document. He was a lousy typist and his anxiety made it even more difficult.

He typed, backed up, crossed out, typed, backed up and crossed out. All the while he shook his head, his hair falling in his eyes. He passed his hands through his hair, pulling it away from his eyes. He may have been doing it badly, but he needed to see what he was doing. The perspiration made his glasses slip just enough to annoy him. It seemed that the more he needed his composure, the more he lost it. He feared he'd lose it forever if he didn't finish this report and run it down to the sheriff immediately.

Finally.

He yanked the sheet out of the machine, the corner sticking and tearing with his final flourish.

"Damn, damn, damn. *Haste makes waste...*I hate it when my mother is right." Relieved to see that none of his hard work had torn off with the corner, he signed it with an illegible scrawl, folded the mangy paper and jammed it into an envelope.

He grabbed his coat off the back of his office chair and headed out the door. His head still shaking.

How, how had he missed this?

***

Jackson came out from the storeroom behind the bar carrying a box of napkins to refill the dispensers, trying to keep himself busy.

"Where did he go? Where's Trevor?" Mike shouted at him from the depths of the alley.

Jackson felt the rebuke like a slap, how had he lost Trevor? But he hadn't, the sheriff had.

"Wait a minute. What do you mean? He was with you," Jackson yelled back.

"I was on the phone! I thought you were keeping an eye on him!"

"I went into the storeroom to give you privacy, that's what I thought you wanted me to do. What the hell…blaming me!"

"I didn't want you to leave. I wanted you to keep an eye out! Damn. Where the hell did he go?" Mike stomped around the alley, looking under every table.

"I'm about done with all this. You want help? Call your deputy. It's bad enough I've got someone breaking in, now I have to play deputy too. Don't you come around here screwing up and blaming me."

Mike ran down the hall to the restrooms.

Despite his anger Jackson helped him look. He didn't want Trevor on the loose any more than the sheriff did. He opened the door to the back room; the pin setting area, maybe he was there. That's where he had found him earlier, hunched in a corner, scared as a child. Jackson felt like a fool having been taken in by that punk.

He heard yelling on the other side of the door. It was Mike. "Jackson, don't go in there. He has a gun! Get out of there!"

Jackson's skin pricked. He froze in place. *Trevor had a gun? What else don't we know about him? Did he kill Sister Elaine? Did Trevor kill that sweet lady for a ring! For the money!* Bile rose in his throat; his legs were rubber. He heard a creak behind him. Still paralyzed, his eyes stung.

Then Mike walked past him with his gun drawn.

Jackson's arms jumped up, his head cleared. Mike made a motion with his head toward the door. Jackson ran out of the room. He didn't want to leave Mike alone in there but Jackson was no hero. Once back in the alley, he leaned over the closest seat and vomited on the newly oiled floor.

***

Mike ignored Jackson's rant, frantically searched the bowling alley and finally ran out the door. He wanted to stop and apologize to Jackson for being out of line and putting him in danger but there wasn't time. Jackson will think he's a jerk for sure and spread the word, but he had no choice. There seemed to be no end to his mis-steps lately.

He jumped into his car, threw on the lights and siren and headed toward the Streat's.

Mike grabbed the car radio and called into his dispatcher. "Shelley, Shelley, this is Mike. Trevor is on the loose again. He is to be considered armed and dangerous. I want everyone on this, and I want them on it now! I'm on my way toward the Streat's, most likely place he will be."

Mike quickly weaved his way through the quiet roads, shocked once again at how everyone can go about their mundane business unaware of the turmoil around them. His sirens made little difference in his progress since the snow banks had so tightened the roadways that cars had nowhere to pull over and clear a path for him. As he rounded the last curve to the Streat farm, Shelley's agitated voice broke in. "Mike, turn around and come back to the office. Trevor is here."

"He's there? At the station? How did he get there?"

"You're not going to believe this, but his father brought him in."

Chapter Thirty-Four

Mike pushed his way through the crowd gathered in front of the sheriff's office. Jake Wilson, the *Gazette* editor, tried to sneak himself in when Vera unlocked the door for the sheriff. Mike pushed him back, gently but firmly. "Not this time, Jake. Don't call us, we'll call you."

"Oh, come on, Mike, how are we supposed to run a paper around here if you refuse to let us in on anything? This is the biggest news we've had in years."

Mike was relieved to see that Jake was the only reporter in sight, but plenty of locals had interrupted their errands to come take a look. Mike was amazed at the turn out. He didn't know so many people worked and shopped on Main Street.

"Not now, Jake. It's not news yet."

Jake finally left but not before snapping a couple of pictures over the sheriff's shoulder.

To Mike's surprise the noise didn't dwindle when he closed the door. The crowd may have been outside, but the chaos was inside.

Deputy Weber called out in relief and started to walk over. "You're here."

But Owen Streat beat her to it. He rushed over to meet Mike at the door. A pistol flailed in one hand, with the other he dragged Trevor by his jacket collar. Trevor was flushed and had been crying. A couple of red splotches led Mike to quickly assess that he had probably been hit, too. Owen was perspiring, the veins bulging near his receding hairline. He looked ready to pass out, no doubt from a combination of drink and adrenalin, Mike assumed.

"Owen, put the gun down. You don't want to be pointing a gun at an officer. Not a good idea," Mike said gently.

"Sheriff, I demand you take my son into custody." Owen yanked Trevor's collar again as he would to a badly behaved dog. Trevor coughed as the jacket zipper strained on his throat.

"Owen, let go of Trevor."

"I won't let go of him until you take him into custody. I won't let him run away again. You lost him once already."

"Owen, Trevor isn't going anywhere. Let him go."

"Stop telling me what to do! I'm sick and tired of everyone telling me what to do. My father, my mother, Rebecca, and now you. I'm done with all of you." With each word Owen yanked at the collar and swung the pistol around like a conductor before his orchestra. Trevor whimpered. Mike stood perfectly still, his muscles aching from the effort of doing nothing.

"Now, take him and straighten him out. You can have him. He's no son of mine."

"Deputy Weber, please take Trevor into custody." Mike motioned with his head to Vera.

"But, Sheriff," Vera started to protest.

"Did you hear me, Deputy? Mr. Streat has brought Trevor in and we need to take him into custody."

Vera carefully approached Owen. She took her cuffs off her belt and slowly put one and then the other of Trevor's arms behind his back. With a click she secured his hands into the cuffs. Only then did Owen release Trevor's collar.

Vera quickly supported Trevor under his arm and led him to her desk at the back of the room to process the paper work.

"Owen, the gun."

"Here, take it." Owen tossed the pistol onto the desk.

Mike lunged, his instincts kicking in. He was in the air for a split second but time stood still. He watched the gun slowly float through the air. He steeled himself for the discharge.

Plunk. Nothing.

Mike allowed himself to exhale. He was straddling the desk. His skin was electric, on alert.

He also felt foolish. He knew most pistols were drop proof and wouldn't discharge, but he was in the air before he could think about it. He scrambled to recompose himself. He needed to regain the upper hand.

At least he had the gun now. And no one was hurt. Yet.

Owen smirked at Mike. "I found the gun in the barn. That's Trevor's hiding place. He thinks I don't know about it. When I went looking for him, I found Rebecca's pistol. Always chasing trouble this one. As if he hasn't done enough harm. I want you to book him."

"What charges are you bringing, Owen?"

"What charges? Take your pick! My son is a liar, a crook and he's probably a murderer. He's in possession of a deadly weapon with the intent to do I don't know what." Owen's face got redder as he spoke. "I owe you an apology, Sheriff. I thought I taught my son right from wrong but apparently he wasn't listening. He acts like he's afraid of me. Well, I'll tell you what, I'm the one who's afraid. I'm afraid he is capable of doing just about anything and whatever he has done, whatever God-awful thing he has done, it's finally time for him to take his consequences."

Owen walked back and forth the short distance between the dispatcher's desk and Vera's desk. He made eye contact with no one.

"He needs to learn his lesson this time for good and pay his dues. He's an ingrate, that's what he is. I gave him so much. He comes from the best family in this puny village. He's a privileged, spoiled, son-of-a-bitch, and I mean son-of-a-bitch. They can both rot in hell as far as I'm concerned." Owen's face was contorted in disgust as if he were smelling something foul. "No more hiding behind mommy's skirt. I don't want him out of here until he accounts for all his trespasses. He disgusts me! I won't call him my son. He's not a Streat. He was on the lake with his filthy friends on the night Elaine was killed. Either they killed her or they saw who did and they're lying to you."

From the back Trevor shouted, "I already told you I didn't see a thing that night."

"Well, now you ask the sheriff if he believes you. Everything you've ever told me and your mom, and for that matter the sheriff, has been a lie."

"Well I'm not lying now."

"And how do we know that now, huh? How? You're just a liar! What you say means nothing. Absolutely nothing. It's what you do that matters. And what you do is damage."

Chapter Thirty-Five

Mike stared at the closed door.

The phone squealed.

After Owen had slammed the door behind him, confident that Trevor was finally going to pay his dues, Mike, Vera and Shelley had stared at the closed door in relief. No one had said a word.

But the persistent ring finally persuaded Shelley to answer it.

Once she hung up with the caller, Shelley walked over to Mike's office with the news. She stood in his doorway waiting. Mike hesitated to wave his dispatcher in. He needed a moment of respite to clear his head and think of his next move. He noticed Shelley didn't rush him. She was very protective even if she was almost half his age.

A little slip of a girl, Shelley was not what most people envisioned as a dispatcher but she was the only one who had applied for the job. Since it required no particular skills, and she had no particular skills, she had gotten the job. Early on he had needed to encourage her to speak up and calm down but over the years he had come to rely on her judgment on countless things, above all her motherly instincts.

"Sorry to say, but this is the day that never ends," Shelley said.

"What now? I still don't know what to do with Trevor."

"Ernie McCrae just called in. He says that from his loft above the carriage house he can see into Agatha's house and it looks like we've got a prowler."

"Is he sure? It's probably just Allison."

"That's what I asked him, but he said he had just seen Allison driving away from town. He can see a light on in the back of the house. Someone's mulling around so he figured you needed to know. He said he would go check it out but I told him to do no such thing. Should I dispatch Vera? Give you a break?"

"No. Thanks anyway, Shelley. Vera's had a tough day too. I don't know what's happened to this town lately but I want to see this day through to the end. Yesterday someone suggested to me that there's more here than meets the eye and I'm afraid I'm beginning to think she's right."

"You're talking about Bianca St. Denis?"

Mike looked at her, startled, but said nothing, not wanting to confirm.

"Don't look so surprised, it's a small town."

***

Mike chose to walk to Agatha's. It was only two blocks away and he would have the element of surprise to his advantage. No car, no sirens.

The wind picked up, flapping his jacket open. He shivered. The cold air coiled around his waist. It cleared his head immediately. He reached down and zipped up without missing a step.

Mike made his way as quickly as possible without arousing suspicion. He was bewildered at the week of turmoil.

Who would need to break in to Agatha's? And why? If not Allison, then who?

Once the house came into view, Mike switched gears. He focused, all his senses were on alert. Perspiration formed in his armpits despite the bitter cold. His eyes darted everywhere. Like a still hunter, he used his eyes and ears to do all the work. He turned off his radio. Mike remembered that one of the bricks was loose at the top of the front stoop. Instead he crept along the side of the house until he could peer into a window. It was the kitchen, and he couldn't see much, but it told him plenty. A light was on and someone's shadow was making its way around Agatha's sick room across the hall.

For the second time today, Mike carefully removed his pistol from its holster. He delicately tried the back door, and was not the least bit surprised when he found it open. No one locked their doors, at least not until two days ago.

His pounding heart drowned out the quiet shuffling in the other room, but he heard enough. He raised his pistol and made his way to the hallway.

Then he stopped, dead.

He saw white before his eyes. He blinked. White. A squeal in his head made him wince.

He couldn't move forward until he could see and hear properly. He tried to draw a breath. A pain in his chest only allowed a short breath. Then another. And finally another breath and the squeal faded, almost gone. He blinked twice and eventually his eyes were able to focus on the vines climbing the yellowed wallpaper. Another breath, another blink and he could hear the movement in the other room again. Was that the intruder or his heartbeat? He had to force himself to stay put another few seconds to make sure he was ready. He couldn't make a mistake now by rushing.

As far as he could tell he was dealing with one person, but he couldn't be sure. Why hadn't he brought backup? He was still operating on the premise that he was the sheriff of a sleepy town, but he would have to reevaluate after all this was over.

He crossed the hallway to Agatha's bedroom. The shadow dancing on the carpet established one person in the room, obviously unaware of Mike's presence.

In one quick motion he turned the corner, raised his pistol and shouted, "Sheriff! Hands up!"

Chapter Thirty-Six

The telephone crashed to the floor as Bianca raised her hands.

"Bianca, what are you doing here?"

"I... I..." Bianca's hands remained above her head. She was shaking. "Can you put your gun down first?"

"What is going on here?" Mike lowered his gun but didn't holster it.

Mike approached her but Bianca could not miss the caution in his gait. She was astonished that he considered her dangerous.

"I didn't mean to do anything wrong but I had to see if I was right."

"Didn't want to do anything wrong? You're breaking and entering." Mike's voice was raw with anger. "You had to see if you were right about what? Wait, that's irrelevant, you shouldn't be here at all."

Bianca had to think fast. "Sheriff, you wouldn't want to hinder the press from getting at the truth, I hope?"

"The press? Since when?"

"Since very recently. I'm...what you call a Reporter at Large. They call me in when they need me or I bring them stories. It's like contract work. I need the money." Bianca thought the last part was a good touch. Added some gravitas to the situation. She guessed this meant that her decision to work for the *Gazette* had been decided. No better time to start than the present.

"I see." Mike was shaking his head but a tiny smirk was forming just the same.

"The door wasn't locked." Bianca decided to push through while she had a tiny advantage. "It's never locked. I didn't think I was trespassing. I mean...she's dead. And I was a friend, I was here all the time."

Mike shook his head and holstered his gun. He picked up his radio, turned it back on and called in to the station, "Shelley, no problem here at Agatha's."

"So, who is it?"

"Never mind, I'll fill you in later."

"You know, you can be exasperating sometimes." Shelley signed off.

Mike was still shaking his head when he finished. Then he motioned with his chin toward Bianca's hands.

Bianca slowly brought her hands down, she was relieved that things had deescalated and besides, she needed her hands to talk. "How did you know I was here?"

"I'm responding to a report of a prowler. Ernie called it in. He can see in here from his place." Bianca's eyes followed Mike's hand pointing out the window and up to Ernie's apartment over the carriage house next door.

"Bianca, you had Ernie worried and I had a gun on you."

"I know, and I'm sorry but you need to see this."

He followed her to Agatha's desk. Papers were in piles, but not neat piles. The drawers were not yawning open but neither were they shut tight.

"What are you showing me?"

"I couldn't swear it, but I think someone has been through her things. Agatha's home is…well, lived in. But her desk has always been neat and tidy. She hasn't been working at her desk since the accident. She has a lap desk for her bed."

Bianca walked over to the corner of the room and stared at the wall. "And then there's this." She pointed to the thermostat and waited for Mike's acknowledgement. When none came she realized he didn't see what she saw. "It's set at seventy-eight degrees."

"So what are you saying?"

"That's awfully warm for someone to die of hypothermia."

"It is high. Has it been touched?"

"Who would have touched it, who would have any reason to come in here?"

"I could say the same to you, if I recall correctly I just found you trespassing."

Bianca blushed at her faux pas.

"Allison could have adjusted the thermostat." Mike walked around the room taking it all in.

"She may have, I suppose, but I'm telling you, it was always too warm in this room. The nurse kept it up high and Agatha complained about it all the time. And the window, it may have been open but I am sure Agatha didn't open it. She just wasn't strong enough. She couldn't open it even a crack, I would do it for her when I arrived each day."

Mike made his way to the window beside the bed. Heavy layers of paint encrusted the frame. He tried to pry it open and had to make two attempts before he finally succeeded.

"I see what you mean. These old houses, layers of paint and swelling make it hard to open the windows. Just like my mother's house. He stood up straight. "You're a natural investigative reporter, aren't you?"

"I'm a historian, remember? I like to piece obscure information together." She walked over to the bed. "And there's something else." Bianca bent to pick up the telephone she had dropped when Mike surprised her. "I also noticed that the telephone was undisturbed."

"You mean until you dropped it?"

"Well, yes, that's true. But that's beside the point."

"If what you're getting at is that this is a murder scene then it's not beside the point at all. It means you have been tampering with evidence."

"What I'm getting at is that I think if Agatha had been cold she would have called someone to help her. Agatha wasn't the shy type, I don't think she would have hesitated to inconvenience someone," Bianca said.

"So, I'll try to ignore the fact that the phone has been dropped, can you tell me how you found the telephone when you arrived?"

"It was right at the end of the night stand, in easy reach of her bed. The handset was firmly on the cradle. She kept it close by her at all times. And all the phone numbers for her caretakers are right here. There is no doubt in my mind that she could have called someone if she were in distress. And she chose not to. It makes no sense. And even if she had been disoriented with hypothermia and she tried to call someone and hadn't succeeded, it seems logical that the handset would have fallen off the cradle. But it was firmly in place, undisturbed like I said."

"So, no sign of distress you're suggesting."

"Yes, I suppose that is what I mean."

"What if she wanted no help?" Mike said with some hesitation in his voice.

"You mean, if she wanted to die? Are you saying you think she committed suicide?" Bianca said the words cautiously, as if the words themselves were dangerous.

"It's not out of the question for a sick person to choose to forgo the pain and welcome a swift end." Mike's eyes glazed over for a brief moment. "She was dying of cancer."

"That's what the doctors said but she wasn't going anywhere. She outlived her prognosis by years. She was not suffering from her cancer. The slip on the ice and her broken hip put her in bed. I don't think she was trying to commit suicide."

"So, Ms. Investigative Reporter, obviously you've given this some thought. What do you think happened?" Mike stared her down, but she didn't feel challenged, rather she felt like his peer. Like he really wanted to know her opinion.

"Reporter at Large," Bianca corrected. "I think she was killed and I think someone opened that window on purpose."

Chapter Thirty-Seven

A creak caused Mike and Bianca to turn.

"Robert, Vera." Mike felt a sting of heat reach his cheeks. He took one step away from Bianca. "What brings you two here?"

Vera stepped directly into the light of the setting sun pooling on Agatha's bed. She raised her hand to shield her eyes from the glare, almost as if she were saluting Mike.

Vera's gaze moved from Mike to Bianca. She nodded curtly to Bianca and quickly turned her attention back to Mike.

"Dr. Spenser came by the station looking for you. He said it was urgent. I was on my way here so I brought him down with me."

"What could possibly be wrong now?" Mike's temple throbbed.

"Mike, look at this. Bianca, I'm glad you're here too." Dr. Spenser held out the first page of his report for Mike to read.

Mike looked it over. "Robert, you did an autopsy? Why didn't I know about this sooner?"

"I didn't do one right away. I'm embarrassed to say that I didn't think it was necessary. Agatha displayed obvious signs of hypothermia and considering the condition of her room, I never questioned it. But Bianca got me thinking. I started to second-guess my findings, so I did an autopsy." Robert's gaze danced around the room, never making direct contact with Mike. "Keep reading."

Mike screwed up his face in an effort to read through the cross outs. "Robert, you're going to need a secretary if you want me to read these reports."

A soft flush swept across Dr. Spenser's face. "I'm sorry, I was never very good at typing."

Despite his off-hand remark Mike kept reading, sensing from Robert's demeanor that he had something important in his hands. "So in layman's language, you want to tell me what this means? What are cyanosis and subconjunctival hemorrhages?" Mike shifted feet, impatient as always with technical jargon.

"It means her skin had a blue tint and her eyes were bloodshot."

"We knew that already, and what does that tell us that's new?"

"It doesn't tell us much by itself. In fact, I ignored it when I was first called to the scene of her death. Both are common in hypothermic patients. But coupled with hypercapnia and Tardieu ecchymosis, it tells a different story." Robert shook his head.

"Hyper what?" Mike tried to repeat after Dr. Spenser. He picked up his hands in exasperation, "Robert, come on...What does it mean? Don't keep me guessing."

"It means we have a problem. Agatha was asphyxiated."

***

Mike's eyes opened wide as it hit him. The doctor continued on in his jargon but Mike had heard enough to understand where this was leading. It seemed that Bianca had been right, but she had been missing some pieces to the puzzle. Robert had just supplied them.

"Hypercapnia means she had excess carbon dioxide in her bloodstream. Tardieu ecchymosis are lung spots indicative of suffocation. Neither definitive on their own." Here Dr. Spenser started shaking his head again. "But in combination point clearly..."

"You're telling me she didn't die from hypothermia, that she suffocated?"

Finally understood, Dr. Spenser relaxed his arms, the remaining pages of the report fluttering to his sides.

Bianca rushed to the bed.

"Bianca, you're not going to touch anything again, I hope?" Mike rushed after her.

"No, but look at this." She pointed to the beam of sunlight on the pillow.

"What about it? What are you looking at? The sun, the pillow?"

"The pillow. There's only one. There's a pillow missing."

"How do you know that?"

"I've been sitting with her for the last few weeks and I distinctly remember two embroidered pillows, they reminded me of the needlework my mother taught me to do as a child. I don't see the other pillow anywhere."

Without consulting each other, the four of them fanned out to search the rooms. After a few futile minutes they reconvened in Agatha's room.

"Mike, I'm so sorry, I don't know how I missed this. I'm a G.P. not a coroner...she had all the signs of hypothermia...but I should have asked more questions." Robert was showing signs of fatigue.

"Stop beating yourself up over this. We all thought she died a natural death," Mike said.

At this pronouncement Bianca started to object. Mike exaggerated a bow with a flourish of his hat. "Except for Miss Marple here, we were all taken in by appearances."

Vera stepped in. "What if the window was only a distraction? If someone suffocated Agatha with her pillow it would explain your autopsy results and the missing pillow."

"And that would also explain why the high thermostat doesn't jive with the hypothermia and —"

Mike turned to Bianca as she finished his thought.

"And why Agatha never tried to call anyone. She was attacked."

"Someone almost succeeded at making this look like an accident," Robert concluded their thinking.

"As horrible as it is to consider this a murder, in a way it makes more sense. But now we have a bigger problem. We have to figure out who murdered Agatha and why? And if there is any connection to Sister Elaine's death. It seems too coincidental to be unrelated."

Mike realized he was reiterating things that Bianca had been saying all along.

Mike turned to Bianca. He felt strangely exhilarated from working out this puzzle with her. What an odd woman, what a persistent and stubborn woman.

Mike stood in silence for a moment as he absorbed the enormity of the situation. They now had a string of murders, the conclusions they had been reaching in Elaine's murder investigation had to be rethought in light of the new information. They were essentially starting from scratch.

***

Bianca stood transfixed in the center of Agatha's room, now a murder scene. The conversation whirled around her head. She barely heard the last few words. A dull ache was welling up behind her eyes, she knew she had not yet properly mourned Richard and her attempts at pretending she was fine were coming unglued. These two deaths couldn't possibly affect her this way; tears stung behind her lids, ready to drop when Mike's last sentence finally settled in her head after a long delay. Was there a connection to Sister Elaine's death?

"Of course!" In all the commotion she had completely forgotten to tell Mike about the revelation that brought her to Agatha's house in the first place.

Mike, Robert and Vera stopped and turned to her.

"Agatha's will. Lester Quirke was reading it this morning. Agatha made a new will and left the bulk of her estate to the Sisters of St. James."

"Are you sure? When was the reading of the will? And why were you there?" Mike looked baffled. Perhaps she wasn't the only one having trouble adapting to the blessings and burdens of an intimate community.

"Don't look so surprised. This is a small town."

"So I've heard."

"It wasn't an official reading. Agatha had given it to me the other day to deliver to Lester. I didn't know what it was at the time. This morning I remembered to give it to him. And he read it to us."

"To us? Who else was there?" Mike asked.

"Eugene. We were at Stella's after breakfast."

"Why am I surprised?" Mike threw up his hands.

"It's possible that whoever killed Elaine did so thinking Elaine was the only one who knew about the bequest," Bianca said.

"Bianca, think very carefully, when did she give it to you?" Mike took a step closer.

"On Friday evening. I'm sure of it." Bianca's eyes turned instinctively to Agatha's calendar on the night stand near the phone.

"And we found Agatha's body on Saturday morning so —"

"Someone acted almost immediately to eliminate her, before the new bequest could be revealed, and that would connect—" Bianca finished.

"Elaine and Agatha's death." Mike finally turned to his deputy. "I need you to find Allison Miller."

Vera started for the door then turned back. "I almost forgot, Mike. We got a hit on Elaine's missing ring. It showed up in a pawnshop report. I called the owner but I had to leave a message. He hasn't gotten back to me." Vera hesitated then said, "I could take a drive up to Albany tomorrow to ask some questions. Or do you want to come with me? You know good cop, bad cop. These guys are not always so cooperative. He's not going to want to give up a diamond, I can tell you that."

"Okay, now we're making progress." Mike smiled for the first time and Vera mirrored his smile.

He turned to Bianca. "I guess I should be saying thank you for your persistence. But I can't say I'm happy about it. I preferred it when Agatha had died a natural death."

"There's one more thing, Sheriff. Allison may not be the only one looking to inherit." Bianca hesitated to complicate things but she couldn't keep this information to herself. "Thomas Brennan is in town. He is probably entitled to—"

"Who?" Mike searched her face for a clue.

"Allison's father."

Now everyone was listening.

"Allison's father? He's alive?"

"Sit down, Sheriff, this is a long story."

Chapter Thirty-Eight

Rebecca Streat stormed into the sheriff's office waving a mangled copy of the newspaper. She threw it in Vera's direction, landing on the deputy's desk. "I can't believe you did this!" Tears streaked Rebecca's makeup. "How could you put cuffs on him? After everything I told you?"

"Mrs. Streat. What is this?" Mike grabbed the newspaper off Vera's desk. Above the fold was a picture of Trevor snapped through the sheriff's office window. Behind Trevor was Vera opening her cuffs.

Mike looked at the paper and then at Rebecca. He could see the anger building on her face. It was always a problem letting Jake anywhere near the sheriff's office. He was a good reporter, Jake was known for getting the scoop, but he was also known for creating a scoop when he needed one. Jake must have done cartwheels in order to get that picture into the paper on time.

"What do you think you're doing? Publishing a photo of my son in the paper! You're treating him like a criminal! You've got nothing on him!" Rebecca blurted out.

"Mrs. Streat, *we* did not publish that photo. Please have a seat. I am as unhappy about this as you are." Mike turned to his dispatcher. "Shelley, get the *Gazette* on the phone. I need to speak to Jake immediately."

"Yes, sir!" Shelley ran to her desk and started dialing.

Rebecca did not take Mike's offer of a seat. She paced and targeted him this time. "Why would you put my son behind bars? Owen is the problem here, not Trevor. You know that!"

231

Mike took a step toward Rebecca but she backed away. "Oh no, don't try to calm me down. Serve and protect? Well, who are you serving? And you're certainly not protecting! Do you even know where Owen is?"

Shelley banged the phone back on the cradle, grabbed her coat off the rack by the door and ran out.

"Rebecca—" Mike started.

"So now I'm Rebecca? Is that something your shrink taught you to do? Call the crazies by their first name, less threatening?"

"Owen brought him in!" Mike yelled over her voice this time. It was as if he had slapped her in the face. She stopped, stunned.

Mike continued. "Look, I'm sorry. We are trying to do the right thing here. Owen brought him in and we took him into custody because Owen was too worked up. We thought it would be safer here for Trevor."

Rebecca sat down, fatigue crossing her face. "So he can come home then?"

"Well, not exactly."

"Why? You have no reason to hold him, you said."

"No, I said Owen brought him in. But Jackson Parker is pressing charges."

"Why would he do that?" Rebecca turned from side to side as if she thought she could find an answer elsewhere.

"Breaking and entering. He made a copy of the bowling alley key."

Rebecca closed her eyes. Inhaled. Shook her head.

Vera walked over. "Sheriff, can I see you a minute?"

"Can you excuse me, Mrs. Str—"

"Rebecca."

"Can you excuse me, Rebecca?" He was making some progress.

Rebecca nodded distractedly.

"Looks like Jackson dropped the charges," Vera whispered holding out a file to Mike.

"Oh no." Mike grabbed the file from her then rubbed his temples.

"I thought you'd be pleased." Vera looked baffled and then the realization seemed to hit her. "That means you have nothing to hold Trevor with. He goes free but he could be in danger."

Mike nodded. "I need him here. He is either dangerous or in danger.

232

Either way I need him to stay. I need to buy some time." Mike slapped the file against the palm of his hand, thinking. "Vera, bring me the charges against Owen."

Mike walked over to the phone on the dispatcher's desk. He dialed and as he turned his back to the room he pressed the flash button on the cradle.

"This is Sheriff Mike Riley, Onanda County. I need to speak to Judge Rawlings. Yes, now. Yes. I'll hold," Mike said to the dial tone.

As he held the line Mike thought about his options. He could release Trevor to Rebecca but he could be in danger, in fact both of them could be in danger. He could hold him and face Streat's attorney, the infamous Winston Tucker, who would probably bring him before Judge Rawlings. Or…he could…Mike ran out of ideas.

He needed to think outside the box. What was he missing? He needed to keep Trevor safe. He was safe in the jail. But if he got Owen behind bars he could let Trevor out. He just needed to get Rebecca to press charges. How hard could that be? He had beaten her up and chased her son with a rifle.

"Tell the sheriff I'm calling my lawyer if I don't see Trevor soon," Rebecca said to Shelley who had just returned.

"Fine, I'll call back." Mike hung up the bogus call and turned back into the room. "Vera, do you have those papers yet?"

Vera handed Mike a crisp manila folder with the name Streat written across a red tab on top.

"Is that my son's file? He doesn't have a record, does he?"

"No, Rebecca, come into my office. I want to show you the possible charges you can file against Owen. There is assault with a deadly weapon—"

"Save your breath, Sheriff. I am not pressing charges against my husband."

"But—"

"No buts, if you think he is out of control now, he would kill someone if—"

"Rebecca, you have to consider your son."

"That's all I do, Sheriff, everything I do is for my son. I am here to get him, aren't I? His father may have brought him in but I'm here to get him out! Now. Sheriff, please. Or do I need to call Winston Tucker?"

"Deputy Weber, please release Trevor." Mike had no choice.

Vera unclasped her keys from her waist, walked down the hall and out of sight. She returned with Trevor, his face tear stained and his shirt crumpled.

Rebecca attempted to hug him but Trevor pushed her away.

"At least let me send a deputy to escort you home." Mike tried to talk some sense into Rebecca.

"Sheriff, I can't show up at home with a sheriff's escort. There is no telling what Owen will do. Thank you for your concern but I can take it from here." Trevor dragged his feet out the door behind Rebecca.

Shelley walked up beside Mike. "Is this wise, Sheriff? I don't mean to second-guess you but—"

"Honestly, I don't know, Shelley. I can't hold Trevor any longer. Jackson dropped the charges, we don't have enough evidence to hold him in the murder, and lying to your parents isn't a crime. My hands are tied."

"Do you think they're in danger?"

"I don't know. I just don't know."

Chapter Thirty-Nine

Mike fumbled with his key. He had to remember to replace the porch lightbulb tomorrow. He was too tired to worry about it tonight. He turned the key in the lock and opened the door. The hallway was dark again today, no warmth came out of the woodstove, nothing simmering in the kitchen.

Without removing his parka, he grabbed a beer out of the fridge, flipped off the cap and left it exactly where it landed since Maggie wasn't at home to complain. He plopped into his favorite chair. Well almost. His favorite chair was stored in the back of the garage along with his old maple roll top desk. He didn't blame Maggie, the chair dated back to his bachelor days when he lived with his cat, Maurice. They would read together in that chair and although Maurice had scratched the arms to shreds, Mike loved the memories. And the desk no longer rolled up, it was jammed three quarters of the way up and one of the drawers was off its track. Mike had gone along with renovating the house, but he had insisted on storing his things in the back of the garage until he was ready to part with them. Occasionally they argued about clearing out the garage but he stuck to his guns.

Mike put his feet up on the coffee table and leaned back in the chair. He surveyed the living room. It was too modern for his taste. A contemporary ranch in a subdivision on the outskirts of town, it was a concession he had made when they had decided to move to the country. He wanted a farmhouse but Maggie wasn't interested. Mike was willing to rent an apartment in one of the turn-of-the-century buildings in the village. He figured he could give up dewy country mornings for the convenience and character of Main

Street. She said drafts weren't character; they were just uncomfortable and the large paned windows made her feel like she was in a fishbowl.

So they had bought a fairly new home with a recently upgraded kitchen. But that hadn't stopped her from tearing it out and starting again. What a waste, he thought, every time he put his beer down on the new counter top.

He left his coat on out of laziness, and truth be told, because he had no one to tell him otherwise. What a day. He thought he had put this craziness behind him when he left the NYPD. Mike had been pulled in so many directions, maybe he wasn't seeing clearly. Dr. Spenser was right to do that autopsy; Mike should have ordered one up front. He had really dropped the ball. But Bianca was able to cut through the distractions and get to the bottom of things. He hated to admit it, but she had really come through today. He could use a deputy like that, someone persistent who could think outside the box. Vera was steady, trustworthy, everyone loved her, but she was by the book.

Mike knew he should be upset with Bianca for interfering. But she produced results and he found her presence calming and exhilarating at the same time, odd since he was yelling at her half the time.

Tomorrow he had a big day. He had two murders on his hands, and he couldn't let that out of the bag, especially to that damned reporter Jake Wilson. Mike could see the headlines now: *Serial Killer Loose on the Streets of Batavia* or *Senior Citizen Serial Killer*. He could wring Jake's neck for publishing Trevor's picture in the Gazette.

Mike considered his suspects. Allison could stand to gain if the new will were kept under wraps, if she thought only Elaine knew then he might have something to work with there.

Trevor was at the scene, could easily have used some bad judgment, especially when you add some beer and peer pressure to the mix, but how did he fit into Agatha's death?

Now Thomas Brennan, Agatha's husband, had appeared out of nowhere. Either this guy had impeccable timing or he was up to no good. If they were never divorced, Brennan could make a claim to Agatha's property, and there was plenty of it, so he would have a motive for both murders. Mike would have Vera check the public records for the marriage and divorce papers tomorrow. And if he were guilty why is he sticking around? Does he have something else up his sleeve? Could someone else be in danger?

Bert's story was full of holes. His only clear motive was Elaine's ring; he obviously needed the money. He couldn't have any reason to kill Agatha. Mike was saddened by the state of his friend's life, Bert needed to sober up or he would be on the skids in no time.

Ishikawa was another one with strange timing. But what possible motive could he have?

Mike shook his head, pressed his temples to stave away the headache that was circling the room, ready to pounce. And then he considered all the lies he had heard this week. Trevor of course, but also Claire and Bert, and Rebecca too. Lying for loved ones rarely produced anything but bitterness and burdens. He could forgive Rebecca. Mike knew that a mother could be expected to do just about anything to protect a child, but Claire? Mike supposed no one really knew the limits of romantic love. Mike certainly hadn't had the pleasure.

Finally, Mike needed to consider the nurse. She had no obvious motive but she had means. No one would find it unusual if the nurse were there at odd hours, and she wouldn't be the first nurse to be named in a will.

Mike had done all that he could do today. He had turned Trevor over to Rebecca, he had had no choice. He had assigned a discreet patrol outside the Streat house, despite what Rebecca wanted. According to Ryan McLoughlin, Owen was tucked into a cot in the back room at the pub. Vera's interview of Allison showed she had alibis for both murders. Those alibis would need to be checked out tomorrow. Mike would need to locate this Brennan fellow too. And then of course there were the funerals. Tomorrow was shaping up to be quite a day.

Last of all, he needed to consider how Bianca might complicate things for him, and she would complicate things, he was sure.

Chapter Forty

Tuesday, December 20

Each afternoon Bianca walked down her long driveway to her mailbox expectantly. Like a child sneaking down the stairs on Christmas morning, heart pounding against her fuzzy robe, hoping against hope that she would find her long-awaited Barbie. Unwrapping with a gleam in her eye. The moment before the gift reveals itself, the expectation, and the mild nausea of anticipation.

Bianca reached her mailbox, excitement mounting. She opened the box and this time her eyes landed on the gift she had been waiting for: her first monthly annuity check from Richard's pension. The gift that would allow her to start paying off her bills and write full time. She paused just long enough to recognize the moment, and like her child self, she tore it open to find her Barbie had the wrong color hair...she wanted the blond...hadn't she been clear in her letter to Santa? Blond, with high heels and a sequin dress: not the brunette with hiking shorts and a backpack. But she had written it down for Santa so carefully...her check was far less than she expected. Where had she miscalculated?

She had waited so long. Probating Richard's estate had taken almost a year. He had never wanted to think about writing wills or assigning death benefits. She had foolishly thought this check would resolve her financial troubles but it wasn't going to be enough.

Now she needed a new strategy. Obviously she wasn't selling her book anytime soon. She needed to look for a job.

Bianca turned toward her driveway and wandered back to the house thinking about her choices.

Will she ever learn that the anticipation is the real gift, the untarnished moment? She should learn to resist opening the package and savor that moment, the precious moment before. The moment that could be perfect because she alone was the architect, and she designed it to please only herself. It was always wasted as she raced to the finish line. The opened gift was reality and it rarely measured up to her dream.

***

Father Liam McCardle entered the cool chapel and slipped into a pew.

The calm before the storm.

He sat in meditation, gathering his thoughts before everyone arrived. A funeral required more than good words, it required stamina. Witnessing pain and suffering in full view was the most harrowing part of his job and he was still not used to it. He didn't plan on ever getting used to it.

Father McCardle knew that Sister Elaine would be greatly missed. He wasn't so sure anyone would mourn for Agatha, but he did know that the church would be full to the brim. He was accustomed to small gatherings every Sunday for the two masses he held. The groups were larger now than when he arrived but they still barely filled the old church. Funerals, however, brought the entire town out. He still got stage fright or performance anxiety, whatever his therapist wanted to call it, a true obstacle for someone who relied on public speaking for his daily work. But this was one of his burdens, one of his offerings; it was not for him to be comfortable in this work, it was for him to do this work.

To further complicate matters, Agatha had requested that her will be read in church today. Based on what Lester had told him, it would raise some eyebrows.

He was sharing the services with Pastor Smythe; they were to have Elaine and Agatha's funerals in tandem. Protestants and Catholics shared the church; the town was too small to support separate buildings for all the denominations. And the nearest synagogue was the next town over. The old Protestant church had been abandoned years ago after a hurricane flooded it out one too many times. They had been hoping to sell to someone and use the proceeds to do repairs at Saint James. But getting a buyer wasn't so easy. So now they alternated services every Saturday and Sunday and combined their fundraisers and community events. It worked better than anyone expected although spirited competition for congregants remained a running joke in the community.

Liam McCardle looked down at the sermon notes in his hand, discouraged. He wasn't happy with what he had prepared, he was never happy with his funeral sermons. This is where his youth betrayed him; he didn't believe he had enough personal experience with loss to comfort others. He was a fraud, never knowing where to put his feet, claiming he had some special salve to assuage the pain, to offer words of faith and wisdom to the community when they needed it most. He had neither. He had tropes, clichés. He did his best to avoid making them sound as if they were exactly that. It was during funeral preparations that he wondered if he was up to this job. He waited for someone to appear from the sacristy and expose him as the imposter that he was.

Liam sidled out of the pew, bent his knee briefly, made the sign of the cross and walked to the back of the silent church, the crunch of crumpled paper in his hands the only sound.

Chapter Forty-One

Bianca sat through the funeral services more anxious than usual. She had asked Father McCardle and Pastor Smythe to allow her to say a few words about Agatha. She had not given a eulogy in years. She had been in no shape to speak at Richard's funeral. Now she almost regretted her decision but she walked up to the sanctuary when she was summoned.

From the podium Bianca scanned the crowded pews and the back of the room. Standing room only.

Everyone in the village was there. The Sisters of St. James were in the first two pews along with Agatha's nurse. Eugene and Ernie were seated next to the two nuns with canes. Allison sat alone at the end of the first pew. Rudy and Trudy snuck in at the last minute, they must have gotten hung up at the store. They plopped down in the two seats the Dekkers had saved for them. Claire picked up her coat and hat to give Bert room to sit. Owen Streat stood in the back of the church behind his mother's wheelchair, the rest of the Streats had taken the last pew near her.

Thomas Brennan was also standing in the back. Olivia had confided that the Gazette had managed to dig up the divorce papers for Agatha and Thomas. Bianca was relieved, that meant he would have no motive for Agatha's death. She was glad she no longer needed to worry about this stranger.

Her eyes settled on Mike off to the side, his eyes in turn were on everyone in the room. Now that he had motive, Bianca could see renewed vigor in his observations. She noticed his gaze bouncing between Allison, Trevor,

Bert, Thomas Brennan and Agatha's nurse.

Just before she started to speak she spotted Mr. Ishikawa in the corner, he acknowledged her with a slight bow of his head. With that nod she launched into her eulogy.

"I don't know why Agatha chose to confide in me, but she did. I didn't know her as well as you all did."

Bianca overheard a quiet "Lucky you" from a nearby pew, followed by a couple of muffled chuckles.

"But I feel blessed to have had a peek into the life of this remarkable woman. Her childhood and young motherhood were riddled with sadness. We laugh and roll our eyes at her grumpiness and impatience, but I witnessed a woman in pain, isolated in youth and choosing to remain so in old age. A woman who walked among us but remained elusive, and we were okay with that. Her death has made me realize the importance of slowing down and taking time to bear witness. In last week's column Olivia Last challenged us to slow down and bear witness to winter and to embrace it as it is with all its inconveniences. She taught us that by opening up and accepting winter, we could then have its beauties and benefits revealed to us. I have taken Olivia's challenge to heart regarding winter, but I would like to apply this challenge to ourselves, to each other, to the community. Let us beware that we might be engaging our neighbors only on the surface, making judgments and choosing sides without truly knowing each other, even those with whom we have grown old. I for one, can think of a few neighbors to whom I would like to offer myself as a witness. And I challenge you, as Olivia did, to bear witness to your neighbors before it is too late."

On the way back to her seat she passed Allison's pew. Bianca kept her head down, no longer willing to make eye contact, hoping she hadn't overstepped her welcome in the village.

Pastor Smythe then took over. He slowly made his way to the lectern.

"Thank you, Bianca St. Denis. Well, it appears that it takes an outsider to view us clearly. Speaking of gifts from Agatha, today we will end services with a few words from Lester Quirke."

Lester was up to the lectern in a flash.

"Agatha has requested that the disposition of her will be read at her funeral. In her letter to me she wrote, 'Although I do not think I will be missed, I know the community will do the right thing and attend my services if only because they are nosey or bored.'"

Some snorts of laughter escaped the audience. How well Agatha knew her neighbors, Bianca thought.

"She expected you would be here and she wanted everyone present to witness her bequests. So here goes," Lester said with a glint in his eye.

I, Agatha Miller, of sound mind and body, bequeath my estate as follows:

To my daughter Allison Miller, I leave the manor at Miller's Point and the surrounding acreage that encompasses the grounds of the manor, approximately five acres. Please do something for yourself and the community.

In gratitude to Elaine Fisher and the Sisters of St. James the Elder, I leave the old Miller Tannery, the company housing and the acreage that encompasses the Tannery grounds, approximately eighty-five acres, on the condition that this property be used to establish a retreat home for women and children in need. In addition, I leave the remaining twenty acres of Miller's Point to the Sisters in order to sell for the initial funding for the retreat.

Mumbles rippled through the church at this news but Lester raised his voice a notch and continued.

From the land bequeathed to the Sisters of Saint James, I reserve the following for the Village of Batavia-on-Hudson: The two-acre bluff of Miller's Point as well as the existing walk along the bluff as it exists today. This property is to remain the property of the Village for use as a public park in perpetuity with funds set aside for maintenance for the first ten years.

In addition, to the Village of Batavia-on-Hudson I leave my current residence and the Miller Carriage House, to be preserved as historical buildings and to be used to the benefit and education of the community.

To Bianca St. Denis, I leave all my books, manuscripts, maps, notes and other miscellaneous papers in the hopes that she will continue my work as Village Historian. Please open yourselves to her.

To my grandson, Trevor Streat—

Gasps and murmurs erupted through the church, and drowned out

Lester's weak voice.

Olivia leaned over to whisper to Bianca, "If Trevor is Agatha's grandson that would make Owen her son!" From the looks of it, everyone was speculating the same thing at the same time. Bianca quickly turned to the back of the room just as everyone else did. The Streats were talking amongst themselves, agitated and obviously uncomfortable with all the attention.

"Ladies and gentlemen, please let Lester finish, we are still in a place of God, please refrain from all this commotion." Father McCardle did his best to quiet the crowd, and slowly the rumblings quieted down.

Lester continued.

To my grandson, Trevor Streat, I leave sufficient funds to cover the cost of four years of state college. These funds will be released every semester exclusively for use as tuition funds in the hopes that you will be educated and open-minded to develop into an honorable man. If you choose not to attend school, the funds will be reallocated to the retreat run by the Sisters. Upon your graduation from a four-year institution, any remaining funds will be released to you to do with as you see fit.

I leave any remaining property not explicitly bequeathed to others, to my daughter, Allison Miller.

The last few words were hardly audible, everyone had returned to mumbles and whispers, absorbing this revelation. Bianca turned to the back of the church again. There she saw Owen Streat with his family and next to them stood Thomas Brennan. Both tall, blue eyed, fair skinned. Putting all the pieces together, she realized why Thomas Brennan looked so familiar, he was an older version of Owen. She had seen something all along, but now it was so obvious. From the sounds in the pews the realization was making its way around the room. Bianca marveled at how some things can be so obvious and yet remained unobserved.

Bianca watched Mike moving in. He motioned to Vera, and from opposite corners they tried to make it to the back of the church. Allison was the first one out of the church. Behind her the aisles were filling up. Mike and Vera were caught in a crush of people. Once Mike finally made it to the door, the

CHAPTER FORTY-ONE

Streats were gone.

Bianca tried to resist the urge to interfere but she couldn't. She gently pushed her way as politely as possible to Mike's side.

"Mi—Sheriff Riley, I wanted to speak to you a minute, if I may?"

Mike turned to her but was not able to focus, his eyes darting around the room.

"Ms. St. Denis, I can't talk at the moment, I'm sure you understand."

"Of course, maybe I can catch you later."

Olivia arrived at her side. "Wow, that's some revelation, Sheriff. Bianca, I thought I lost you in this crowd, are you coming to the cemetery?"

"I am but then I'm heading right home. I have a meeting with Rebecca. She already has a buyer for my land, I'm amazed. I'm nervous too. She may have a buyer for my house and—"

"For your house? What are you doing that for?" The disappointment on Olivia's face made Bianca feel better. Maybe she was making a home for herself here, after all.

When Bianca turned back to the sheriff, all she caught was his back as he followed Vera down the church steps.

Chapter Forty-Two

B ianca was perched on the top step of the stool, reaching for her chai tea bags. They were right there, she could see them, behind the rice and oatmeal. The kettle squealed as if annoyed. She lifted her weight onto her toes, still not quite there. She stretched a bit more. The stool rocked slightly as she lifted one foot. Just another inch and she would reach it.

She stretched, she wiggled her foot, and almost lost her footing. She grabbed the tea bags and held on to the cabinet as the stool fell off to the side. The kettle reached a higher pitch. This time the cat had had enough and scooted from the room. Bianca put her knee down on the counter, turned and jumped down. A lot of good the step stool had done her.

The last time Rebecca had visited, Bianca had anticipated a lovely afternoon developing a friendship and discussing business. And it had proven to be just that. This time her nerves were on edge. Rebecca was supposed to have brought listing papers for her to sign but she already had an offer on her property. Bianca was initially thrilled, then Rebecca dropped the bomb.

"Bianca, hang on to your hat, not only do they want the land but they are interested in the house! They made you a generous offer. I think you need to consider it." Rebecca's enthusiasm was contagious. "This way you can move on. Clean slate. It's perfect! No more worrying about maintenance and taxes, no more paying Bert for his work. It would save you a bundle. You could pay off most of your debt. You would be sitting pretty. Bianca, do I envy you!"

Rebecca had a way of bringing you on board. Bianca had no intention of selling the house yet. But she had intimated to Rebecca that it might be her only solution. She wasn't ready...and yet...the timing of this offer was tempting. She couldn't seem to extricate herself from the mortgage arrears, and the unexpected shortfall of her annuity check made her head spin.

"Maybe if I just let go of the farmhouse and the property it would help me move on." Bianca addressed Richard's photograph but couldn't bring herself to look him in the eyes. "I could rent an apartment; life would be so simple. I could write. The rents on Main street are so reasonable, I could get a two bedroom with a courtyard for very little. Think and simplify, that's always been your motto, Richard." She said it, but she knew she wasn't fooling him.

Now that she was preparing for Rebecca's visit, Bianca had a deeper understanding of the expression *getting butterflies*. It was the perfect description of the fluttering and irregular flits she felt deep in her gut. It made her slightly nauseous and mildly dizzy. She paced the kitchen waiting for her guest. She began to hope that all the inevitable commotion at the Streat's after the bombshell of Agatha's will would force Rebecca to reschedule.

"But they didn't even get to see the inside of the house," Bianca had reminded Rebecca on the phone.

"Oh that doesn't matter, they want to gut it and start again, but they love the location!"

That thought had stopped Bianca in her tracks. Bianca felt Richard's presence everywhere throughout the house and the property. As if his essence mingled here with her, still vibrant. He had built or repaired every inch of this place, he had nurtured the trees that shaded her in summer, he had planted and weeded the raspberry brambles until they produced bowls and bowls of berries to be mashed on her toast in the morning or her ice cream at night.

The timer on her oven rang. Her Java Cakes are just coming out of the oven for tomorrow night's Solstice Festival, she would serve one to Rebecca as a preview. They go beautifully with the chai tea. Bianca put another log on the fire and steeped the tea leaves.

The doorbell rang. Rebecca was right on time. Bianca opened the door to greet her and helped her off with her winter things, then offered her a pair of slippers.

"Rebecca, how lovely these gloves are. A robin's egg blue. How unusual."

"They are nice, aren't they? But they don't match my coat and boots. I ruined the mauve suede ones, they were my favorite. I'll need to replace them. Now that we have a deal I can treat myself to a few new things, right? And so can you."

"Shopping's not really my thing. But I do love those gloves," Bianca said.

"Let me take you, I'd love to play personal shopper," Rebecca said with what looked like genuine enthusiasm.

Rebecca took off her high-heeled boots and slipped into a pair of crocheted slippers. She sat at the table and took out her papers.

"Oh no, Rebecca. Let's start with some tea, I don't want to start with business. I have a luscious chai for us today."

"I love chai, and what do I smell baking?"

Bianca had prepared two plates. Each held a mini Java Cake, a flourish of orange-infused whipped cream, topped with curls of orange zest. Bianca enjoyed serving these cakes to her guests, they never failed to get rave reviews and, truth be told, she enjoyed the compliments.

Rebecca took her fork and broke off a tiny sliver and savored it.

"Bianca, if you want to make friends in this town you may not want to broadcast your baking skills. The ladies will not be happy about this development!"

Bianca smiled but wasn't sure she liked the compliment. She hoped that Rebecca's teasing was just that. Bianca didn't want to jeopardize her fragile relationships with the ladies in town. Friendships have been broken over less. She remembered the baking feuds between her grandmothers. Such nice ladies and yet…

But this was silly, she was just on edge.

Bianca wanted to talk about how lucky Trevor was with Agatha's bequest. This was just what Rebecca had been saving for, the ability to send Trevor to college. But it wasn't her place to bring it up. There was so much baggage attached to this bequest. Revelations about Owen's natural parents, Trevor's grandmother, Thomas Brennan returning to town. Who knew how Owen was taking all of this.

Rebecca nibbled at the cake as she talked about the weather. Maybe she was looking to avoid the subject of the will, Bianca thought, maybe that was why she wanted to start with business right away.

Bianca watched Rebecca push the crumbs around her plate. Maybe she didn't like it? But everybody loved this cake usually. Rebecca made a lot of crumbs but didn't eat very much. The bites she did bring to her mouth were small and deliberate motions. Could she be avoiding the calories, Bianca wondered.

Bianca looked more closely at the lovely lady sitting beside her. It saddened her that Rebecca couldn't be more relaxed. Bianca should be more careful with her own weight but she believed that food was something to enjoy.

And all the makeup Rebecca wore, was it her imagination or was Rebecca wearing more makeup than usual? She found herself staring under Rebecca's left eye. Bianca noticed that she was covering a bruise on her face.

Sorrow seeped into their little coffee klatch. Was this Owen's handiwork? Although she didn't know her very well, this revelation made Bianca feel instantly close and protective of Rebecca. No man had ever hit Bianca.

For all Rebecca's involvement in the village, Bianca wondered if Rebecca had a close friend, someone to confide in, someone to cry with. As far as she could recall, she had never seen her giggling with a friend in town. Bianca needed to consider her own words from her eulogy today. She needed to make sure she had her eyes open and that she was offering an open friendship to Rebecca.

Chapter Forty-Three

Mike walked into McLoughlin's Pub and stood by the door for a moment until his eyes adjusted to the darkness. He stepped further in. Ryan McLoughlin was behind the bar slicing lemons. The place was quiet. A couple of hunters in the corner with a pitcher and some wings. And Owen at the counter.

He took a seat at the bar next to Owen.

"Ryan, let me have a Coke."

"You sure you want to do that, Sheriff? You're still on the clock. Isn't there a rule about drinking on the job?"

"Very funny. Just get me the Coke or I'll take a look in the back room." Mike motioned with his head to where the weekend poker games took place.

"Coming right up. Nobody can take a joke around here anymore."

Mike turned to Owen. "Quite a day, huh, Owen?"

"You don't know the half of it," Owen replied.

Ryan brought Mike's Coke and plopped a slice of lemon in it.

Mike sipped quietly. The hunters paid their tab and left.

"Owen, we need to talk."

"Can't a man drink in peace?"

"Owen, these new developments—"

"Are you here to question me again? You must really have it in for my family. Or are you just trying to get us all out of the way so you can hit on my Rebecca?"

"Owen, we need to be serious here. We can talk here, now, or at the station. You decide. But decide quick or I'll make the decision for you."

Owen threw back the rest of his drink, waved Ryan over. Mike stopped his hand in midair. "Not until we finish talking."

"Fine," Owen said. He swung around on his stool and yanked his arm out of Mike's hand. "What do you need to know now? What sordid detail from my life do you want to unearth?" Owen's eyes were glassy. Mike wondered how many drinks he had already consumed.

"Owen, you're Agatha's son."

"What about it, Sherlock? Proud of yourself that you were able to figure that one out? That my parents didn't want me? That doesn't make me a criminal."

"No, but it makes you an heir, and that makes you a suspect in a murder."

"A suspect to what? Elaine has nothing to do with this."

"I'm not talking about Elaine. Agatha was murdered. And you have a motive. Where were you on Friday night?"

***

Bianca added some cream to her chai and Rebecca passed her the sugar bowl. As she did, her sleeve fell back off her wrist revealing a glittering marcasite bracelet.

"Rebecca, your bracelet, the one that matches your broach. You got it back. I'm so glad. Let me get a closer look."

"I know, isn't it beautiful? It broke my heart when I had to give it up last year but I was determined, and I got it back." Rebecca stretched out her arm toward Bianca so she could properly admire it.

Bianca twirled it delicately on Rebecca's arm.

"This looks so much like my grandmother's," Bianca mused aloud.

"As soon as I had a chance yesterday I ran over to my dealer and redeemed it. It was a close call. He had sent me a letter that he had a buyer if I wanted to let it go. I almost did," Rebecca said.

Bianca sipped her chai. After a couple of sips, she pushed it to the side. It wasn't sitting well with her. The spices did that to her sometimes.

"Rebecca, let me see what you brought for me today."

"Great. But can you do me a favor and get the survey maps you showed me last week?"

"Of course. They're upstairs, it will take me just a second. Unless you want to come up too? I'll give you the grand tour I promised you. I'll show you the work Richard did. We uncovered all the original wood floors, and we stole some space out of the little bedroom to make a tiny bathroom, we actually made it out of the closet. It's small but it works."

"I see you redid the stairs too, you painted them. How clever."

At the top of the stairs, Richard's rifle leaned in the corner.

"Bianca, I thought you were against hunting."

"I am, that's Richard's. He always kept it around for the bear that had been attacking his beehives. It never did any good, the bear never showed his face when we were around. I should unload it and clean it. But as long as it is still leaning there I feel like Richard could come by and pick it up at any time. I have a few issues letting go as you can see." Bianca motioned to Richard's corner of the library still intact, with all his books and cherished items, his desk just as he left it.

Bianca realized how quickly she was warming toward Rebecca. It wasn't everyday she let someone into Richard's space. She went over to her filing cabinet. "The surveys are in here. Take a look around while I fish them out."

Rebecca walked around admiring the handiwork that had turned the old farmhouse from worn to nostalgic.

"So sad about Elaine. I didn't know her well, but she was hard not to admire. I would never have guessed her age. She was a dynamo," Rebecca said.

"I agree and it's pretty disturbing to have a murder in Batavia," Bianca said.

"I wonder what could have happened to her. You're friendly with the sheriff—"

Bianca bristled. "Why does everyone keep saying that? We hardly know each other."

"Well, it just seems that you two are always huddled together... anyway, what does he think? Any ideas? Any motives?"

Bianca pulled back. Why was she so sensitive about Mike? "I don't know much…but it seems that it was a mugging. Her ring was valuable, I heard." Bianca knew Mike would be furious if she talked about the investigation.

"It must have been horrible for her out there in the cold all night. Bleeding into the water. What a way to go," Rebecca said.

Bianca's stomach clenched at the clear image Rebecca had drawn, she looked around for the comfort of Richard's face. She looked into his eyes in the photo but she couldn't shake off her discomfort. Her eyes continued to skitter around the room, her nerves ragged. Her gaze landed on her Timberland boots, the yellow nubuc suede stained beyond help with three drops of blood. She had cut her finger on firewood that morning and the blood had landed right on the toe box. She had tried to clean it but to no avail. She would never get that stain out, blood was unforgiving.

Bile rose up in Bianca's throat. Blood on suede. Unforgiving, unwearable. She felt pin pricks of sweat under her arms.

Richard's mantle clock ticked, echoing, now that they were both standing still on the landing, not saying a word. Silent.

Flashes, images, clicked in her head to the sound of the clock; Rebecca's pink suede gloves, her marcasite bracelet out of hock, and Vera Weber's report about the diamond ring from the pawn broker.

Her breathing no longer steady, she gulped a breath and tried to force herself to be calm and think straight.

She tried to unthink, unremember, reverse her understanding to ten minutes ago when she chatted over tea with a new friend. But her instinct knew better and her senses were on high alert.

Chapter Forty-Four

Mike repeated himself, "Where were you on Friday night?"

Owen seemed reluctant but answered anyway. "After work on Friday I did the usual. I was here at the pub, I ordered a cheeseburger and fries and two bourbons."

"What time was that?"

"From about six to…well, I'm not sure. Those bourbons sometimes turn into three or four." Owen shrugged. "Maybe midnight?"

"You're sure?"

"Look, I had a few drinks but I remember it. I'm always here on Friday night. Ask Ryan."

Mike looked up and Ryan nodded, not pretending he couldn't overhear.

"What about afterwards?"

"Home to bed. What can I say? And don't even bother to look for corroboration on that, Rebecca and I haven't shared a bedroom in years. I bet the town will enjoy that nugget of information. Once that gets out…and don't think about moving in on her."

"Owen, please." Mike turned his hands over, palms up, in a gesture to discourage Owen's line of thinking. It wasn't working.

"I've seen the way you look at her. For that matter, I've seen how everyone looks at her. Why do you think I get so crazy? Wouldn't you if she were your wife? Why do you think I don't want her to work? I don't want Rebecca to be successful because she will leave me. I was abandoned once. It won't happen again. Maybe I come on a little too strong, but how else am I supposed to keep her in line? She says I stifle her and Trevor. I'm just trying to keep us together as a family."

Owen was getting agitated but Mike knew better than to interrupt. Finally, he was getting some answers.

"I know she will leave as soon as she has the money. She cares more about her business than she does for me. She has been working on this condo sale for years. I'm glad it's all gone to the church. Maybe she will give up this ridiculous job. Now that she doesn't stand to make any money from this deal, maybe she will settle down. I refuse to give her money. I know what she does. She squirrels it away. She's waiting for the chance to escape, she says. Well, she's not going anywhere. Not as long as I have anything to say about it."

Owen waved for a drink. This time Mike didn't stop him.

"It's all about her and Trevor. They never made any room for me. You should have seen him when he was a kid, he was such a momma's boy. Shadowed her everywhere. I don't know what happened lately but for years I had to worry that she would leave me and take my only son with her. She was so concerned about college. Who needs college? I didn't have any. I just want to work side by side with my son, have a legacy, leave the farm to him, change the name to Streat and Son. But she turned him against me."

Owen rattled on, the floodgates open.

"Now Agatha has done me a favor, gave away the land and now Rebecca can't leave. And she can't take my son either. He may go to college but the farm will be here waiting for him when he gets back." Owen shook his head. "Agatha, my mother. How about that. She was here the whole time. She lived right here and never told me."

Owen kept talking and Mike didn't interfere. The trick to interrogating was letting them think they wanted to tell you, then it's one revelation after another.

"I'm telling you, Mike, I was abandoned once; I am not going to be abandoned again. I always knew I was adopted I just never knew who my mother was and I didn't care. She didn't want me so I didn't go looking for her. Mom and Dad were always good to me but I never let them get close. I guess I assumed they couldn't love me properly like real parents.

So stupid of me, they were probably the best people I ever had in my life and I resented them for helping my mother dispose of me. They told me I was adopted, they wanted to be upfront. They told me my mother had no choice, that my father was a drunk, a crazy man. That he beat her and gave her nothing, she had to leave him. So now I know. I know that the stranger lurking around town is my father. I know that Agatha is my mother. And I know that we're all beyond help. What goes around, comes around."

With that last sentence Owen swiped his arm across the bar, throwing both glasses across the room.

***

Bianca stared out the landing window behind Rebecca. The icicles had reached the window frame and dripped in the heat of the southern sun. Before her eyes, one broke off, crashing to the ground.

She took a half step back, startled.

"Rebecca, suddenly I'm not feeling well…would you mind if we continue this meeting tomorrow?" Bianca said with an attempt to level her voice. Was it believable? She closed her eyes and tried to calculate the distance to the rifle but couldn't do it. She opened her eyes and turned her head slightly to sneak a peek.

Rebecca followed her gaze, and when she saw that it rested on the rifle her shoulders sunk, as if she had deflated. She was two steps closer to the rifle than Bianca. Bianca lunged but it was a futile attempt and she knew it before she even tried. Rebecca swept the rifle up easily in a brisk motion.

"Bianca, what are you doing? What are you thinking?" Rebecca asked, holding the rifle out of reach.

"Rebecca, please put the gun down, this isn't the way to solve anything," Bianca managed to say, the words spilling out, unplanned. They sounded muffled in her own ears, as if someone else had just spoken. She hadn't wanted to show her cards, but now she had.

"I'm not doing anything, I'm just admiring Richard's rifle, aren't I?"

"Rebecca, please…" Bianca edged a couple of inches away from Rebecca, the stairs and the rifle.

"What gave me away? It was those damn gloves, right? See where vanity gets you? If I wore plain gloves like everyone else, you would never have noticed they were missing."

"Rebecca." Bianca heard the pleading in her own voice.

"Or was it the bracelet? Of course, the bracelet. Vanity once again."

"Why, Rebecca?" This time Bianca knew she was the one speaking. She was incredulous and needed to know how a life could go this wrong.

"Why? Why? I'll tell you why. Because Owen beats me, because Owen is destroying my son, because we need to get away from him and he will never let that happen. I needed money. I could never get away from him without money."

"But Rebecca, Elaine's ring couldn't possibly bring you enough money to change your life."

"You think this was about Elaine's ring? I thought you had it all figured out, but you don't, do you? I needed to close this deal with Janus. That commission is worth tens of thousands, it would have changed my life, but she refused to die..." Rebecca ran her free wrist across her upper lip to wipe away the sweat.

"I could have waited a little longer, I had waited this long, but she changed her will! She changed her will," Rebecca repeated, deflated. "Allison was on board to sell. Then Wednesday, when I was ready to leave Agatha's, I overheard her call Sister Elaine and promise her all the waterfront land. There I sat, in the alcove, powerless while she squandered what was rightfully mine. I had worked on this deal for years. It was my last hope. I begged Elaine to change Agatha's mind, she wouldn't listen.

"Friday Agatha called Lester Quirke and told him she would get a new will to him on Saturday. Well, I couldn't allow Saturday to arrive. I was out of time. I had to protect my Trevor." Rebecca started to shake but it didn't stop her confession.

"I didn't start out wanting to kill Agatha. I went to talk to her. I tried to change her mind. But she wouldn't listen. I pleaded with her. She said she wanted to open a refuge for battered women. What about me? She was so selfish. Couldn't she see she could have helped me and Trevor?"

257

Rebecca paused. Bianca scrambled for ideas but Rebecca wasn't finished.

"I've been trying to leave Owen for years, but I couldn't do it without money. I couldn't afford for this deal to fall through. And now it has fallen through. This is all your fault. You had the will. I looked everywhere for it. You had it all along." Rebecca's face flushed deep red, visible through the makeup.

"I didn't want it to be this way. Agatha forced my hand." Rebecca was crying now. "Why did she have to go and do that? I couldn't stay anymore in that house with Owen. It was killing me, and watching what he was doing to Trevor was even worse. He turned him into a rebellious, awful teenager. He used to be such a sweet child. And school. I needed to get Trevor to college. I was going crazy. You don't understand, do you? You had Richard. Loving Richard. Good Richard. Smart Richard. Oh god, at first I enjoyed hearing you tell your stories, but then..."

Rebecca stopped mid-sentence.

"Rebecca let's talk to Mike, he will look out for you. He'll know what to do."

"You are so naïve, Bianca, no wonder he's infatuated with you. A breath of fresh air you must be for that guy. It's too late, what could he do for me? You will not turn me in! I thought we could be friends. Now you want to call the sheriff. I have nothing to lose now that the deal fell through."

Rebecca lifted the rifle.

Bianca's instinct kicked in and she threw herself at Rebecca's legs. The sound of the gunshot echoed in the stairwell.

Bianca landed on top of Rebecca, the rifle thrown off to the side.

Rebecca's legs found their mark in Bianca's gut. With a grunt she heaved Bianca off her.

Thrown off balance, Bianca fumbled for the bannister, but only caught air. Her body rolled back. She floated in midair flailing as gravity yanked her down the stairs.

She bounced from side to side until she landed with a crash at the foot of the stairs. The pain in her leg blinding her for a moment. Then she scrambled to her feet, and yelping in pain, she stumbled into the mudroom.

She threw herself on the door, grabbed the knob. The door was locked. Her fingers fumbled but couldn't release the lock.

She persisted until she heard the click. She turned the knob and hobbled out the back door.

Chapter Forty-Five

Mike jumped off the barstool, staring at Owen, the pieces falling into place.

"Owen, you're telling me that Rebecca would have made a nice commission on this sale if it went through?"

"Yeah, the whole reason she went into real estate was because she said that this town would be booming in a few years. The condo was just the beginning."

"How significant would her take be?"

"That's why I wanted this deal to fall through. She would make a six percent commission on a two-million-dollar deal. Enough for her to leave me! That's all I know."

"Are we talking a hundred and twenty-thousand-dollar commission?" Mike asked stunned.

"At least, because she would get another hefty sum as a finder's fee from the developer for bringing the parties together."

"Owen, where is Rebecca now?"

"I'm not sure. She was supposed to go to the burial and the luncheon and then she had a sale to close."

"Where, who with?" Mike realized with brutal clarity that he had been interrogating the wrong Streat.

"I don't remember."

Mike grabbed Owen's arm. "Think."

"She was going to the old farm, the Van Rouse's."

"You mean Bianca St. Denis?"

"Yeah, maybe, that's the one."

Mike threw a ten-dollar bill on the bar and ran out of McLoughlin's.

He lifted himself into his truck and slammed the door. He fumbled with the ignition. The engine refused to turn over.

"This damn cold."

Mike tried again. Nothing.

"Come on, come on."

He caught his breath and tried again. This time he heard the engine catch. He turned out of the lot and on to Main Street.

His dispatcher crackled through immediately. "Claire Koop heard a gunshot across the way from her house. She said it sounded like it came from the Van Rouse property or maybe from the quarry. Hard to tell because of the way the sound bounces at this time of year. I told her she had nothing to worry about, it's hunting season. But she insisted that I call you. She thinks someone must be trespassing because the quarry's closed and no one hunts—"

"Send backup to meet me at Bianca's house, that's where I'm heading now."

"For a trespassing hunter, Mike? Shouldn't we just call the DEC?"

"Shelley, just do it!"

Mike flipped on his lights and siren and raced through the only stop light in the village.

***

Bianca made it to the edge of the woods before she heard another shot. Too afraid to look over her shoulder, she pressed on. She wanted to stay on the path but that would make it too easy to be pursued. She dragged her bad leg to the left, off the path and into the depths of the woods. Immediately she faced a roadblock. She gingerly stepped over a downed tree, on the other side the snow gave way to a thick layer of soft leaves and she lost her footing. She winced in pain, her left leg throbbing. She picked herself up and kept going deeper into the forest.

She slowed down just enough to avoid losing her footing again. Looking down, she found drops of blood in the snow at her feet. She looked herself over and realized that her left arm was bleeding. She must have been hit. She never felt it. Adrenalin or the pain of her leg must have distracted her. The blood would leave a trail. She pressed her hand against the wound to staunch the bleeding. She had no scarf, or coat. Nothing to wrap around her arm. She wasn't even wearing her boots, just her knitted slippers.

She needed to get deeper into the woods. She didn't slow down. She knew that speed was everything. Alternating between sweating and shivering, she dragged her leg as fast as she could. She heard a crack behind her to the left. She stopped to gauge the danger. She could hear nothing but her own shallow breathing. She carefully rested her back on the tree behind her to remove some weight off her leg, catch her breath, and reassess.

No more noise. She pushed off the tree and continued.

As she ventured deeper she saw to her right an entrance to the thick pine stand. The snow was almost nonexistent there. Her blood would not be as visible. It was safer. Bianca knew there were two hunting blinds left behind by the Van Rouse boys. They had hunted together, one blind was in a tree, she could never get up there in this condition, but there was also one in a gulley. She needed to find that blind.

She found a spot with some cover and with her back against the tree lowered herself to the soft pine needle floor. She expected the pain to lessen after getting off her leg but the throbbing was excruciating. She saw white and smelled something like ammonia. She was passing out. She dipped her head between her knees and immediately her vision focused and the smell subsided.

A crash to her left made her jump. The pain reignited. She started to scramble to her feet, but they found no purchase in the slippery pine needles. She put her arms out to steady herself, her left arm inflamed. She finally grabbed the tree and pulled her leg under her and up. She ran in the opposite direction of the noise, looking over her shoulder this time. Two deer leapt from the forest floor and loped into the woods in front of her. She had inadvertently snuck up on their bedding site and startled them. Relieved, she slowed down. She looked around the woods, and then she spotted it, a hunting blind on the other side of the frozen brook. She could rest there and keep a look out at the same time.

There was a small wooden bridge crossing the brook farther north. She considered going up there but the pain in her leg was more than she could bear. She needed to get off it soon. She picked up a broken tree limb to use as a staff. She timidly crossed the brook. She tested the ice with the staff before each step and used it to lean her weight from her left side like a crutch. Two more steps and she would be across. Her feet were starting to tingle with numbness and she couldn't gauge her footing. Slowly she transferred her weight to her bad leg so she could make the last step and then rest the bulk of her weight on her good leg. Done. Now one more step.

Her right leg fell through the ice and into the brook beneath. The frigid water pulled a yelp out of her chest. She stopped dead, had Rebecca heard her? After a minute she couldn't feel her foot. She hadn't heard anything so she scrambled out, the pain in her leg obscured by numbness.

She reached the blind and hunkered in. She dropped herself onto the soft bedding that still remained and closed a flap of thick burlap that made her camouflage complete. She leaned her head against the side.

She heard a whimper.

Then realized it was her own voice. She closed her eyes and cried quietly.

Chapter Forty-Six

Mike searched Bianca's house from top to bottom, Bianca was nowhere.

Vera had Rebecca in cuffs. They had met her car head-on in Bianca's driveway. There had been nowhere for her to escape, especially in her high heels. She sat crumpled in the driver's seat with the rifle by her side.

But now where to find Bianca? Rebecca told them nothing. Mike continued his search until he found the mud room door ajar. Out back the snow was trampled. Tracks led to the woods. He took off running. The rifle had been discharged. He had no idea what he would find. Or how much time he had to find her.

He couldn't let her down, not like he had let Sal down. His partner had needed him and he hadn't been there. He hadn't made it on time. Sal, his mangled body on the pavement, if Mike had only gotten there on time.

He could never regain that time, but he wouldn't let it happen again. He needed to harness all his reserves and do this. How long had she been out there?

A sweat broke out on his neck, he could hear his own breath, short and shallow. His vision blurred. He stopped. With his hands on his knees, Mike bent over and dropped his head. He breathed in for seven seconds, he held for seven, he released his breath slowly. He closed his eyes and pictured an ocean. His body swayed.

I can do this. Calm down, calm down. His breathing slowed. *I will not give in to this. She will not die out there.*

***

Bianca awoke with a start. Her leg so swollen it wouldn't move, thankfully she couldn't feel it. Her arm pulsated. She looked around to get her bearings. Raw wood walls enclosed her, then she remembered she was in the blind. Had she fallen asleep here? How could that be possible? She was running for her life. Her teeth chattered. Her hands were numb, she blew on them, her breath created a mist but could not warm them. Tears filled her eyes again. She leaned her head against the back of the blind, trying to remember the scene at the house, it seemed like it was days ago. What time could it be? She peeked outside without making a sound. The sun was gone but it wasn't night yet.

She needed to get herself out of there before dark, but she felt weak and needed to rest a little longer. She would just close her eyes for a minute.

***

Mike spotted a drop of blood where the tracks led into the woods. He didn't know whether to be relieved that he had a trail or worried about the wound. It couldn't be too bad he told himself, there wasn't that much blood. He followed the trail, a drop here and there. Veered off to the left and then the right. And then he lost the trail. No blood, no snow. He was in the pine stand. And no hints to where she was.

He was baffled. He stood there choosing a path. Where would she go?

He heard a noise. A squirrel chattering? No, a voice.

As if tracking a deer, he tiptoed to the sound.

***

A squirrel scurried past the blind. Bianca woke up.

She sat upright.

Where had all this heat come from. The Java Cakes must be ready. I need to test them. Where did the toothpicks go?

She rummaged around in her pockets and found a mint.

Oh, thank goodness. I can't go up to give the eulogy without a mint.

Richard, can you zip me up? You know I can never reach the zipper on this black dress. Please hurry or we'll be late for the funeral.

Don't forget to turn off the oven.

Bianca opened a couple of buttons on her blouse.

Aren't those cakes ready yet? I can't stand the heat.

Please open the window. Rebecca, can you take the cakes out of the oven, I'm going to take a nap. I just need to close my eyes.

She rested her head. As she dozed, her head hit the wooden frame and jolted her.

Where was she? She shivered and found her blouse open. Why was she dressed this way?

She couldn't control the shivering. Then suddenly it stopped and in a flash, heat rose to her face. Doctor Spenser said that hypothermia caused a heat sensation. And sleepiness. She slapped her face. She needed to keep her eyes open...

Robert, don't you think Monica is pretty?

Her head slipped forward, she jerked her head up again.

Stay awake, Bianca...she shook her hands and banged her toes with her fists. She just needed to stay awake until someone found her. But who would know she was even there? Bianca pinched her cheeks. She needed to get out of there, she tried to stand up but fell back immediately. The pain! Rebecca would be looking for her. She needed to stay here where it was safe. She needed to stay and sleep to the rhythmic sound of coyotes.

***

Mike crouched half in and half out of the hunting blind.

"Bianca, wake up!"

He tried to get his arms under her limp body. She was barely dressed, blood congealed on her arm and hand. He got some leverage and picked her up a few inches. Her eyes shot open as she screamed.

He placed her down again, relieved. A scream was better than unresponsive. But her eyes were closed again.

"Bianca, please try to wake up."

She opened her eyes and closed them again.

"Tell me where you're hurt. Bianca!"

He slapped her, he hated to do it but he couldn't shake her, he didn't know what was broken.

Her eyes popped open. She smiled weakly. "I'm so glad you're here."

"I'm here to help you, don't worry." Mike returned the smile.

"Thank you, Richard, you are always here when I need you." Her head nodded as she fell back to sleep.

He touched each leg carefully, first right and then left. When he touched the left leg it jerked. He ran out of the blind. In the fading light he searched until he found a straight tree limb and broke it into two pieces over his knee. He used his scarf to make a splint, trying to maneuver in the tiny blind. Luckily, Bianca was small, he could never have done this to Eugene in here.

Once her leg was secure he wrapped his arms under her armpits. "Bianca, I'm going to pick you up now, this might hurt but we will make your leg better soon." He dragged her out as carefully as possible.

Once outside with more room, he picked her up in his arms like a child and walked across the brook. His footing was weak and his right foot slipped. He lost his grip on her right side. He picked up his knee to support her and to reposition his hands.

The jolt awakened Bianca. She squinted at him.

"Mike, is that you? Rebecca? Where is she? Mike!"

"Yes, Bianca, I'm getting you to the hospital. We have Rebecca."

He managed to make it to the edge of the woods, but his breath was short and his heart was racing. He was out of shape. He hadn't needed to be in shape in a long time. This would teach him a lesson.

Bianca's arm slipped from his neck.

"Bianca, please, I need you to stay awake." He stopped in his tracks to gain some balance and helped her place her hand back over his neck for support.

She looked up at him, his warm breath seemed to revive her momentarily, then she turned away, rested her head on his chest and closed her eyes.

Chapter Forty-Seven

Wednesday, December 21

Bianca hobbled into the Community Center, balancing on her crutches. She was not very good at it yet, but she hadn't wanted to miss the event. Ernie was standing immediately to her right to help her with the rough spots and Eugene was carrying her Java Cakes.

"Bianca's here!" Olivia's voice announced as she ran over to help.

Bianca looked up to greet Olivia. Over her shoulder Bianca could see that the entire village was already there. Her eyes focused as she took in each face, all smiling. Lester was there. Bert and Claire, Mike and Vera, Emily and Monica, Robert and Ben, they were all there. She didn't see the Streats but that was no surprise. Everyone was beaming and clapping. She snuck a peek behind her to see what they were clapping at. Her crutch wiggled precariously as she turned. Ernie grabbed her elbow to right her.

"What are you looking at? They're clapping for you," Eugene said with a twinkle in his eye.

"For me? What did I do but make a fool of myself?"

Olivia hugged her and found her a seat. With a thump Bianca plopped in a chair. Her face tingled from embarrassment. She had briefly considered not attending, she was a little self-conscious about how she had made a mess of things. And Dr. Spenser wasn't pleased with her either after she had discharged herself from the hospital this morning. But there he was cheering her on.

269

Olivia motioned to the group that the applause was enough. Eventually the clapping died down and everyone returned to chatting.

Olivia went to find her an eggnog and Ernie went off with Eugene to help with serving the meal. Bianca took a moment to look around. Tables packed the room, she had no idea so many people would be attending.

Ben walked over and took the seat next to her. He handed her a cup of nog. "Olivia asked me to give you this. She has a mashed potato emergency."

"Thank you, Ben." Bianca indulged in a sip of creamy eggnog. She enjoyed the warmth of the rum as it coated her throat and ran into her empty belly. The cold had not left her yet. It had been hard to bundle up properly and maneuver the crutches.

"So many tables, so many people," Bianca said.

"Well," Ben said, "we will be feeding a lot of people today. Our venison roasts are the main event. One roast for every table and then we have frozen packages for those in need to take home. We are pretty proud of ourselves, the Hunting Club, I mean. We broke all records this year with our take. This season has been particularly hard on folks. There are a lot of needy people in the area, I hate to admit it. We are all doing our best to help, though. We've been out hunting every day we've had free. Almost ran out of freezer space around town. But we did it. Every needy family will take home a bag full of venison. Enough to feed a small family for the winter."

Bianca was shocked by this unexpected revelation. She had judged Ben as an insensitive hunter, when in fact he and his buddies had been doing a good deed all along. "I have to confess I never liked the thought of hunting, but in this case I think you're doing a good thing."

"Great. Hurry up and heal and I'll take you out hunting myself. You've got some great hunting land on your property."

"Well, wait a minute, I may find some redeeming qualities but I doubt I will hunt."

Ben took a swig of eggnog and then turned to her with renewed attention.

"Bianca, I have another purpose for sitting here with you. As you know I am on the Board of Trustees for the Library and—"

"Actually, I didn't know that. You have your hands in everything, don't

270

you?"

"Well, it's a small town, lots of overlapping responsibilities. So, as President of the Board I wanted to mention to you that our librarian, Mrs. Abernathy, will be retiring after the new year and we haven't found a replacement yet. I was wondering if you might want to consider interviewing for the job? It's not very high paying, but it's not too many hours either."

"Ben, I'm flattered you thought of me, but unfortunately I don't have any library credentials." Bianca's heart had skipped a beat for the brief moment when she thought she had found herself the perfect job, but she quickly knew it was only wishful thinking.

"This is a small independent village library. If we waited for a candidate with credentials the library would never open. Mrs. Abernathy has been a dedicated librarian for over thirty years and she had no credentials either, other than having read every volume in the library. It was all on the job training. Everyone has to give a little. I figure your teaching background and your history degree must count for something. I suppose you had to work with one or two books to do that, huh?" Ben treated her to one of his famous smiles and nudged her gently with his elbow.

"Yes, one or two if I recall correctly." Bianca's heart leapt again. Maybe, just maybe, this could work. She imagined being paid for spending time with books. Too good to be true, or was it? "I have to say that I would be foolish not to interview for the job. I would love to work in the library. What does it entail? When could I interview?"

"I'd say your interview went well. The job is yours if you want it."

"Doesn't the board have to vote or something?"

"Or something." Ben chuckled. "Think about it and let me know. We can talk details whenever you want."

With some fanfare, the roasts came out of the kitchen. The servers placed one bacon wrapped roast on each table along with platters and platters of sides: roasted root vegetables, mashed potatoes, stuffed mushrooms, string beans, candied yams. The food stretched out as far as she could see.

Ben stood up to make a toast.

"Let us all raise our glasses to our sheriff, his deputies and to our newest villager, Bianca St. Denis."

"Here, here."

"Speech, speech! Mike, get up!"

Vera and Bianca blushed. Mike half stood, gave a quick wave and sat back down. When he did, the woman beside him linked her arm in his and pecked him on the cheek.

Bianca looked away, fidgeting with her crutch.

Ernie reached over and stabilized the crutch for her. "Do you need some help? Are you okay?"

Bianca nodded without looking at him. "Yes, I'm fine," she mumbled into her glass.

***

Mike was startled by the kiss. Maggie never kissed him in public anymore. Then again, they were rarely in public together lately.

He quickly turned toward Ben, and raised his glass with a nod before taking a healthy swig. At a loss after that, he stood up but had no where to go.

"Speech, speech," his friends started again. He had passed on saying a few words earlier but now that he found himself standing he felt cornered.

"I want to thank everyone who contributed to today's feast with a special thanks to the Hunting Club and all their efforts for the community."

Mike turned to sit but thought better of it.

"Maggie, I'm going to help with carving the roasts. Start without me, I'll be back in a bit."

As he turned toward the kitchen he snuck a peek at Bianca sitting next to Ernie, chatting. He willed her to look up but she never saw him.

Chapter Forty-Eight

The clinking of glasses lasted for several minutes as everyone stretched across tables to those out of reach.

The platters were passed around the tables until everyone's plate overflowed. The clatter and clang of dishes and forks drowned out the voices at first. Eventually everyone settled in to eat and chat. Bianca ate with gusto, enjoying this meal in communion with her new neighbors.

Once dessert was served Freddie came over with Claire. They brought a slice of apple pie for Bianca, and they each settled in to enjoy the Java Cakes. Olivia came over next, dragging Mike behind her.

"Okay, you two. Let's hear the whole thing," Olivia said.

"Off the record?" Mike asked the journalist with a smirk on his face.

"Off the record," Olivia said.

Mike turned a hand to Bianca. "You should start."

Bianca blushed but she put her coffee down and got comfortable. "Well, Rebecca's story started to unravel when she arrived at my house. I noticed that she wasn't wearing her regular gloves, those wonderful pink suede gloves that I always admire." The ladies all nodded vigorously in agreement.

"We found those gloves at her house in the bottom of the garbage, ruined with blood stains," Mike clarified.

"But how did you make a connection between her new gloves and her guilt? Lots of ladies change purses and gloves to match outfits," Olivia asked.

"That's just it, they didn't match her outfit. You know how fashion conscious she is. And then at one point I saw my Timberland boots. I ruined them recently with blood when I cut my finger. I was thinking how

273

the suede was ruined, and how the blood stain would never come out."

"Hell to get out of corduroy too," Claire added.

"Rebecca is fit and she could easily have overpowered Elaine. The blood on the gloves would never have come out," Mike continued.

"Also, Rebecca had recently confided in me that she used to hock jewelry in Albany for cash." Bianca picked up the thread of the story.

"Right, and Vera had reported to us that she had found Elaine's ring at a pawnbroker in Albany," Mike interjected.

The ladies' heads bobbed back and forth between Mike and Bianca as the story bounced from one and then the other.

"Exactly! And when she arrived at my house, Rebecca had reclaimed her grandmother's bracelet from her dealer. I thought that was strange because she had just told me a few days ago that she was broke, and that she would need to hock another piece of jewelry soon," Bianca said.

"Who knew that Rebecca needed to sell off her jewelry to make ends meet? It seemed the Streats always had everything they needed," Claire said.

"Rebecca was desperate to get out of her marriage but couldn't liberate herself. She couldn't put enough money together to do it, Owen kept her on a short leash. This condo deal would have made her a tidy sum and she could have started all over," Bianca explained.

"I'd have never guessed that she was having such a bad time in her marriage," Freddie said with sadness in her voice.

"None of us did. Sad to think of it, but she really didn't have any friends, did she? Appearances are deceiving. She was so upbeat and involved that we never noticed she had a problem, we never really let her in. I feel bad about that," Freddie said.

"She hid her plight well. I think she felt she had no choice, that no one would do business with her if she were open about her problems," Bianca said. "In fact, I noticed that she had a lot of makeup under her left eye covering a bruise, that's the kind of thing that could ruin a saleswoman's career."

"I think we were all blinded by their looks. Owen is so handsome and she is so striking. Maybe we mistook the surface for the substance. Glossy outside but rotten inside," Olivia said. "From what you're both telling us, it seems that for years Rebecca was a desperate woman. Yet we never saw it. It's true what Bianca said in her eulogy. It's possible to live in full view of others but with no one to see our loneliness or despair, even in such an intimate community as this. Living with others requires honesty and acceptance of those around us, with all their good and bad qualities."

Everyone's desserts sat half-finished on the table in front of them, the reality of the last few days starting to set in.

Bianca continued, "Rebecca had been trying to save money to send Trevor to college because Owen wouldn't pay for it. She knew she needed a new life. Agatha's will ended up having a provision for Trevor's college but there was no way for Rebecca to know that. No one knew that Agatha was Owen's mother and Trevor's grandmother."

"But still, Owen had abused her, verbally even more than physically. Doctor Spenser says that a diagnosis of Post-Traumatic Stress Disorder may give her a break in sentencing. If I've learned anything in this profession, it's that anyone can do anything if the motivation is strong enough," Mike said.

"I don't think Rebecca was a cold-hearted killer. She was trapped and saw an opportunity to fix things and acted on impulse. Robert says victims of abuse can behave in strange ways. Rebecca lied to the sheriff to cover up for Trevor because she was afraid he would become a suspect. She was frantic that she had set her son up for a murder rap. And to complicate things, Trevor lied about being on the lake all night because he didn't want anyone to know he had broken into Lois Lanes."

In the momentum of telling her story Bianca never noticed that someone had joined their group. When everyone turned to greet her, Bianca saw a young woman with long curls take a seat next to Mike.

"Honey, please introduce me," she said.

Mike turned to her. "Maggie, this is Bianca St. Denis. Bianca, this is Maggie, my wife." Mike got up. "Excuse me ladies, Ben needs me."

Maggie extended her hand to Bianca. "So happy to meet you. Mike's told me so much about you."

Bianca was at a loss, she knew nothing about Maggie. Why would Mike put her in this awkward situation?

But Bianca quickly learned that she was charming and disarming. Maggie complimented her on her help in the investigation but quickly dropped the subject when she noticed Bianca's discomfort. She moved on to the delicious desserts and Bianca's writing.

"Mike tells me you're working on a book. How exciting. Not often we get writers right here in Batavia."

"Well, like I told Mike, I'm not published yet."

"But you're a writer. That's what counts. Tell me about your book."

Maggie seemed genuinely interested and easy to talk to. Bianca told her about her plans for Agatha's story, about Roosevelt, about the local history and the tannery. She bubbled about all the notebooks and maps and about the ideas she had for developing a historical series based on Agatha's life.

"Well, here's what I have to say. This sounds fascinating. Get to your desk and start writing. Then send me the first fifty pages and a synopsis." Maggie pulled out a business card from her bag.

"I don't understand," Bianca said, baffled.

"Didn't Mike tell you I'm a literary agent? That's why he wanted me to meet you. He called me in New York the other day and went on and on about you. To tell you the truth, I was a little jealous for a minute. But he is right, this is exactly what we are looking for. My agency is growing and we have just started building our stable of historical novelists. Your series sounds promising. You never know, you might have something we can market. Let me have a look and we can discuss it. I'm excited to start reading."

"I don't know what to say. I didn't know I was pitching. You haven't even read any of my writing."

"Well, your pitch was terrific, maybe all pitches should be done this way. Removes the anxiety, I guess. And I have done my homework. I got my hands on a couple of your short stories and I loved them. You are a talented writer. All you need for a good book is good writing and a good story, and you have both."

Maggie stood up. She offered her hand and they shook on it.

"Well, it's been a pleasure Bianca, now I'm going to get another Java Cake. Simply the best thing on the dessert table."

Bianca watched her walk to the desserts. Maggie picked up two mini cakes, and walked one over to Mike. She handed it to him and whispered in his ear. Mike looked up at Bianca, his eyes wide in an unspoken question.

Bianca smiled back and mouthed the words, "Thank you."

Chapter Forty-Nine

The lights dimmed. Bianca found herself alone, the eggnog and wine had started to take effect and she was excited about the library job and her new book project. Things were starting to fall into place. "Can I have your attention, everyone?" Ben was once again where he was most comfortable, at the head of the room. "It's time for our candlelight vigil. Emily is handing out your candles. We will meet outside for the lunar eclipse; it is almost complete now. If you have lighters or matches please bring them outside for the lighting later."

The villagers bundled up and stepped out onto the field of the Community Center. The last person to leave the room was Allison. She switched off the lights as she walked out the door. Bianca felt a tug of compassion for Allison. After being recently overlooked for a promotion, Allison had quit her job at the Tavers Hotel. She was grieving and starting over, something Bianca understood very well. Should she say something to Allison? She could think of nothing, so instead, nodded to Allison and received a nod in return.

The air out on the field was cold and still, but not frigid. Bianca noticed that the darkness was so rich and deep it seemed to have a weight of its own.

She leaned on the door frame and watched as the moon finished its disappearing act.

Next to her, Bianca could barely make out Mr. Ishikawa leaning on the other door frame. Once again he offered her a slight bow. They remained silent. In complete darkness they watched the black sky and the moon, rust colored in the completed eclipse.

It was as dark as Bianca had ever seen it in Batavia, she could easily have believed that she was all alone. But she wasn't. She knew that she was sharing this moment with an entire village.

Slowly, a lighted candle made its way to Bianca. One by one, like a string of Christmas lights, they brightened up the darkness. Everyone slowly passed Bianca as they entered the Community Center. Mr. Ishikawa offered to take her candle so she could maneuver her crutches. Once inside, he settled her into a seat.

"Thank you. Please join me," Bianca offered.

Mr. Ishikawa took the seat next to her. "Thank you for what you did for me," he said with a mild trace of a Japanese accent.

"What did I do?"

"You discovered the truth, and I am grateful. I know the villagers suspected me. Eventually they would have figured it out, but sooner is better than later." He smiled a tiny smile.

"You're welcome."

Bianca found it natural to sit in silence with this quiet man.

"This is a beautiful ceremony. It is the one event I attend each year in the village," he said.

"It is special. I wish Richard and I had come to one sooner."

"A famous Japanese author, Junichiro Tanizaki wrote that, 'were it not for shadows, there would be no beauty.' He also praises silence. Both mostly lost in modern life. Darkness and silence." As if to prove his point, Mr. Ishikawa stopped talking for several minutes before he continued.

"The Solstice reminds us to be in communion with nature and with each other. The darkest longest night is also when it is easiest to see Polaris, the North Star. It is the guiding light, and it is always there, but only if we allow the darkness to envelop us can we see it and be guided. Like silence, it quiets our minds. Some people never have a quiet mind, you can see it on their faces."

Bianca thought about Agatha and Rebecca, and Owen. They all had unquiet minds.

Bianca watched the moon outside the window over Mr. Ishikawa's shoulder. The rusty orange slipping away slowly to reveal a sliver of the bright moon beneath. Then a flash of light streamed over his shoulder. An Ursid meteor, only visible because of the darkness, Bianca realized.

They continued to sit in silence until whispers of music floated to them, the party had just started. The first song was a mellow ballad, a slow transition from the silence and darkness.

Bianca witnessed the room come to life. The village postman, Pieter, walked over to Claire and asked her to dance. Bianca could see Claire watching Bert in the corner by the bar. Claire hesitated at first then accepted Pieter's offer.

Bianca was pleased to see Robert approach Monica, they easily found a comfortable rhythm. Big Ben swooped Emily onto the floor.

Then Maggie tapped Mike on the shoulder. He looked around uncomfortably, and at first shook his head, but eventually Mike gave in and walked onto the floor with her.

Rudy and Trudy Bauer, Kurt and Freddie Dekker joined the others. Slowly the dance floor filled up.

The tempo picked up and the lights went from dim to disco.

A shadow crossed over Bianca. Eugene stood there with her crutches.

"Come on, little lady, let's show them how it's done."

"Eugene, I can't—"

"Chicken?" Eugene handed her the crutches. With his help, she leaned on them and hobbled to the dance floor. Once there, all she could do was swivel on her crutches but she enjoyed herself just the same.

As the village danced, nobody noticed the eclipse receding, the orange disappeared until all that remained was the light of the full moon, bathing the dance floor in light.

Acknowledgements

"The knowledge of how little you can do alone teaches you humility."
Eleanor Roosevelt

How lucky am I to be writing the acknowledgments to my debut novel? Not only am I fulfilling my dream, but I have had such a beautiful journey along the way. So many individuals and organizations have been a part of the process that brought this book to fruition.

Thank you to Verena Rose, Shawn Reilly Simmons and Harriette Sackler at Level Best Books for making *Winter Witness* a reality. From the first moment, all three have been there cheering me on, offering advice and improving my book every step of the way. Thank you, Arleen Trundy, for seeing something special in my manuscript and recommending it for publication.

Those early readers of my fledgling manuscript always believed it was just a matter of time before this book was published. What faith! Thank you to Michele Cippitelli, Betsabé Montoya, Emily Munger, and Sandra Yanowitch.

Stefani Dana-Langel read chapter after chapter and gave me honest criticism and full-throated praise as she read. You are a true friend like no other. I love you like a sister. And thank you to Stefani's daughter Sarah for her careful proofreading.

Mally Becker is my partner in crime. She commiserates or celebrates with me at every juncture. How perfect that we are at the next stage together at Level Best Books. I am so blessed to be traveling this journey with you.

Many thanks to Sisters in Crime, Mavens of Mayhem and Mystery Writers of America, the writing organizations and the authors who welcomed me, schooled me in the vagaries of the publishing world, critiqued my work, encouraged me, recognized me, made me feel like I was not just another face in the crowd.

Thank you to Jeff Markowitz for introducing me to the MWA-NY Mentor Program and to Erica Obey, the first author to suggest that my work had merit. Special thanks to Bethany Blake, my assigned mentor, who offered such an insightful and compassionate critique.

Thank you to Bob Knightly, who read and critiqued page after page. Thanks also to Carol Pouliot, Marni Graff, Frankie Bailey, and Eleanor Kuhns, who have all allowed me to pick their brains, and offered generous guidance and support.

I am grateful to Annette Dashofy, whose kind words are always forthcoming when I need them most; Liz Milliron for her sound, and practical advice; Gabriel Valjan, for his constant support and guidance.

And who else but the dynamic Hank Phillippi Ryan could be so generous of her time and expert advice? She can't know how much her encouragement over the past few years has meant to me.

Writers in Kyoto recently welcomed me with open arms. Thank you for broadening my writing horizons.

I owe so much to the Catskill Public Library. Thank you to my office sisters and daughters for your unrelenting support: Sue, Crystal, Allie, Heather, Nita, Cressa, Peggy, Joy, Ashley, Bathsheba, Joan, Beth and Bianca. I love you and miss you all.

Thank you to Sachi Mulkey, the talented artist whose vision of my book cover made it her unique work of art.

I am so very grateful to my in-laws, Cheryl and Claude Jean, for all they have done for me. Thank you to the entire Jean clan for their encouragement and support.

So much of my love and gratitude goes to my parents Delfina and Vincenzo Tersigni. They made me believe I had superpowers. In fact, they are the superheroes, raising three children and making us each feel unique, and unstoppable. I love you. And I am incredibly grateful to my siblings, Michael and Patrizia. It's a privilege being your sister.

And finally, thank you to my men. To my son Alessandro, who makes me believe that being his mother was the most perfect thing I have ever done. Who else would brainstorm story ideas with me at 3:00 a.m. from across the ocean in Japan? He is such an inspiration to me in all that he does. Thank you for believing in me every day. I love you.

To my husband Denis, whose support for my writing has never wavered. Who, along with his brother Claude, built me my writing cottage long before I realized I would need one. His confidence in my work was so unshakeable that he waited until the manuscript was completed before reading a word. He continues to build me bookshelves, and every day he manages to make me believe that I am his sunlight. You have made this all possible. I love you.

I thought writing my first novel was difficult until I tried distilling the story into summaries, blurbs and pitches, and realized that writing the novel was easy in comparison. But sitting down to write my acknowledgements has been the hardest by far. I have so many wonderful people to thank and I fear I have not mentioned them all. Thank you isn't nearly enough, I am indebted to you all.

About the Author

Tina deBellegarde lives in Catskill, New York, with her husband Denis and their cat Shelby. *Winter Witness* is the first book in the Batavia-on-Hudson Mystery Series. Tina also writes short stories and flash fiction. When she isn't writing, she is helping Denis tend their beehives, harvest shiitake mushrooms, and cultivate their vegetable garden. She travels to Japan regularly to visit her son Alessandro. Tina did her graduate studies in history. She is a former exporter, paralegal, teacher, and library clerk. Visit her website at www.tinadebellegarde.com

FIC DEBELLEGARDE

Debellegarde, Tina
Winter witness : a
Batavia-on-Hudson

10/08/20

CPSIA information can be obtained
at www.ICGtesting.com
Printed in the USA
LVHW022318150920
666084LV00005B/992